WARD'S VALLEY

WRITTEN BY
BOBBY CURNOW

ART BY
BRENDA HICKEY

Top Shelf® PRODUCTIONS

Chapter One

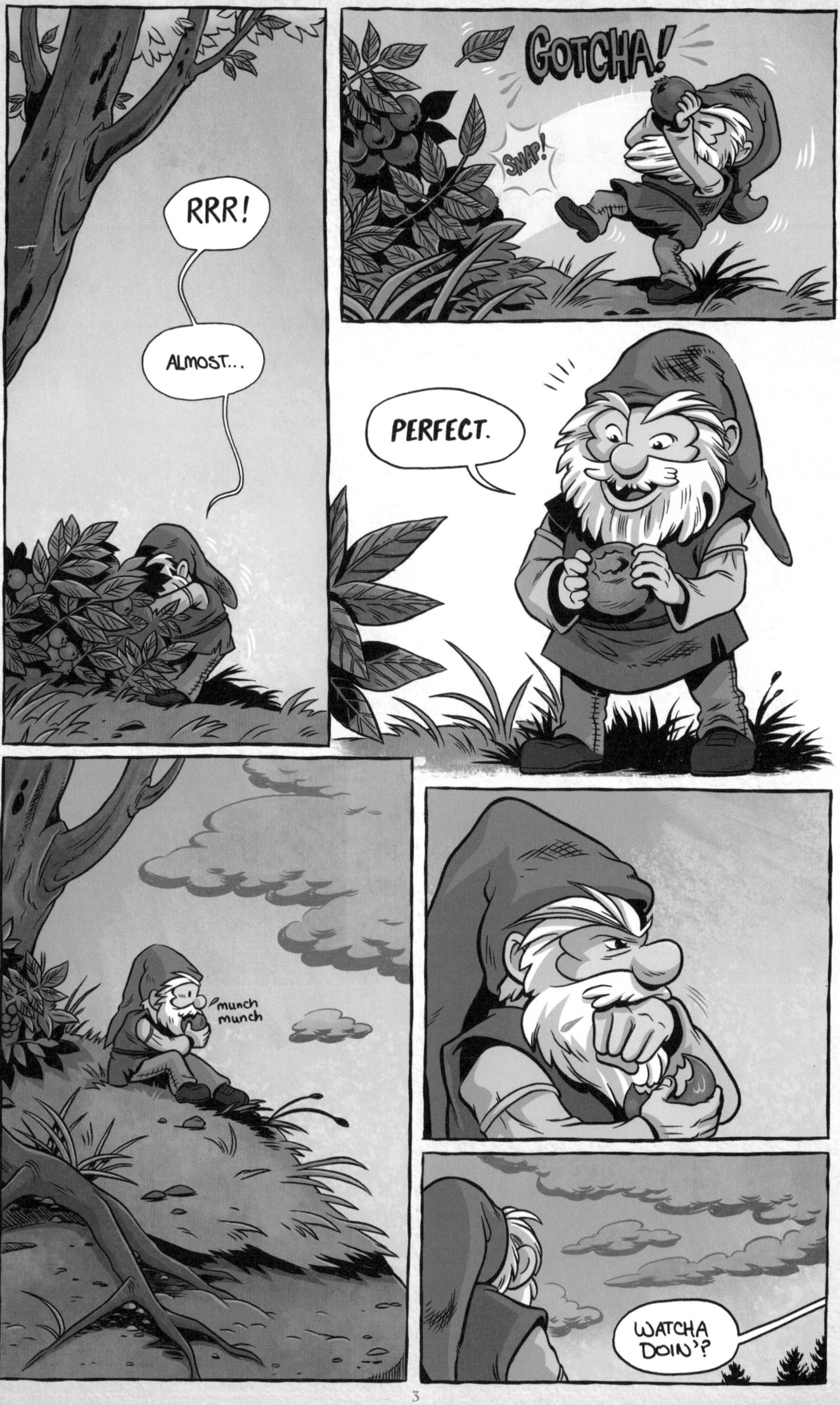
RRR!
ALMOST...
GOTCHA!
SNAP!
PERFECT.
munch munch
WATCHA DOIN'?

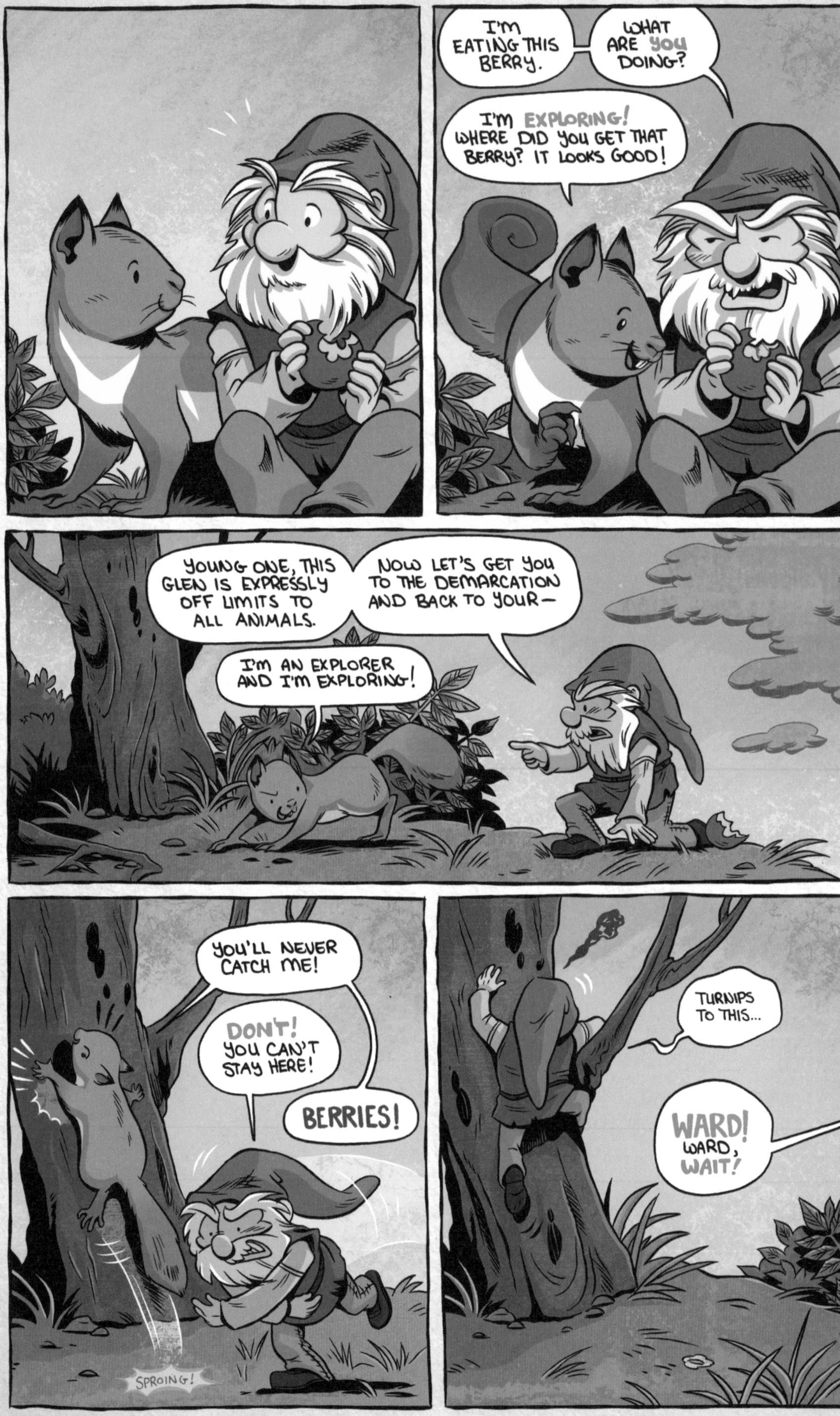
I'M EATING THIS BERRY.
WHAT ARE YOU DOING?
I'M EXPLORING! WHERE DID YOU GET THAT BERRY? IT LOOKS GOOD!
YOUNG ONE, THIS GLEN IS EXPRESSLY OFF LIMITS TO ALL ANIMALS.
NOW LET'S GET YOU TO THE DEMARCATION AND BACK TO YOUR—
I'M AN EXPLORER AND I'M EXPLORING!
YOU'LL NEVER CATCH ME!
DON'T! YOU CAN'T STAY HERE!
BERRIES!
SPROING!
TURNIPS TO THIS...
WARD! WARD, WAIT!

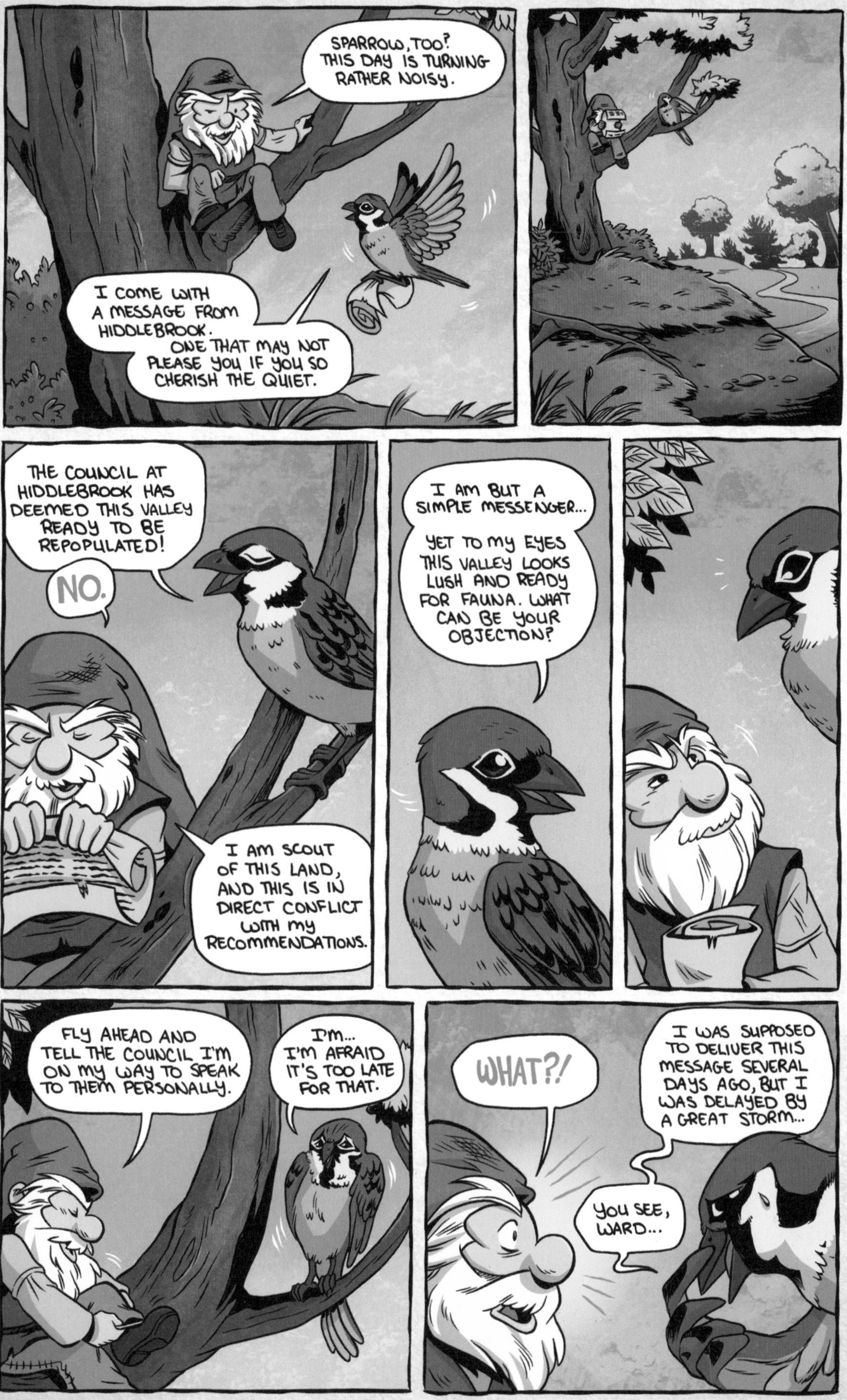
SPARROW, TOO? THIS DAY IS TURNING RATHER NOISY.
I COME WITH A MESSAGE FROM HIDDLEBROOK.
ONE THAT MAY NOT PLEASE YOU IF YOU SO CHERISH THE QUIET.
THE COUNCIL AT HIDDLEBROOK HAS DEEMED THIS VALLEY READY TO BE REPOPULATED!
NO.
I AM SCOUT OF THIS LAND, AND THIS IS IN DIRECT CONFLICT WITH MY RECOMMENDATIONS.
I AM BUT A SIMPLE MESSENGER...
YET TO MY EYES THIS VALLEY LOOKS LUSH AND READY FOR FAUNA. WHAT CAN BE YOUR OBJECTION?
FLY AHEAD AND TELL THE COUNCIL I'M ON MY WAY TO SPEAK TO THEM PERSONALLY.
I'M... I'M AFRAID IT'S TOO LATE FOR THAT.
WHAT?!
I WAS SUPPOSED TO DELIVER THIS MESSAGE SEVERAL DAYS AGO, BUT I WAS DELAYED BY A GREAT STORM...
YOU SEE, WARD...

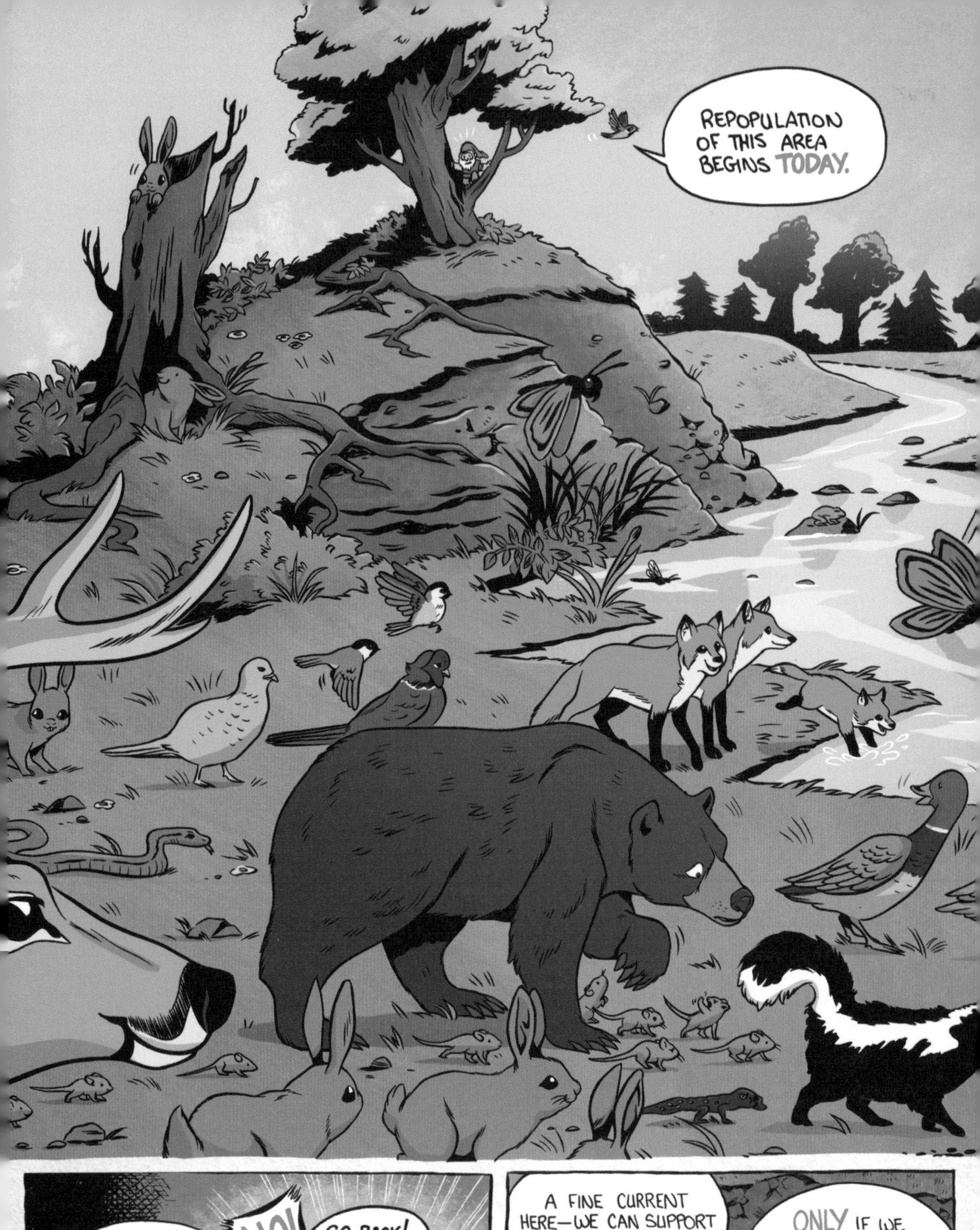
REPOPULATION OF THIS AREA BEGINS TODAY.

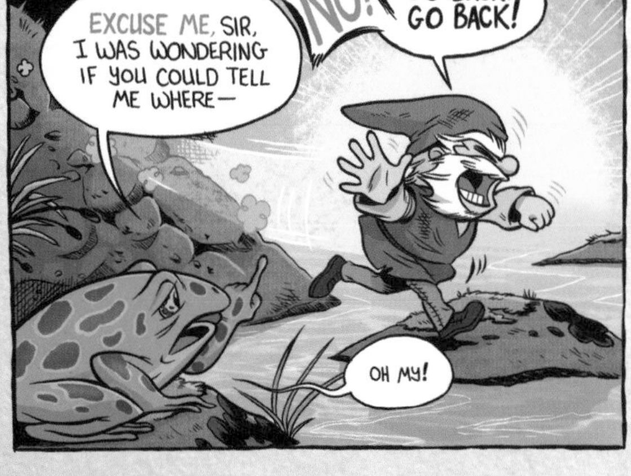
EXCUSE ME, SIR, I WAS WONDERING IF YOU COULD TELL ME WHERE—
NO!
GO BACK! GO BACK!
OH MY!

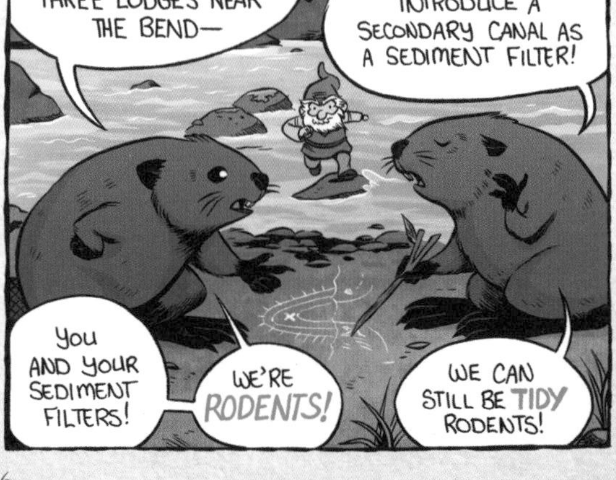
A FINE CURRENT HERE—WE CAN SUPPORT THREE LODGES NEAR THE BEND—
ONLY IF WE INTRODUCE A SECONDARY CANAL AS A SEDIMENT FILTER!
YOU AND YOUR SEDIMENT FILTERS!
WE'RE RODENTS!
WE CAN STILL BE TIDY RODENTS!

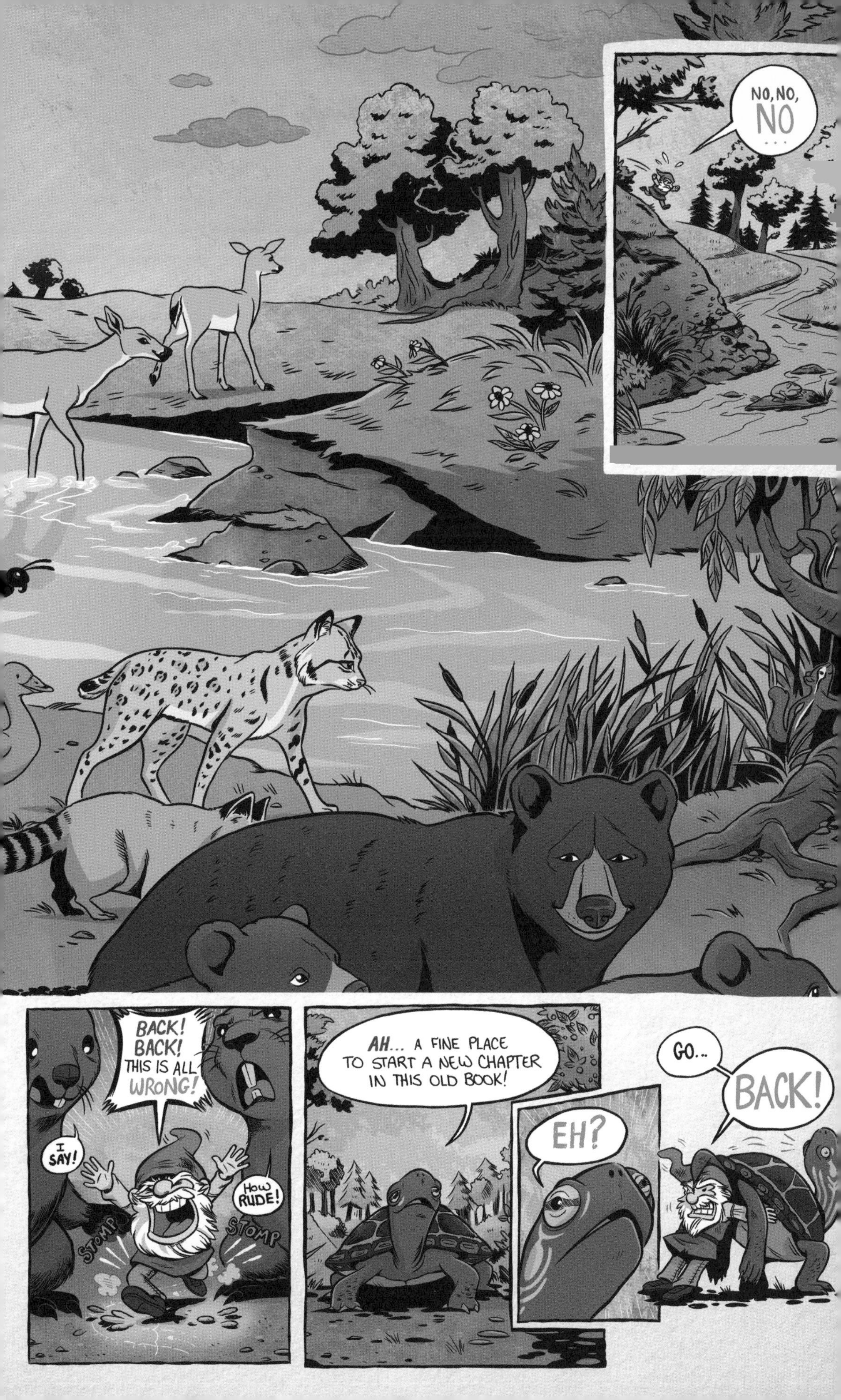
NO, NO, NO ...
BACK! BACK! THIS IS ALL WRONG!
I SAY!
HOW RUDE!
STOMP
STOMP
AH... A FINE PLACE TO START A NEW CHAPTER IN THIS OLD BOOK!
EH?
GO...
BACK!

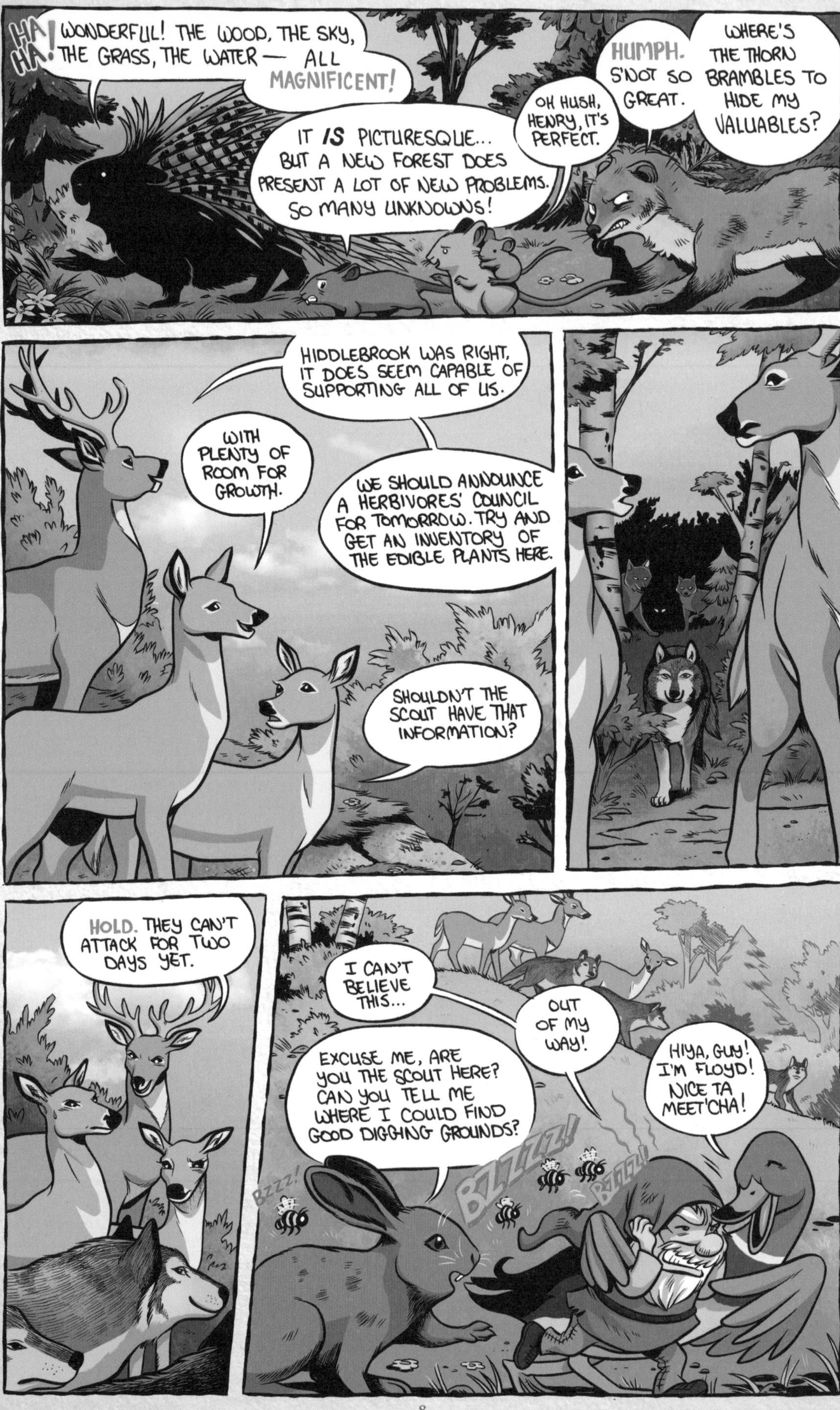
HA HA!
WONDERFUL! THE WOOD, THE SKY, THE GRASS, THE WATER— ALL MAGNIFICENT!
IT IS PICTURESQUE... BUT A NEW FOREST DOES PRESENT A LOT OF NEW PROBLEMS. SO MANY UNKNOWNS!
OH HUSH, HENRY, IT'S PERFECT.
HUMPH. S'NOT SO GREAT.
WHERE'S THE THORN BRAMBLES TO HIDE MY VALUABLES?
HIDDLEBROOK WAS RIGHT, IT DOES SEEM CAPABLE OF SUPPORTING ALL OF US.
WITH PLENTY OF ROOM FOR GROWTH.
WE SHOULD ANNOUNCE A HERBIVORES' COUNCIL FOR TOMORROW. TRY AND GET AN INVENTORY OF THE EDIBLE PLANTS HERE.
SHOULDN'T THE SCOUT HAVE THAT INFORMATION?
HOLD. THEY CAN'T ATTACK FOR TWO DAYS YET.
I CAN'T BELIEVE THIS...
OUT OF MY WAY!
EXCUSE ME, ARE YOU THE SCOUT HERE? CAN YOU TELL ME WHERE I COULD FIND GOOD DIGGING GROUNDS?
HIYA, GUY! I'M FLOYD! NICE TA MEET'CHA!
BZZZ!
BZZZZZ!

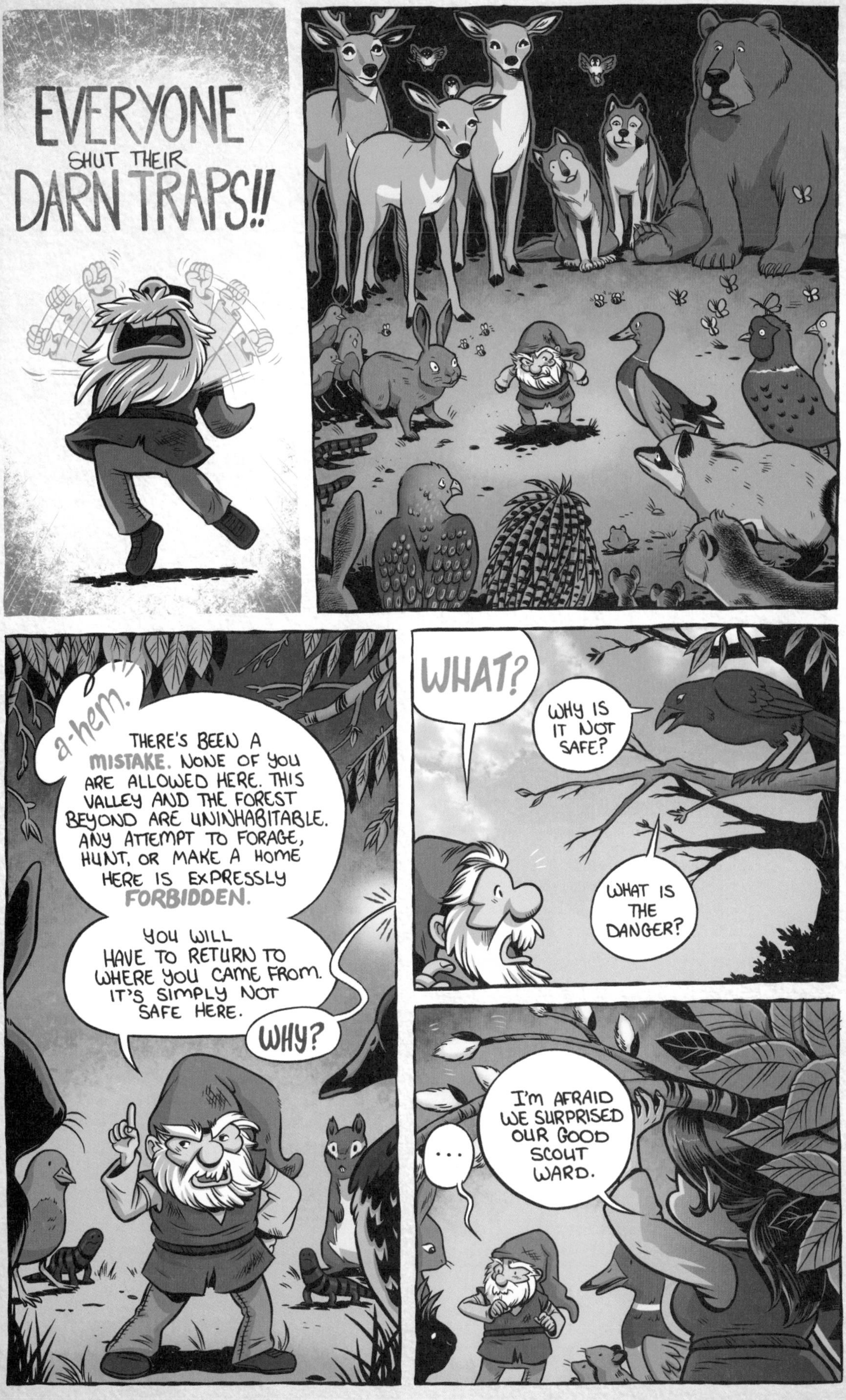
EVERYONE SHUT THEIR DARN TRAPS!!
a-hem.
THERE'S BEEN A MISTAKE. NONE OF YOU ARE ALLOWED HERE. THIS VALLEY AND THE FOREST BEYOND ARE UNINHABITABLE. ANY ATTEMPT TO FORAGE, HUNT, OR MAKE A HOME HERE IS EXPRESSLY FORBIDDEN.
YOU WILL HAVE TO RETURN TO WHERE YOU CAME FROM. IT'S SIMPLY NOT SAFE HERE.
WHY?
WHAT?
WHY IS IT NOT SAFE?
WHAT IS THE DANGER?
...
I'M AFRAID WE SURPRISED OUR GOOD SCOUT WARD.

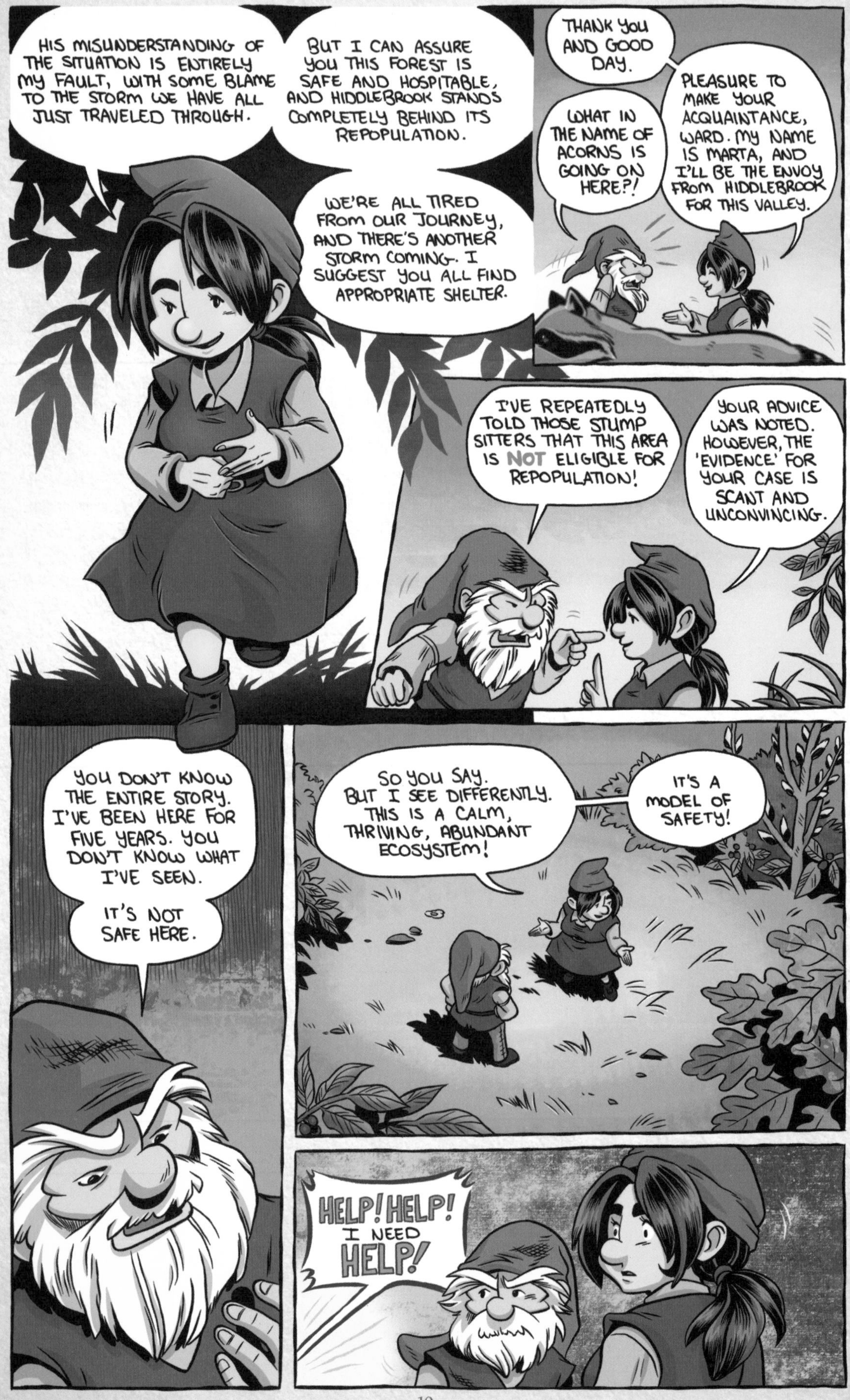
HIS MISUNDERSTANDING OF THE SITUATION IS ENTIRELY MY FAULT, WITH SOME BLAME TO THE STORM WE HAVE ALL JUST TRAVELED THROUGH.
BUT I CAN ASSURE YOU THIS FOREST IS SAFE AND HOSPITABLE, AND HIDDLEBROOK STANDS COMPLETELY BEHIND ITS REPOPULATION.
WE'RE ALL TIRED FROM OUR JOURNEY, AND THERE'S ANOTHER STORM COMING. I SUGGEST YOU ALL FIND APPROPRIATE SHELTER.
THANK YOU AND GOOD DAY.
WHAT IN THE NAME OF ACORNS IS GOING ON HERE?!
PLEASURE TO MAKE YOUR ACQUAINTANCE, WARD. MY NAME IS MARTA, AND I'LL BE THE ENVOY FROM HIDDLEBROOK FOR THIS VALLEY.
I'VE REPEATEDLY TOLD THOSE STUMP SITTERS THAT THIS AREA IS NOT ELIGIBLE FOR REPOPULATION!
YOUR ADVICE WAS NOTED. HOWEVER, THE 'EVIDENCE' FOR YOUR CASE IS SCANT AND UNCONVINCING.
YOU DON'T KNOW THE ENTIRE STORY. I'VE BEEN HERE FOR FIVE YEARS. YOU DON'T KNOW WHAT I'VE SEEN.
IT'S NOT SAFE HERE.
SO YOU SAY. BUT I SEE DIFFERENTLY. THIS IS A CALM, THRIVING, ABUNDANT ECOSYSTEM!
IT'S A MODEL OF SAFETY!
HELP! HELP! I NEED HELP!

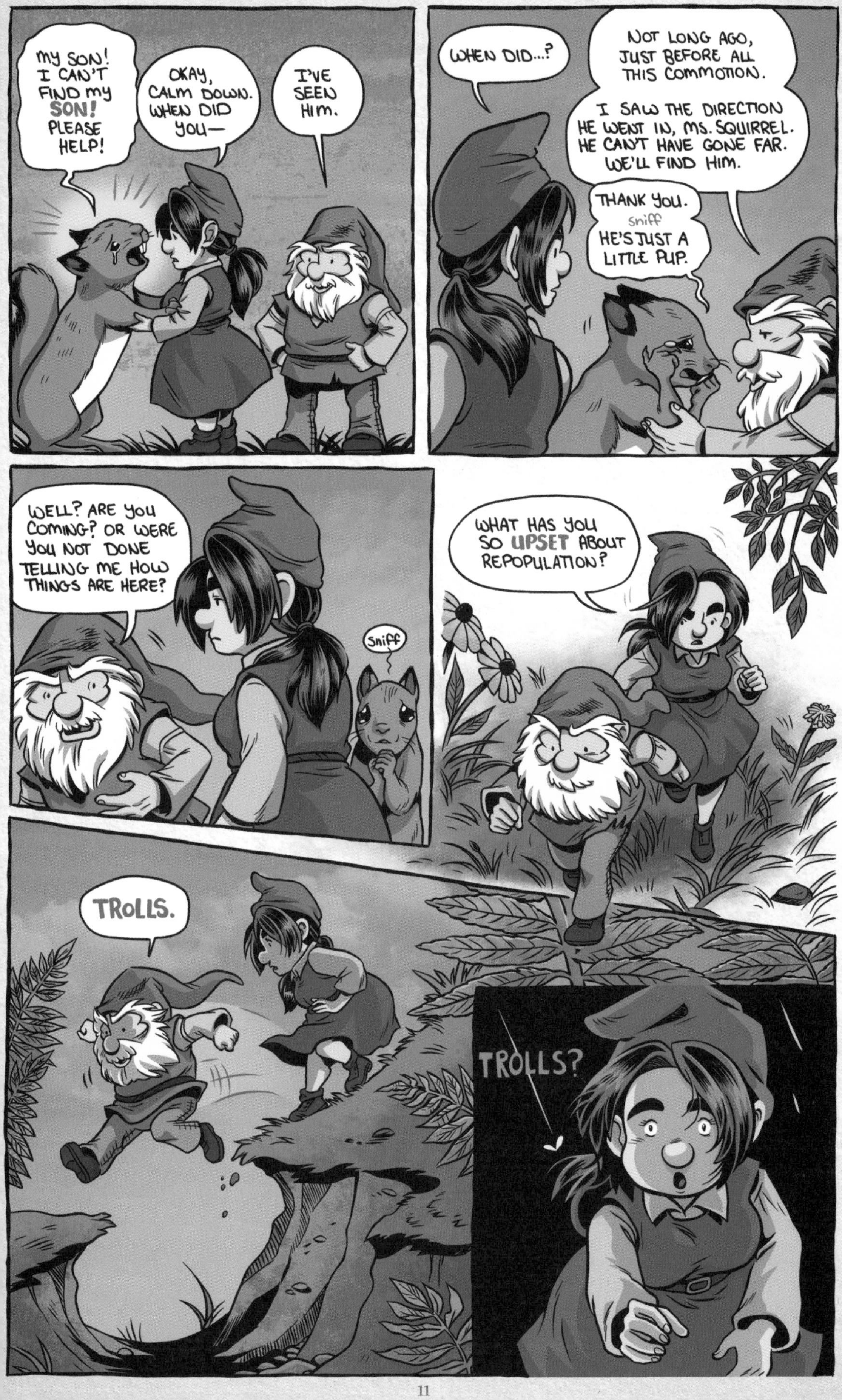
MY SON! I CAN'T FIND MY SON! PLEASE HELP!
OKAY, CALM DOWN. WHEN DID YOU—
I'VE SEEN HIM.
WHEN DID...?
NOT LONG AGO, JUST BEFORE ALL THIS COMMOTION.
I SAW THE DIRECTION HE WENT IN, MS. SQUIRREL. HE CAN'T HAVE GONE FAR. WE'LL FIND HIM.
THANK YOU. sniff HE'S JUST A LITTLE PUP.
WELL? ARE YOU COMING? OR WERE YOU NOT DONE TELLING ME HOW THINGS ARE HERE?
sniff
WHAT HAS YOU SO UPSET ABOUT REPOPULATION?
TROLLS.
TROLLS?

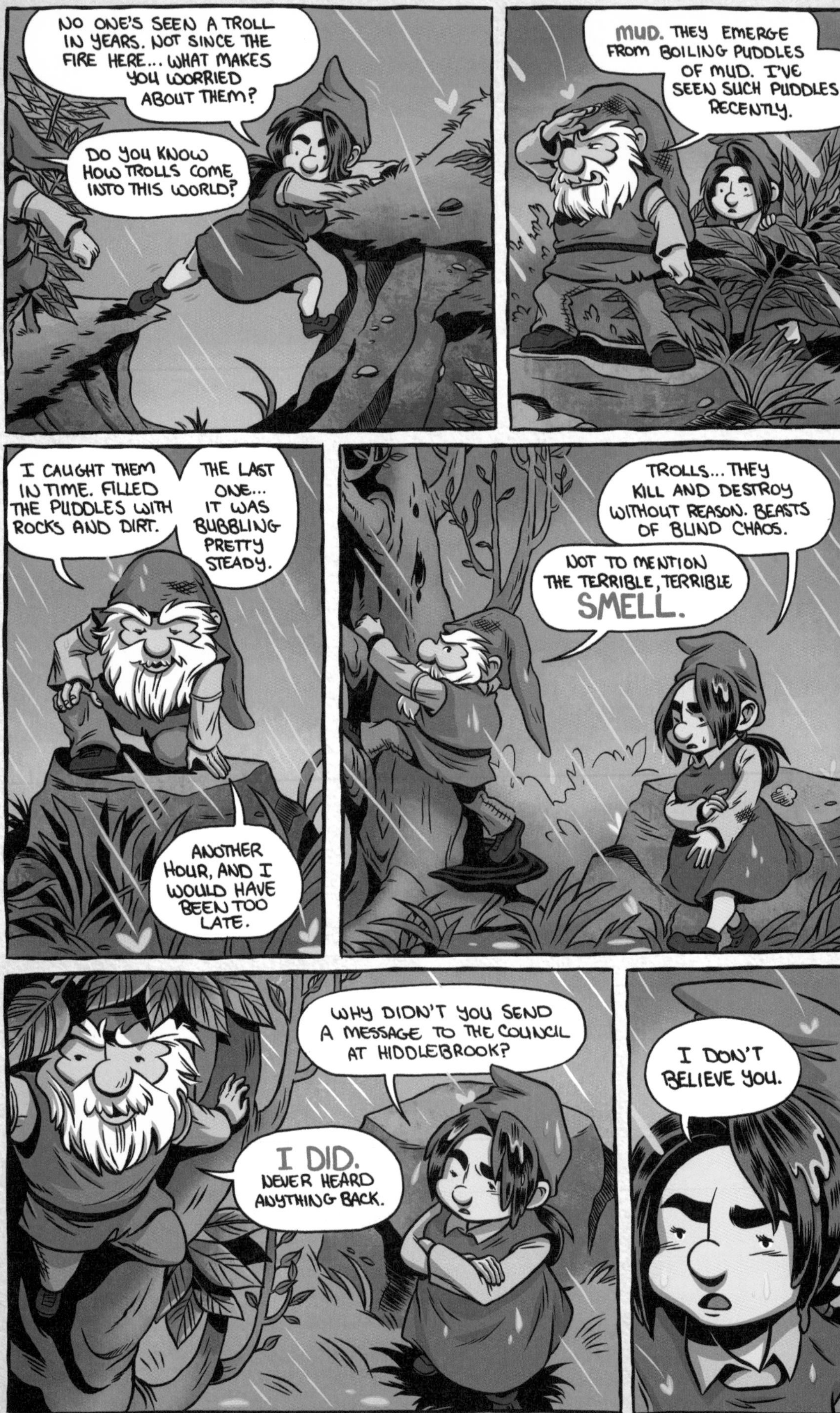
NO ONE'S SEEN A TROLL IN YEARS. NOT SINCE THE FIRE HERE... WHAT MAKES YOU WORRIED ABOUT THEM?
DO YOU KNOW HOW TROLLS COME INTO THIS WORLD?
MUD. THEY EMERGE FROM BOILING PUDDLES OF MUD. I'VE SEEN SUCH PUDDLES. RECENTLY.
I CAUGHT THEM IN TIME. FILLED THE PUDDLES WITH ROCKS AND DIRT.
THE LAST ONE... IT WAS BUBBLING PRETTY STEADY.
ANOTHER HOUR, AND I WOULD HAVE BEEN TOO LATE.
TROLLS... THEY KILL AND DESTROY WITHOUT REASON. BEASTS OF BLIND CHAOS.
NOT TO MENTION THE TERRIBLE, TERRIBLE SMELL.
WHY DIDN'T YOU SEND A MESSAGE TO THE COUNCIL AT HIDDLEBROOK?
I DID. NEVER HEARD ANYTHING BACK.
I DON'T BELIEVE YOU.

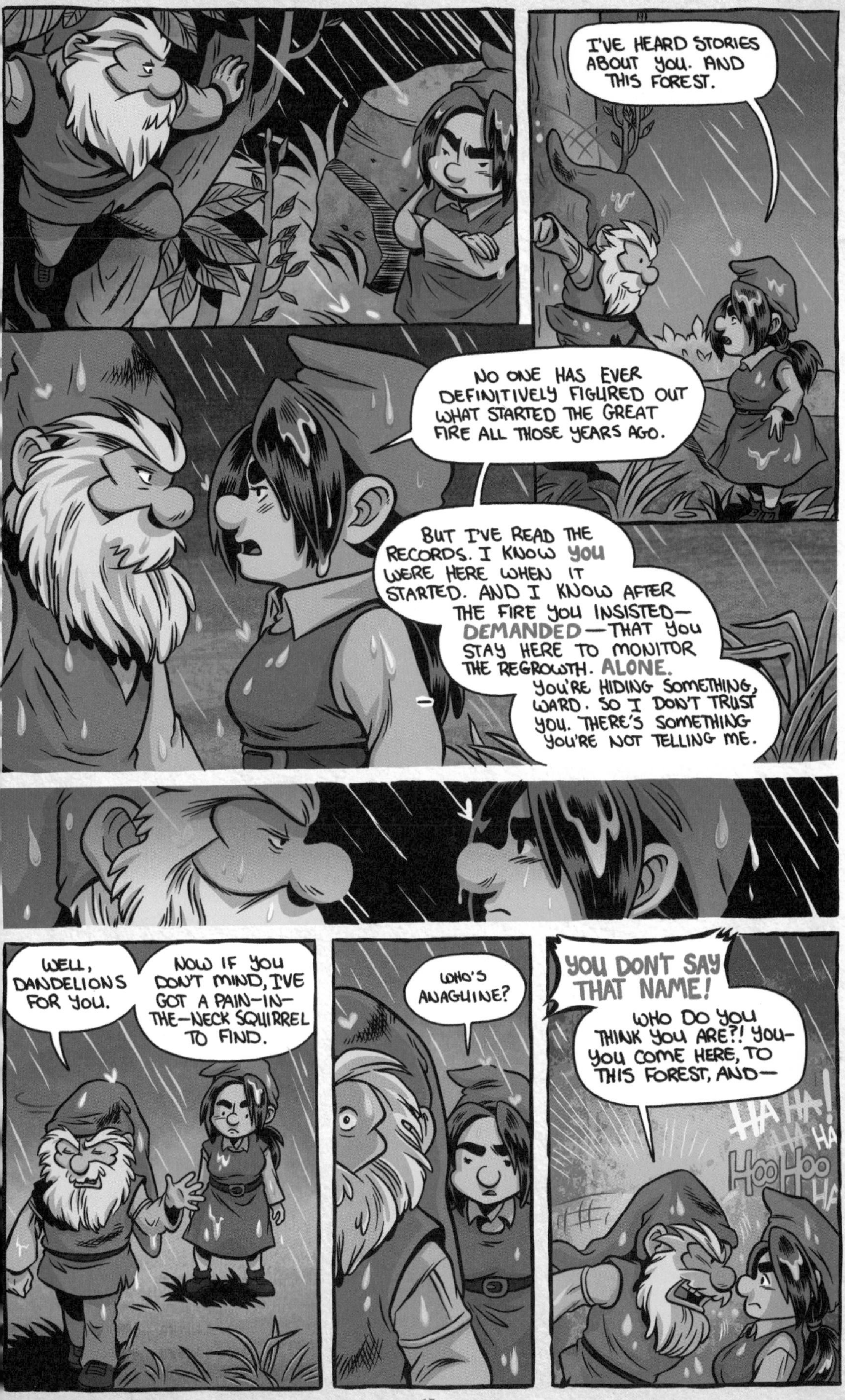

I'VE HEARD STORIES ABOUT YOU. AND THIS FOREST.
NO ONE HAS EVER DEFINITIVELY FIGURED OUT WHAT STARTED THE GREAT FIRE ALL THOSE YEARS AGO.
BUT I'VE READ THE RECORDS. I KNOW YOU WERE HERE WHEN IT STARTED. AND I KNOW AFTER THE FIRE YOU INSISTED—DEMANDED—THAT YOU STAY HERE TO MONITOR THE REGROWTH. ALONE.
YOU'RE HIDING SOMETHING, WARD. SO I DON'T TRUST YOU. THERE'S SOMETHING YOU'RE NOT TELLING ME.
WELL, DANDELIONS FOR YOU.
NOW IF YOU DON'T MIND, I'VE GOT A PAIN-IN-THE-NECK SQUIRREL TO FIND.
WHO'S ANAGUINE?
YOU DON'T SAY THAT NAME!
WHO DO YOU THINK YOU ARE?! YOU-YOU COME HERE, TO THIS FOREST, AND—
HA HA! HA HA
HOO HOO HA

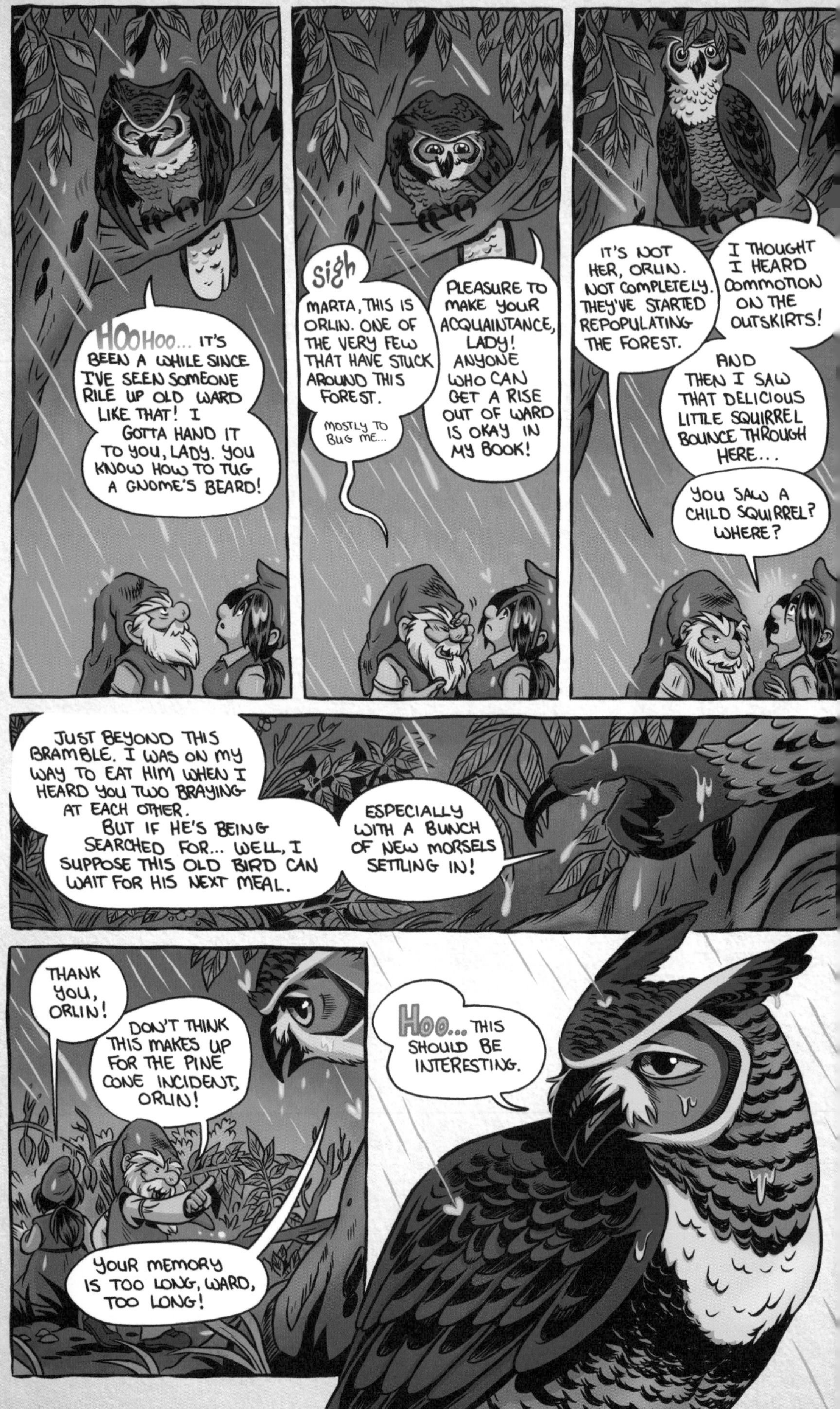
HOOHOO... IT'S BEEN A WHILE SINCE I'VE SEEN SOMEONE RILE UP OLD WARD LIKE THAT! I GOTTA HAND IT TO YOU, LADY. YOU KNOW HOW TO TUG A GNOME'S BEARD!
SIGH
MARTA, THIS IS ORLIN. ONE OF THE VERY FEW THAT HAVE STUCK AROUND THIS FOREST.
MOSTLY TO BUG ME...
PLEASURE TO MAKE YOUR ACQUAINTANCE, LADY! ANYONE WHO CAN GET A RISE OUT OF WARD IS OKAY IN MY BOOK!
IT'S NOT HER, ORLIN. NOT COMPLETELY. THEY'VE STARTED REPOPULATING THE FOREST.
I THOUGHT I HEARD COMMOTION ON THE OUTSKIRTS!
AND THEN I SAW THAT DELICIOUS LITTLE SQUIRREL BOUNCE THROUGH HERE...
YOU SAW A CHILD SQUIRREL? WHERE?
JUST BEYOND THIS BRAMBLE. I WAS ON MY WAY TO EAT HIM WHEN I HEARD YOU TWO BRAYING AT EACH OTHER.
BUT IF HE'S BEING SEARCHED FOR... WELL, I SUPPOSE THIS OLD BIRD CAN WAIT FOR HIS NEXT MEAL.
ESPECIALLY WITH A BUNCH OF NEW MORSELS SETTLING IN!
THANK YOU, ORLIN!
DON'T THINK THIS MAKES UP FOR THE PINE CONE INCIDENT, ORLIN!
YOUR MEMORY IS TOO LONG, WARD, TOO LONG!
HOO... THIS SHOULD BE INTERESTING.

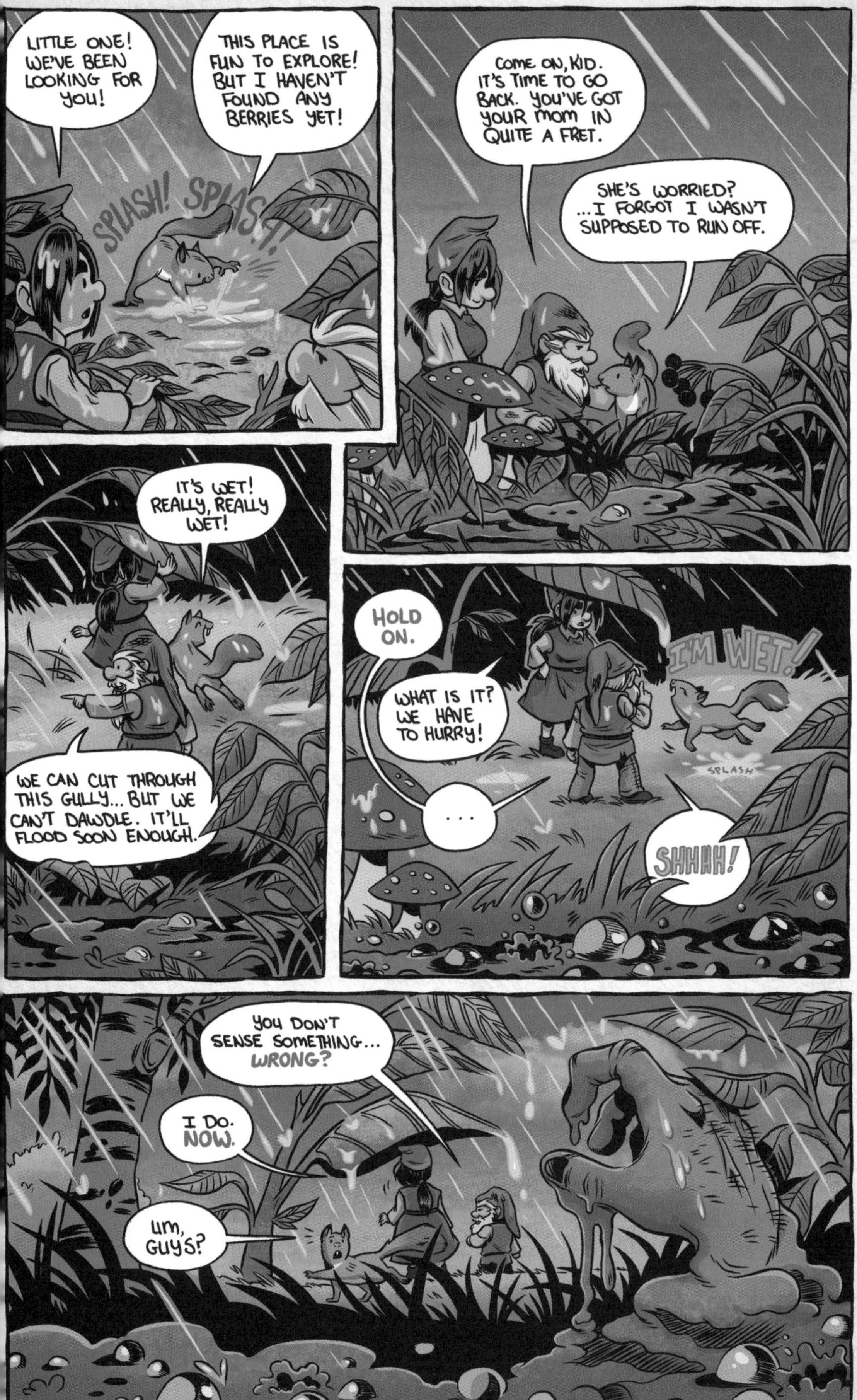
LITTLE ONE! WE'VE BEEN LOOKING FOR YOU!
THIS PLACE IS FUN TO EXPLORE! BUT I HAVEN'T FOUND ANY BERRIES YET!
SPLASH! SPLASH!
COME ON, KID. IT'S TIME TO GO BACK. YOU'VE GOT YOUR MOM IN QUITE A FRET.
SHE'S WORRIED? ...I FORGOT I WASN'T SUPPOSED TO RUN OFF.
IT'S WET! REALLY, REALLY WET!
WE CAN CUT THROUGH THIS GULLY... BUT WE CAN'T DAWDLE. IT'LL FLOOD SOON ENOUGH.
HOLD ON.
WHAT IS IT? WE HAVE TO HURRY!
I'M WET!
SPLASH
. . .
SHHHH!
YOU DON'T SENSE SOMETHING... WRONG?
I DO. NOW.
UM, GUYS?

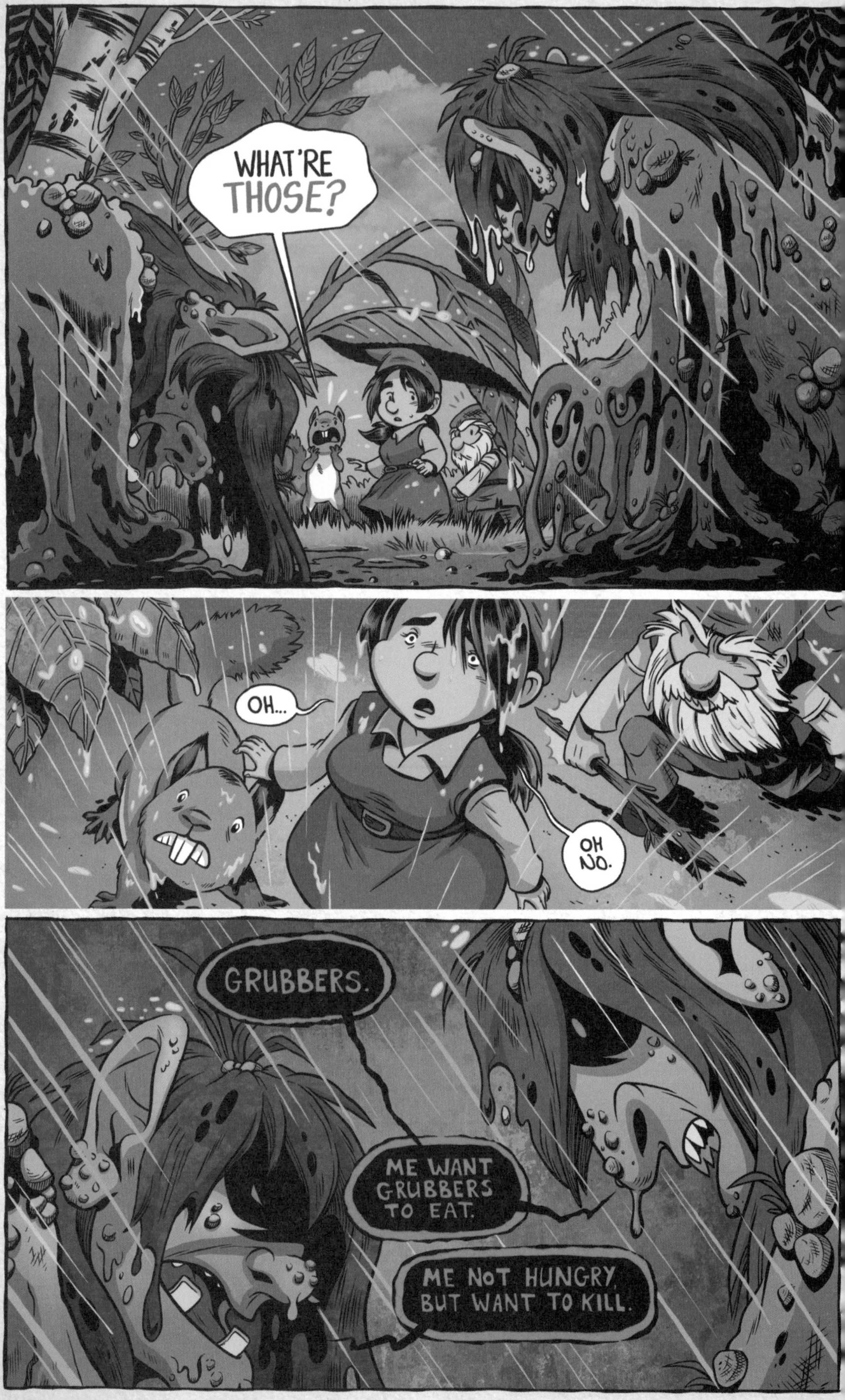
WHAT'RE THOSE?
OH...
OH NO.
GRUBBERS.
ME WANT GRUBBERS TO EAT.
ME NOT HUNGRY, BUT WANT TO KILL.

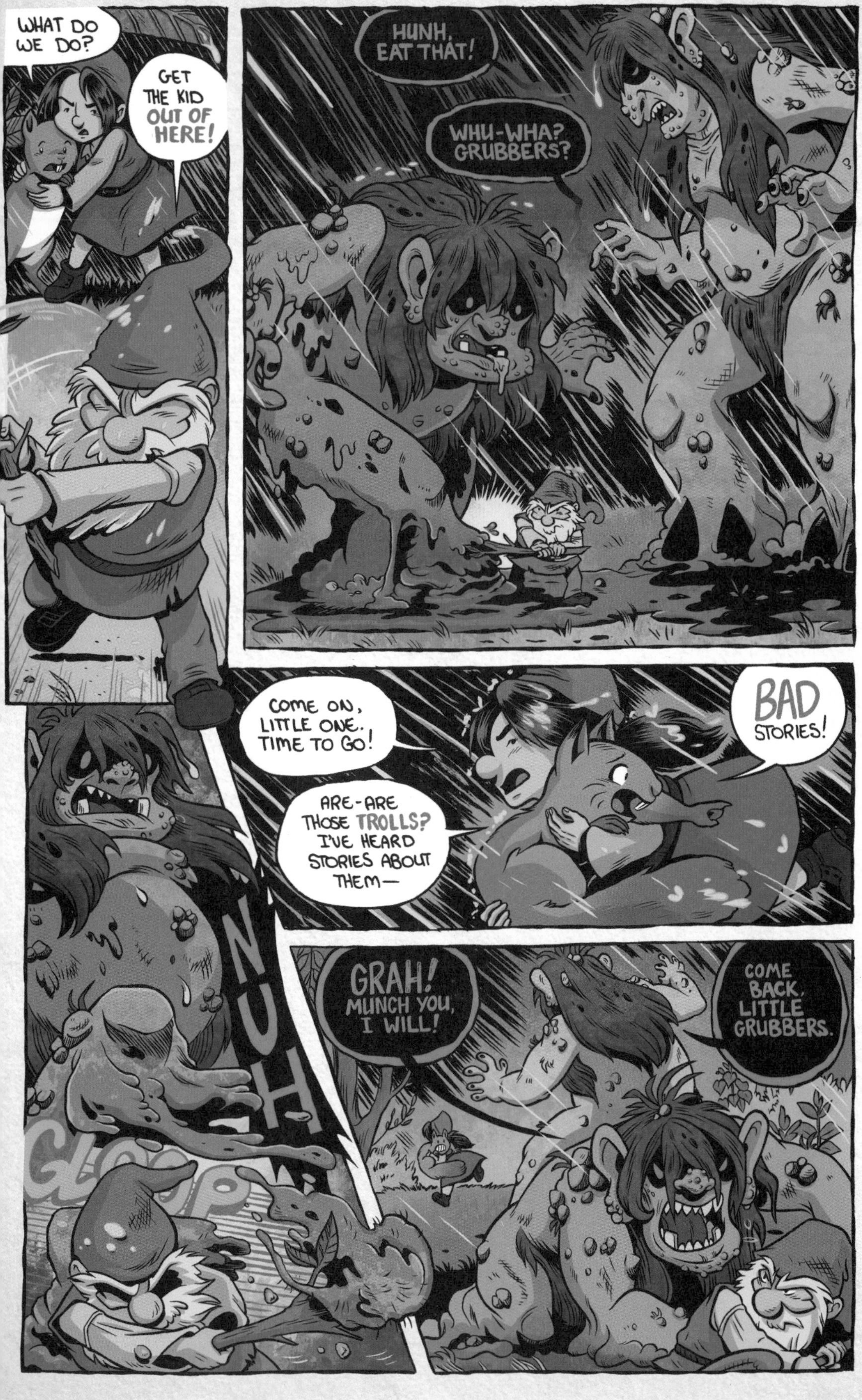
WHAT DO WE DO?
GET THE KID OUT OF HERE!
HUNH, EAT THAT!
WHU-WHA? GRUBBERS?
COME ON, LITTLE ONE. TIME TO GO!
ARE-ARE THOSE TROLLS? I'VE HEARD STORIES ABOUT THEM—
BAD STORIES!
GRAH! MUNCH YOU, I WILL!
COME BACK, LITTLE GRUBBERS.

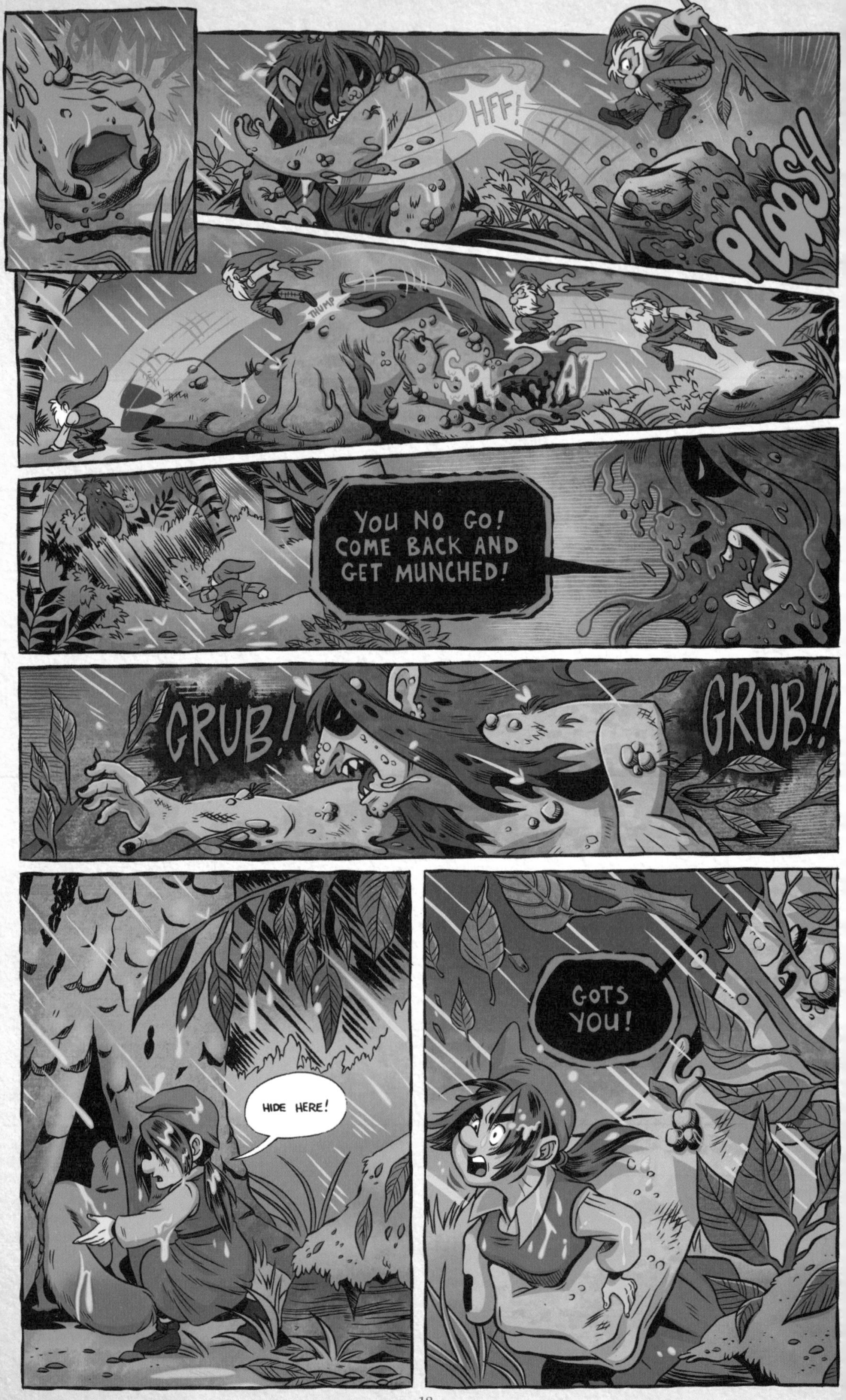
GRUMPH!
HFF!
PLOOSH
THUMP
SPLAT
YOU NO GO! COME BACK AND GET MUNCHED!
GRUB!
GRUB!!
HIDE HERE!
GOTS YOU!

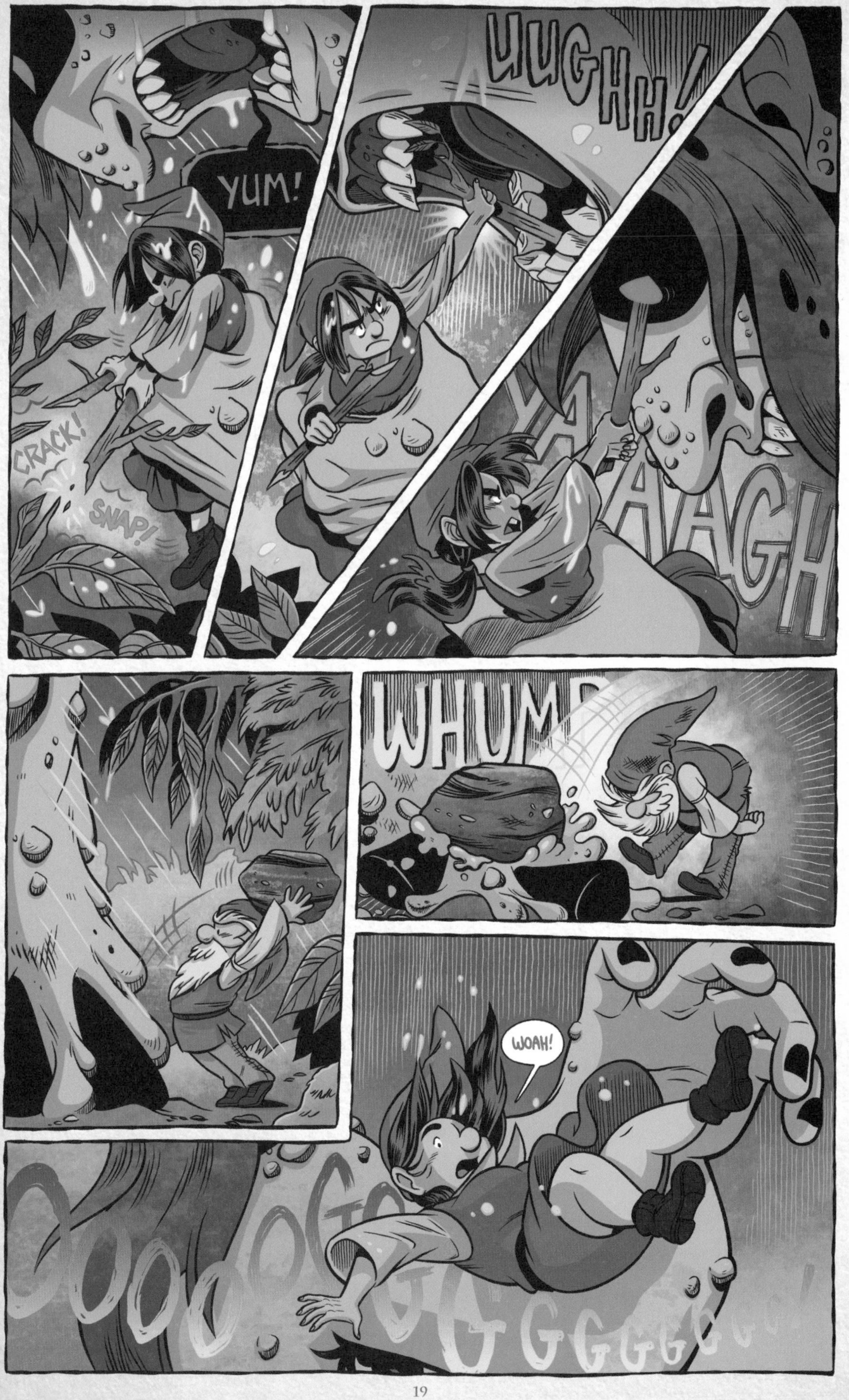
YUM!
CRACK!
SNAP!
UUGHH!
YAAAGH
WHUMP
WOAH!
OOOOOGGGGGGGG!

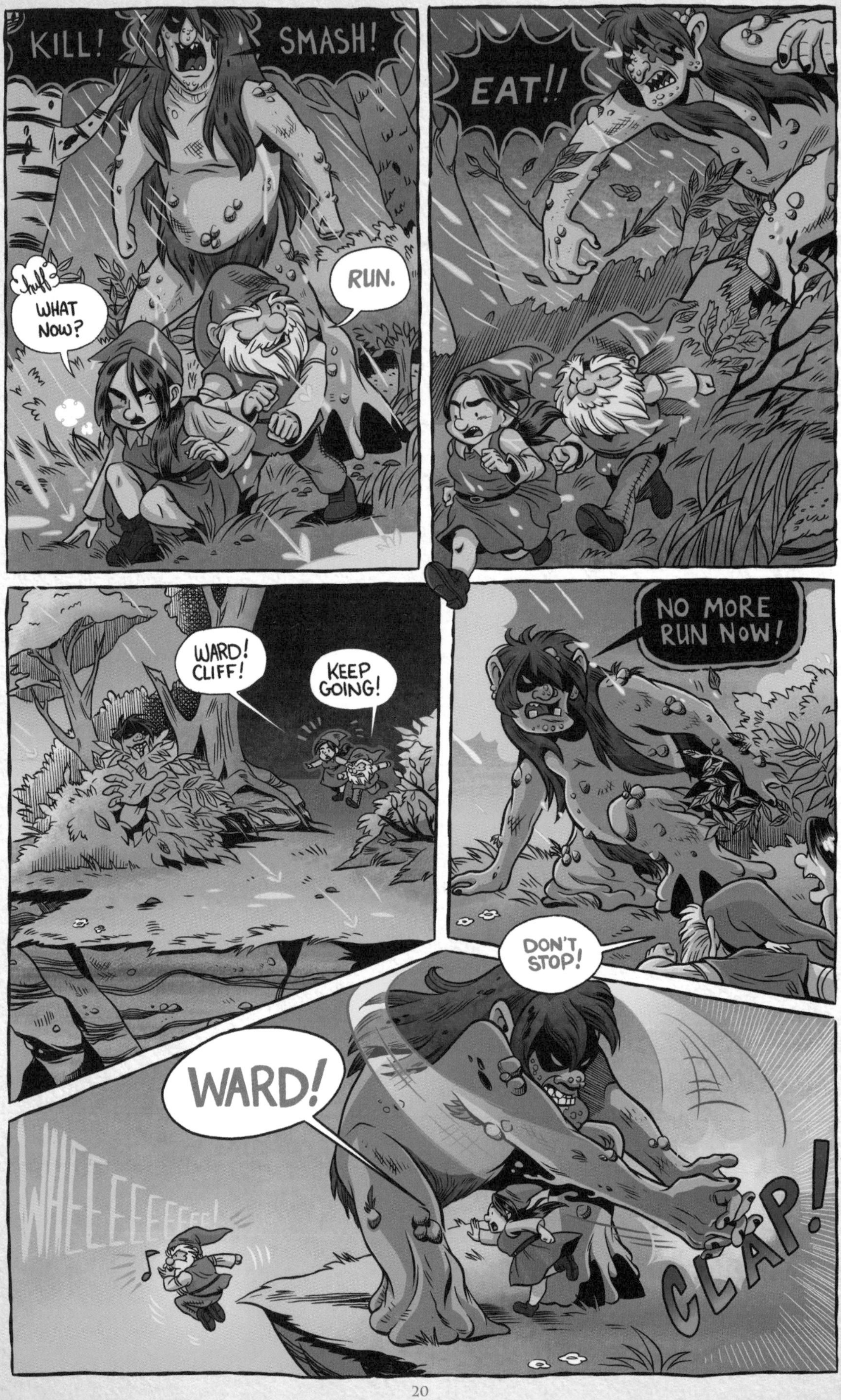
KILL!
SMASH!
huff
WHAT NOW?
RUN.
EAT!!
WARD! CLIFF!
KEEP GOING!
NO MORE RUN NOW!
DON'T STOP!
WARD!
WHEEEEEEEEEE!
CLAP!

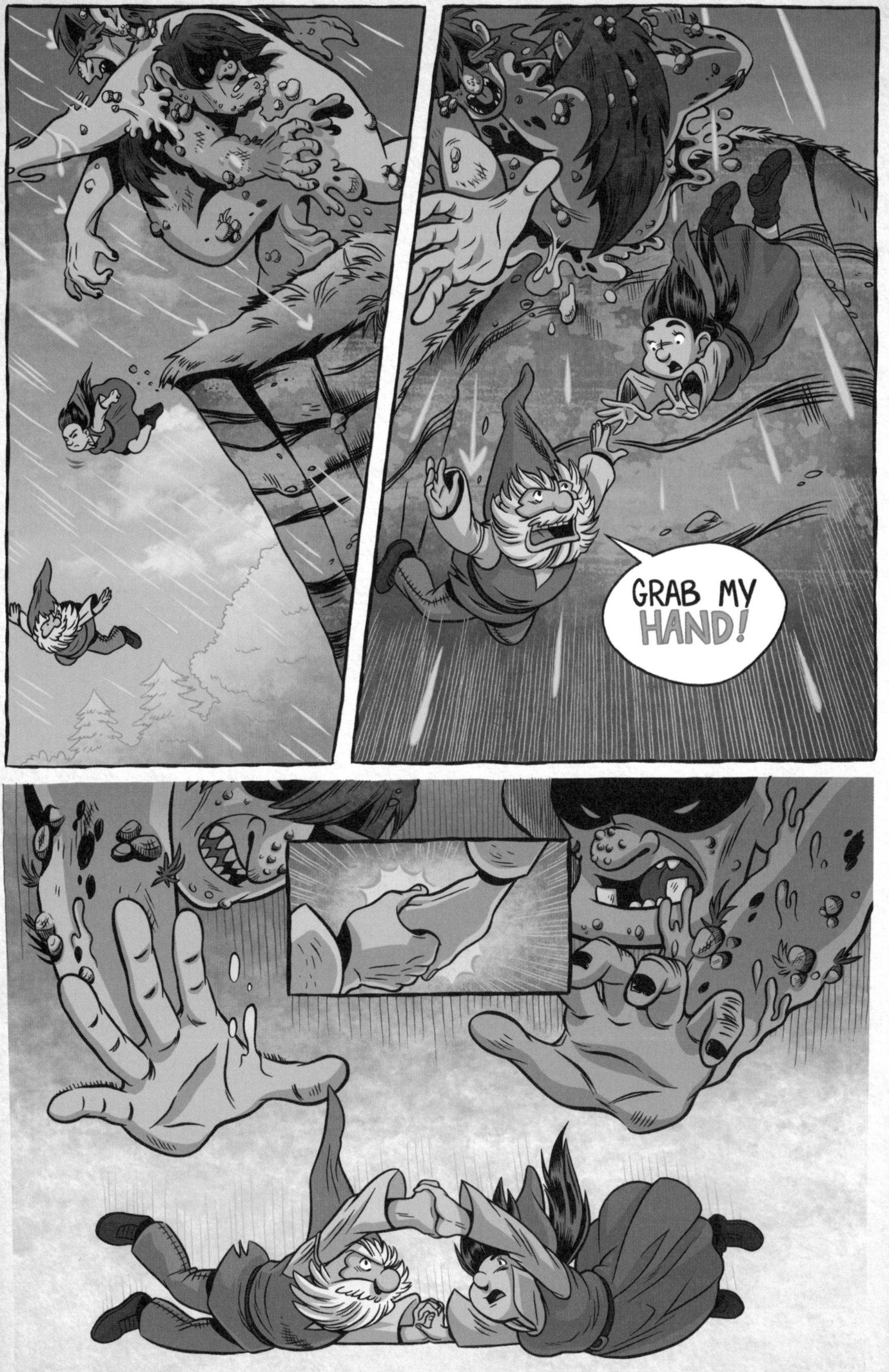
GRAB MY HAND!

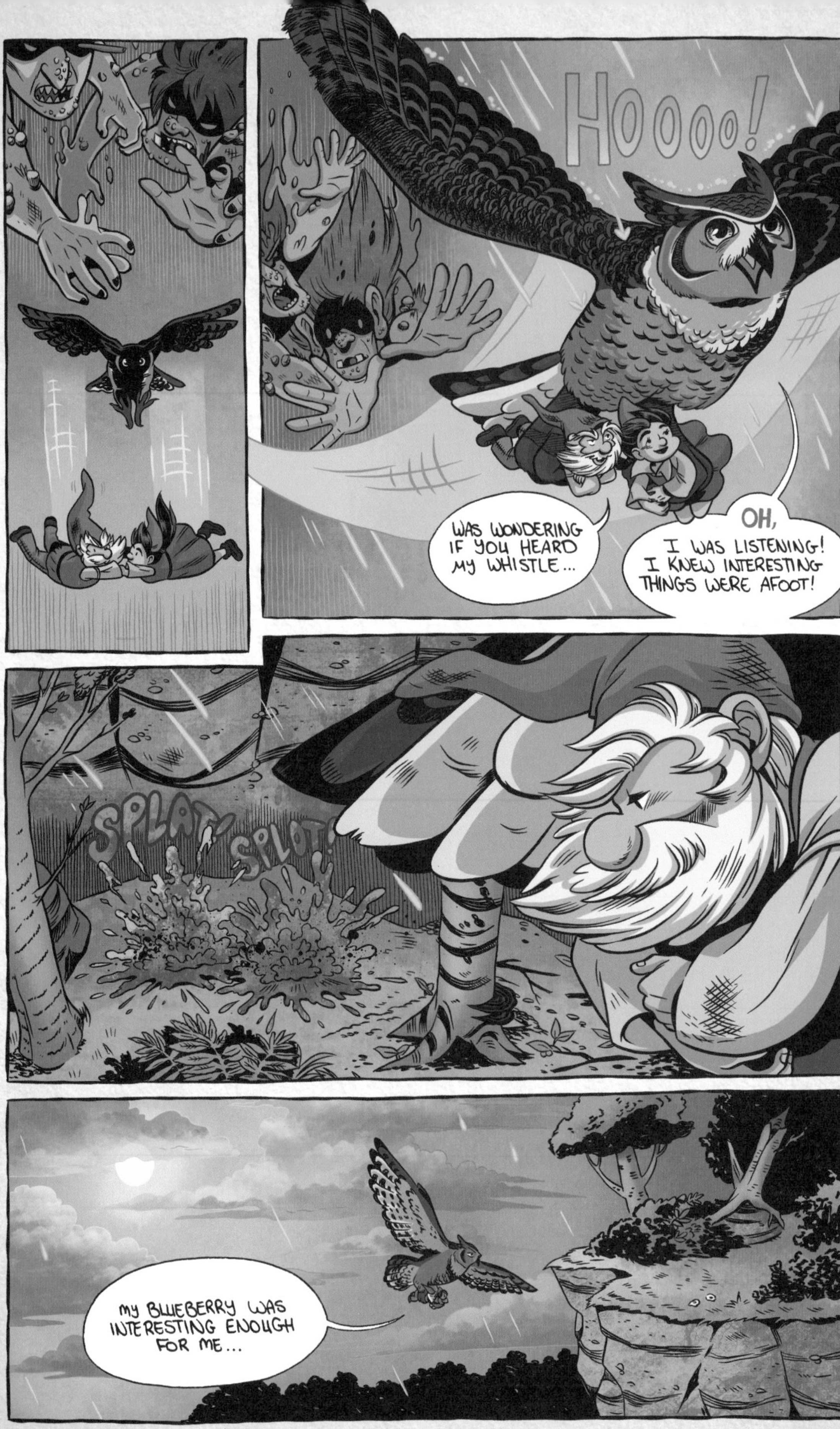
HOOOO!
WAS WONDERING IF YOU HEARD MY WHISTLE...
OH, I WAS LISTENING! I KNEW INTERESTING THINGS WERE AFOOT!
SPLAT!
SPLOT!
MY BLUEBERRY WAS INTERESTING ENOUGH FOR ME...

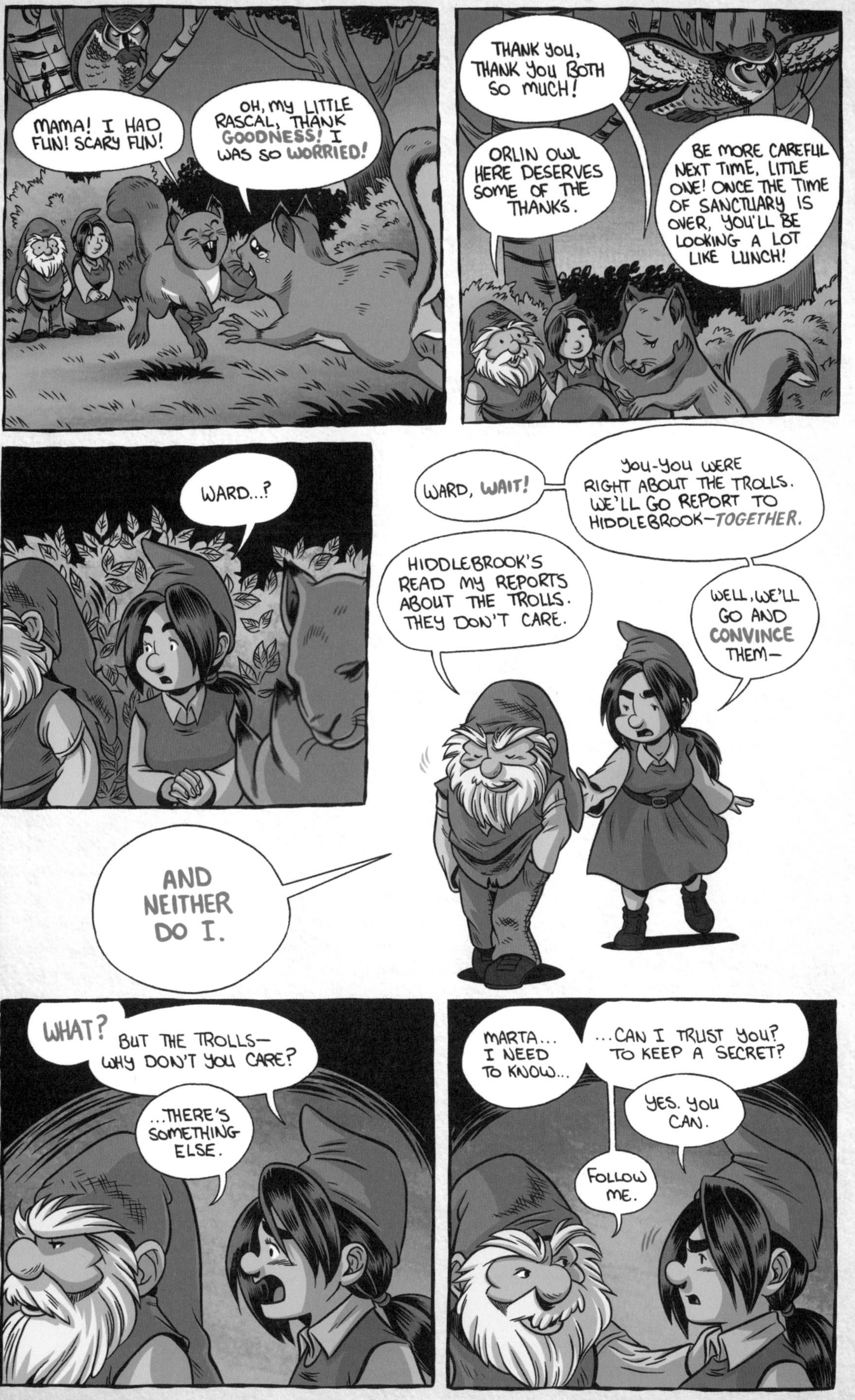
MAMA! I HAD FUN! SCARY FUN!
OH, MY LITTLE RASCAL, THANK GOODNESS! I WAS SO WORRIED!
THANK YOU, THANK YOU BOTH SO MUCH!
ORLIN OWL HERE DESERVES SOME OF THE THANKS.
BE MORE CAREFUL NEXT TIME, LITTLE ONE! ONCE THE TIME OF SANCTUARY IS OVER, YOU'LL BE LOOKING A LOT LIKE LUNCH!
WARD...?
WARD, WAIT!
YOU-YOU WERE RIGHT ABOUT THE TROLLS. WE'LL GO REPORT TO HIDDLEBROOK—TOGETHER.
HIDDLEBROOK'S READ MY REPORTS ABOUT THE TROLLS. THEY DON'T CARE.
WELL, WE'LL GO AND CONVINCE THEM—
AND NEITHER DO I.
WHAT? BUT THE TROLLS— WHY DON'T YOU CARE?
...THERE'S SOMETHING ELSE.
MARTA... I NEED TO KNOW...
...CAN I TRUST YOU? TO KEEP A SECRET?
YES. YOU CAN.
FOLLOW ME.

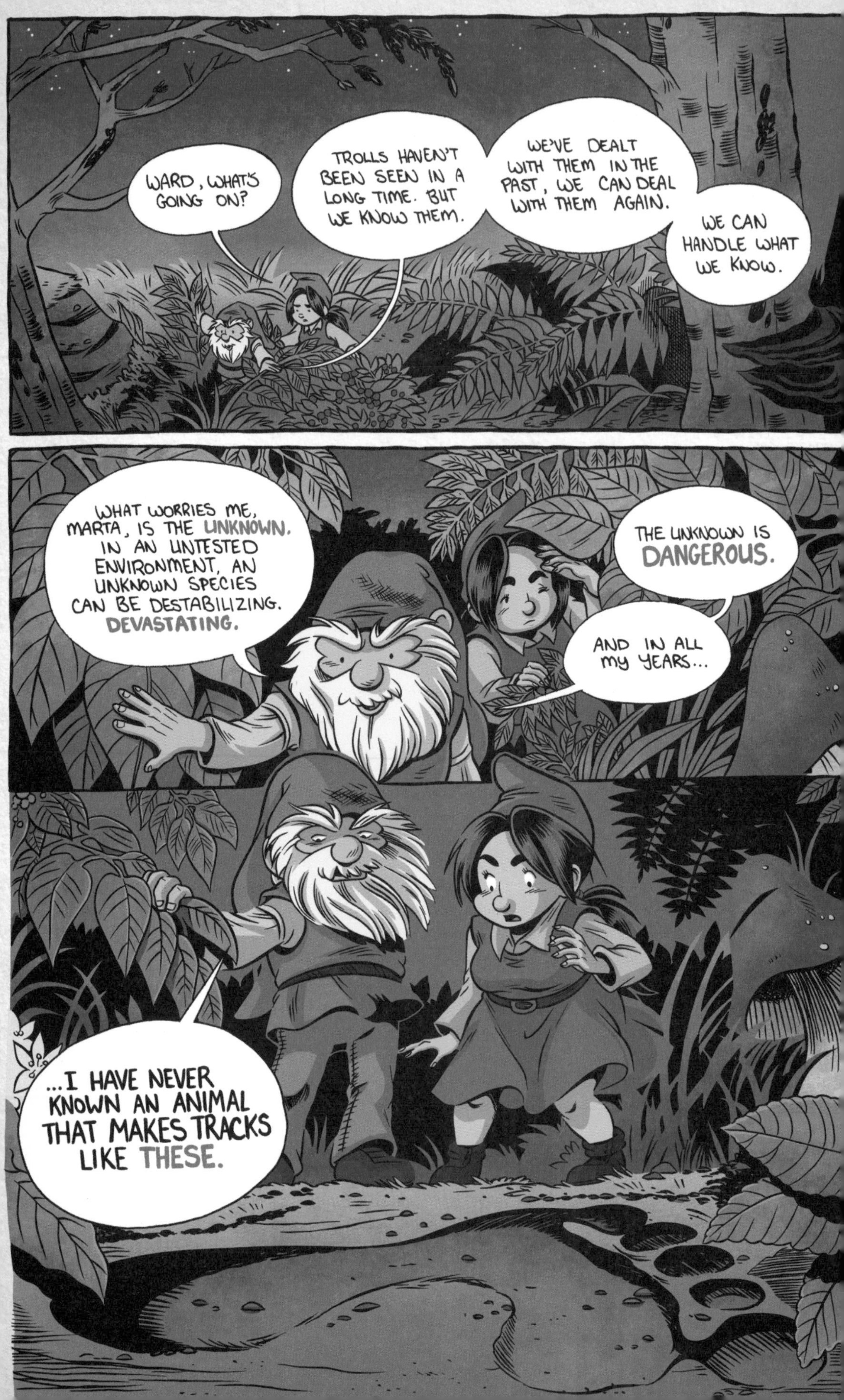

WARD, WHAT'S GOING ON?
TROLLS HAVEN'T BEEN SEEN IN A LONG TIME. BUT WE KNOW THEM.
WE'VE DEALT WITH THEM IN THE PAST, WE CAN DEAL WITH THEM AGAIN.
WE CAN HANDLE WHAT WE KNOW.
WHAT WORRIES ME, MARTA, IS THE UNKNOWN. IN AN UNTESTED ENVIRONMENT, AN UNKNOWN SPECIES CAN BE DESTABILIZING. DEVASTATING.
THE UNKNOWN IS DANGEROUS.
AND IN ALL MY YEARS...
...I HAVE NEVER KNOWN AN ANIMAL THAT MAKES TRACKS LIKE THESE.

Chapter Two

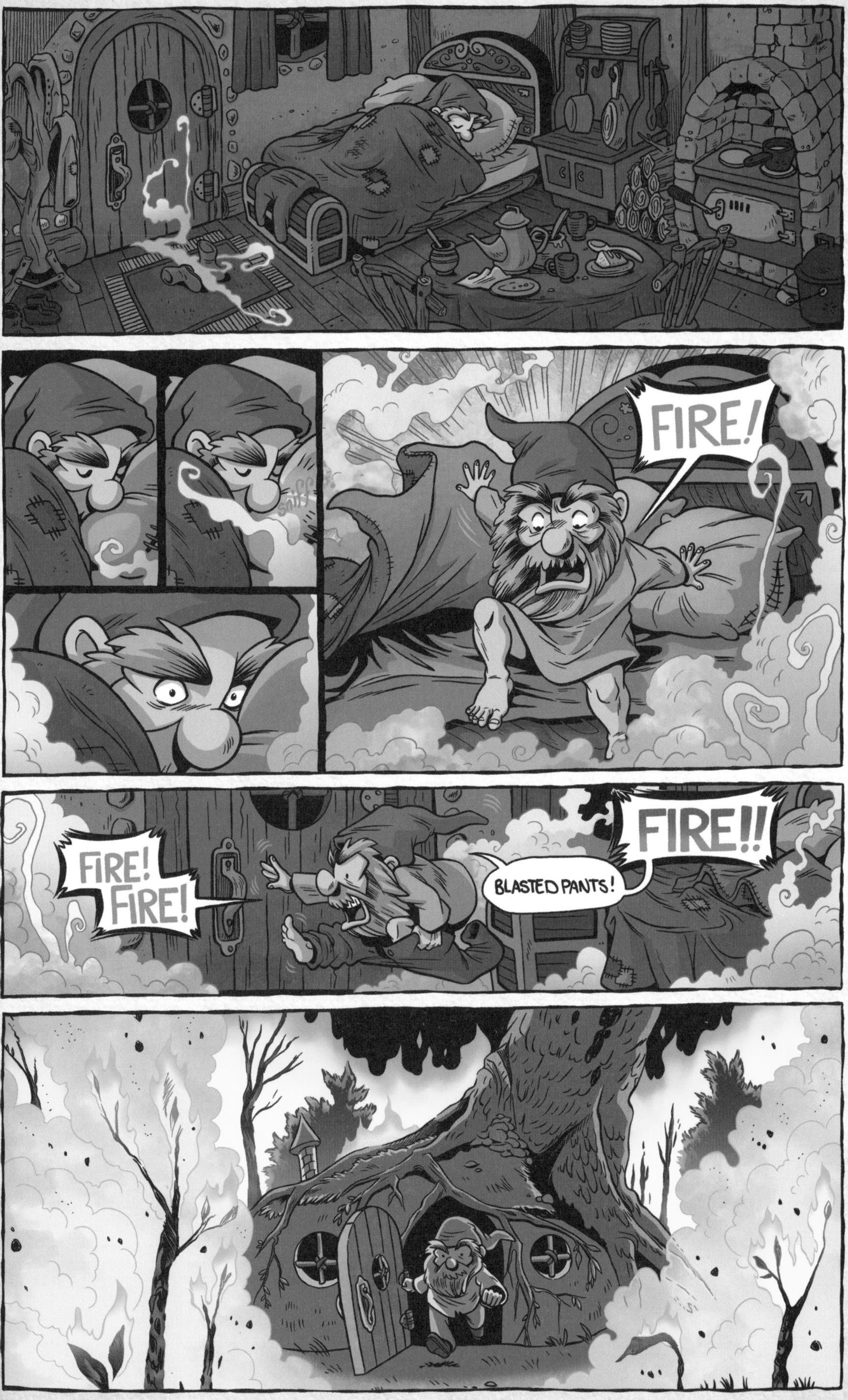
FIRE!
FIRE! FIRE!
BLASTED PANTS!
FIRE!!

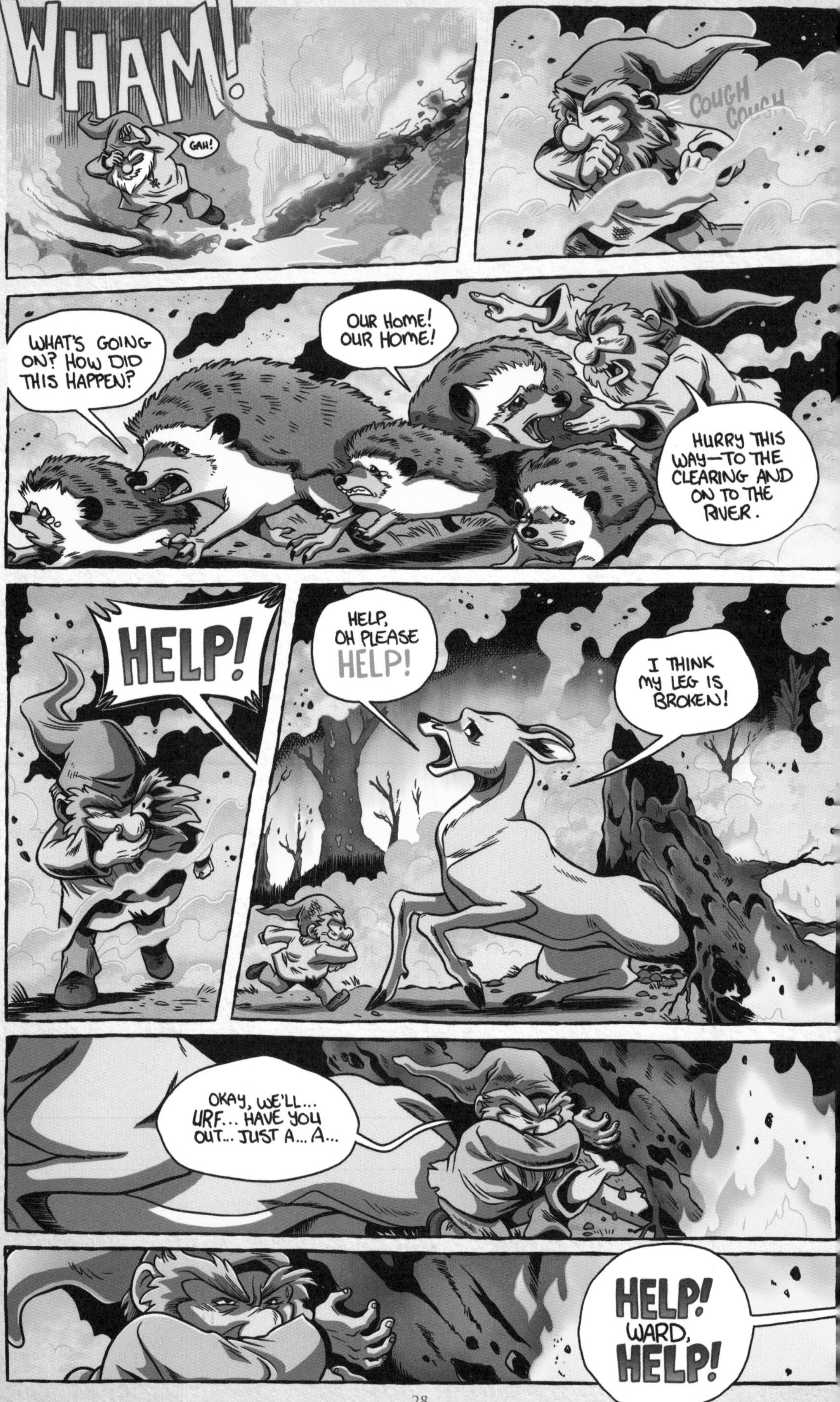

WHAM!
GAH!
COUGH COUGH
WHAT'S GOING ON? HOW DID THIS HAPPEN?
OUR HOME! OUR HOME!
HURRY THIS WAY—TO THE CLEARING AND ON TO THE RIVER.
HELP!
HELP, OH PLEASE HELP!
I THINK MY LEG IS BROKEN!
OKAY, WE'LL... URF... HAVE YOU OUT... JUST A... A...
HELP! WARD, HELP!

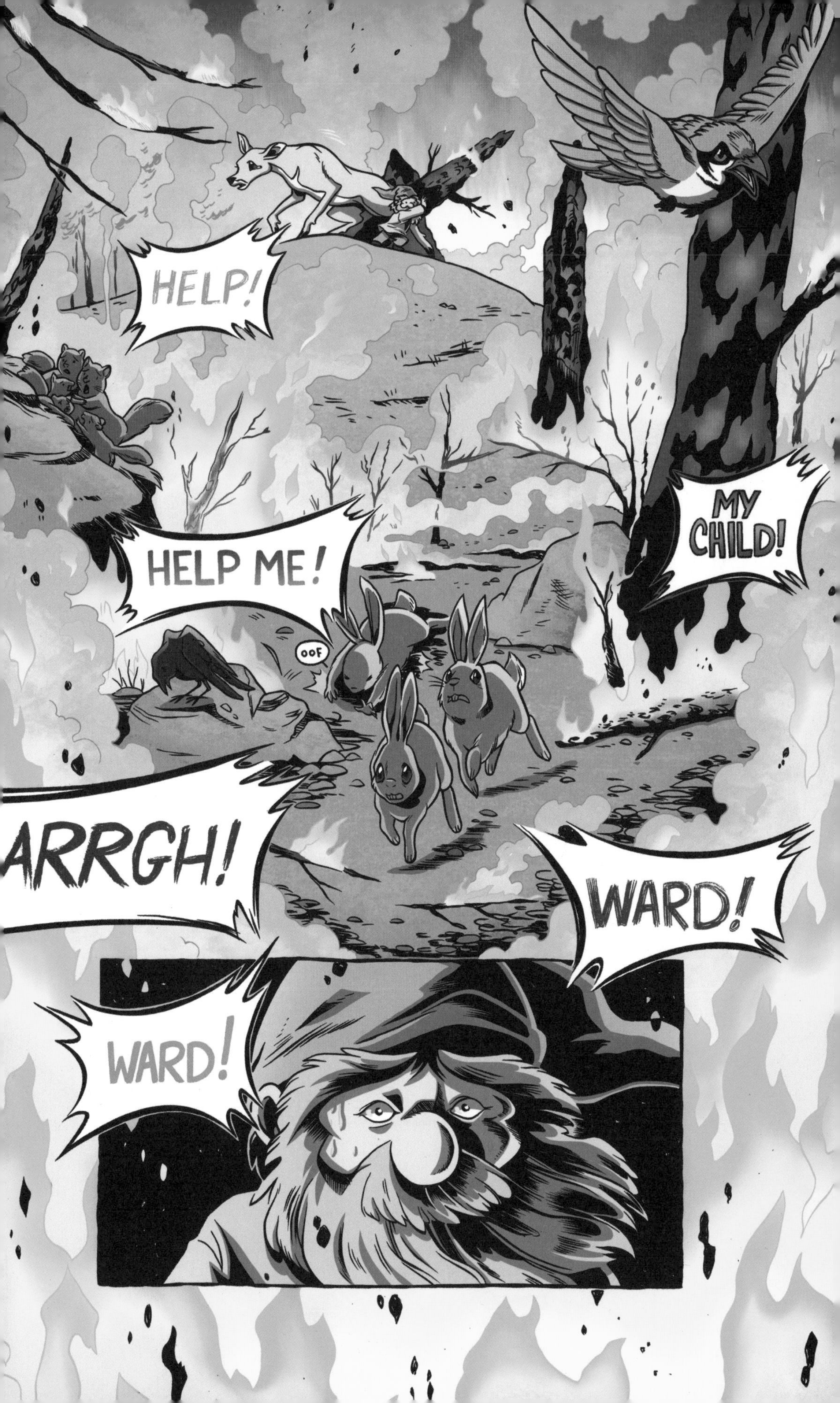
HELP!
MY CHILD!
HELP ME!
OOF
ARRGH!
WARD!
WARD!

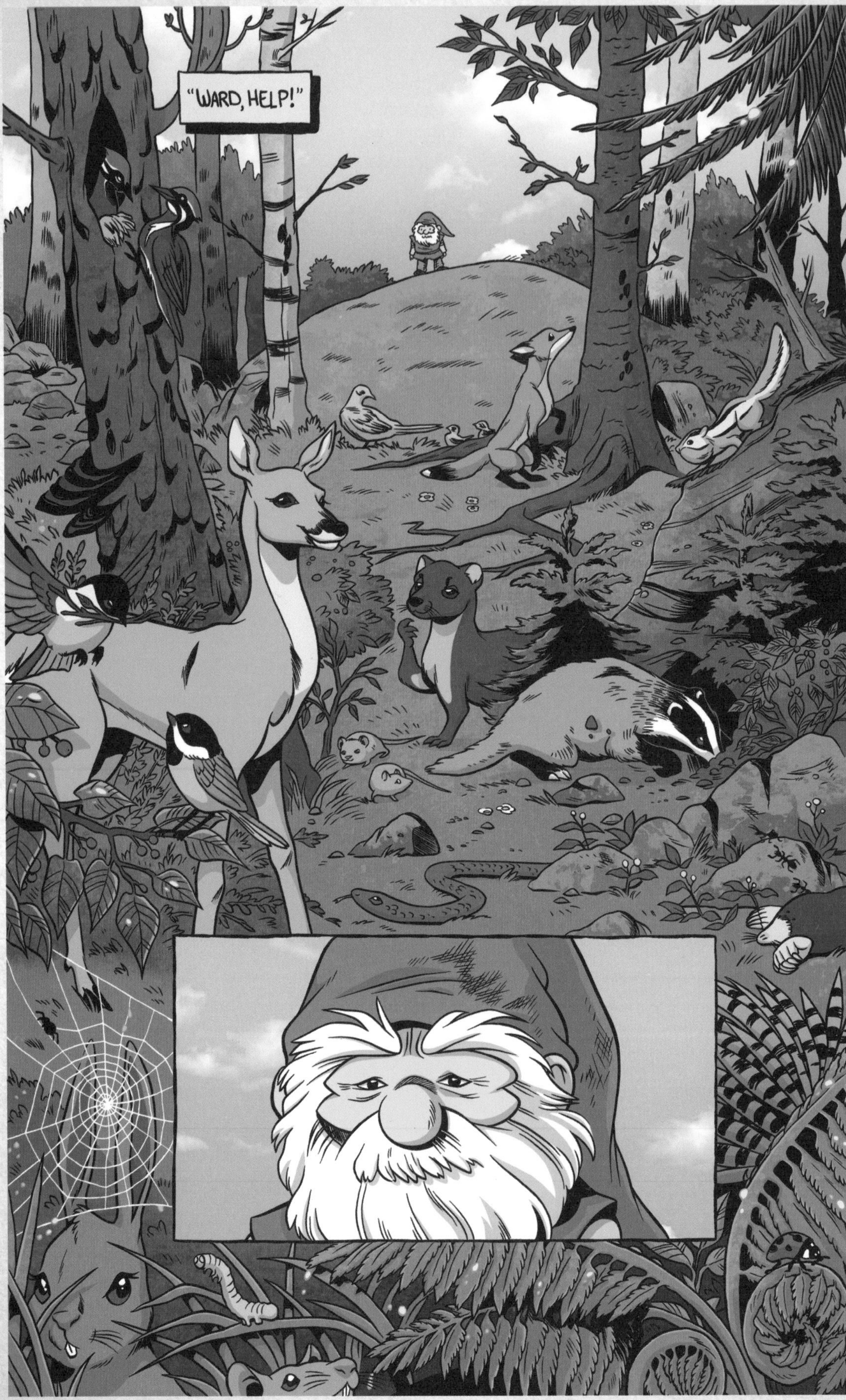
"WARD, HELP!"

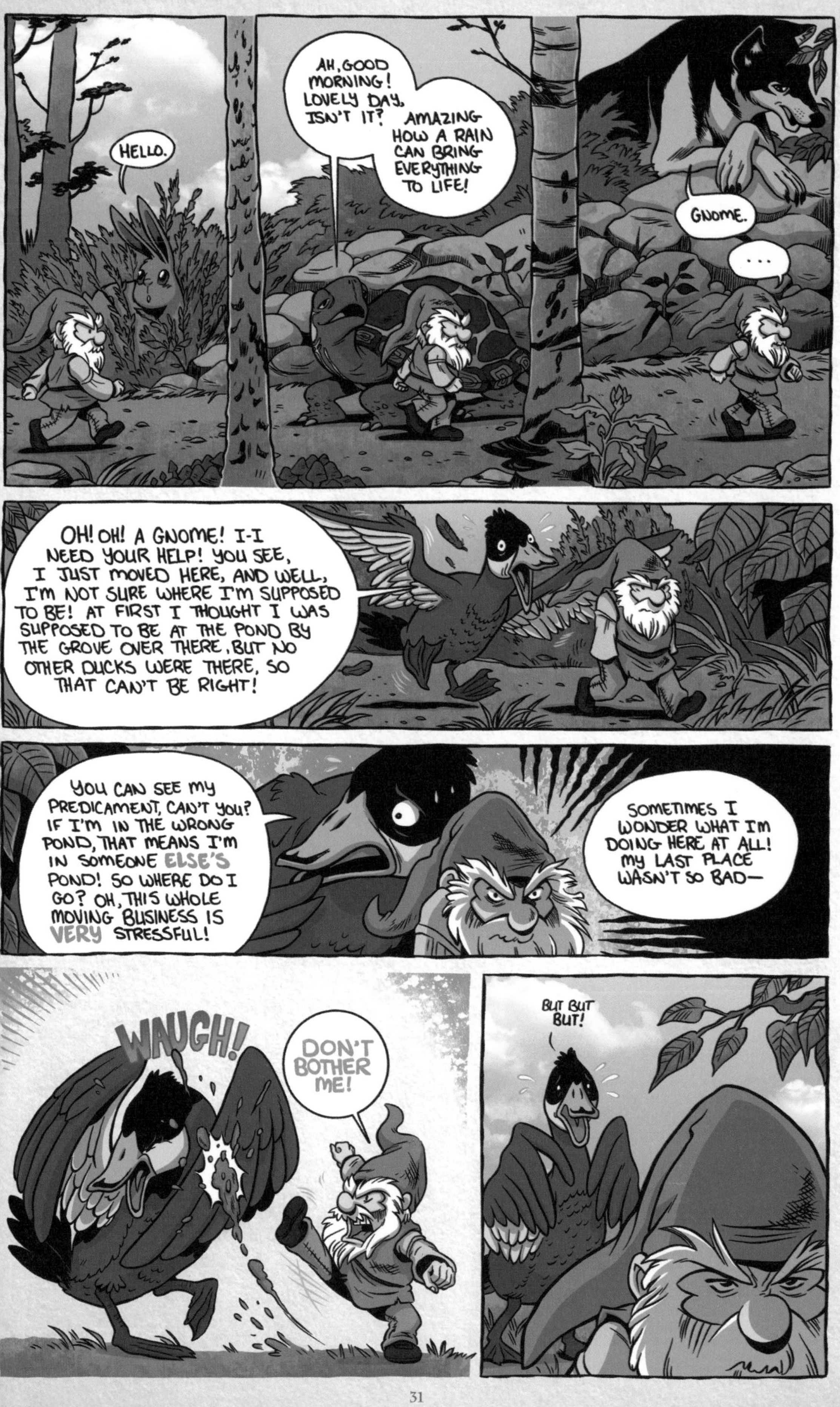
HELLO.
AH, GOOD MORNING! LOVELY DAY, ISN'T IT?
AMAZING HOW A RAIN CAN BRING EVERYTHING TO LIFE!
GNOME.
...
OH! OH! A GNOME! I-I NEED YOUR HELP! YOU SEE, I JUST MOVED HERE, AND WELL, I'M NOT SURE WHERE I'M SUPPOSED TO BE! AT FIRST I THOUGHT I WAS SUPPOSED TO BE AT THE POND BY THE GROVE OVER THERE, BUT NO OTHER DUCKS WERE THERE, SO THAT CAN'T BE RIGHT!
YOU CAN SEE MY PREDICAMENT, CAN'T YOU? IF I'M IN THE WRONG POND, THAT MEANS I'M IN SOMEONE ELSE'S POND! SO WHERE DO I GO? OH, THIS WHOLE MOVING BUSINESS IS VERY STRESSFUL!
SOMETIMES I WONDER WHAT I'M DOING HERE AT ALL! MY LAST PLACE WASN'T SO BAD—
WAUGH!
DON'T BOTHER ME!
BUT BUT BUT!

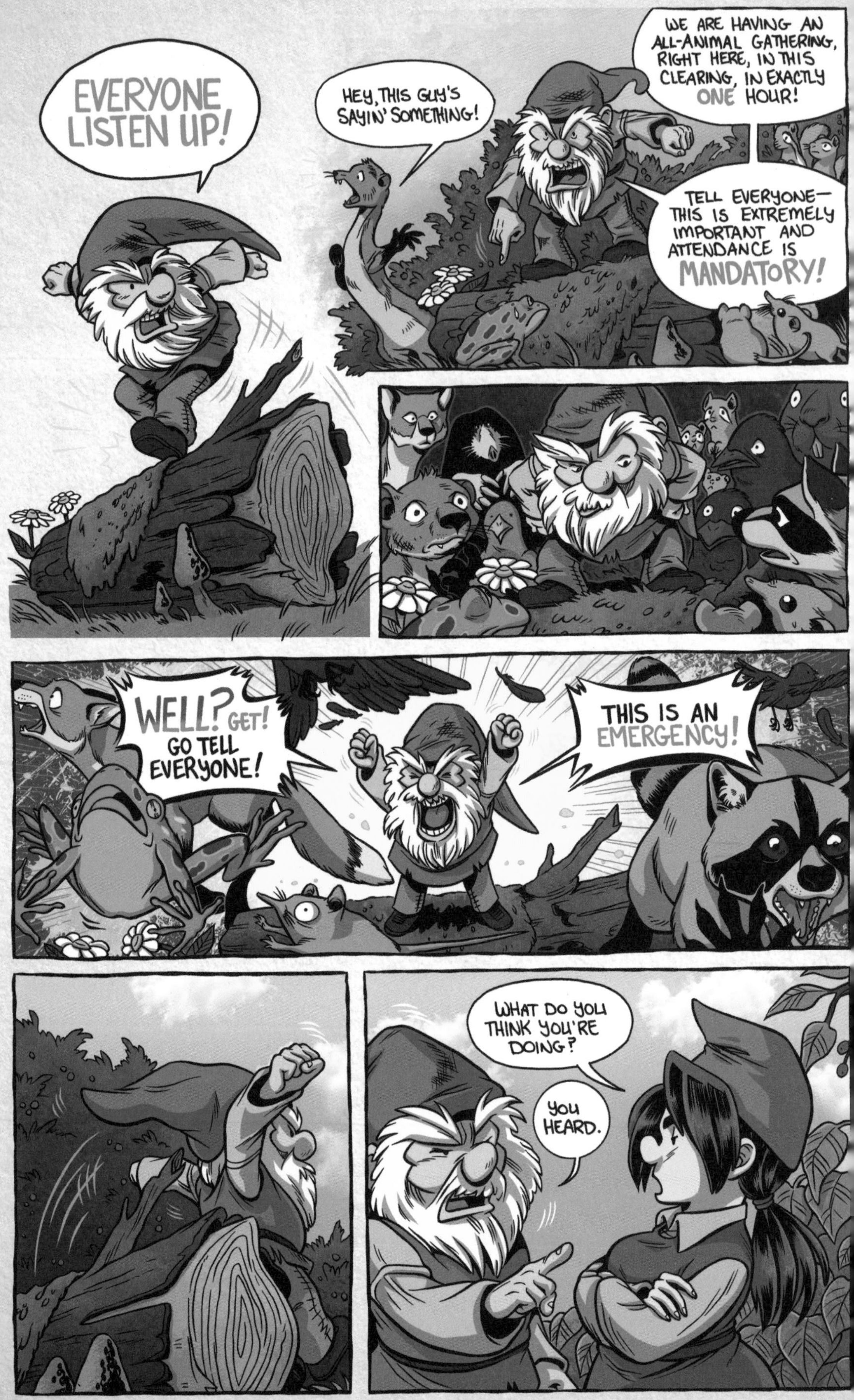

EVERYONE LISTEN UP!
HEY, THIS GUY'S SAYIN' SOMETHING!
WE ARE HAVING AN ALL-ANIMAL GATHERING, RIGHT HERE, IN THIS CLEARING, IN EXACTLY ONE HOUR!
TELL EVERYONE— THIS IS EXTREMELY IMPORTANT AND ATTENDANCE IS MANDATORY!
WELL? GET! GO TELL EVERYONE!
THIS IS AN EMERGENCY!
WHAT DO YOU THINK YOU'RE DOING?
YOU HEARD.

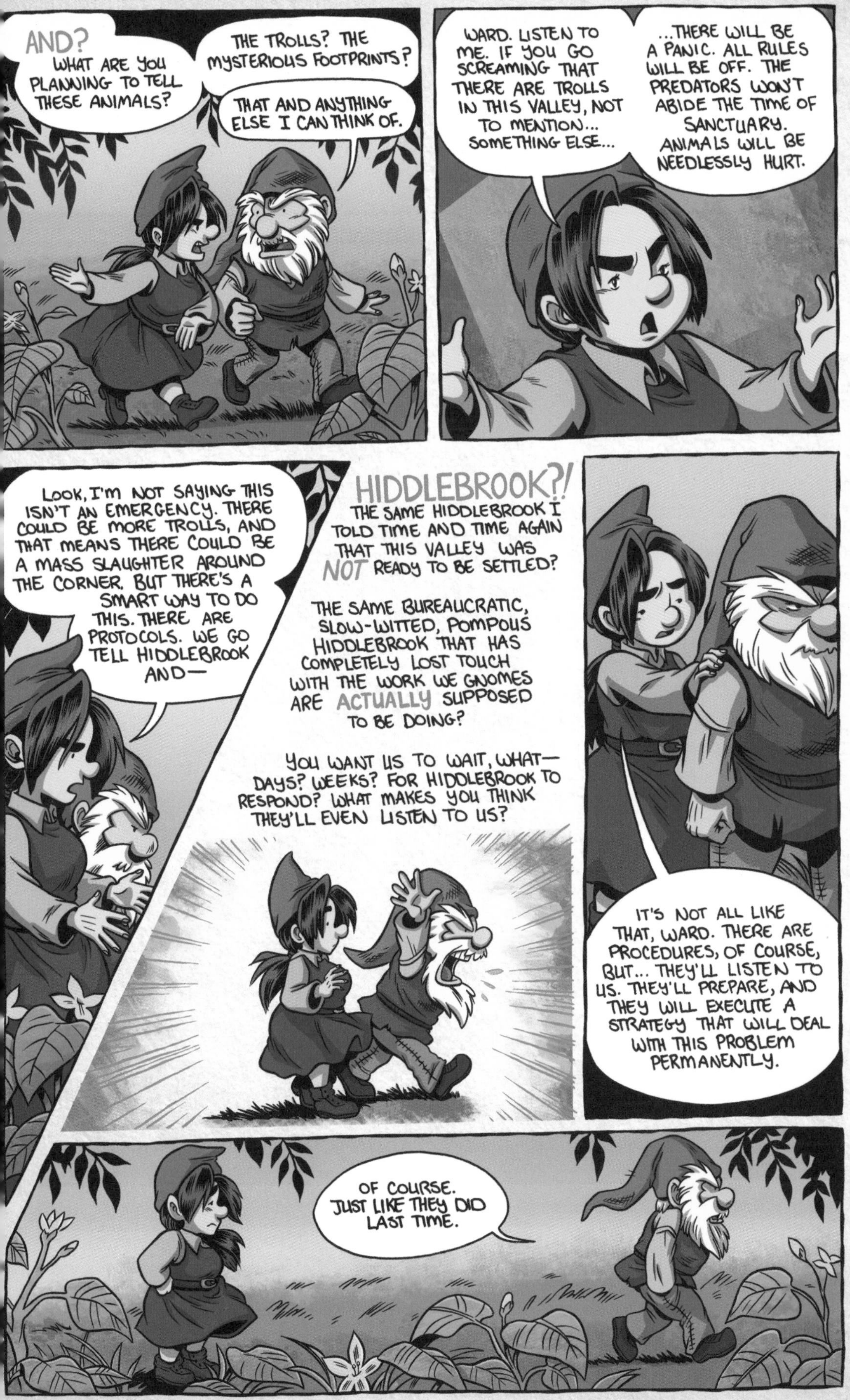
AND? WHAT ARE YOU PLANNING TO TELL THESE ANIMALS?
THE TROLLS? THE MYSTERIOUS FOOTPRINTS?
THAT AND ANYTHING ELSE I CAN THINK OF.
WARD. LISTEN TO ME. IF YOU GO SCREAMING THAT THERE ARE TROLLS IN THIS VALLEY, NOT TO MENTION... SOMETHING ELSE...
...THERE WILL BE A PANIC. ALL RULES WILL BE OFF. THE PREDATORS WON'T ABIDE THE TIME OF SANCTUARY. ANIMALS WILL BE NEEDLESSLY HURT.
LOOK, I'M NOT SAYING THIS ISN'T AN EMERGENCY. THERE COULD BE MORE TROLLS, AND THAT MEANS THERE COULD BE A MASS SLAUGHTER AROUND THE CORNER. BUT THERE'S A SMART WAY TO DO THIS. THERE ARE PROTOCOLS. WE GO TELL HIDDLEBROOK AND—
HIDDLEBROOK?! THE SAME HIDDLEBROOK I TOLD TIME AND TIME AGAIN THAT THIS VALLEY WAS NOT READY TO BE SETTLED?
THE SAME BUREAUCRATIC, SLOW-WITTED, POMPOUS HIDDLEBROOK THAT HAS COMPLETELY LOST TOUCH WITH THE WORK WE GNOMES ARE ACTUALLY SUPPOSED TO BE DOING?
YOU WANT US TO WAIT, WHAT— DAYS? WEEKS? FOR HIDDLEBROOK TO RESPOND? WHAT MAKES YOU THINK THEY'LL EVEN LISTEN TO US?
IT'S NOT ALL LIKE THAT, WARD. THERE ARE PROCEDURES, OF COURSE, BUT... THEY'LL LISTEN TO US. THEY'LL PREPARE, AND THEY WILL EXECUTE A STRATEGY THAT WILL DEAL WITH THIS PROBLEM PERMANENTLY.
OF COURSE. JUST LIKE THEY DID LAST TIME.

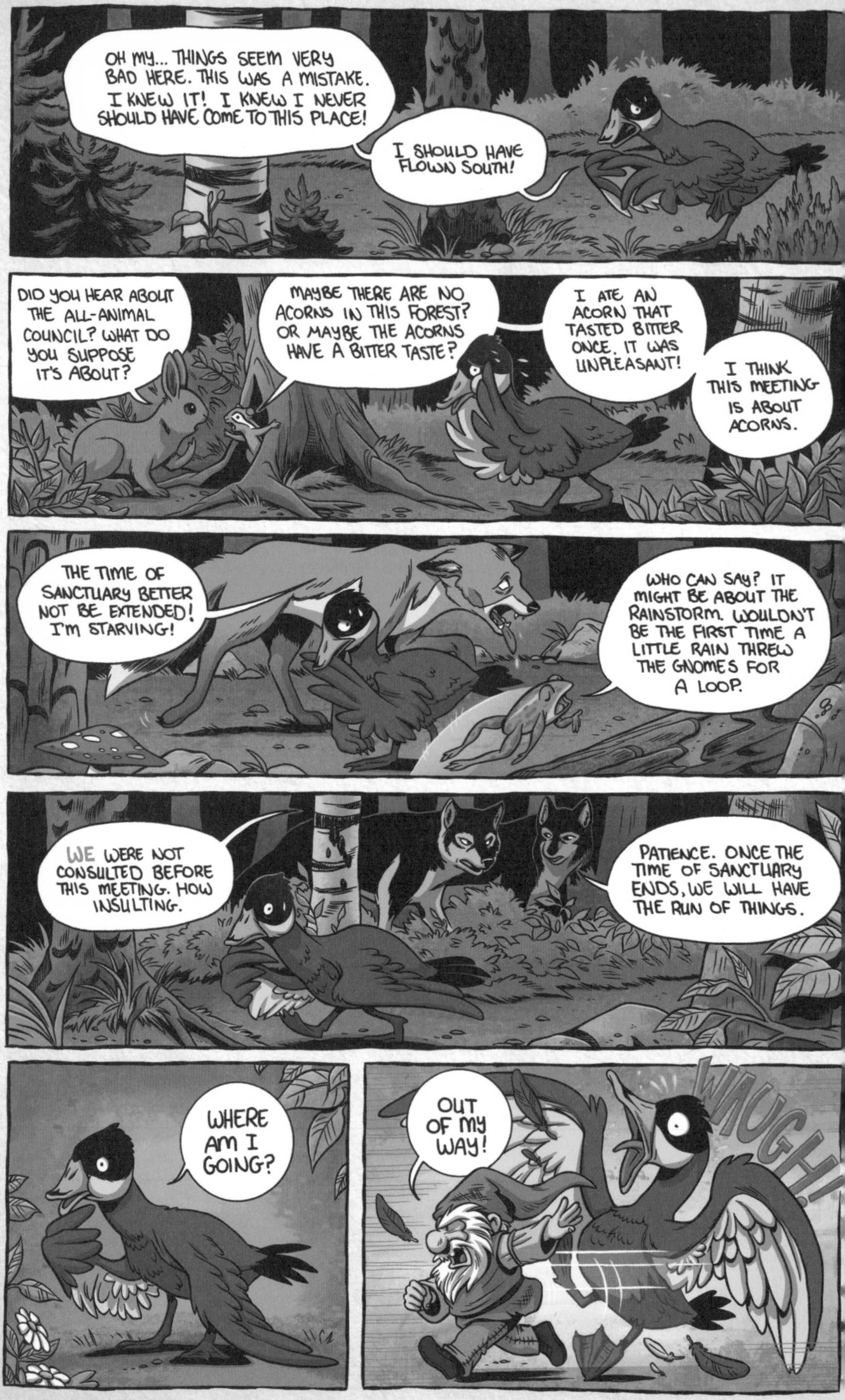
OH MY... THINGS SEEM VERY BAD HERE. THIS WAS A MISTAKE. I KNEW IT! I KNEW I NEVER SHOULD HAVE COME TO THIS PLACE!
I SHOULD HAVE FLOWN SOUTH!
DID YOU HEAR ABOUT THE ALL-ANIMAL COUNCIL? WHAT DO YOU SUPPOSE IT'S ABOUT?
MAYBE THERE ARE NO ACORNS IN THIS FOREST? OR MAYBE THE ACORNS HAVE A BITTER TASTE?
I ATE AN ACORN THAT TASTED BITTER ONCE. IT WAS UNPLEASANT!
I THINK THIS MEETING IS ABOUT ACORNS.
THE TIME OF SANCTUARY BETTER NOT BE EXTENDED! I'M STARVING!
WHO CAN SAY? IT MIGHT BE ABOUT THE RAINSTORM. WOULDN'T BE THE FIRST TIME A LITTLE RAIN THREW THE GNOMES FOR A LOOP.
WE WERE NOT CONSULTED BEFORE THIS MEETING. HOW INSULTING.
PATIENCE. ONCE THE TIME OF SANCTUARY ENDS, WE WILL HAVE THE RUN OF THINGS.
WHERE AM I GOING?
OUT OF MY WAY!
WAUGH!!

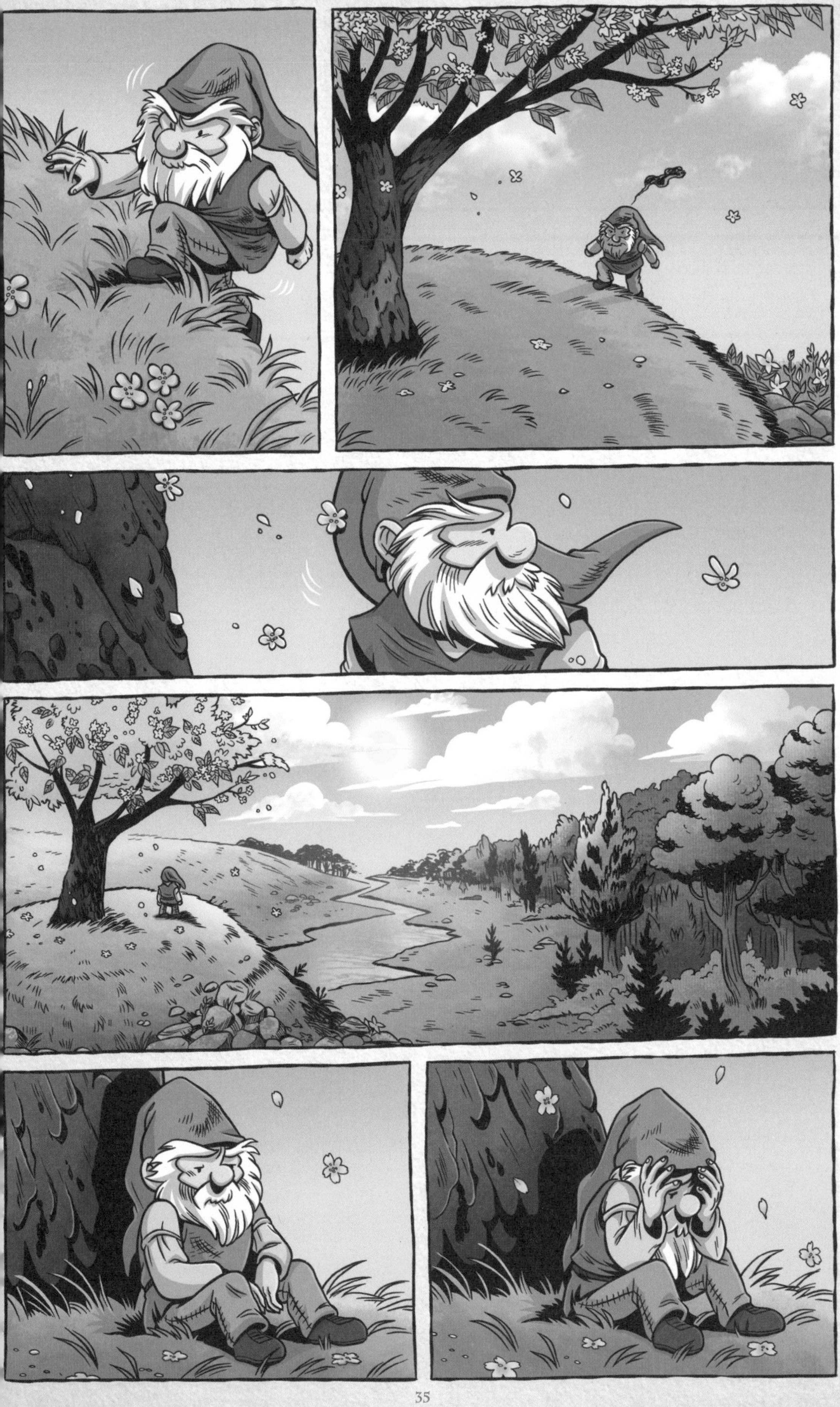

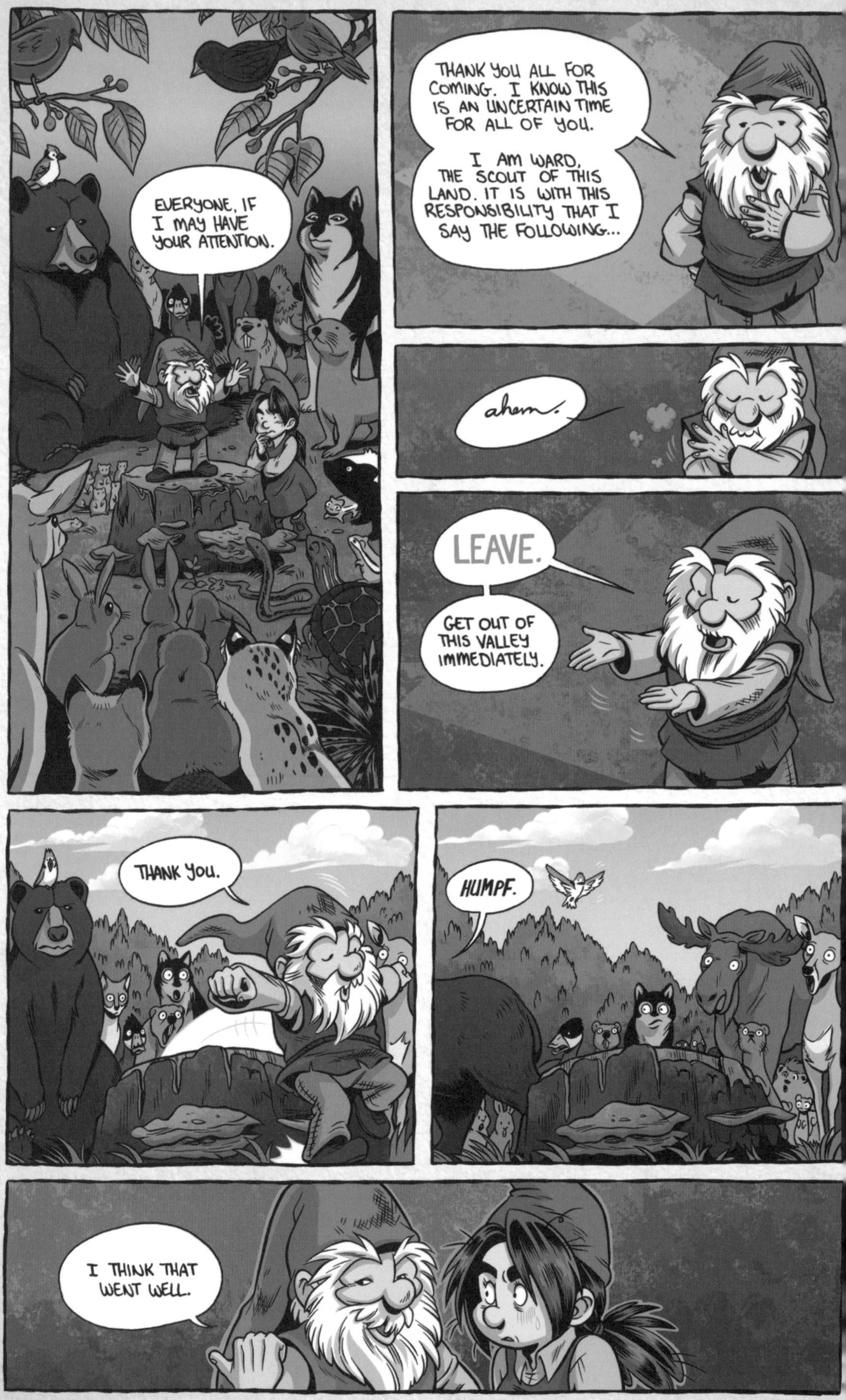
EVERYONE, IF I MAY HAVE YOUR ATTENTION.
THANK YOU ALL FOR COMING. I KNOW THIS IS AN UNCERTAIN TIME FOR ALL OF YOU.
I AM WARD, THE SCOUT OF THIS LAND. IT IS WITH THIS RESPONSIBILITY THAT I SAY THE FOLLOWING...
ahem.
LEAVE.
GET OUT OF THIS VALLEY IMMEDIATELY.
THANK YOU.
HUMPF.
I THINK THAT WENT WELL.

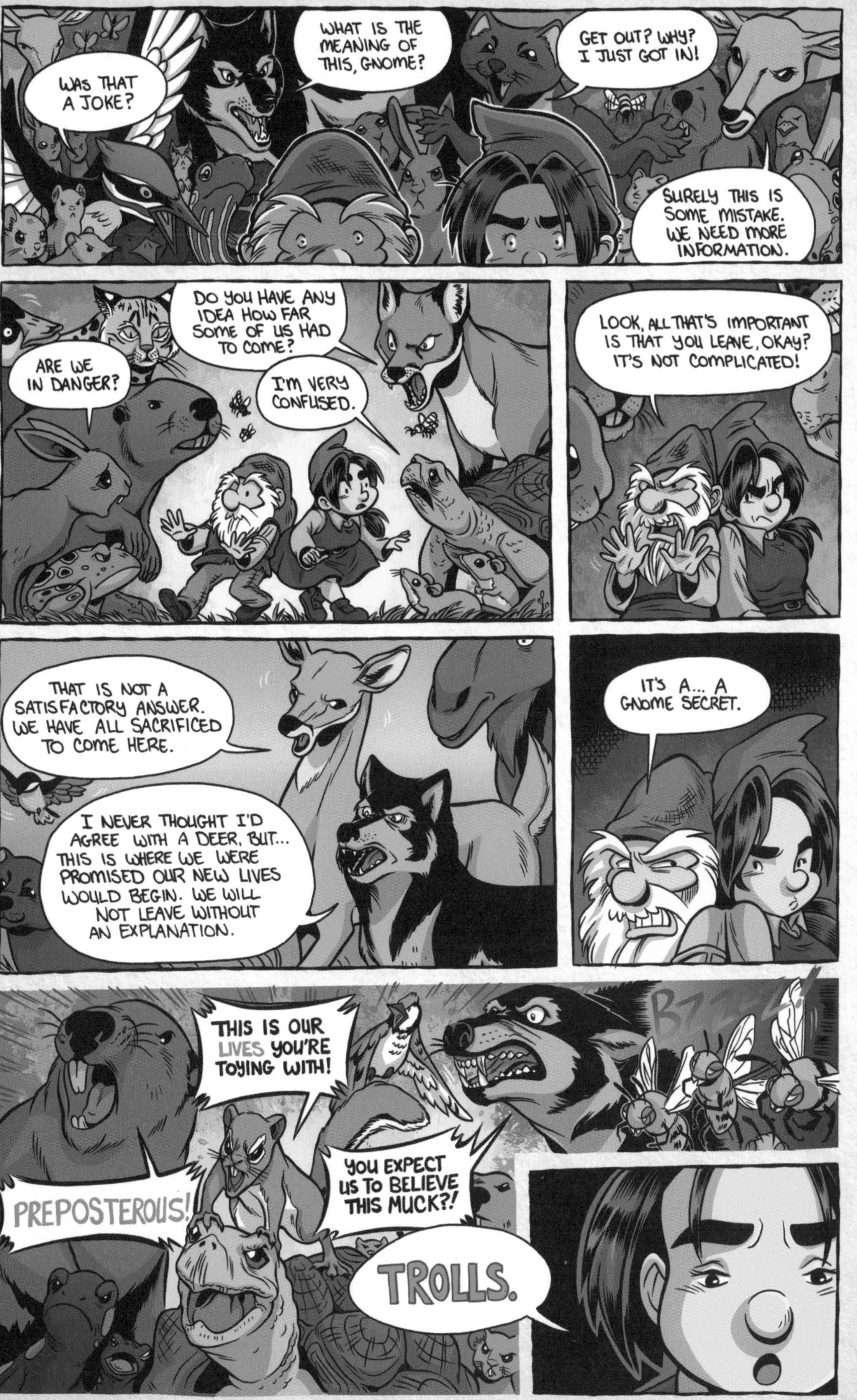

WAS THAT A JOKE?
WHAT IS THE MEANING OF THIS, GNOME?
GET OUT? WHY? I JUST GOT IN!
SURELY THIS IS SOME MISTAKE. WE NEED MORE INFORMATION.
ARE WE IN DANGER?
DO YOU HAVE ANY IDEA HOW FAR SOME OF US HAD TO COME?
I'M VERY CONFUSED.
LOOK, ALL THAT'S IMPORTANT IS THAT YOU LEAVE, OKAY? IT'S NOT COMPLICATED!
THAT IS NOT A SATISFACTORY ANSWER. WE HAVE ALL SACRIFICED TO COME HERE.
I NEVER THOUGHT I'D AGREE WITH A DEER, BUT... THIS IS WHERE WE WERE PROMISED OUR NEW LIVES WOULD BEGIN. WE WILL NOT LEAVE WITHOUT AN EXPLANATION.
IT'S A... A GNOME SECRET.
THIS IS OUR LIVES YOU'RE TOYING WITH!
BZZZZ
PREPOSTEROUS!
YOU EXPECT US TO BELIEVE THIS MUCK?!
TROLLS.

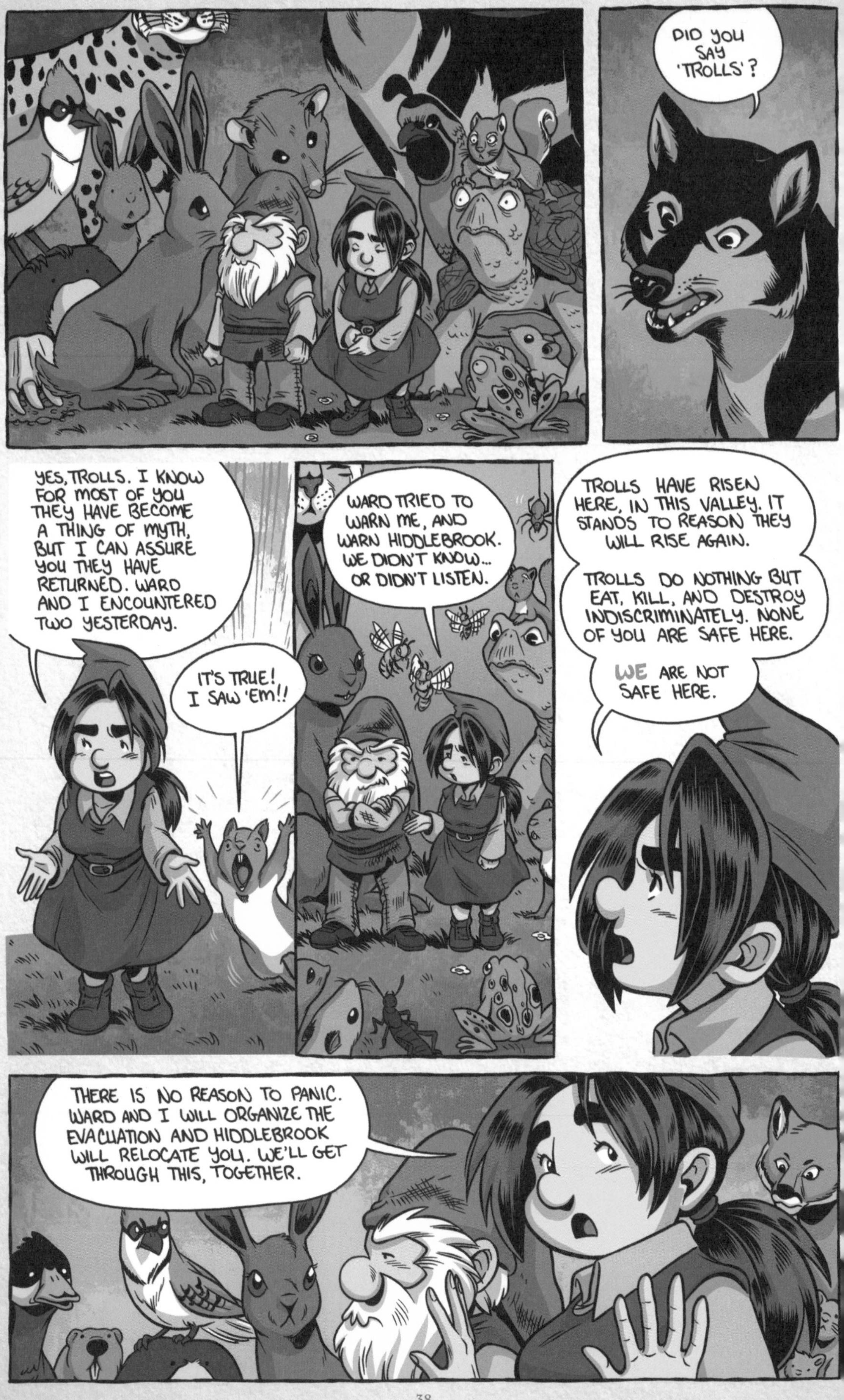
DID YOU SAY 'TROLLS'?
YES, TROLLS. I KNOW FOR MOST OF YOU THEY HAVE BECOME A THING OF MYTH, BUT I CAN ASSURE YOU THEY HAVE RETURNED. WARD AND I ENCOUNTERED TWO YESTERDAY.
IT'S TRUE! I SAW 'EM!!
WARD TRIED TO WARN ME, AND WARN HIDDLEBROOK. WE DIDN'T KNOW... OR DIDN'T LISTEN.
TROLLS HAVE RISEN HERE, IN THIS VALLEY. IT STANDS TO REASON THEY WILL RISE AGAIN.
TROLLS DO NOTHING BUT EAT, KILL, AND DESTROY INDISCRIMINATELY. NONE OF YOU ARE SAFE HERE.
WE ARE NOT SAFE HERE.
THERE IS NO REASON TO PANIC. WARD AND I WILL ORGANIZE THE EVACUATION AND HIDDLEBROOK WILL RELOCATE YOU. WE'LL GET THROUGH THIS, TOGETHER.

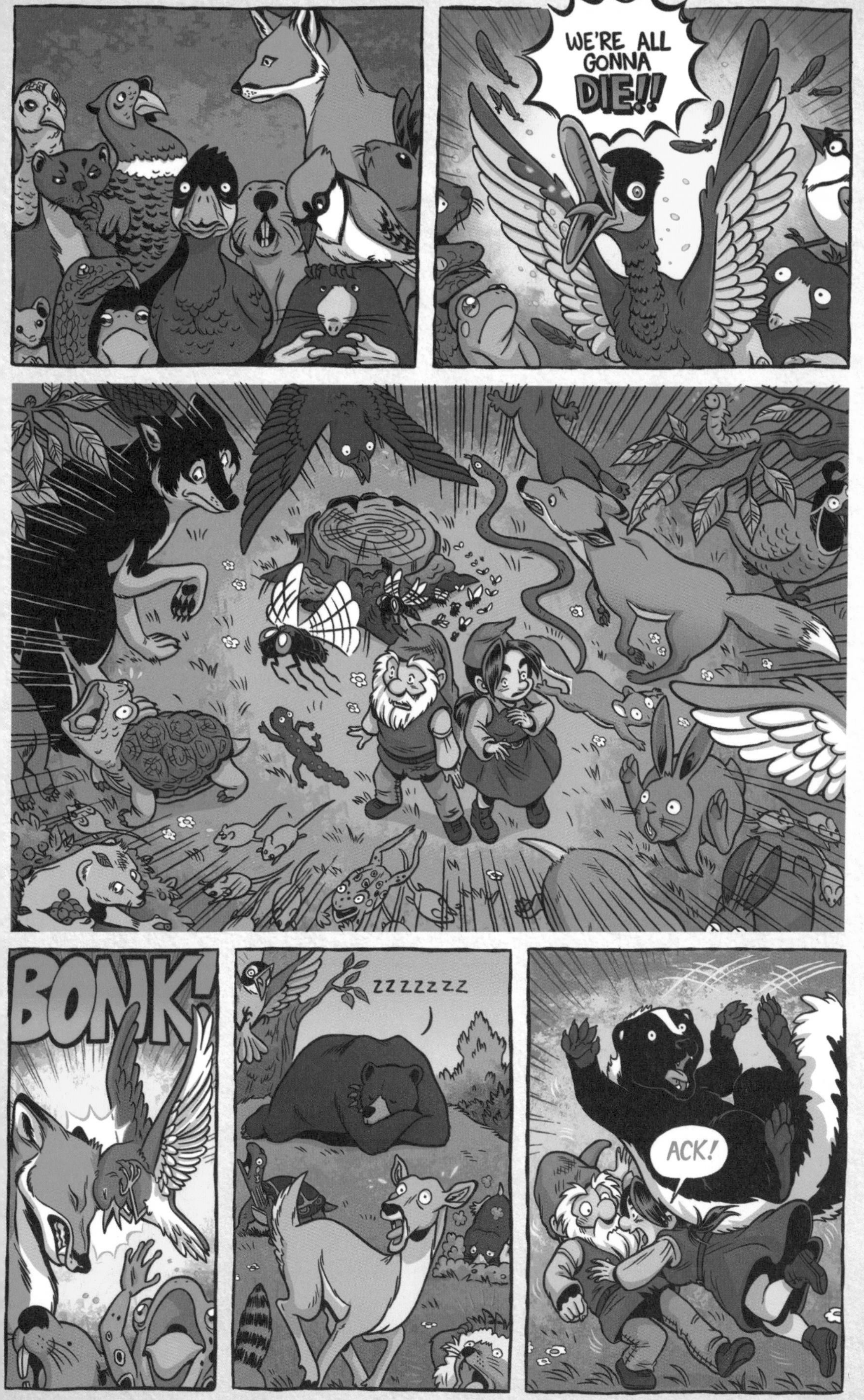
WE'RE ALL GONNA DIE!!
BONK!
ZZZZZZZ
ACK!

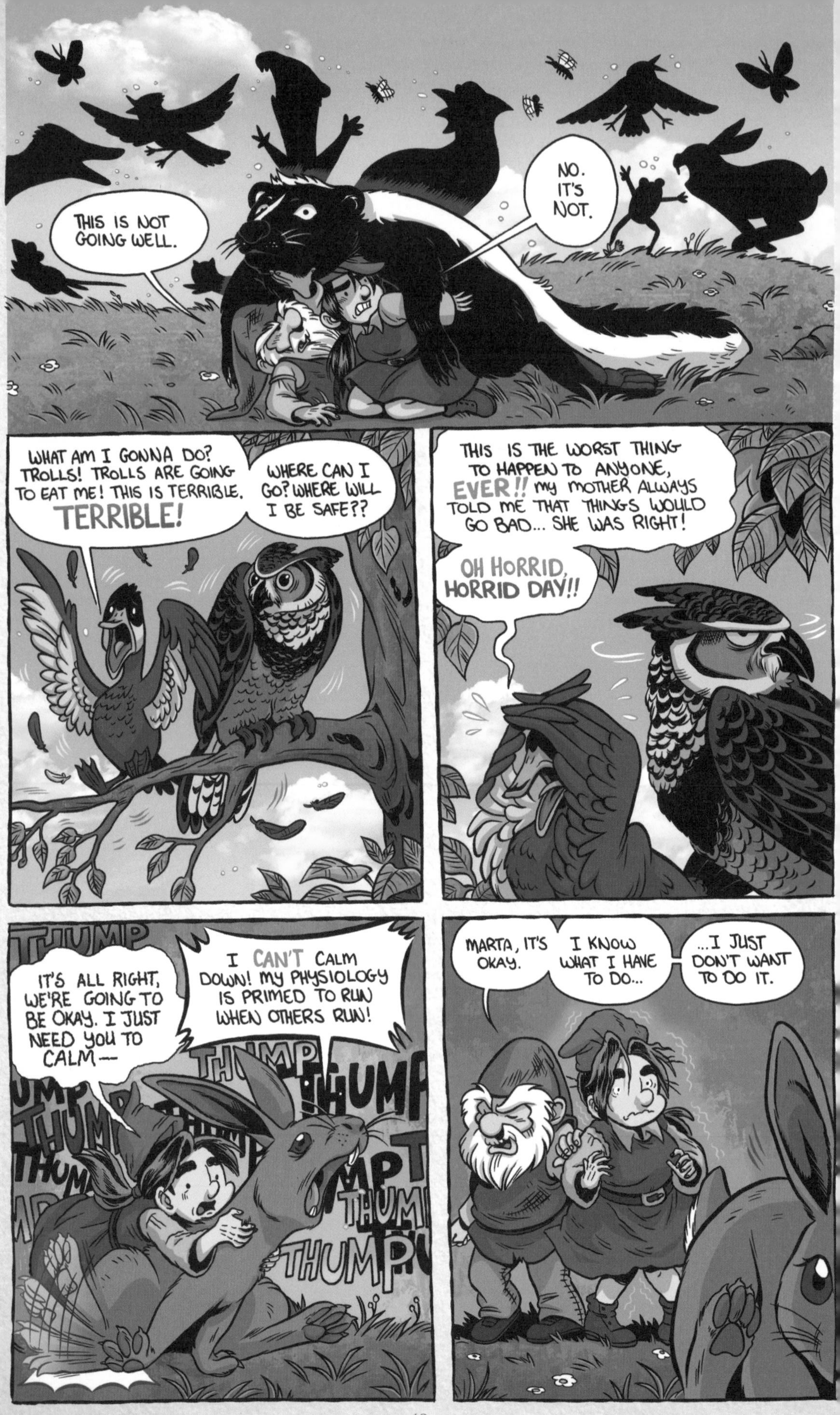
THIS IS NOT GOING WELL.
NO. IT'S NOT.
WHAT AM I GONNA DO? TROLLS! TROLLS ARE GOING TO EAT ME! THIS IS TERRIBLE. TERRIBLE!
WHERE CAN I GO? WHERE WILL I BE SAFE??
THIS IS THE WORST THING TO HAPPEN TO ANYONE, EVER!! MY MOTHER ALWAYS TOLD ME THAT THINGS WOULD GO BAD... SHE WAS RIGHT!
OH HORRID, HORRID DAY!!
THUMP
IT'S ALL RIGHT, WE'RE GOING TO BE OKAY. I JUST NEED YOU TO CALM—
I CAN'T CALM DOWN! MY PHYSIOLOGY IS PRIMED TO RUN WHEN OTHERS RUN!
THUMP THUMP THUMP
MARTA, IT'S OKAY.
I KNOW WHAT I HAVE TO DO...
...I JUST DON'T WANT TO DO IT.

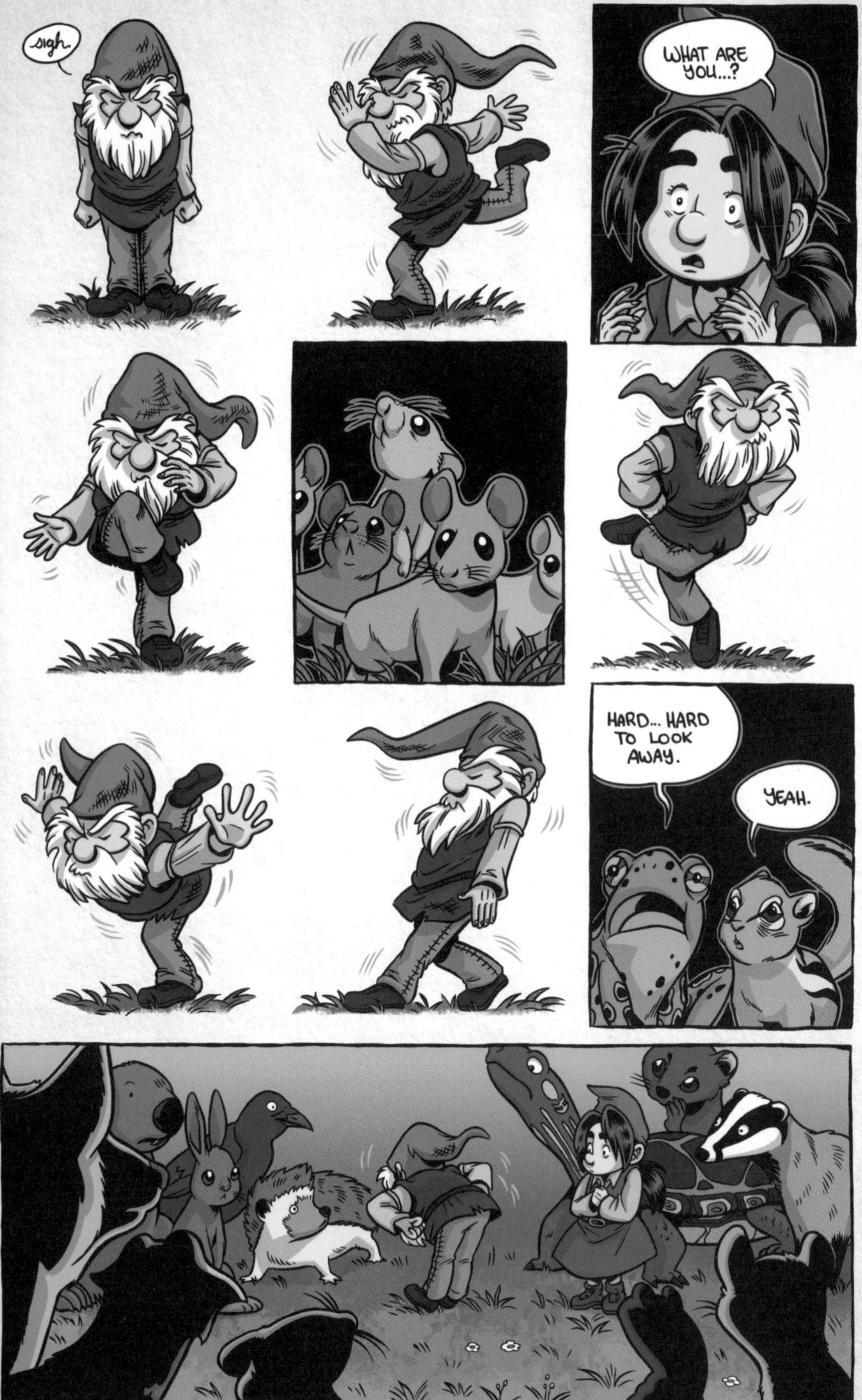
sigh.
WHAT ARE YOU...?
HARD... HARD TO LOOK AWAY.
YEAH.

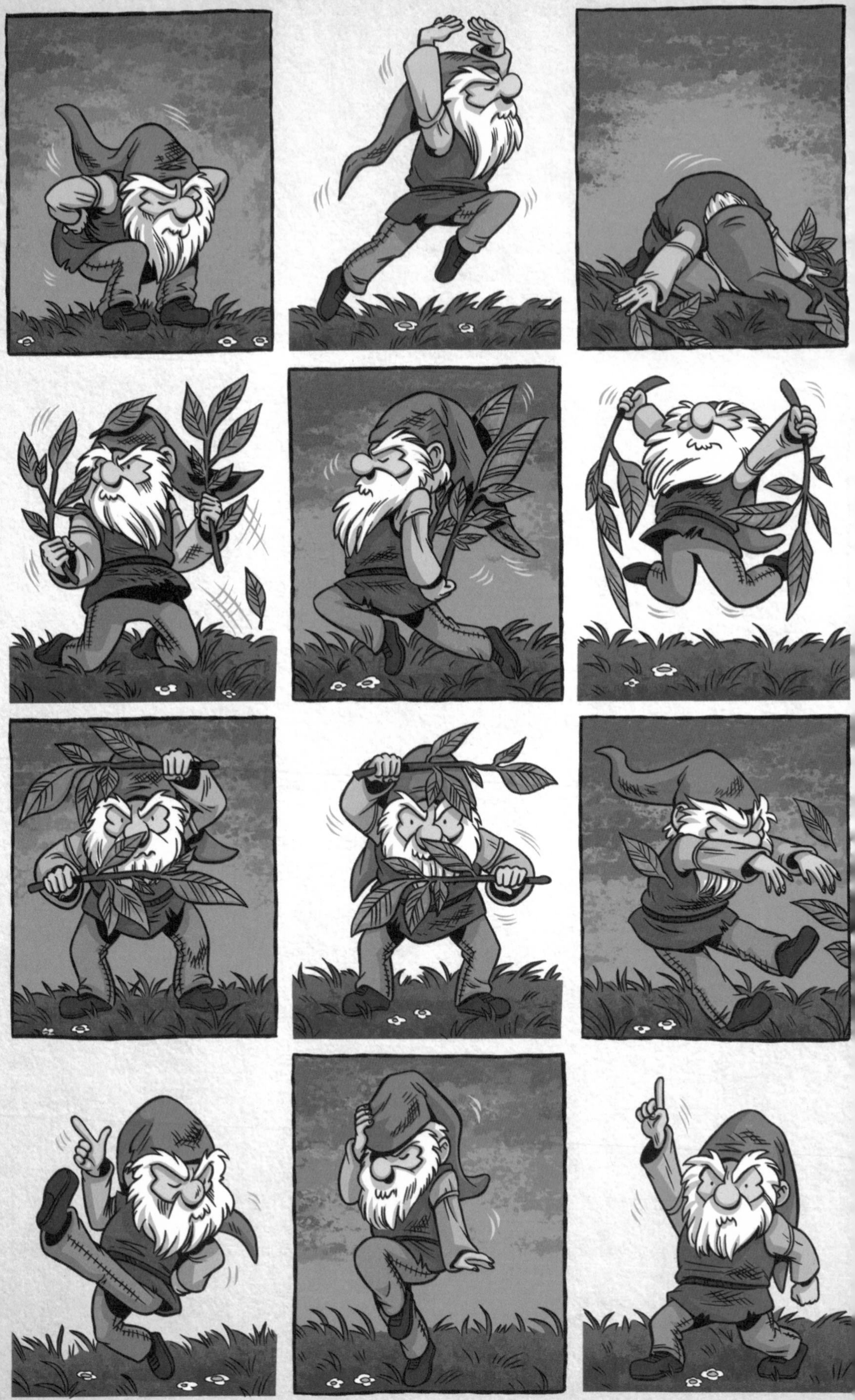

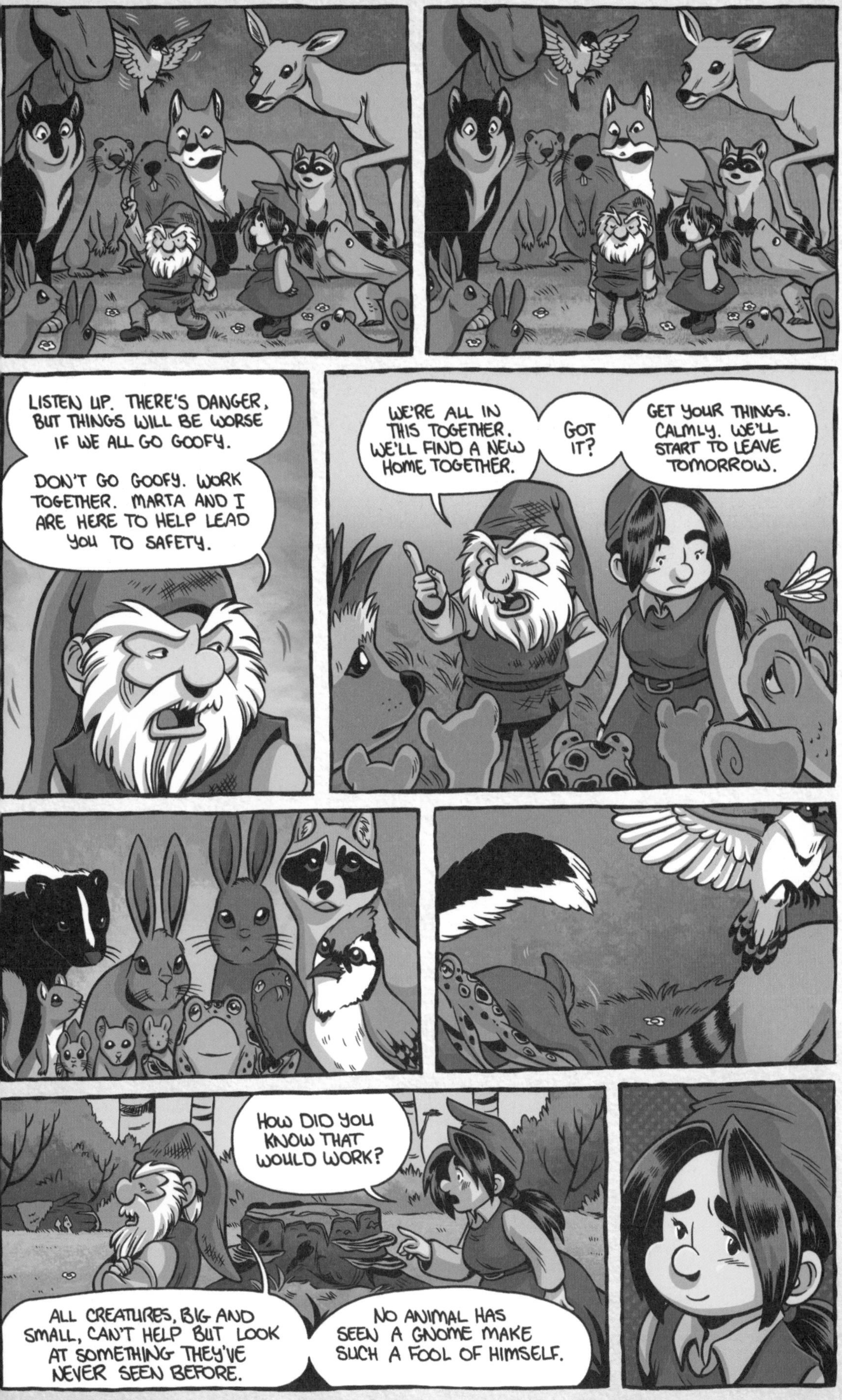
LISTEN UP. THERE'S DANGER, BUT THINGS WILL BE WORSE IF WE ALL GO GOOFY.
DON'T GO GOOFY. WORK TOGETHER. MARTA AND I ARE HERE TO HELP LEAD YOU TO SAFETY.
WE'RE ALL IN THIS TOGETHER. WE'LL FIND A NEW HOME TOGETHER.
GOT IT?
GET YOUR THINGS. CALMLY. WE'LL START TO LEAVE TOMORROW.
HOW DID YOU KNOW THAT WOULD WORK?
ALL CREATURES, BIG AND SMALL, CAN'T HELP BUT LOOK AT SOMETHING THEY'VE NEVER SEEN BEFORE.
NO ANIMAL HAS SEEN A GNOME MAKE SUCH A FOOL OF HIMSELF.

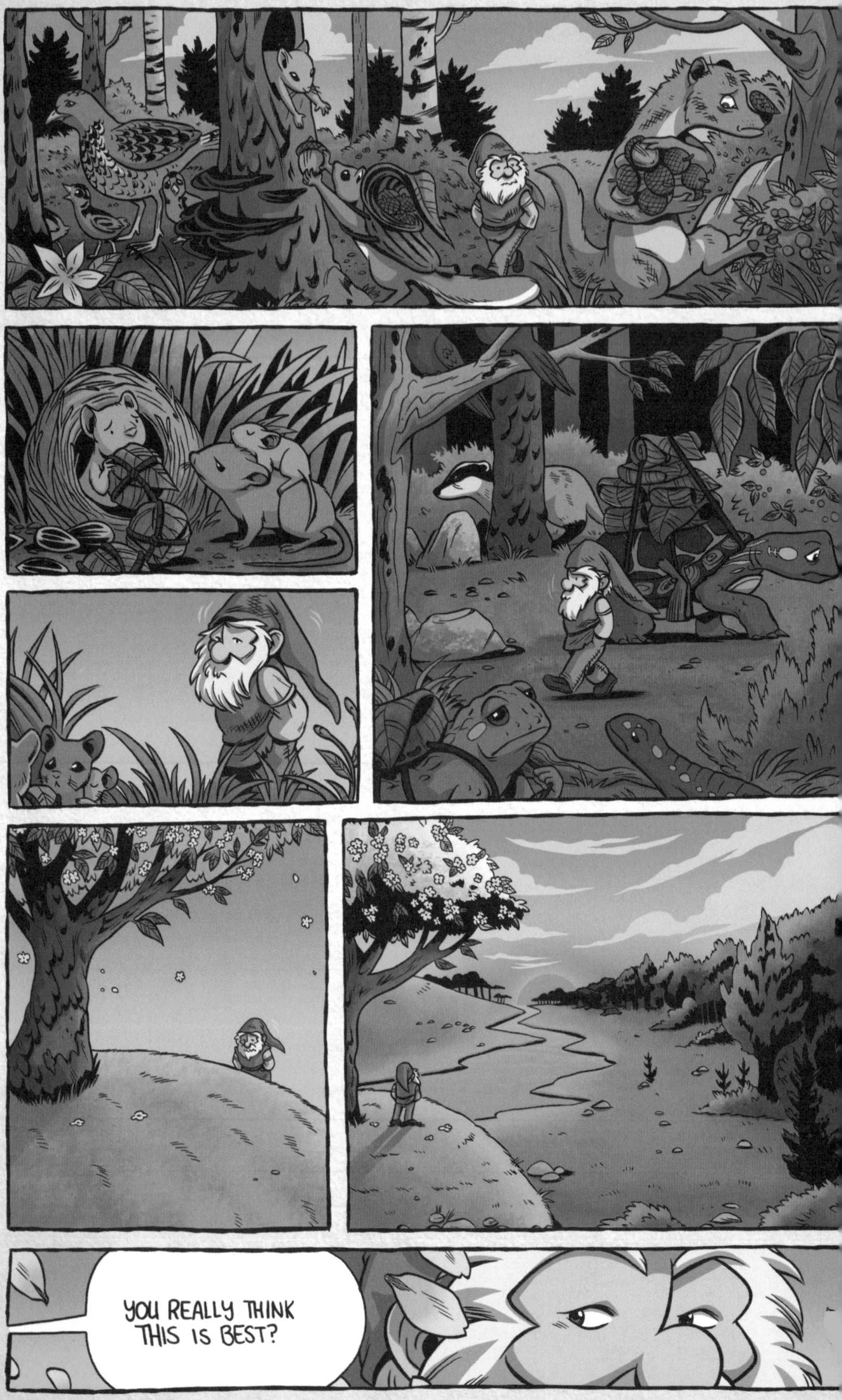
YOU REALLY THINK THIS IS BEST?

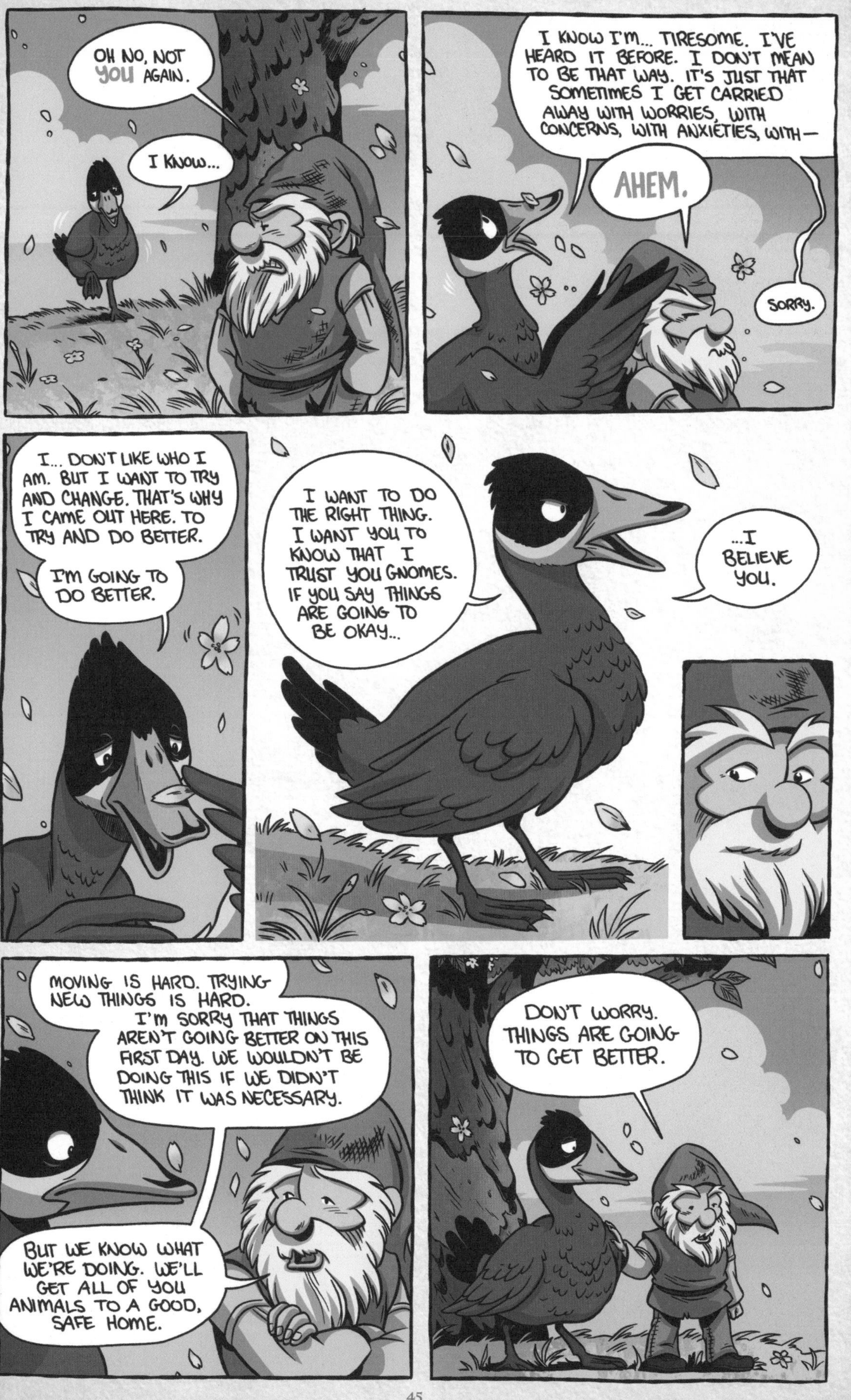
OH NO, NOT YOU AGAIN.
I KNOW...
I KNOW I'M... TIRESOME. I'VE HEARD IT BEFORE. I DON'T MEAN TO BE THAT WAY. IT'S JUST THAT SOMETIMES I GET CARRIED AWAY WITH WORRIES, WITH CONCERNS, WITH ANXIETIES, WITH—
AHEM.
SORRY.
I... DON'T LIKE WHO I AM. BUT I WANT TO TRY AND CHANGE. THAT'S WHY I CAME OUT HERE. TO TRY AND DO BETTER.
I'M GOING TO DO BETTER.
I WANT TO DO THE RIGHT THING. I WANT YOU TO KNOW THAT I TRUST YOU GNOMES. IF YOU SAY THINGS ARE GOING TO BE OKAY...
...I BELIEVE YOU.
MOVING IS HARD. TRYING NEW THINGS IS HARD.
I'M SORRY THAT THINGS AREN'T GOING BETTER ON THIS FIRST DAY. WE WOULDN'T BE DOING THIS IF WE DIDN'T THINK IT WAS NECESSARY.
BUT WE KNOW WHAT WE'RE DOING. WE'LL GET ALL OF YOU ANIMALS TO A GOOD, SAFE HOME.
DON'T WORRY. THINGS ARE GOING TO GET BETTER.

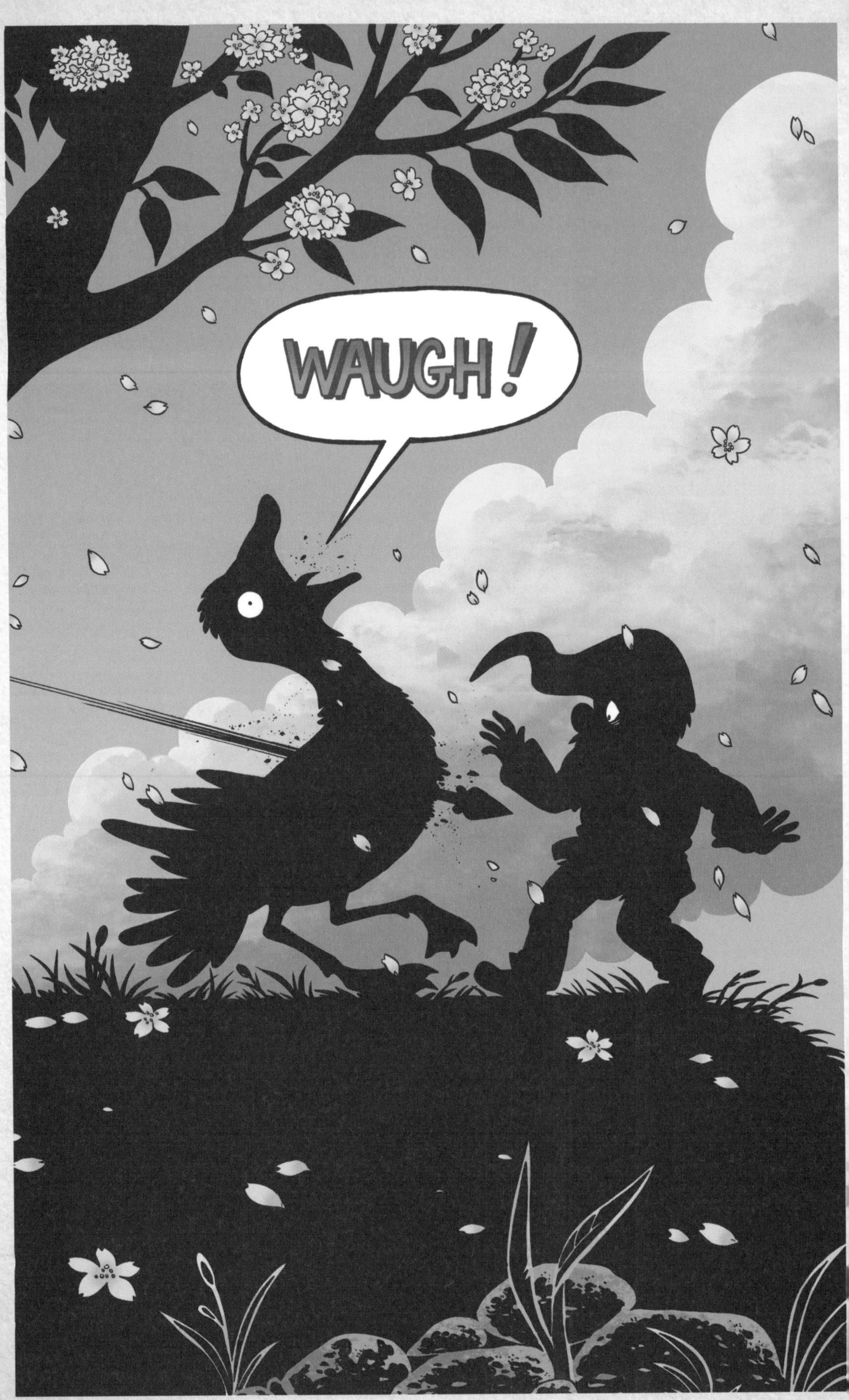
WAUGH!

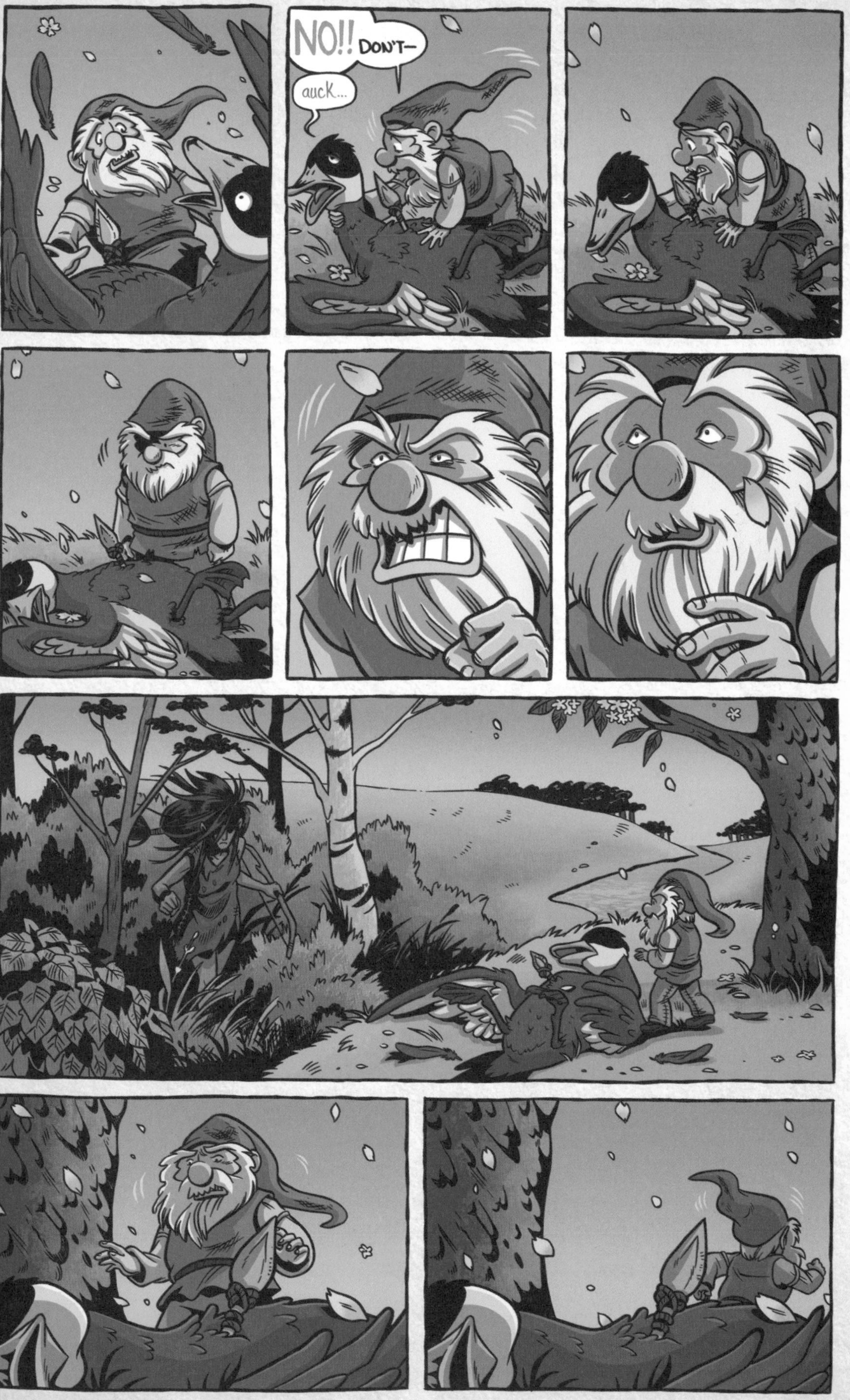
NO!! DON'T—
auck...

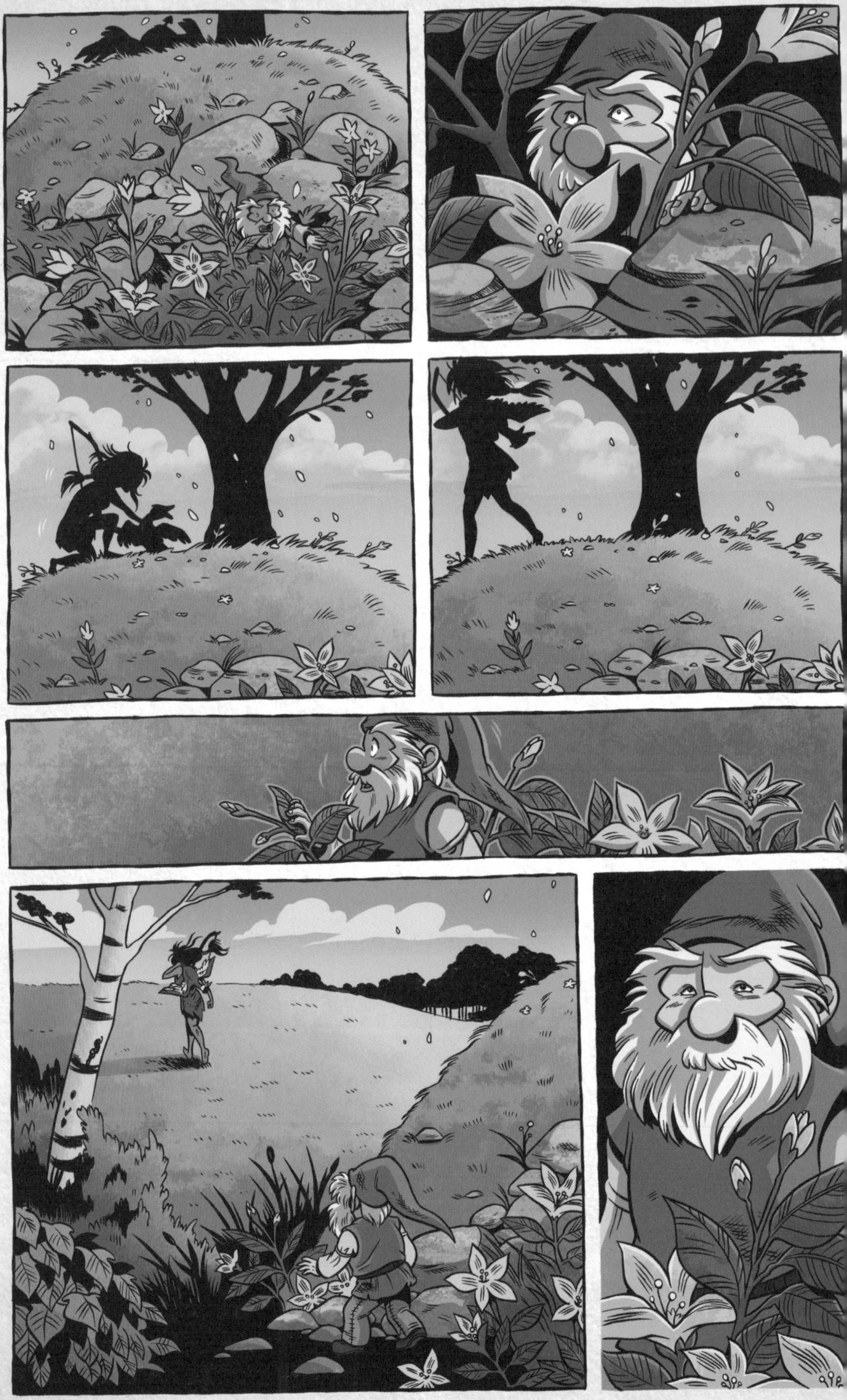

Chapter Three

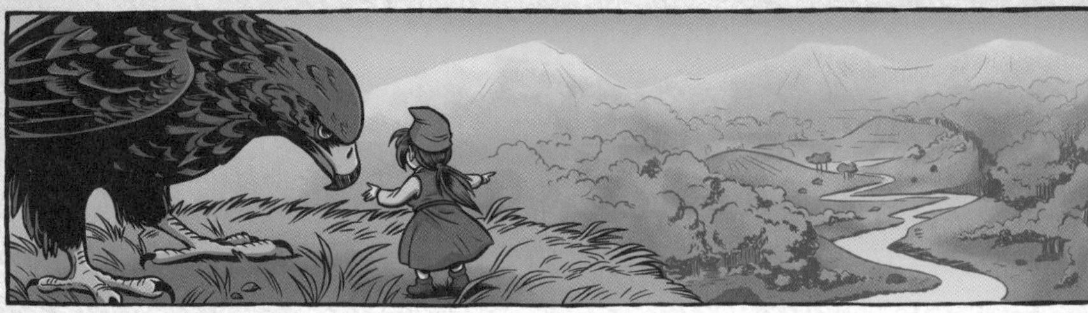

"THANK YOU FOR HEARING ME. I AM AS SURPRISED AS YOU
THAT I HAVE RETURNED TO HIDDLEBROOK SO QUICKLY."

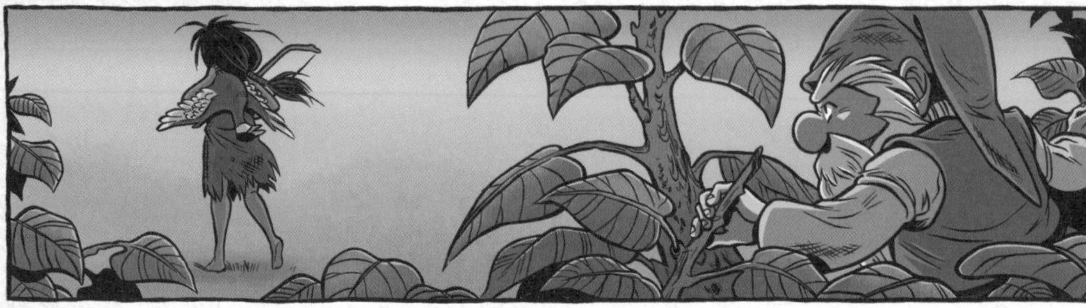

"I HAVE MET WARD. HE IS... DIFFICULT, AS ANTICIPATED.
BUT HE IS NOT WRONG."

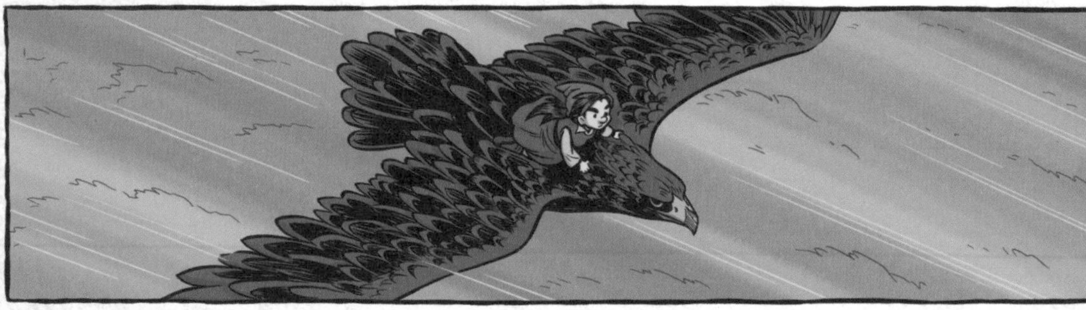

"BY ALL CONVENTIONAL MEASURES,
THE VALLEY IS READY FOR REPOPULATION."

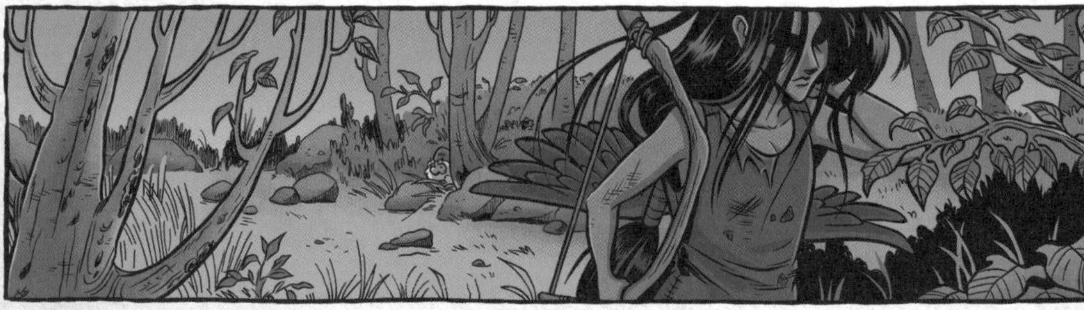

"YET THERE IS MORE TO
THE VALLEY THAN IT SEEMS."

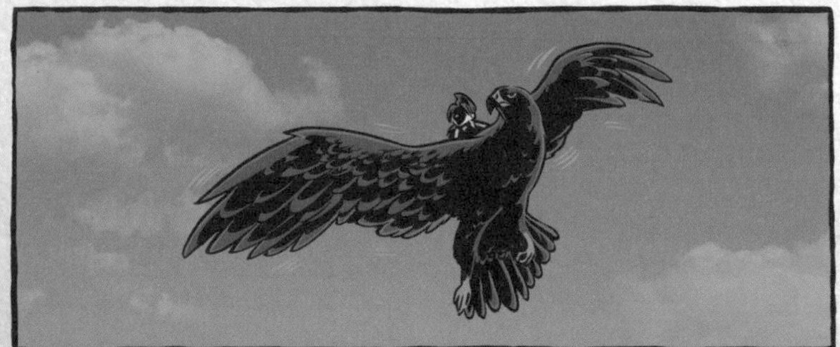

"THERE ARE THINGS WE
DID NOT ANTICIPATE.
THINGS WE COULD
NOT ANTICIPATE."

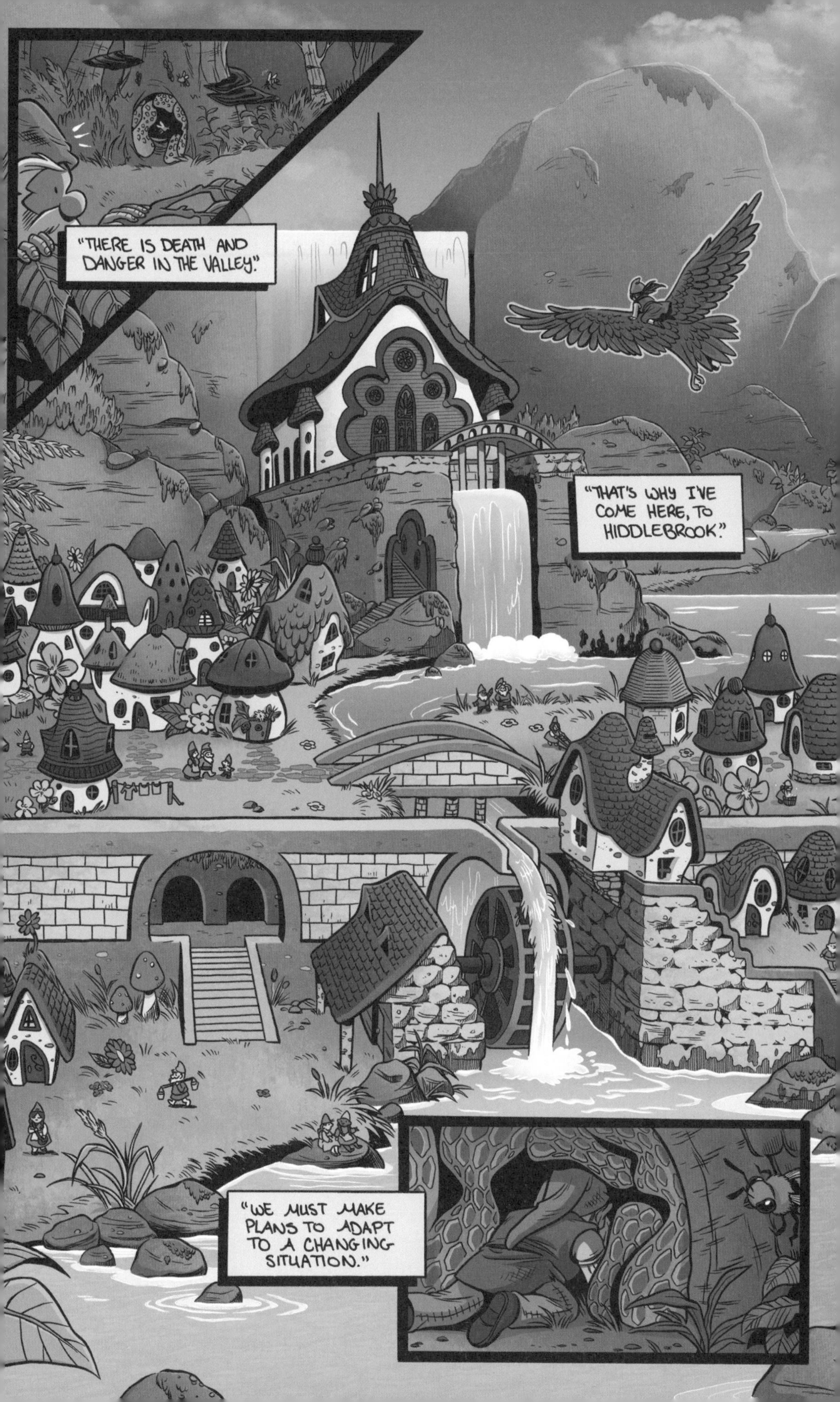
"THERE IS DEATH AND DANGER IN THE VALLEY."
"THAT'S WHY I'VE COME HERE, TO HIDDLEBROOK."
"WE MUST MAKE PLANS TO ADAPT TO A CHANGING SITUATION."

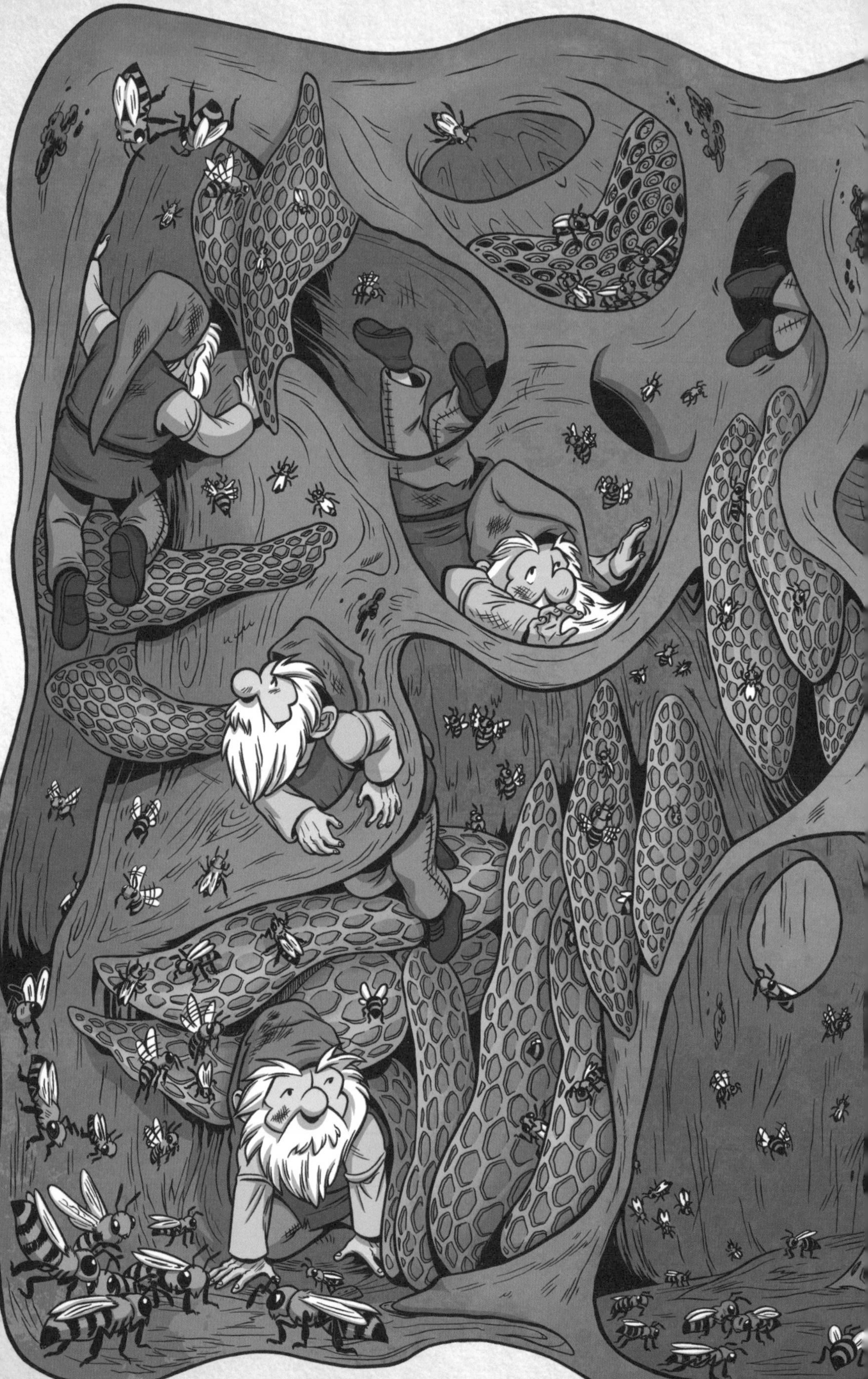

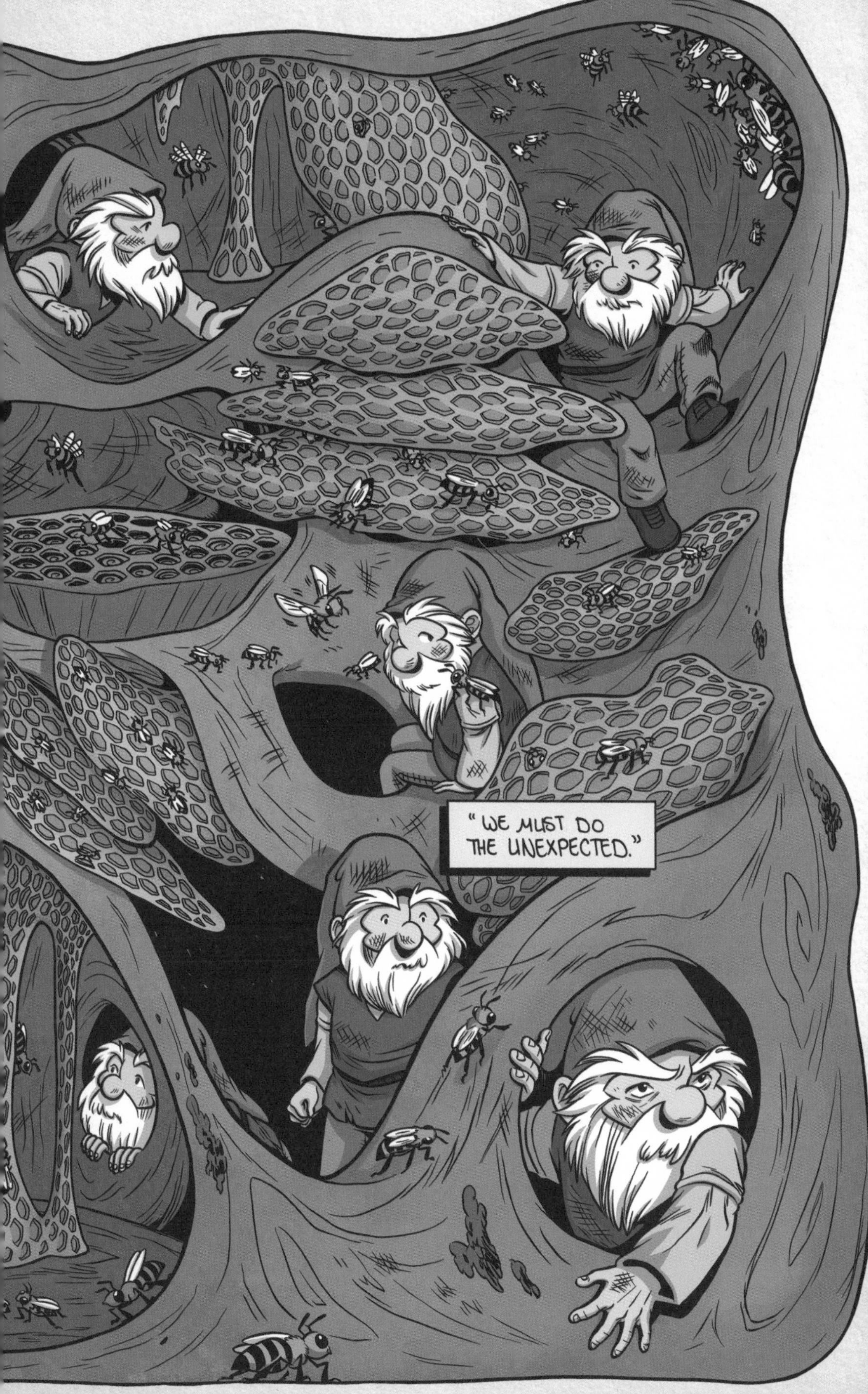
"WE MUST DO THE UNEXPECTED."

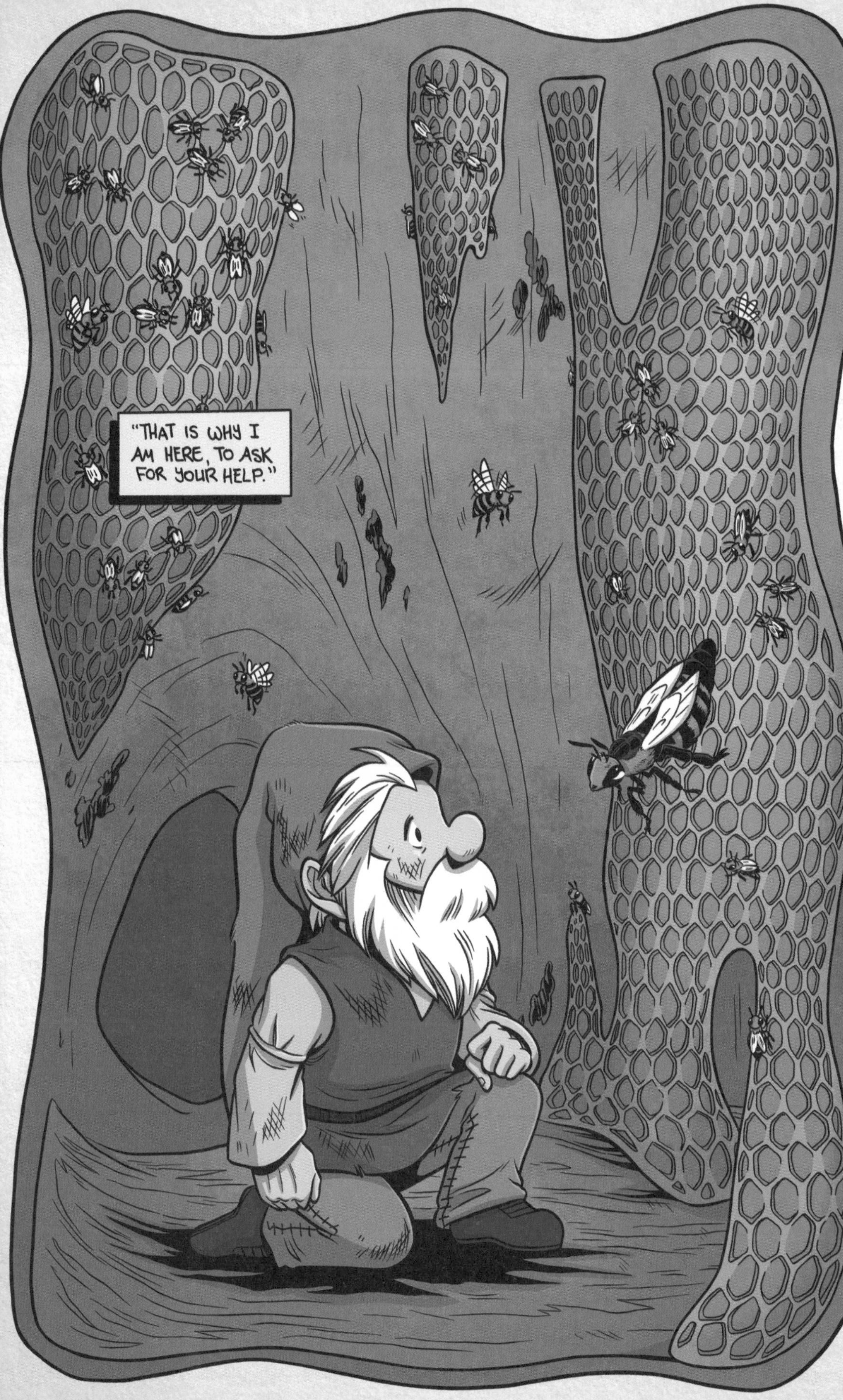
"THAT IS WHY I AM HERE, TO ASK FOR YOUR HELP."

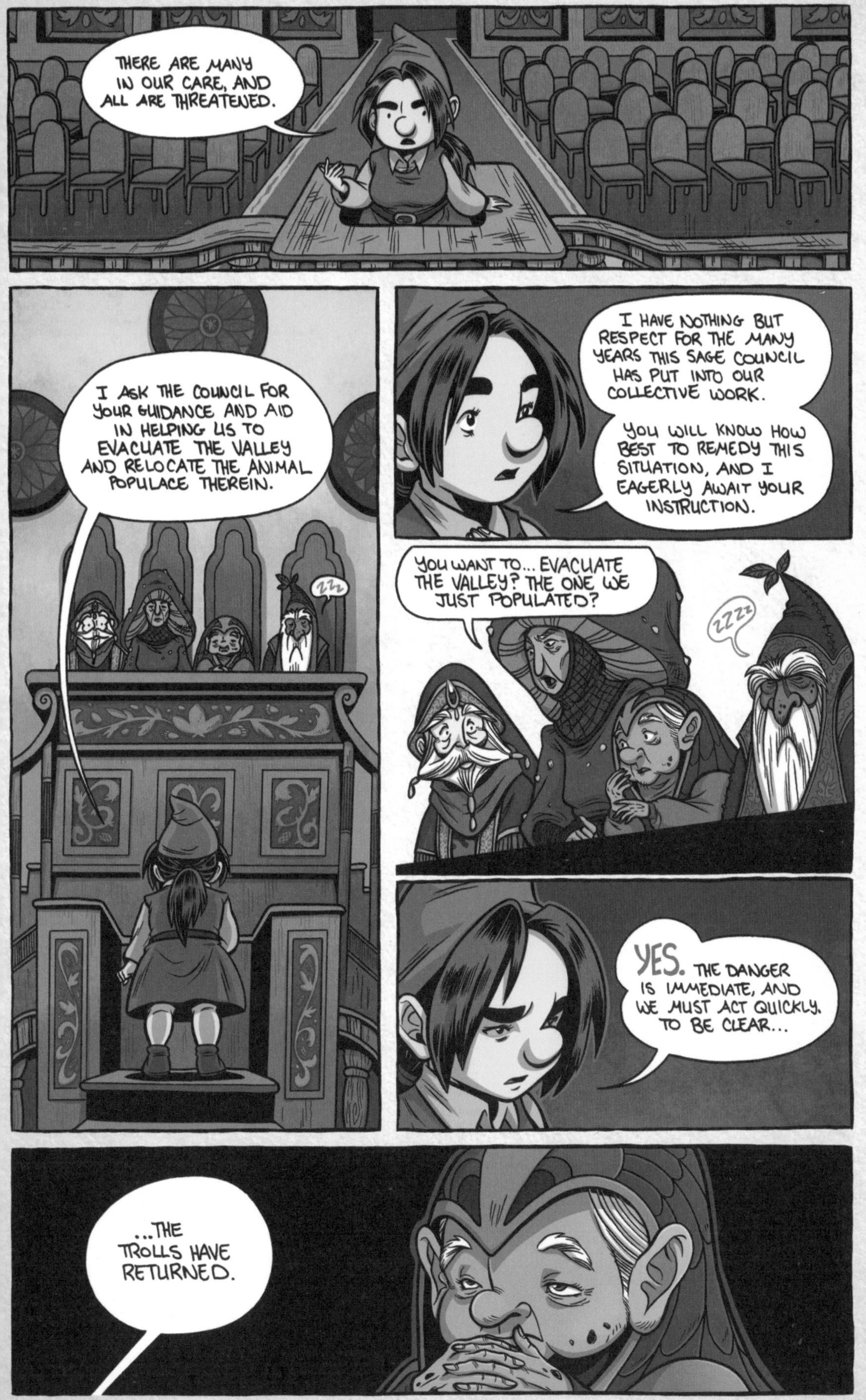

THERE ARE MANY IN OUR CARE, AND ALL ARE THREATENED.
I ASK THE COUNCIL FOR YOUR GUIDANCE AND AID IN HELPING US TO EVACUATE THE VALLEY AND RELOCATE THE ANIMAL POPULACE THEREIN.
ZZZ
I HAVE NOTHING BUT RESPECT FOR THE MANY YEARS THIS SAGE COUNCIL HAS PUT INTO OUR COLLECTIVE WORK.
YOU WILL KNOW HOW BEST TO REMEDY THIS SITUATION, AND I EAGERLY AWAIT YOUR INSTRUCTION.
YOU WANT TO... EVACUATE THE VALLEY? THE ONE WE JUST POPULATED?
ZZZZ
YES. THE DANGER IS IMMEDIATE, AND WE MUST ACT QUICKLY. TO BE CLEAR...
...THE TROLLS HAVE RETURNED.

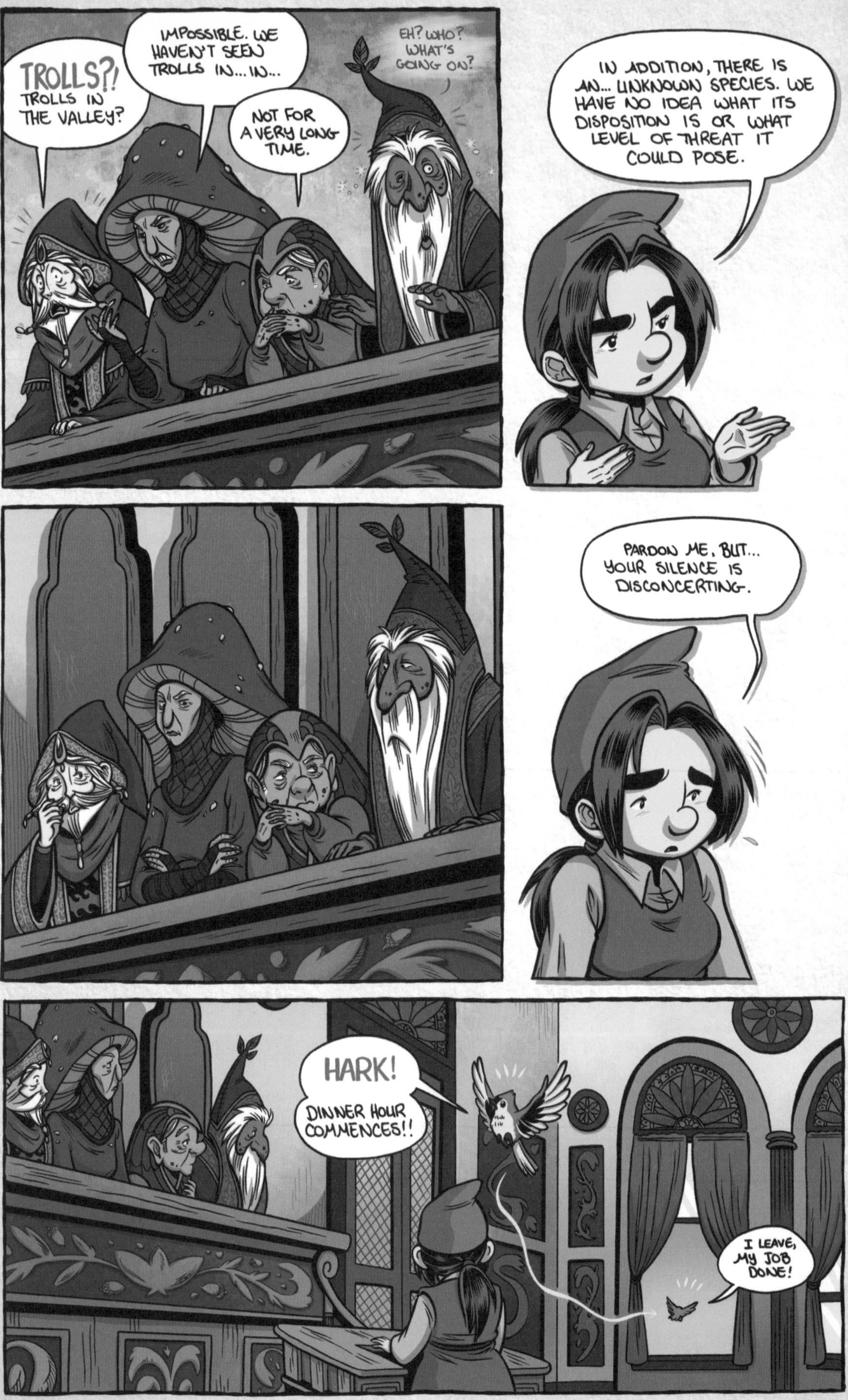
TROLLS?! TROLLS IN THE VALLEY?
IMPOSSIBLE. WE HAVEN'T SEEN TROLLS IN... IN...
NOT FOR A VERY LONG TIME.
EH? WHO? WHAT'S GOING ON?
IN ADDITION, THERE IS AN... UNKNOWN SPECIES. WE HAVE NO IDEA WHAT ITS DISPOSITION IS OR WHAT LEVEL OF THREAT IT COULD POSE.
PARDON ME, BUT... YOUR SILENCE IS DISCONCERTING.
HARK!
DINNER HOUR COMMENCES!!
I LEAVE, MY JOB DONE!

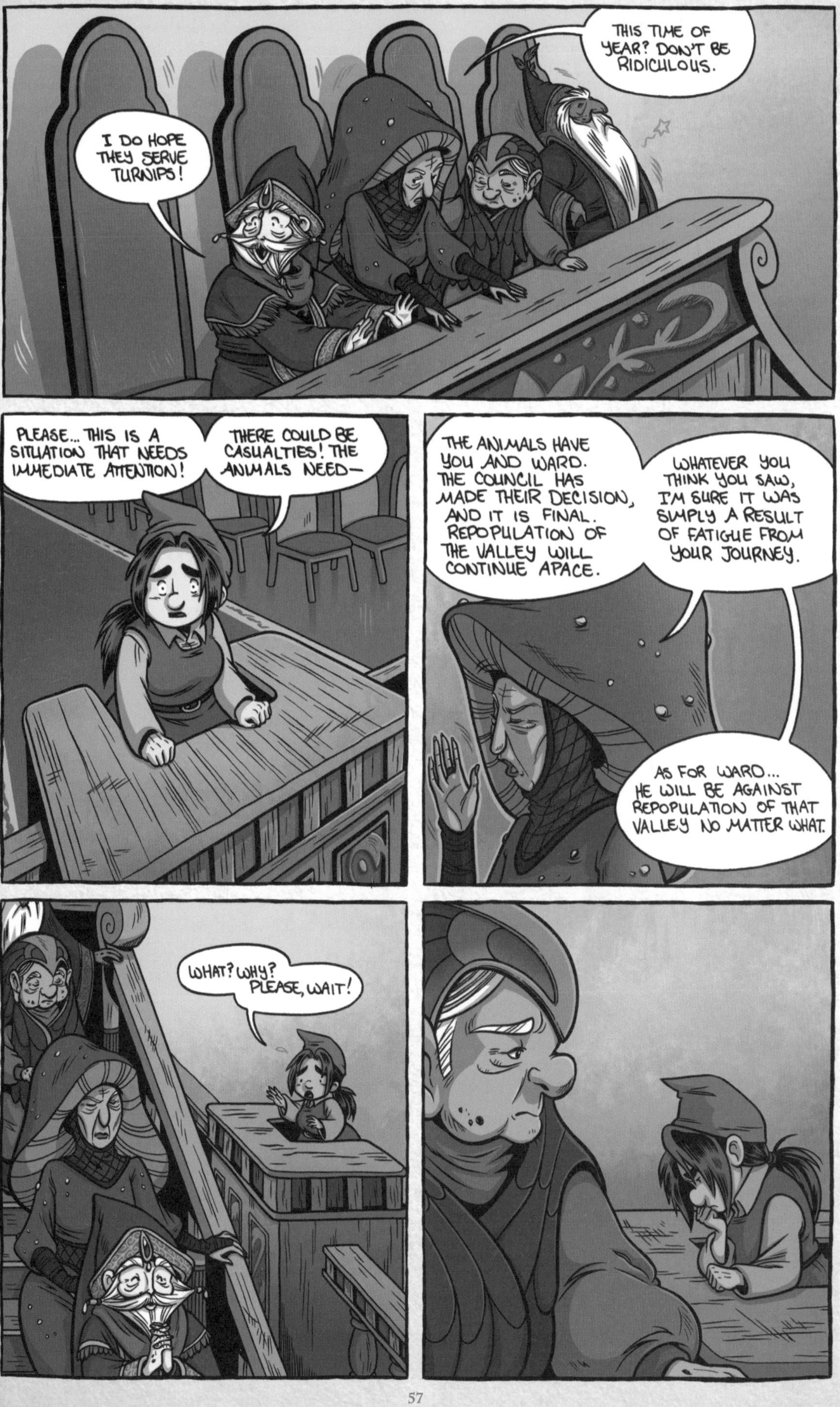
I DO HOPE THEY SERVE TURNIPS!
THIS TIME OF YEAR? DON'T BE RIDICULOUS.
PLEASE... THIS IS A SITUATION THAT NEEDS IMMEDIATE ATTENTION!
THERE COULD BE CASUALTIES! THE ANIMALS NEED—
THE ANIMALS HAVE YOU AND WARD. THE COUNCIL HAS MADE THEIR DECISION, AND IT IS FINAL. REPOPULATION OF THE VALLEY WILL CONTINUE APACE.
WHATEVER YOU THINK YOU SAW, I'M SURE IT WAS SIMPLY A RESULT OF FATIGUE FROM YOUR JOURNEY.
AS FOR WARD... HE WILL BE AGAINST REPOPULATION OF THAT VALLEY NO MATTER WHAT.
WHAT? WHY? PLEASE, WAIT!

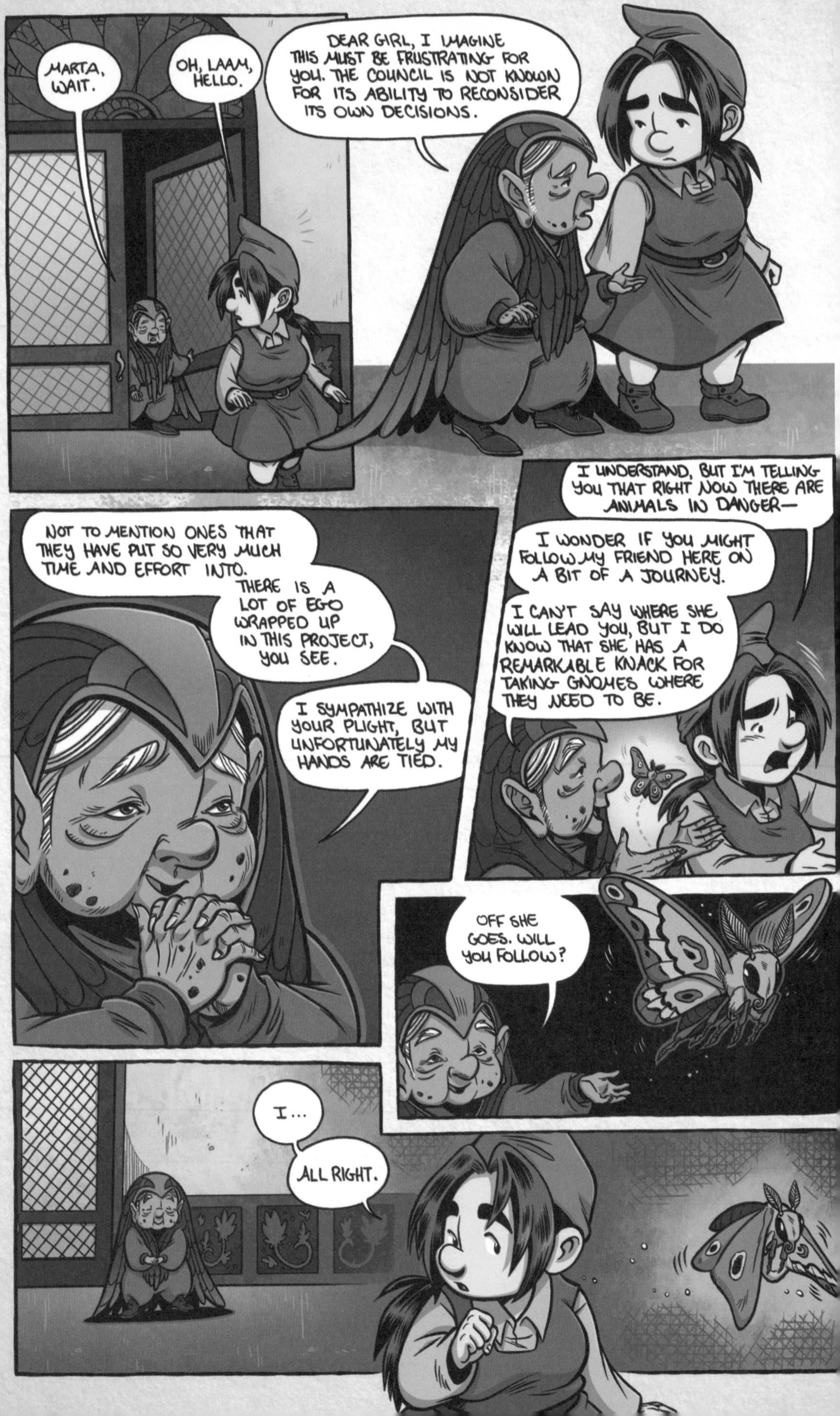
MARTA, WAIT.
OH, LAAM, HELLO.
DEAR GIRL, I IMAGINE THIS MUST BE FRUSTRATING FOR YOU. THE COUNCIL IS NOT KNOWN FOR ITS ABILITY TO RECONSIDER ITS OWN DECISIONS.
NOT TO MENTION ONES THAT THEY HAVE PUT SO VERY MUCH TIME AND EFFORT INTO.
THERE IS A LOT OF EGO WRAPPED UP IN THIS PROJECT, YOU SEE.
I UNDERSTAND, BUT I'M TELLING YOU THAT RIGHT NOW THERE ARE ANIMALS IN DANGER—
I SYMPATHIZE WITH YOUR PLIGHT, BUT UNFORTUNATELY MY HANDS ARE TIED.
I WONDER IF YOU MIGHT FOLLOW MY FRIEND HERE ON A BIT OF A JOURNEY.
I CAN'T SAY WHERE SHE WILL LEAD YOU, BUT I DO KNOW THAT SHE HAS A REMARKABLE KNACK FOR TAKING GNOMES WHERE THEY NEED TO BE.
OFF SHE GOES. WILL YOU FOLLOW?
I...
ALL RIGHT.

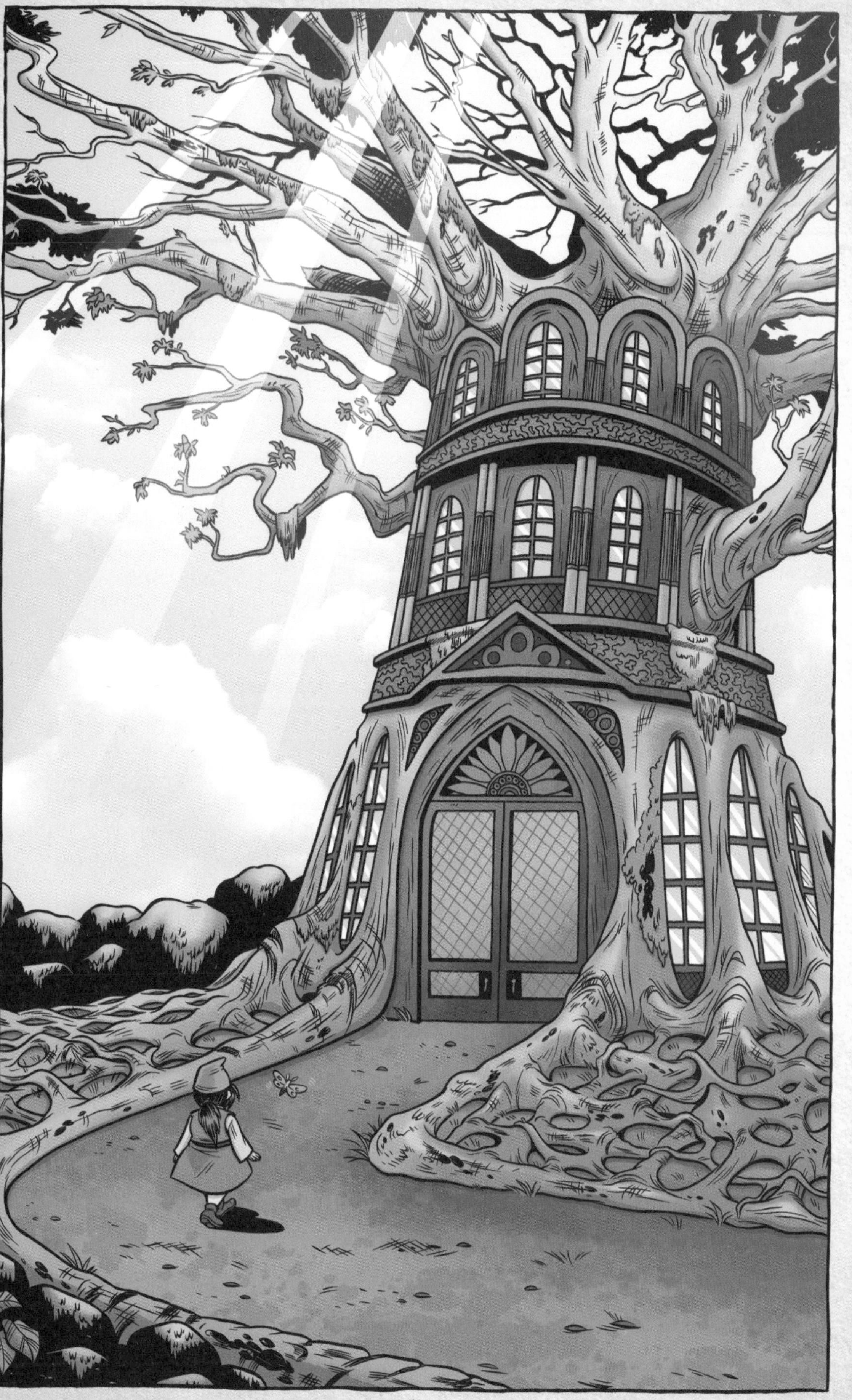

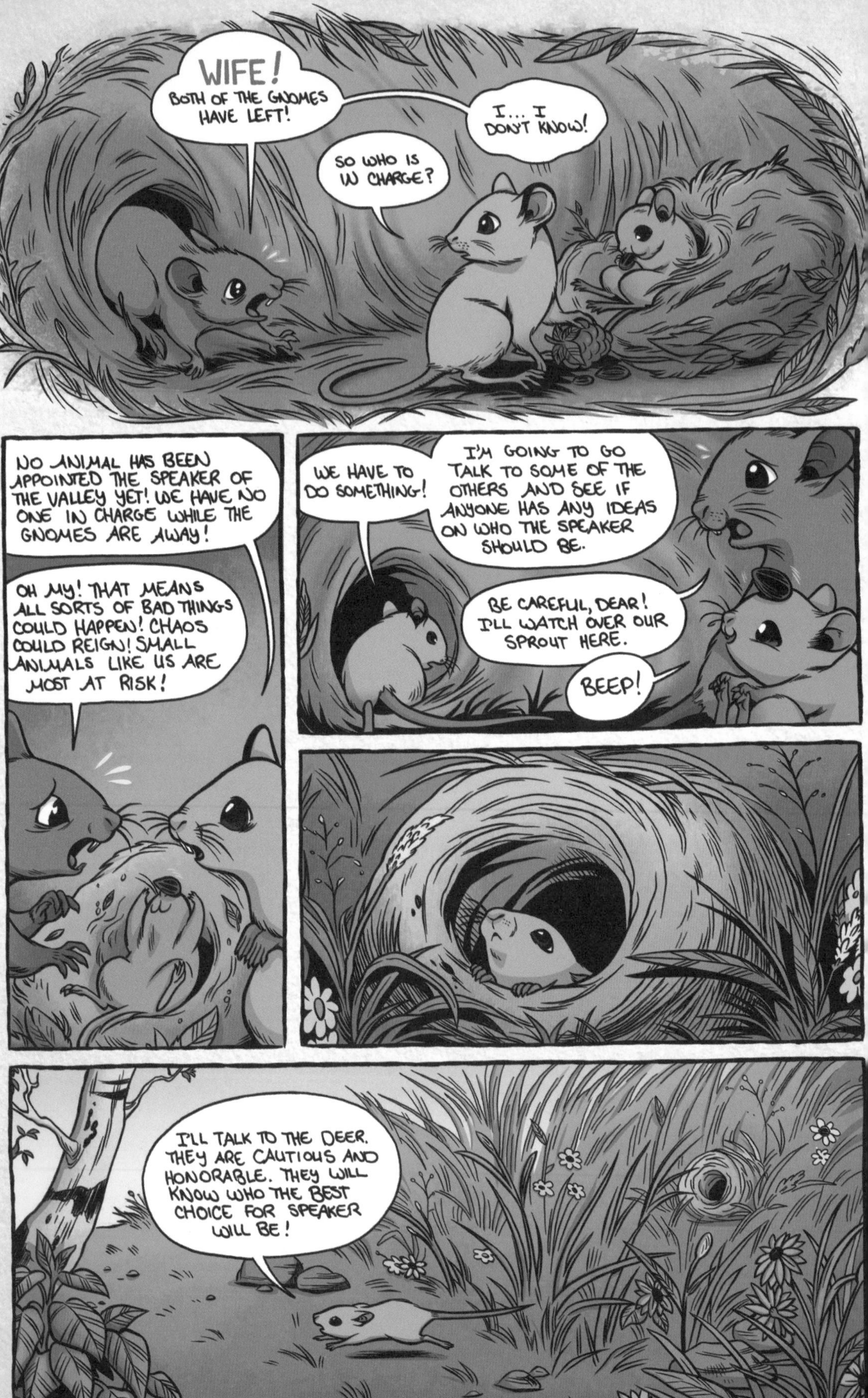

WIFE! BOTH OF THE GNOMES HAVE LEFT!
SO WHO IS IN CHARGE?
I... I DON'T KNOW!
NO ANIMAL HAS BEEN APPOINTED THE SPEAKER OF THE VALLEY YET! WE HAVE NO ONE IN CHARGE WHILE THE GNOMES ARE AWAY!
OH MY! THAT MEANS ALL SORTS OF BAD THINGS COULD HAPPEN! CHAOS COULD REIGN! SMALL ANIMALS LIKE US ARE MOST AT RISK!
WE HAVE TO DO SOMETHING!
I'M GOING TO GO TALK TO SOME OF THE OTHERS AND SEE IF ANYONE HAS ANY IDEAS ON WHO THE SPEAKER SHOULD BE.
BE CAREFUL, DEAR! I'LL WATCH OVER OUR SPROUT HERE.
BEEP!
I'LL TALK TO THE DEER. THEY ARE CAUTIOUS AND HONORABLE. THEY WILL KNOW WHO THE BEST CHOICE FOR SPEAKER WILL BE!

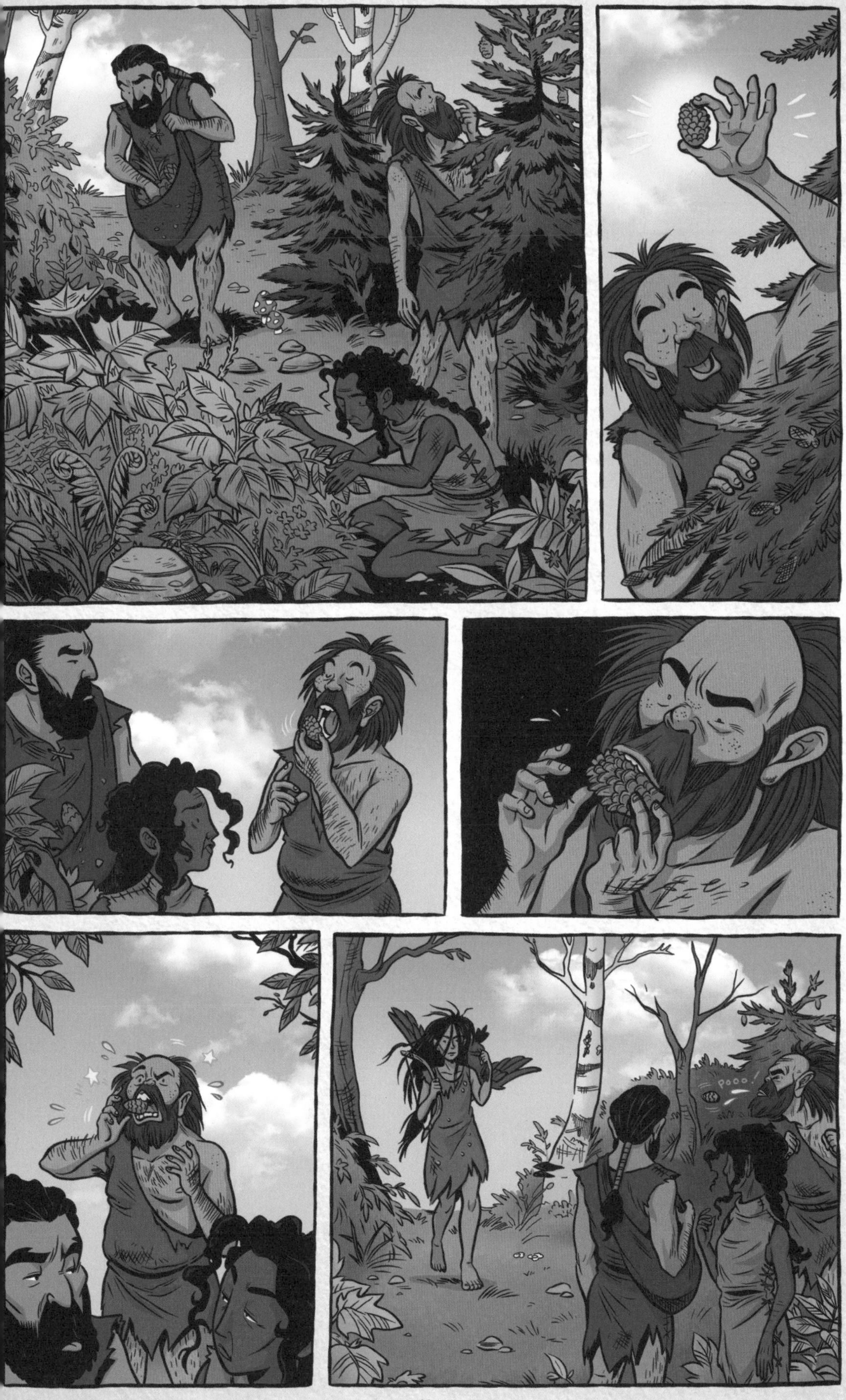
POOO!

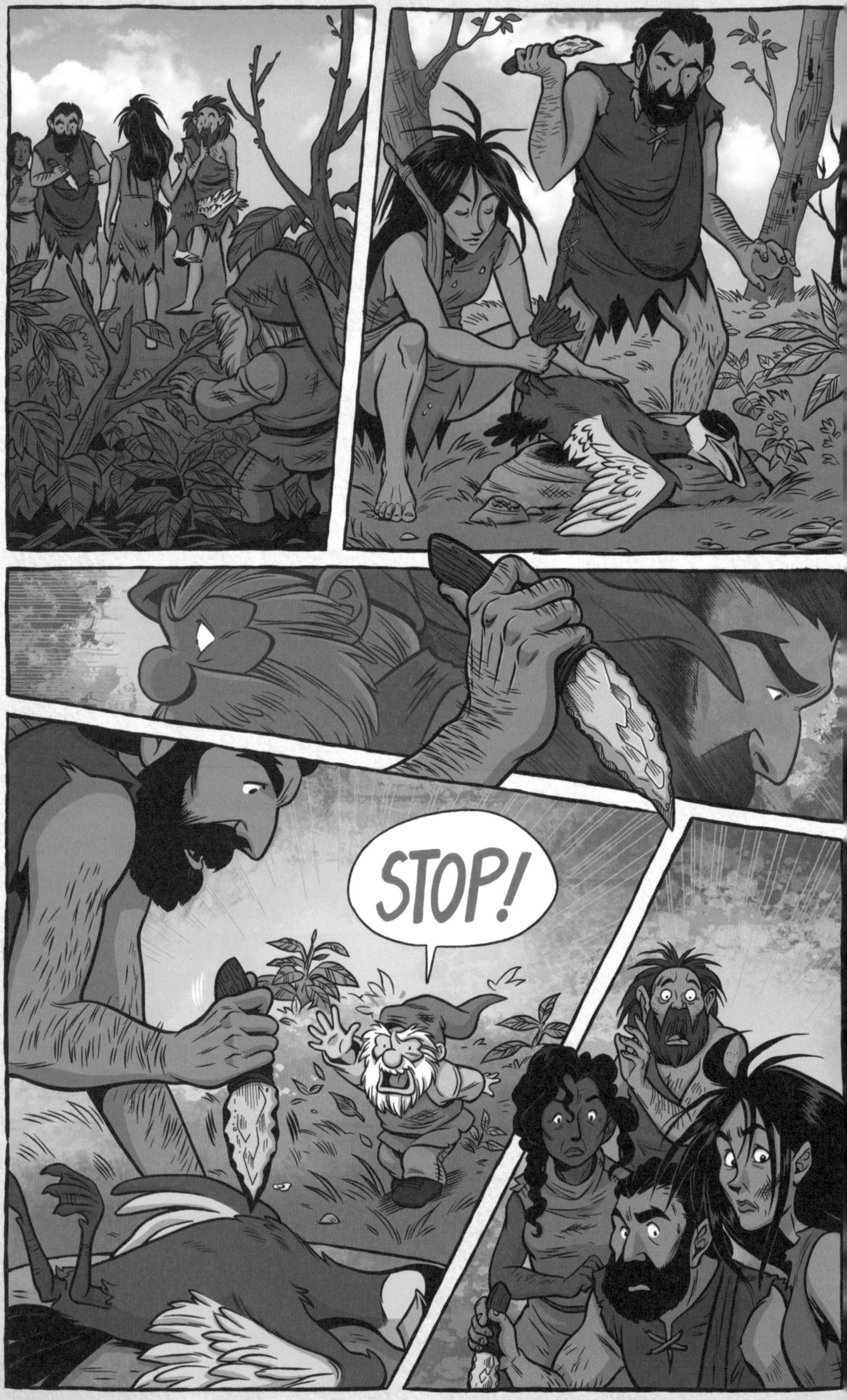
STOP!

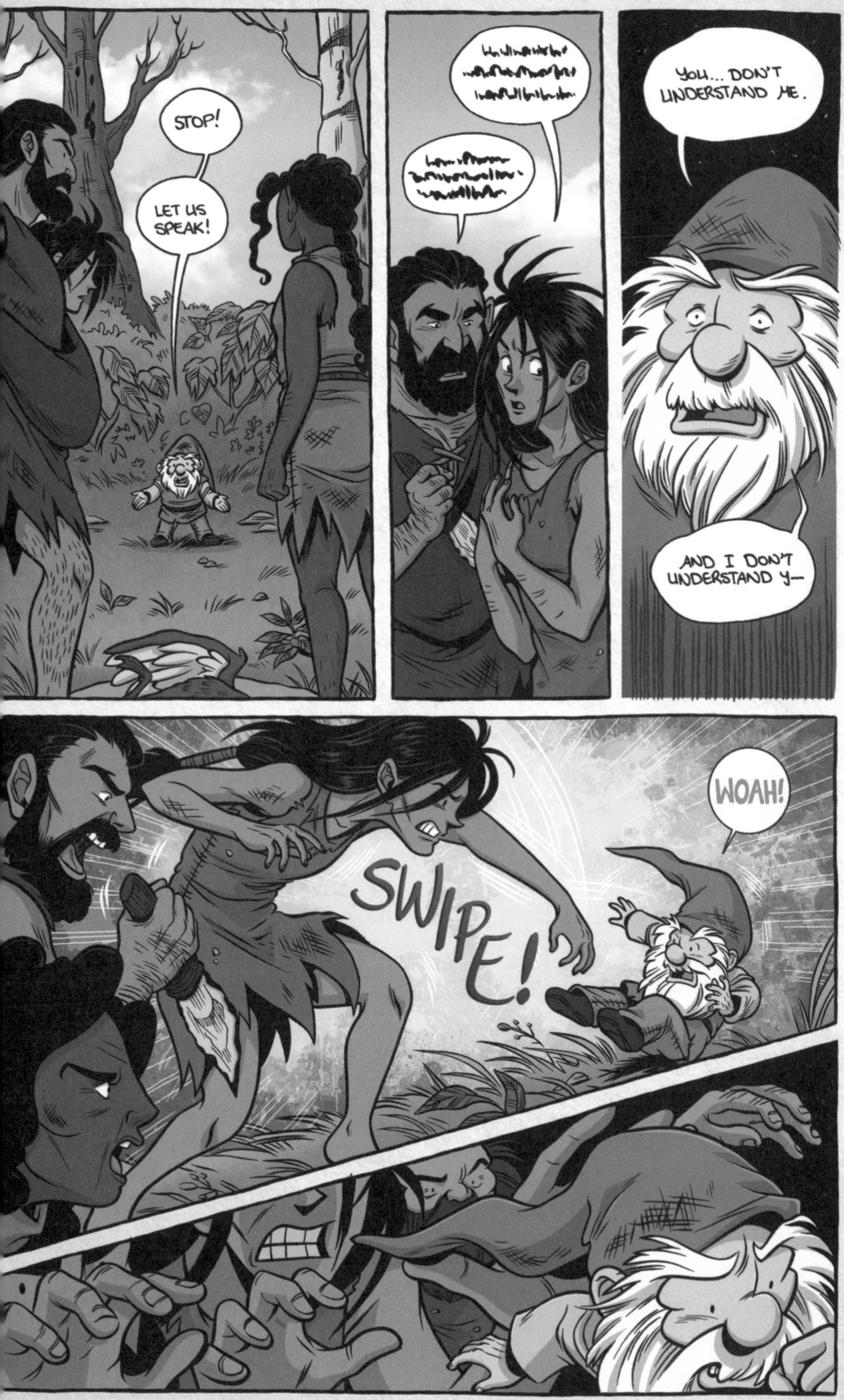
STOP!
LET US SPEAK!
YOU... DON'T UNDERSTAND ME.
AND I DON'T UNDERSTAND Y—
SWIPE!
WOAH!

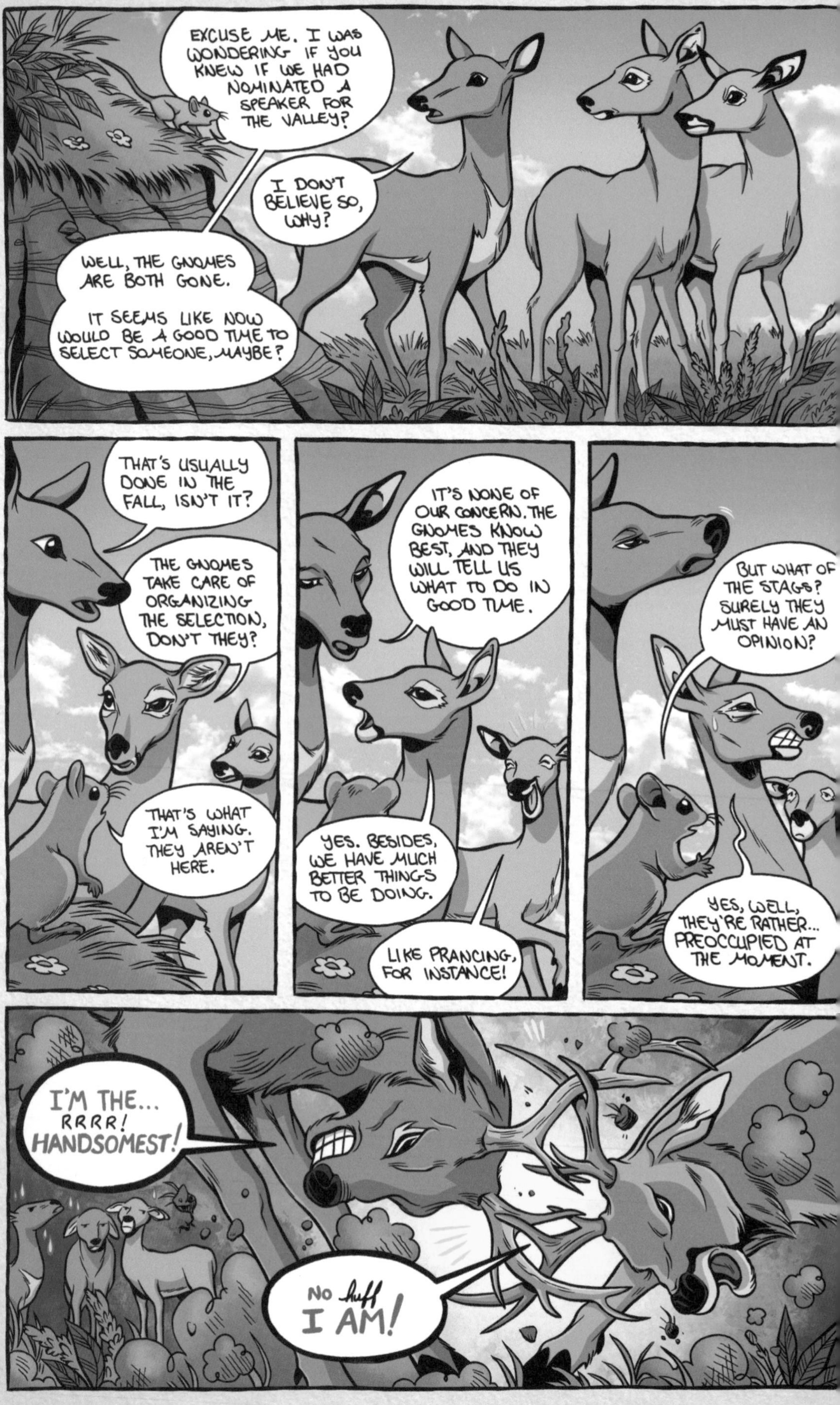
EXCUSE ME. I WAS WONDERING IF YOU KNEW IF WE HAD NOMINATED A SPEAKER FOR THE VALLEY?
I DON'T BELIEVE SO, WHY?
WELL, THE GNOMES ARE BOTH GONE.
IT SEEMS LIKE NOW WOULD BE A GOOD TIME TO SELECT SOMEONE, MAYBE?
THAT'S USUALLY DONE IN THE FALL, ISN'T IT?
THE GNOMES TAKE CARE OF ORGANIZING THE SELECTION, DON'T THEY?
THAT'S WHAT I'M SAYING. THEY AREN'T HERE.
IT'S NONE OF OUR CONCERN. THE GNOMES KNOW BEST, AND THEY WILL TELL US WHAT TO DO IN GOOD TIME.
YES. BESIDES, WE HAVE MUCH BETTER THINGS TO BE DOING.
LIKE PRANCING, FOR INSTANCE!
BUT WHAT OF THE STAGS? SURELY THEY MUST HAVE AN OPINION?
YES, WELL, THEY'RE RATHER... PREOCCUPIED AT THE MOMENT.
I'M THE... RRRR! HANDSOMEST!
No huff I AM!

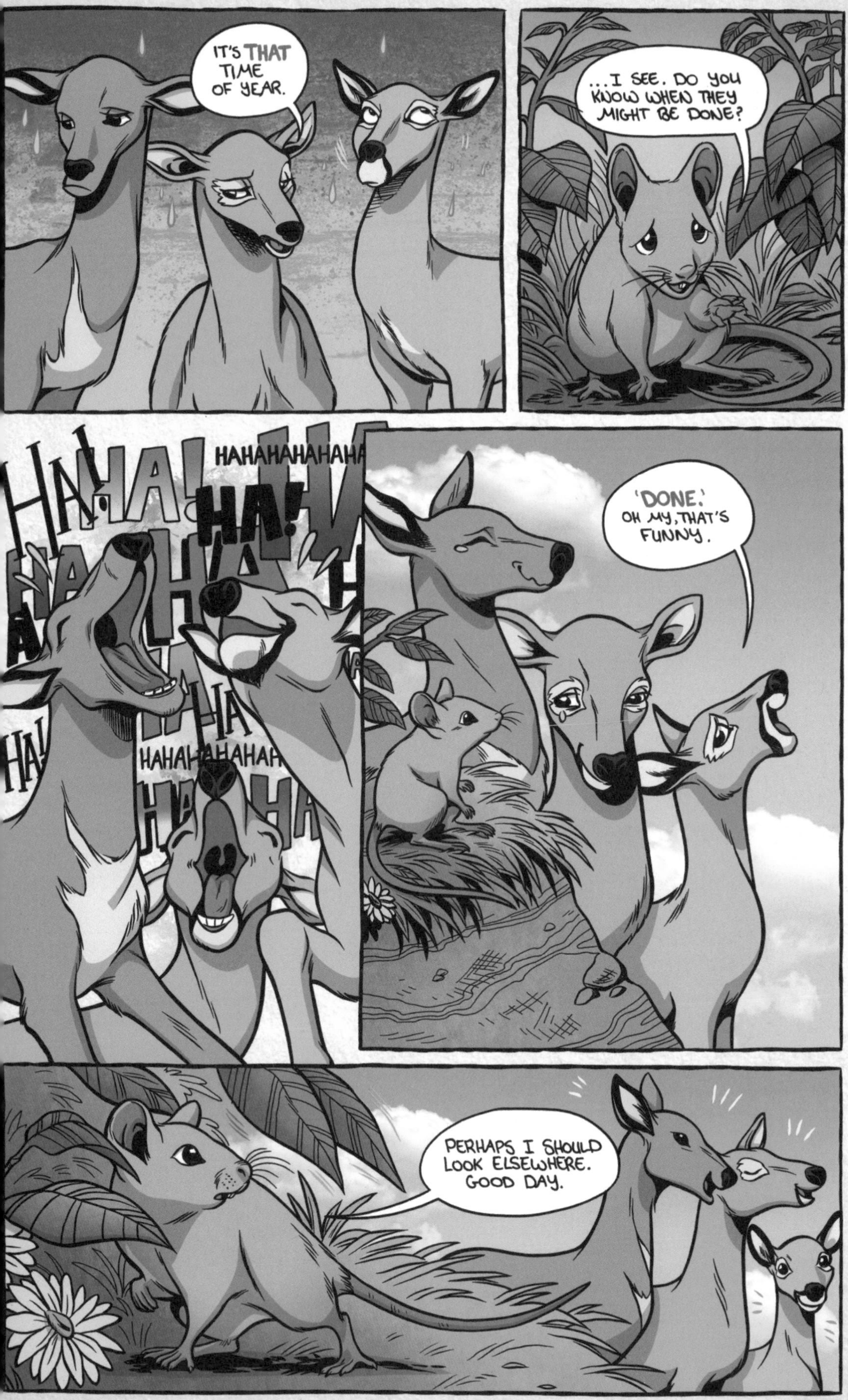

IT'S THAT TIME OF YEAR.
...I SEE. DO YOU KNOW WHEN THEY MIGHT BE DONE?
HA! HA! HA! HA! HA!
HAHAHAHAHAHAHA
HAHAHAHAHAH
'DONE.' OH MY, THAT'S FUNNY.
PERHAPS I SHOULD LOOK ELSEWHERE. GOOD DAY.

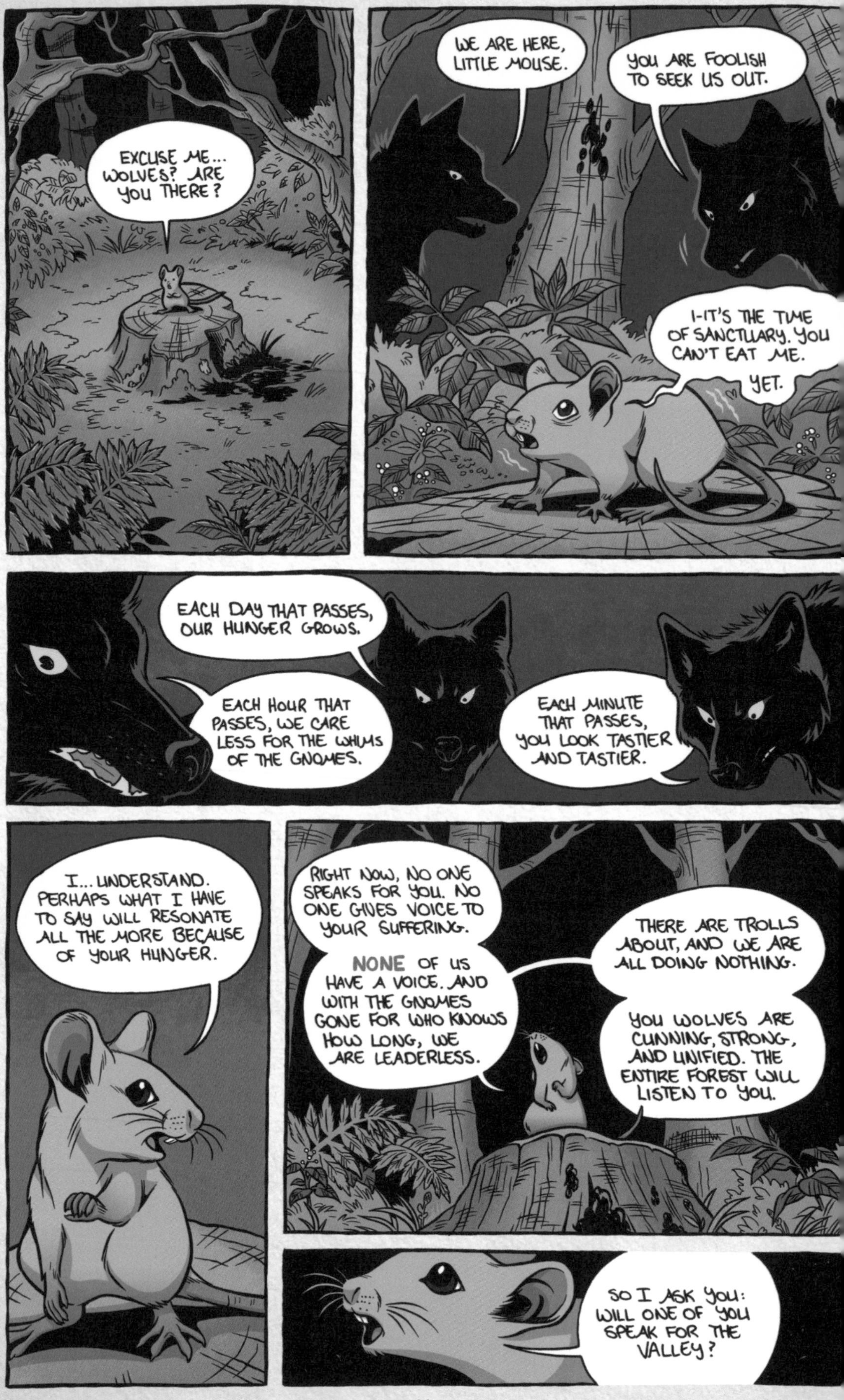
EXCUSE ME... WOLVES? ARE YOU THERE?
WE ARE HERE, LITTLE MOUSE.
YOU ARE FOOLISH TO SEEK US OUT.
I-IT'S THE TIME OF SANCTUARY. YOU CAN'T EAT ME.
YET.
EACH DAY THAT PASSES, OUR HUNGER GROWS.
EACH HOUR THAT PASSES, WE CARE LESS FOR THE WHIMS OF THE GNOMES.
EACH MINUTE THAT PASSES, YOU LOOK TASTIER AND TASTIER.
I... UNDERSTAND. PERHAPS WHAT I HAVE TO SAY WILL RESONATE ALL THE MORE BECAUSE OF YOUR HUNGER.
RIGHT NOW, NO ONE SPEAKS FOR YOU. NO ONE GIVES VOICE TO YOUR SUFFERING.
NONE OF US HAVE A VOICE. AND WITH THE GNOMES GONE FOR WHO KNOWS HOW LONG, WE ARE LEADERLESS.
THERE ARE TROLLS ABOUT, AND WE ARE ALL DOING NOTHING.
YOU WOLVES ARE CUNNING, STRONG, AND UNIFIED. THE ENTIRE FOREST WILL LISTEN TO YOU.
SO I ASK YOU: WILL ONE OF YOU SPEAK FOR THE VALLEY?

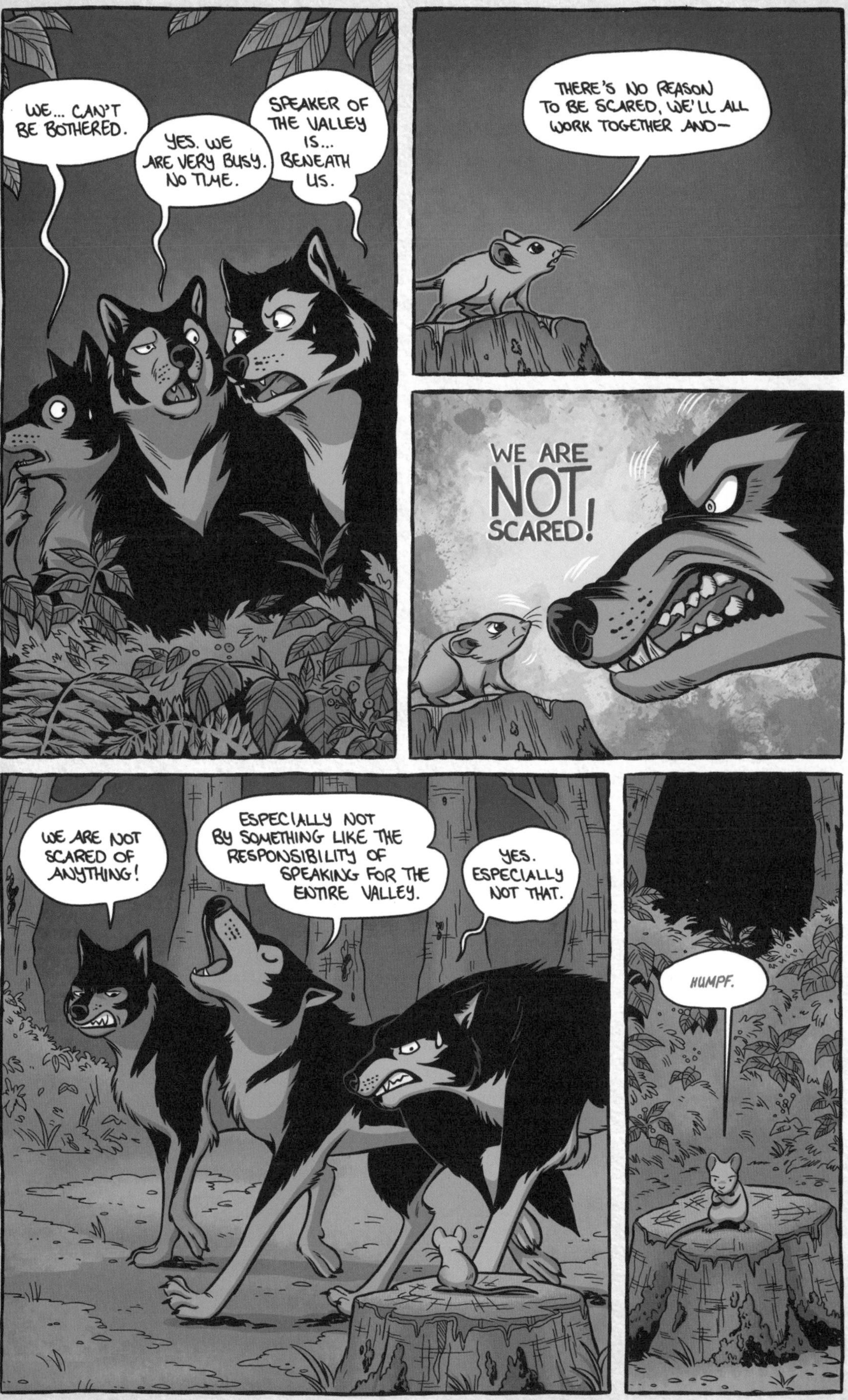
WE... CAN'T BE BOTHERED.
YES. WE ARE VERY BUSY. NO TIME.
SPEAKER OF THE VALLEY IS... BENEATH US.
THERE'S NO REASON TO BE SCARED. WE'LL ALL WORK TOGETHER AND—
WE ARE NOT SCARED!
WE ARE NOT SCARED OF ANYTHING!
ESPECIALLY NOT BY SOMETHING LIKE THE RESPONSIBILITY OF SPEAKING FOR THE ENTIRE VALLEY.
YES. ESPECIALLY NOT THAT.
HUMPF.

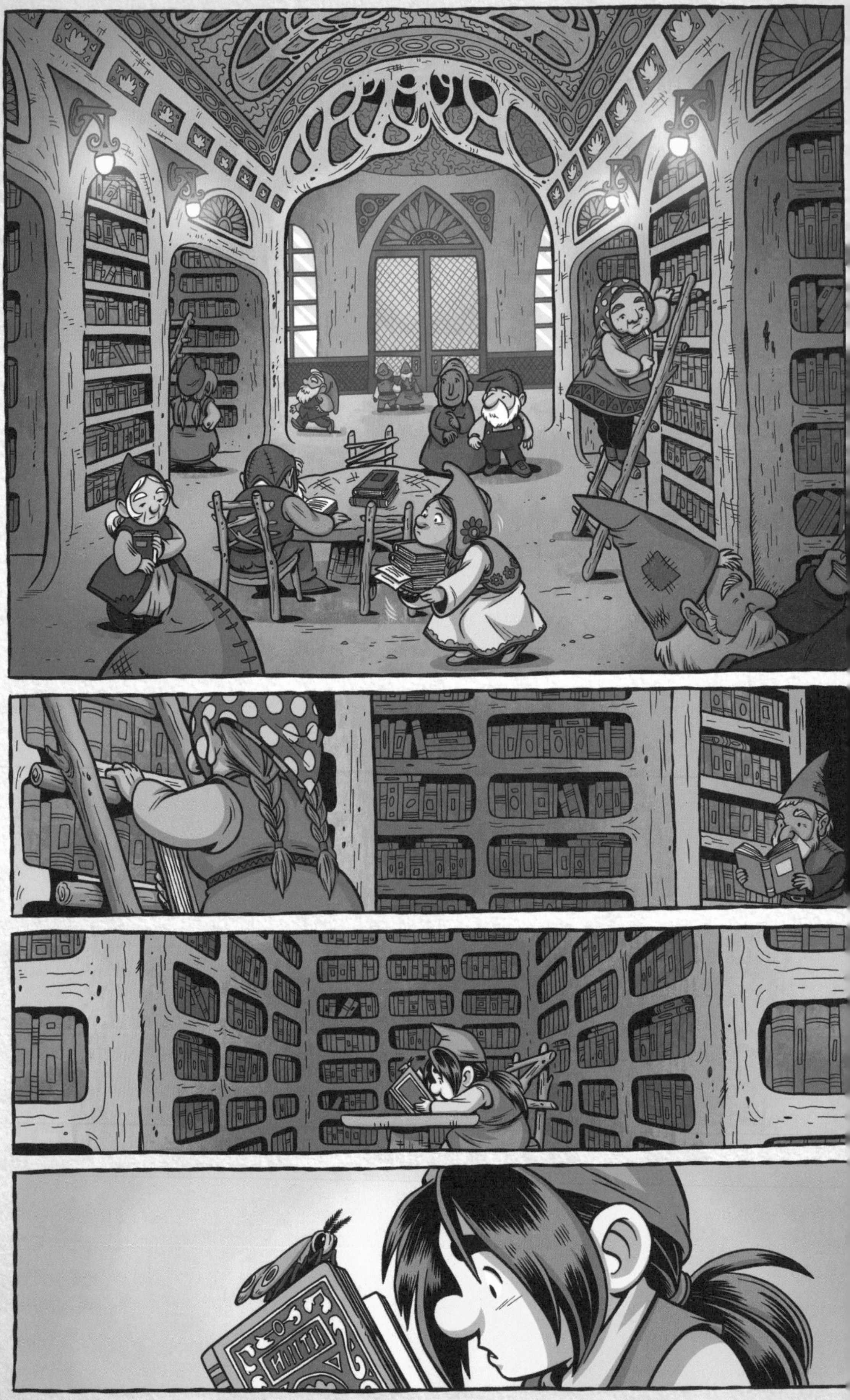

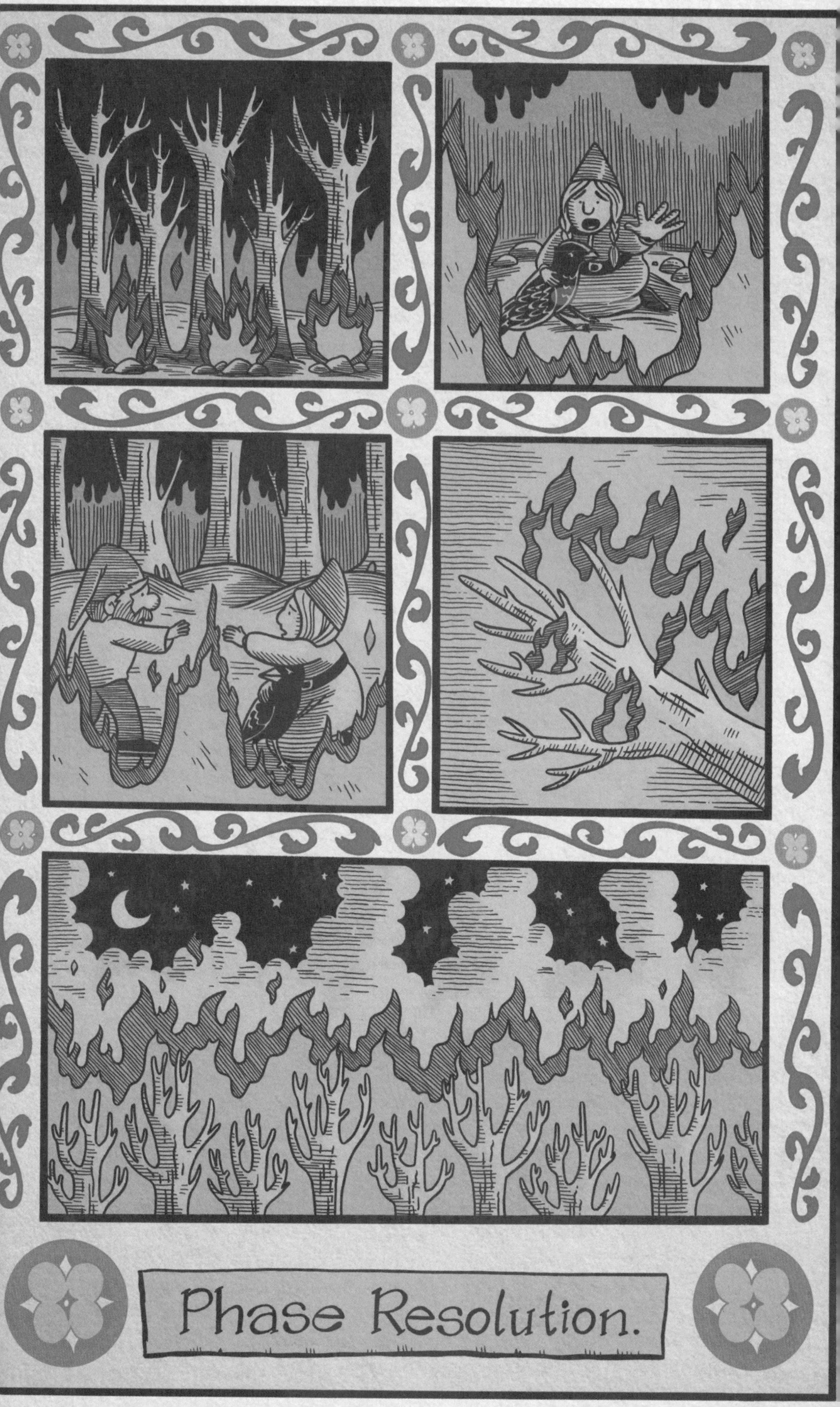
Phase Resolution.

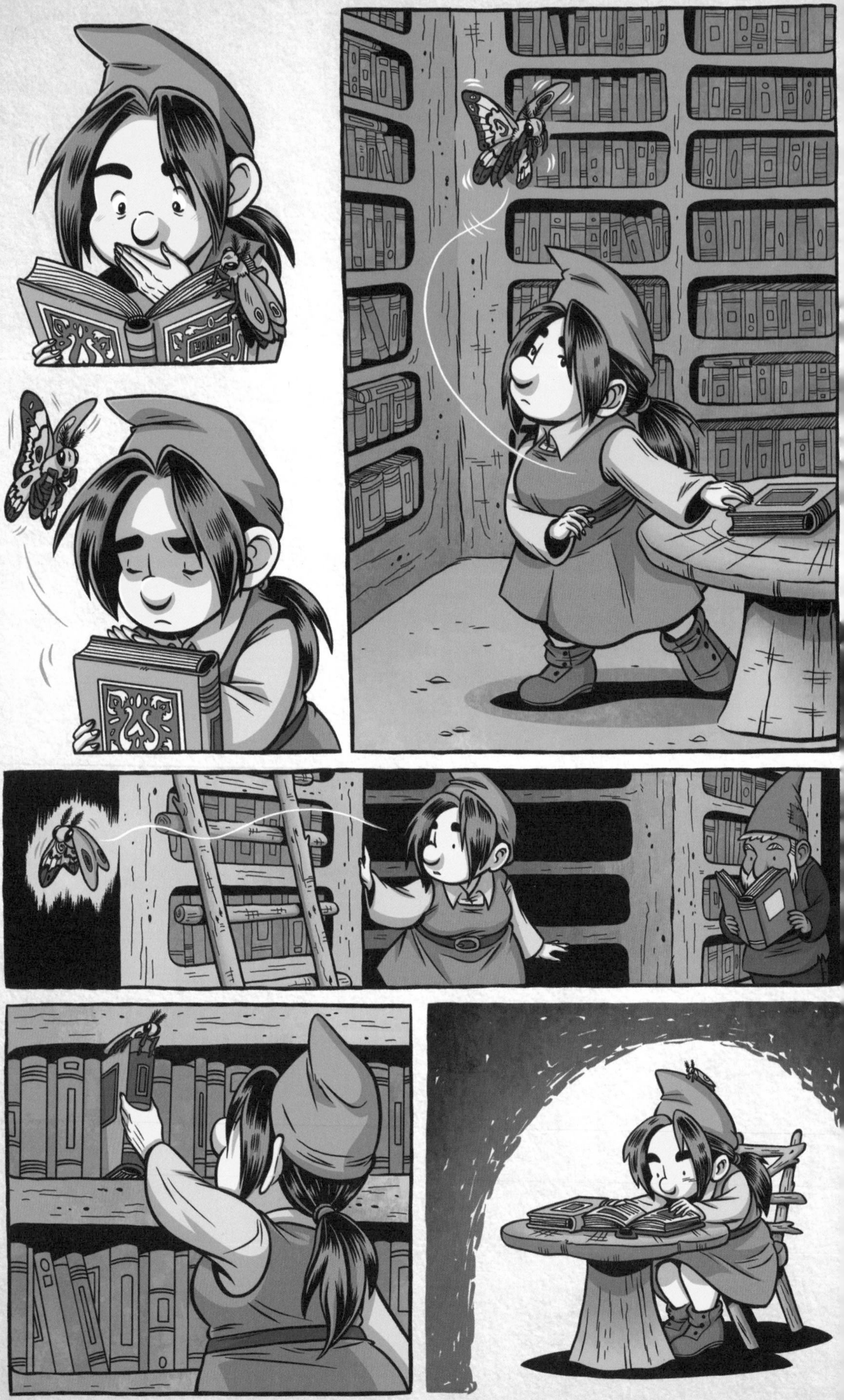

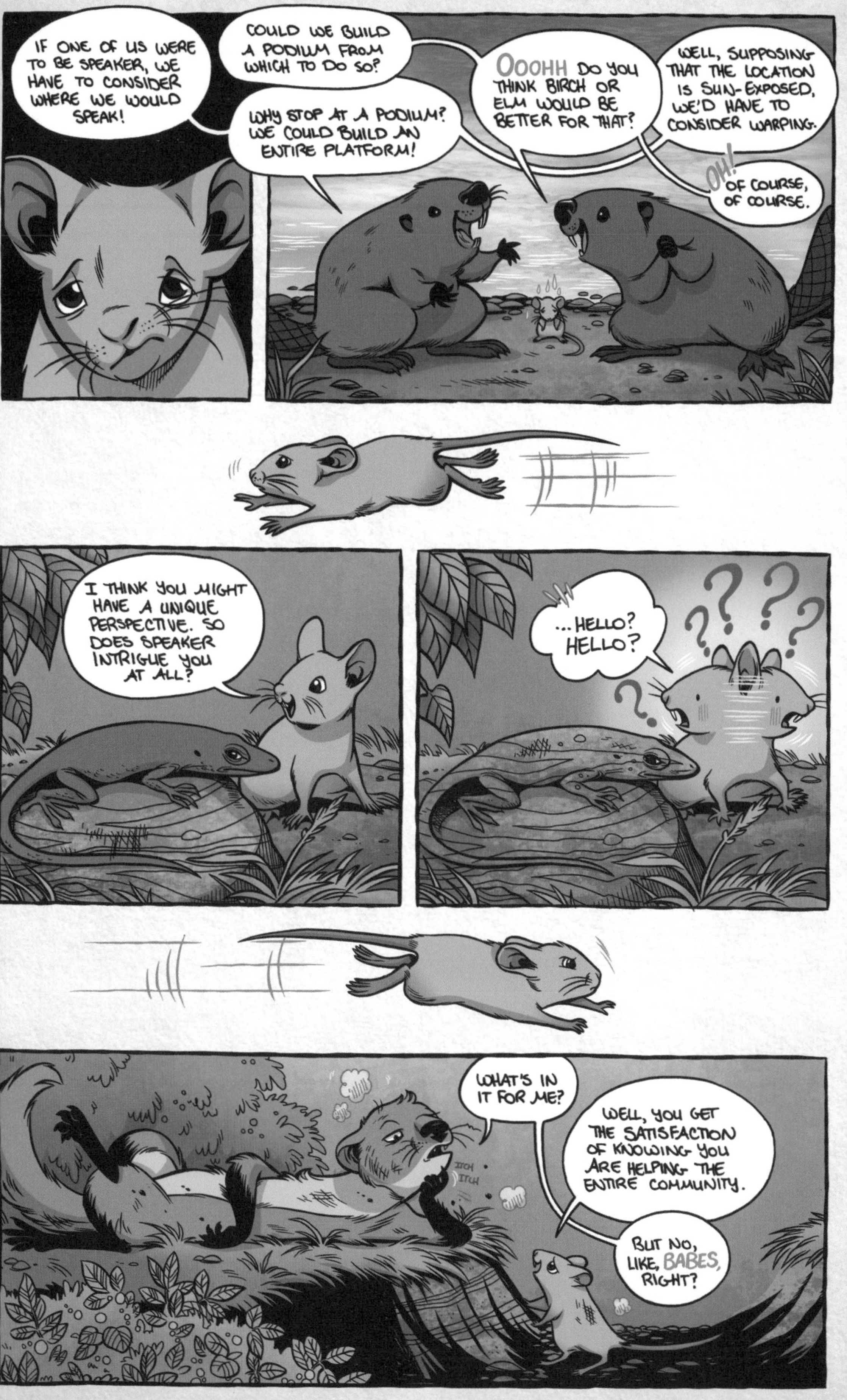
IF ONE OF US WERE TO BE SPEAKER, WE HAVE TO CONSIDER WHERE WE WOULD SPEAK!
COULD WE BUILD A PODIUM FROM WHICH TO DO SO?
WHY STOP AT A PODIUM? WE COULD BUILD AN ENTIRE PLATFORM!
OOOHH DO YOU THINK BIRCH OR ELM WOULD BE BETTER FOR THAT?
WELL, SUPPOSING THAT THE LOCATION IS SUN-EXPOSED, WE'D HAVE TO CONSIDER WARPING.
OH!
OF COURSE, OF COURSE.
I THINK YOU MIGHT HAVE A UNIQUE PERSPECTIVE. SO DOES SPEAKER INTRIGUE YOU AT ALL?
...HELLO? HELLO?
WHAT'S IN IT FOR ME?
WELL, YOU GET THE SATISFACTION OF KNOWING YOU ARE HELPING THE ENTIRE COMMUNITY.
BUT NO, LIKE, BABES, RIGHT?

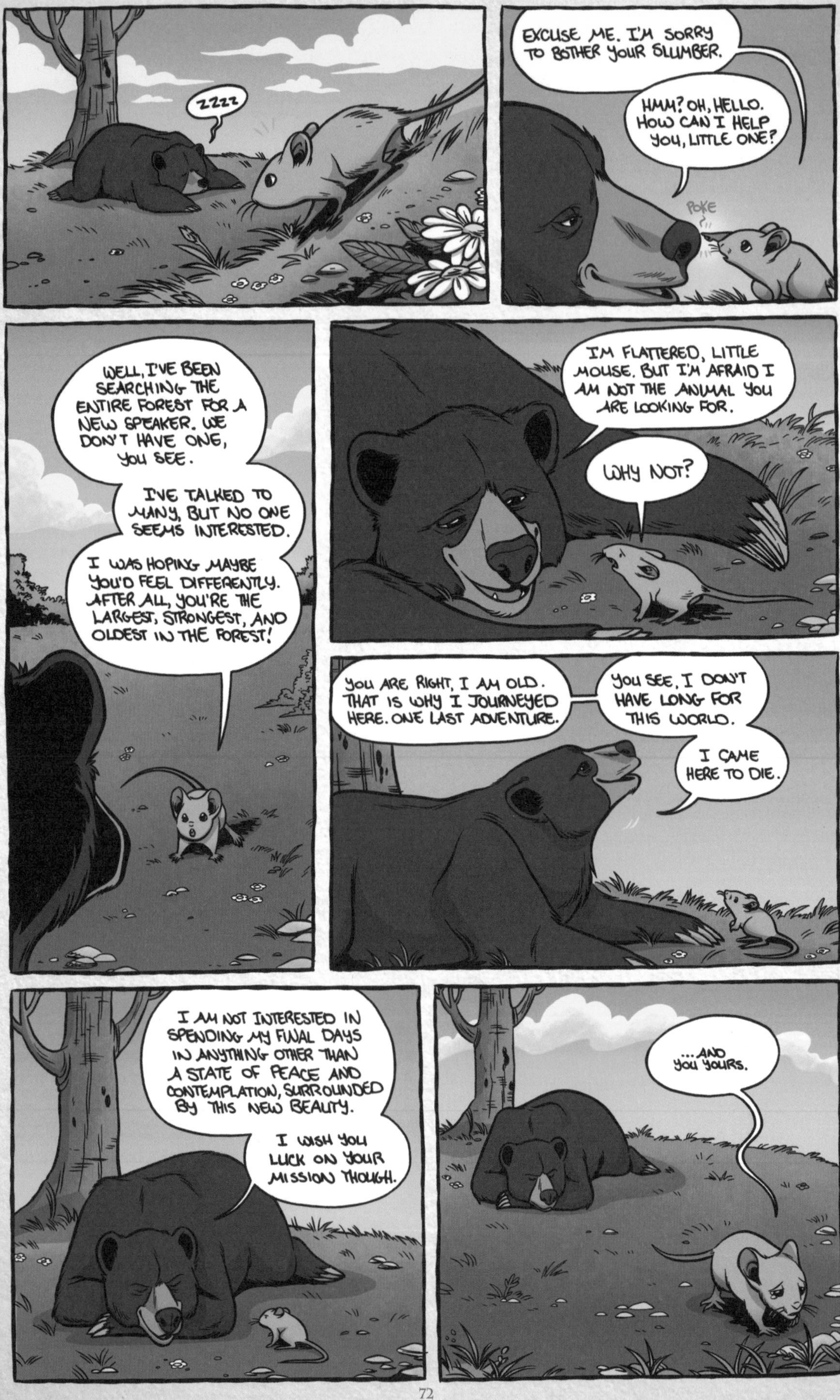

ZZZZ
EXCUSE ME. I'M SORRY TO BOTHER YOUR SLUMBER.
HMM? OH, HELLO. HOW CAN I HELP YOU, LITTLE ONE?
POKE
WELL, I'VE BEEN SEARCHING THE ENTIRE FOREST FOR A NEW SPEAKER. WE DON'T HAVE ONE, YOU SEE.
I'VE TALKED TO MANY, BUT NO ONE SEEMS INTERESTED.
I WAS HOPING MAYBE YOU'D FEEL DIFFERENTLY. AFTER ALL, YOU'RE THE LARGEST, STRONGEST, AND OLDEST IN THE FOREST!
I'M FLATTERED, LITTLE MOUSE. BUT I'M AFRAID I AM NOT THE ANIMAL YOU ARE LOOKING FOR.
WHY NOT?
YOU ARE RIGHT, I AM OLD. THAT IS WHY I JOURNEYED HERE. ONE LAST ADVENTURE.
YOU SEE, I DON'T HAVE LONG FOR THIS WORLD.
I CAME HERE TO DIE.
I AM NOT INTERESTED IN SPENDING MY FINAL DAYS IN ANYTHING OTHER THAN A STATE OF PEACE AND CONTEMPLATION, SURROUNDED BY THIS NEW BEAUTY.
I WISH YOU LUCK ON YOUR MISSION THOUGH.
...AND YOU YOURS.

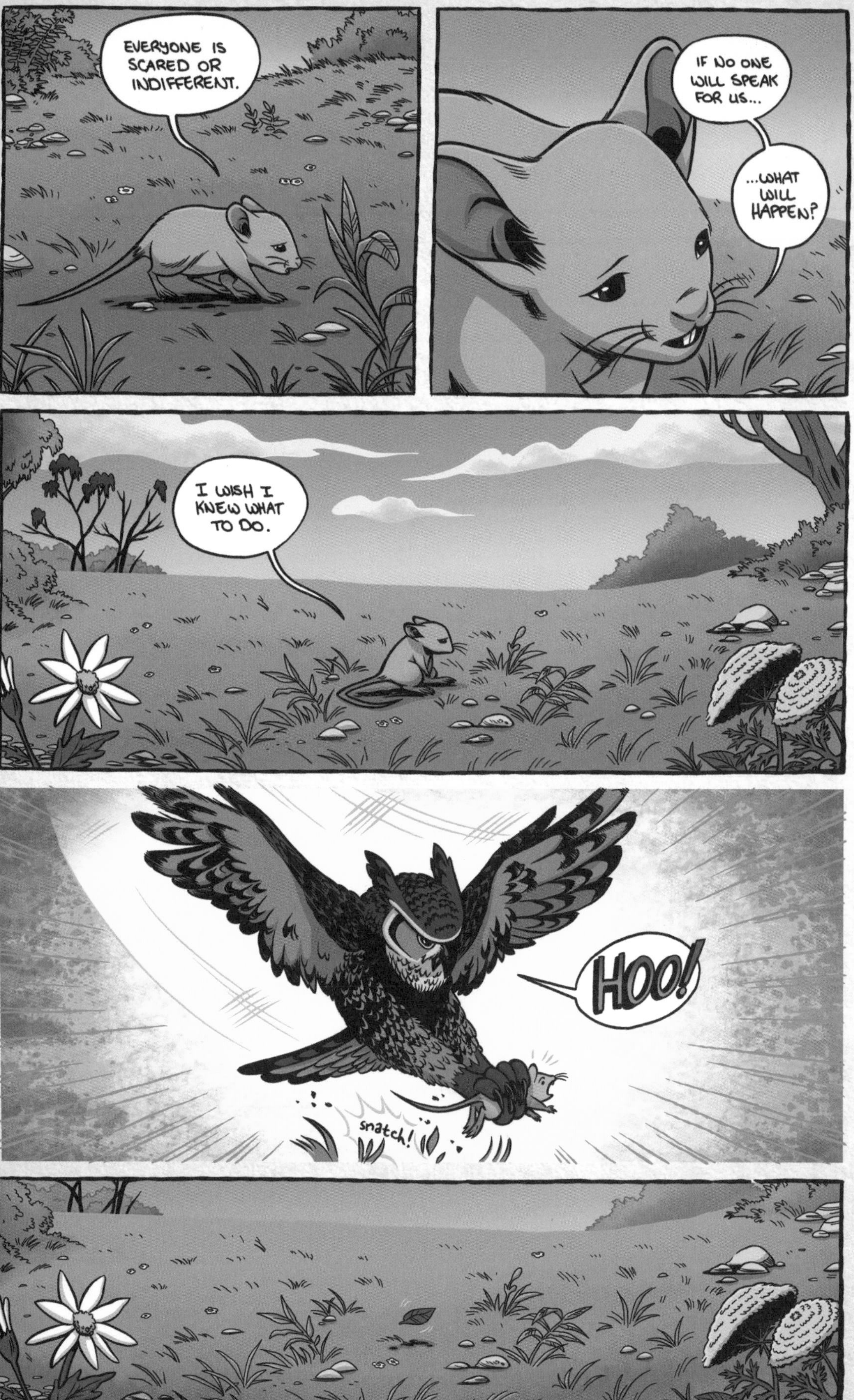
EVERYONE IS SCARED OR INDIFFERENT.
IF NO ONE WILL SPEAK FOR US...
...WHAT WILL HAPPEN?
I WISH I KNEW WHAT TO DO.
HOO!
snatch!

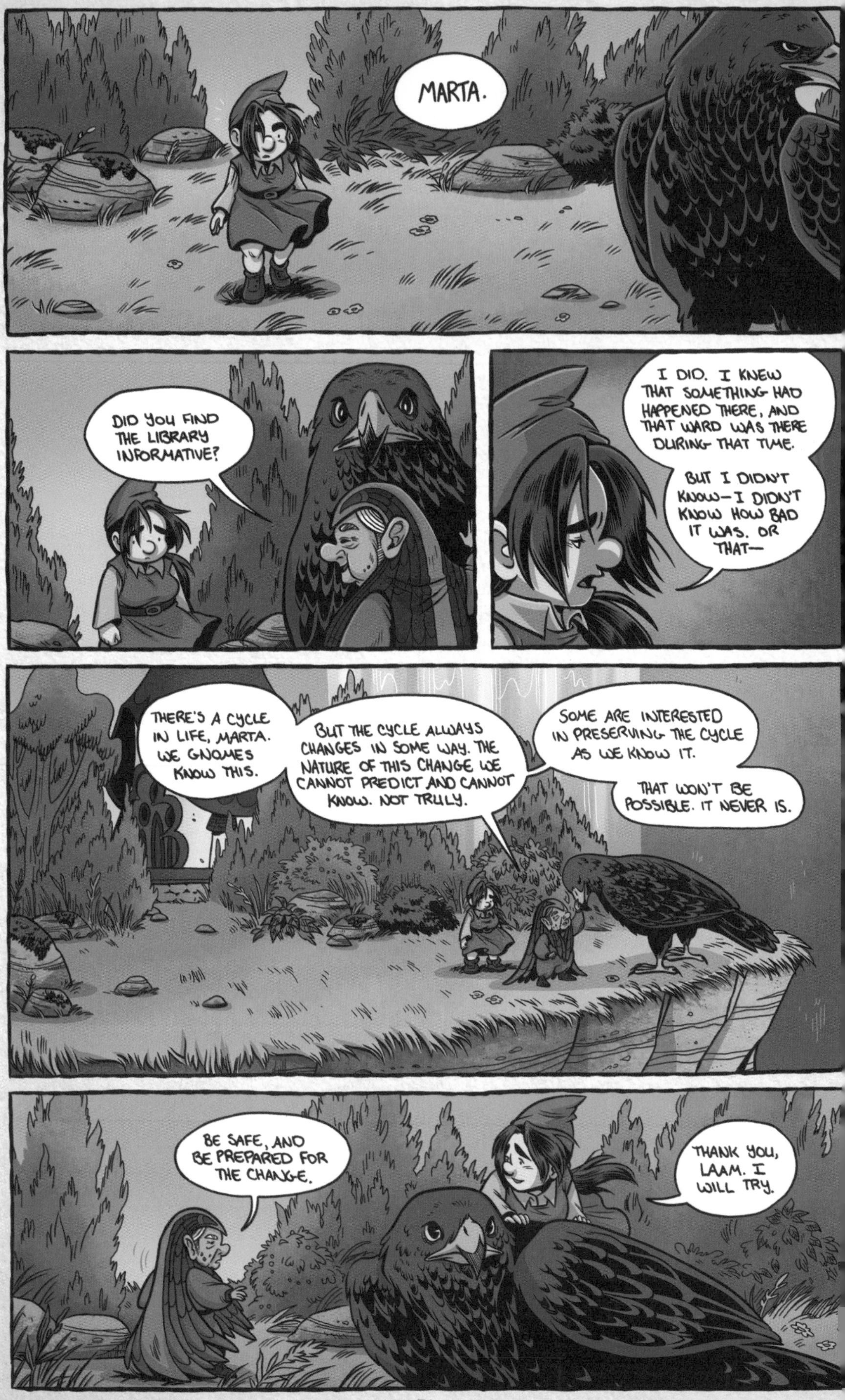
MARTA.
DID YOU FIND THE LIBRARY INFORMATIVE?
I DID. I KNEW THAT SOMETHING HAD HAPPENED THERE, AND THAT WARD WAS THERE DURING THAT TIME.
BUT I DIDN'T KNOW—I DIDN'T KNOW HOW BAD IT WAS. OR THAT—
THERE'S A CYCLE IN LIFE, MARTA. WE GNOMES KNOW THIS.
BUT THE CYCLE ALWAYS CHANGES IN SOME WAY. THE NATURE OF THIS CHANGE WE CANNOT PREDICT AND CANNOT KNOW. NOT TRULY.
SOME ARE INTERESTED IN PRESERVING THE CYCLE AS WE KNOW IT.
THAT WON'T BE POSSIBLE. IT NEVER IS.
BE SAFE, AND BE PREPARED FOR THE CHANGE.
THANK YOU, LAAM. I WILL TRY.

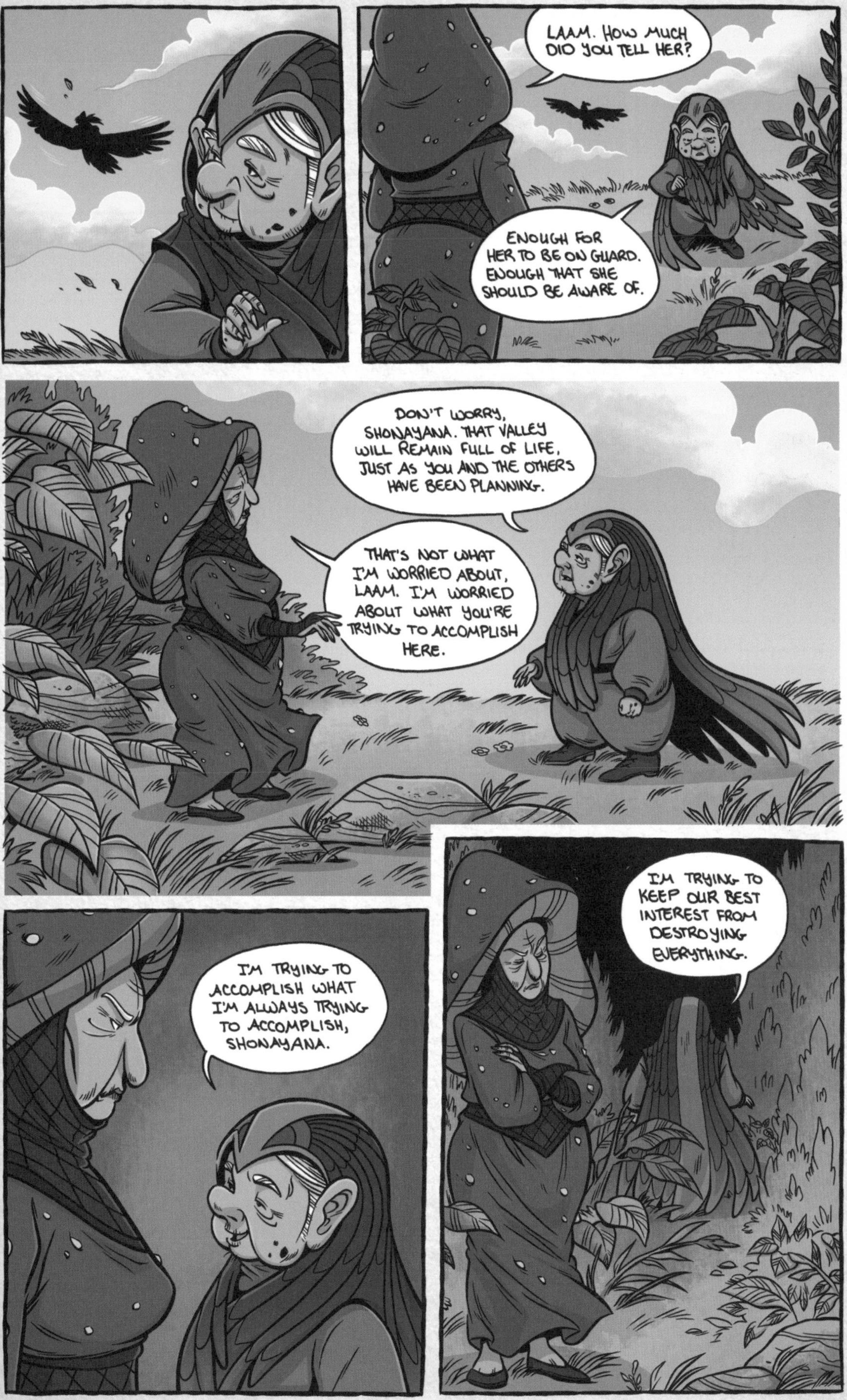

LAAM. HOW MUCH DID YOU TELL HER?
ENOUGH FOR HER TO BE ON GUARD. ENOUGH THAT SHE SHOULD BE AWARE OF.
DON'T WORRY, SHONAYANA. THAT VALLEY WILL REMAIN FULL OF LIFE, JUST AS YOU AND THE OTHERS HAVE BEEN PLANNING.
THAT'S NOT WHAT I'M WORRIED ABOUT, LAAM. I'M WORRIED ABOUT WHAT YOU'RE TRYING TO ACCOMPLISH HERE.
I'M TRYING TO ACCOMPLISH WHAT I'M ALWAYS TRYING TO ACCOMPLISH, SHONAYANA.
I'M TRYING TO KEEP OUR BEST INTEREST FROM DESTROYING EVERYTHING.

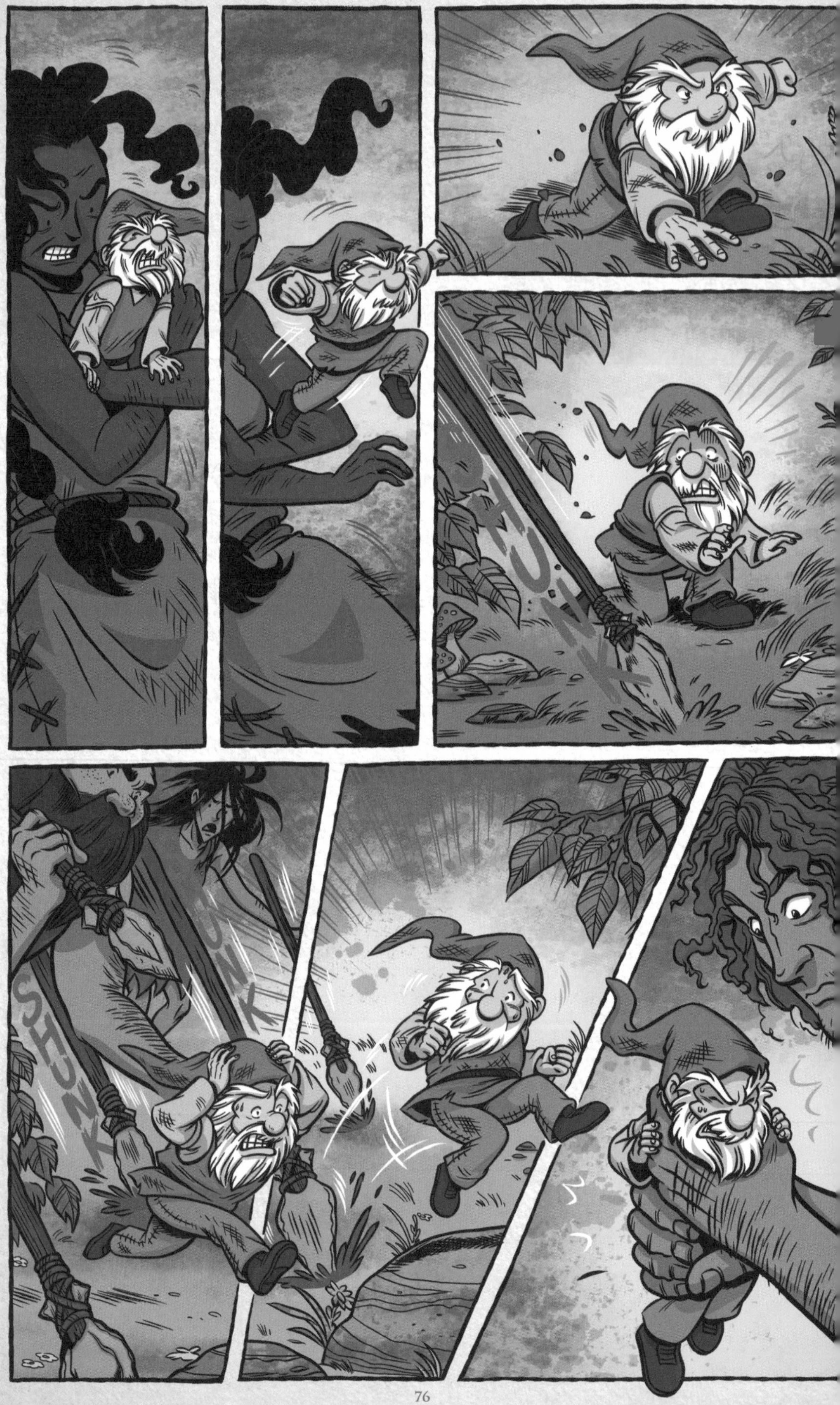
SHUNK
SHUNK

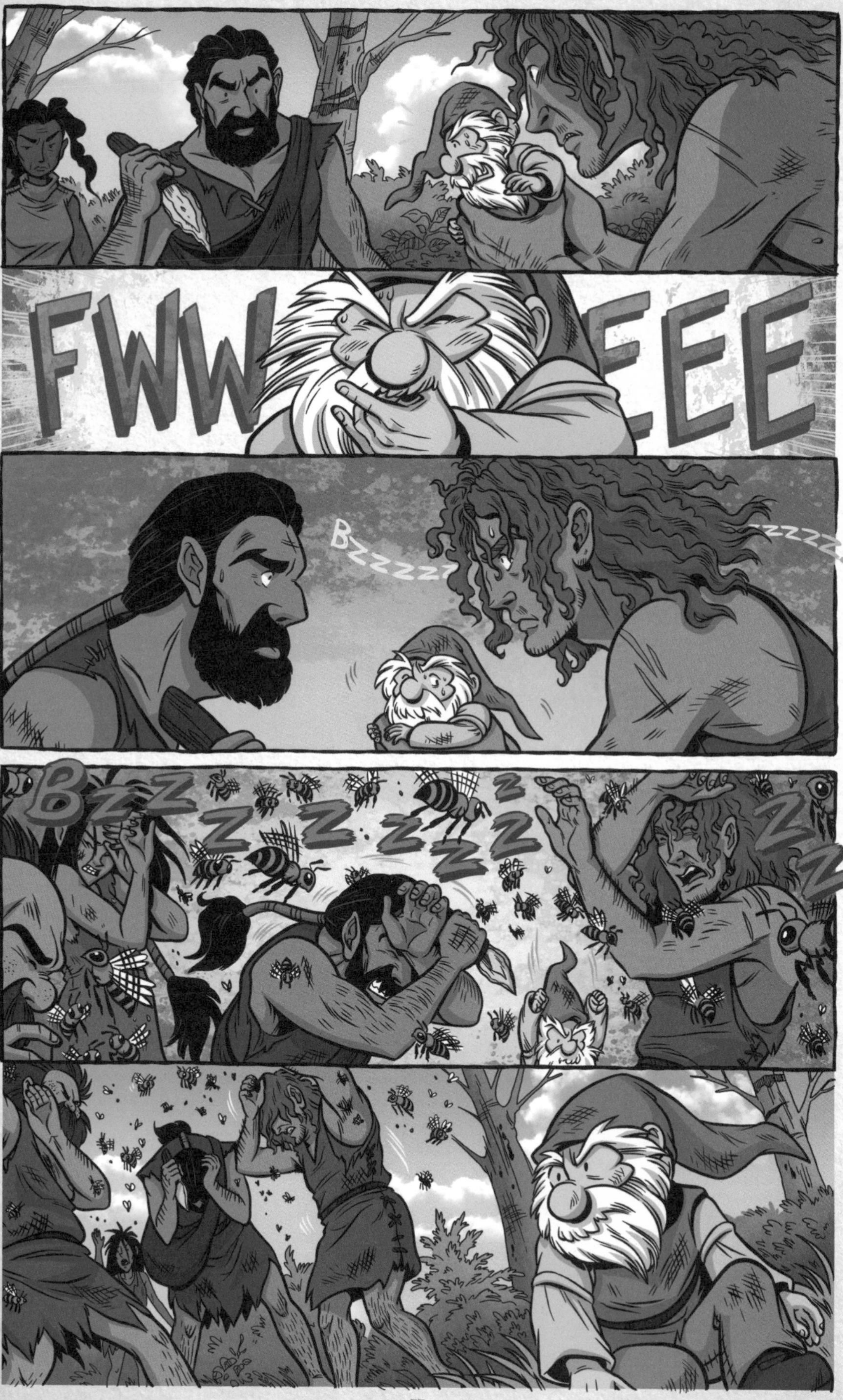
FWWEEE
BZZZZZT
ZZZZZZ
BZZZZZZZZZ

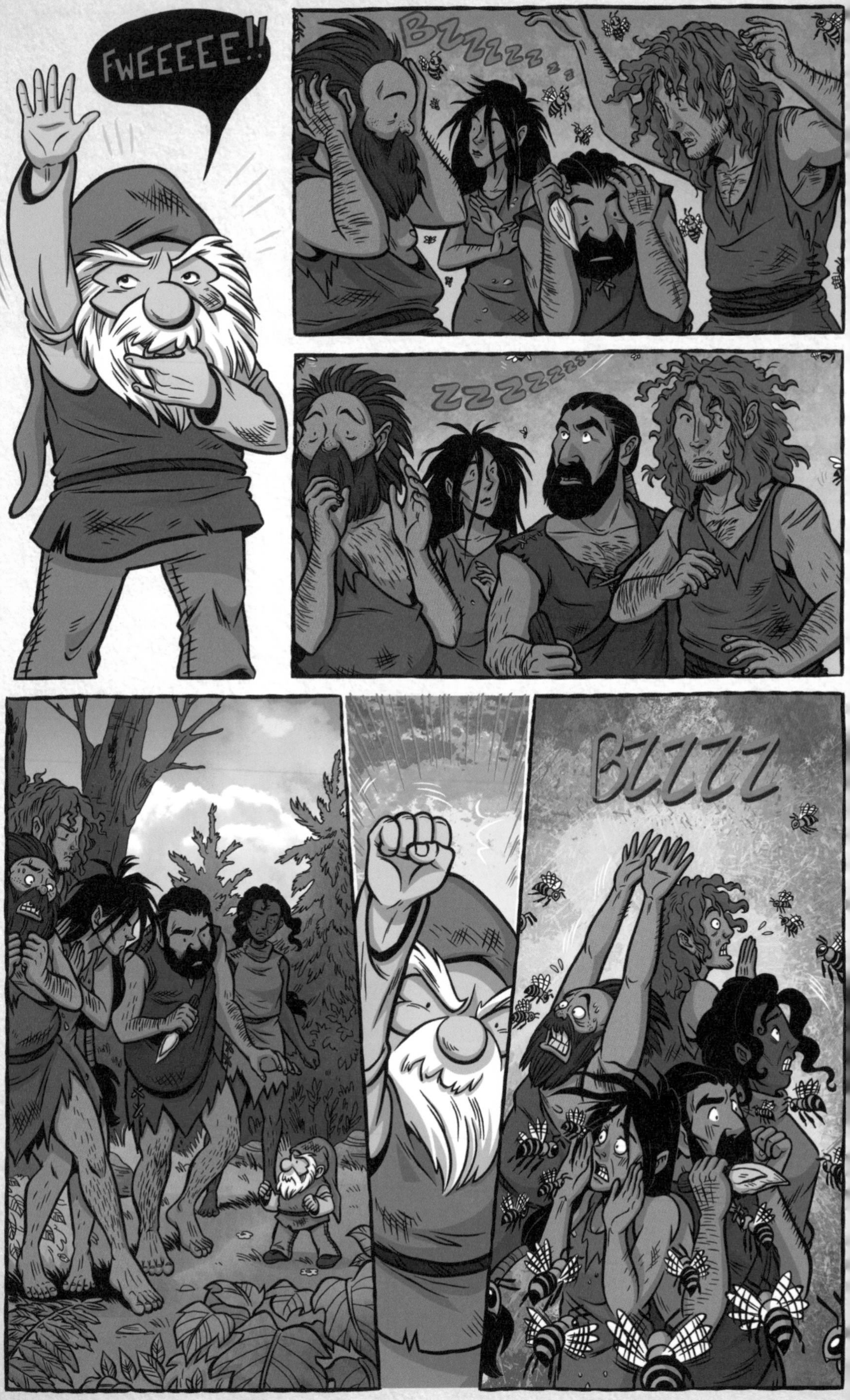
FWEEEEE!!
BZZzzz
ZZZZZZZZ
BZZZZ

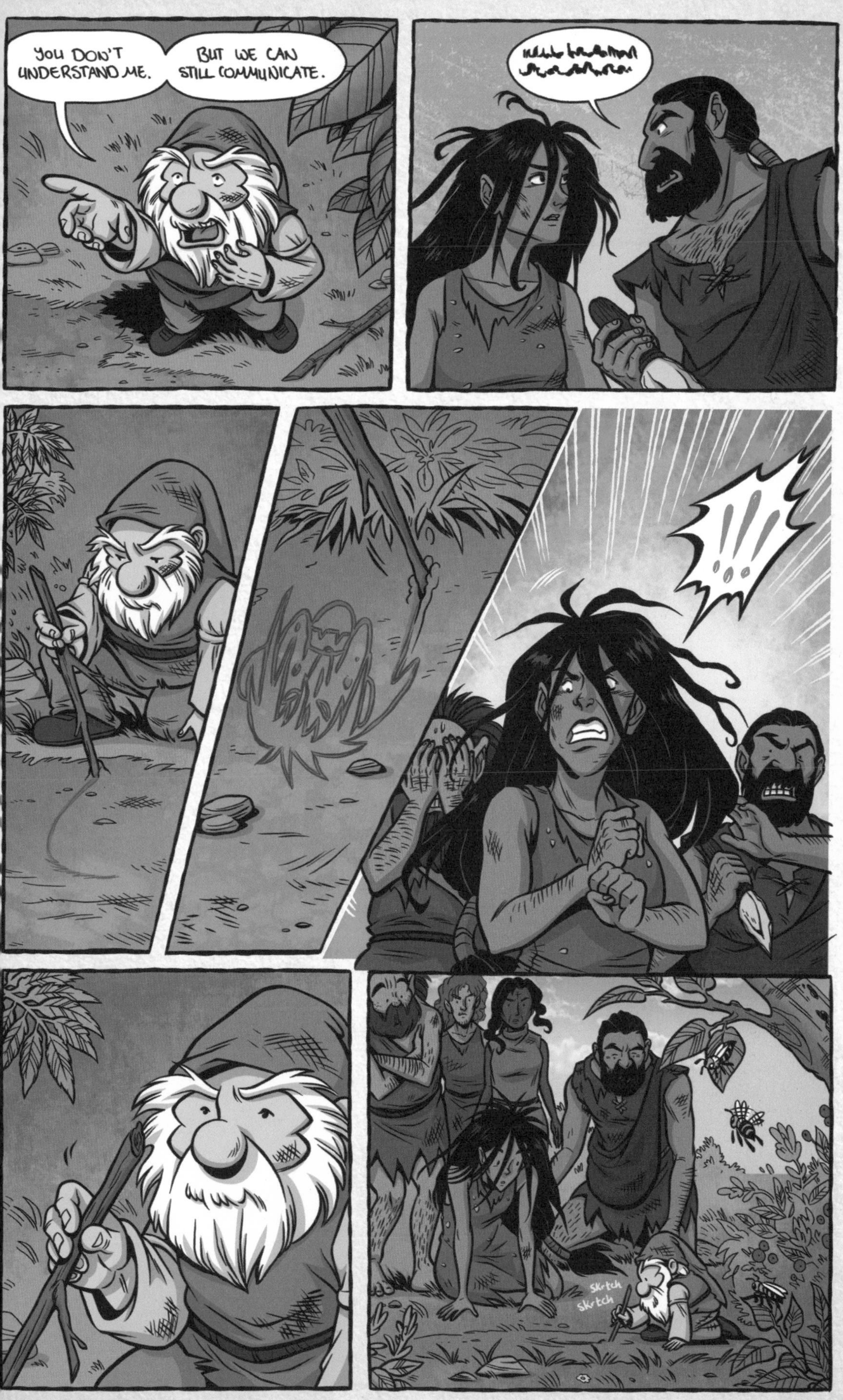
YOU DON'T UNDERSTAND ME.
BUT WE CAN STILL COMMUNICATE.
!!!
SKrtch SKrtch

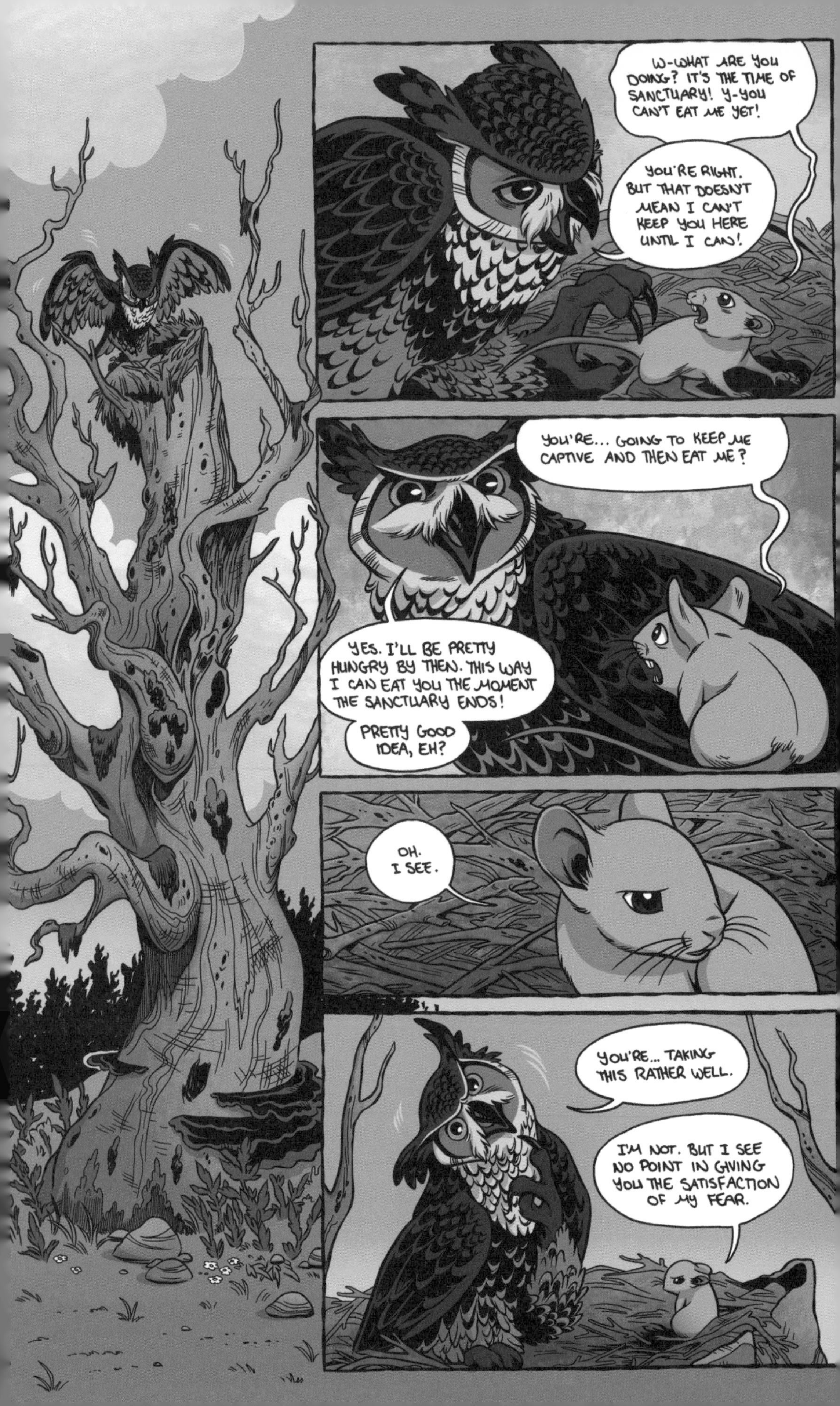
W-WHAT ARE YOU DOING? IT'S THE TIME OF SANCTUARY! Y-YOU CAN'T EAT ME YET!
YOU'RE RIGHT. BUT THAT DOESN'T MEAN I CAN'T KEEP YOU HERE UNTIL I CAN!
YOU'RE... GOING TO KEEP ME CAPTIVE AND THEN EAT ME?
YES. I'LL BE PRETTY HUNGRY BY THEN. THIS WAY I CAN EAT YOU THE MOMENT THE SANCTUARY ENDS!
PRETTY GOOD IDEA, EH?
OH. I SEE.
YOU'RE... TAKING THIS RATHER WELL.
I'M NOT. BUT I SEE NO POINT IN GIVING YOU THE SATISFACTION OF MY FEAR.

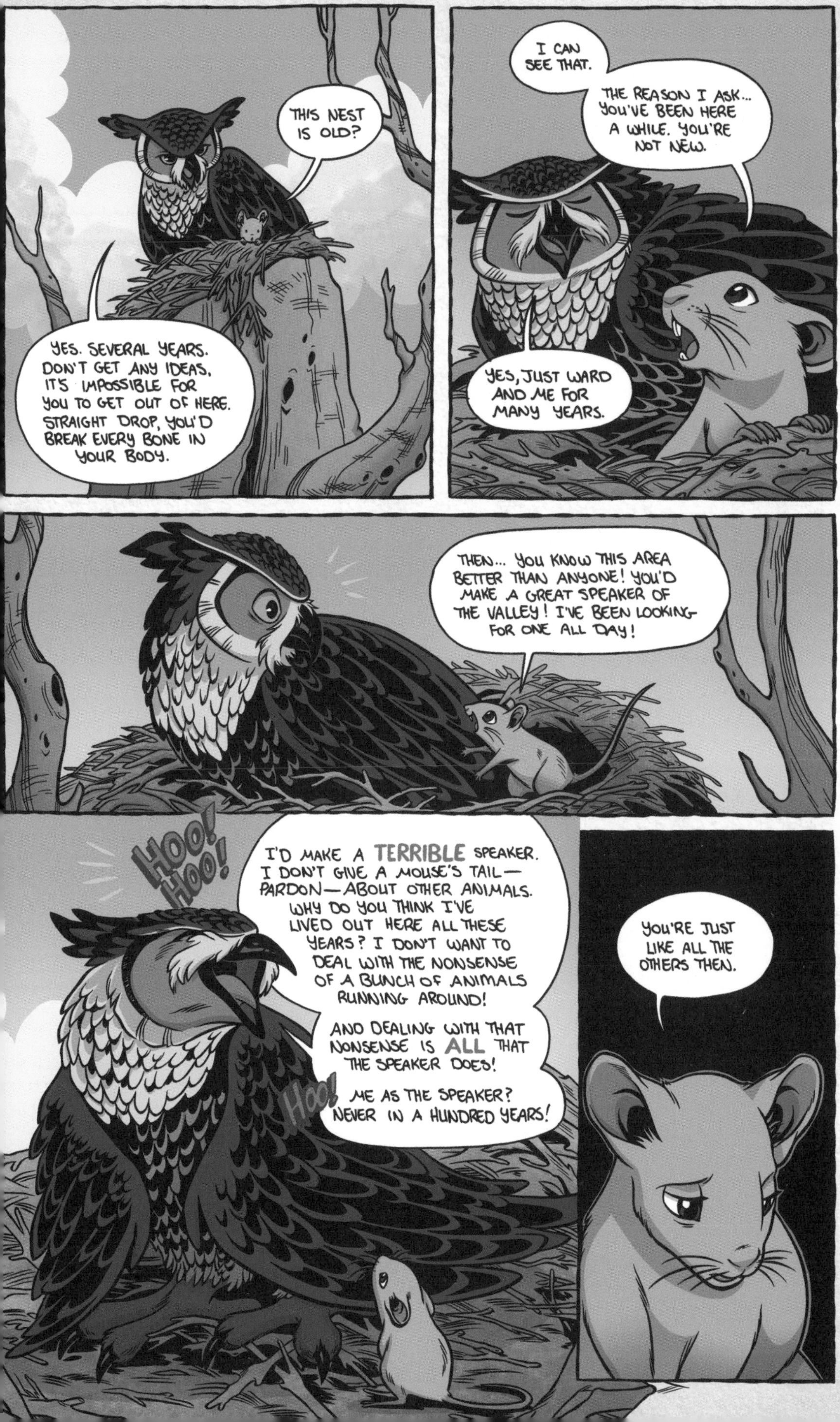

THIS NEST IS OLD?
YES. SEVERAL YEARS. DON'T GET ANY IDEAS. IT'S IMPOSSIBLE FOR YOU TO GET OUT OF HERE. STRAIGHT DROP, YOU'D BREAK EVERY BONE IN YOUR BODY.
I CAN SEE THAT.
THE REASON I ASK... YOU'VE BEEN HERE A WHILE. YOU'RE NOT NEW.
YES, JUST WARD AND ME FOR MANY YEARS.
THEN... YOU KNOW THIS AREA BETTER THAN ANYONE! YOU'D MAKE A GREAT SPEAKER OF THE VALLEY! I'VE BEEN LOOKING FOR ONE ALL DAY!
HOO! HOO!
I'D MAKE A TERRIBLE SPEAKER. I DON'T GIVE A MOUSE'S TAIL— PARDON—ABOUT OTHER ANIMALS. WHY DO YOU THINK I'VE LIVED OUT HERE ALL THESE YEARS? I DON'T WANT TO DEAL WITH THE NONSENSE OF A BUNCH OF ANIMALS RUNNING AROUND!
AND DEALING WITH THAT NONSENSE IS ALL THAT THE SPEAKER DOES!
HOO!
ME AS THE SPEAKER? NEVER IN A HUNDRED YEARS!
YOU'RE JUST LIKE ALL THE OTHERS THEN.

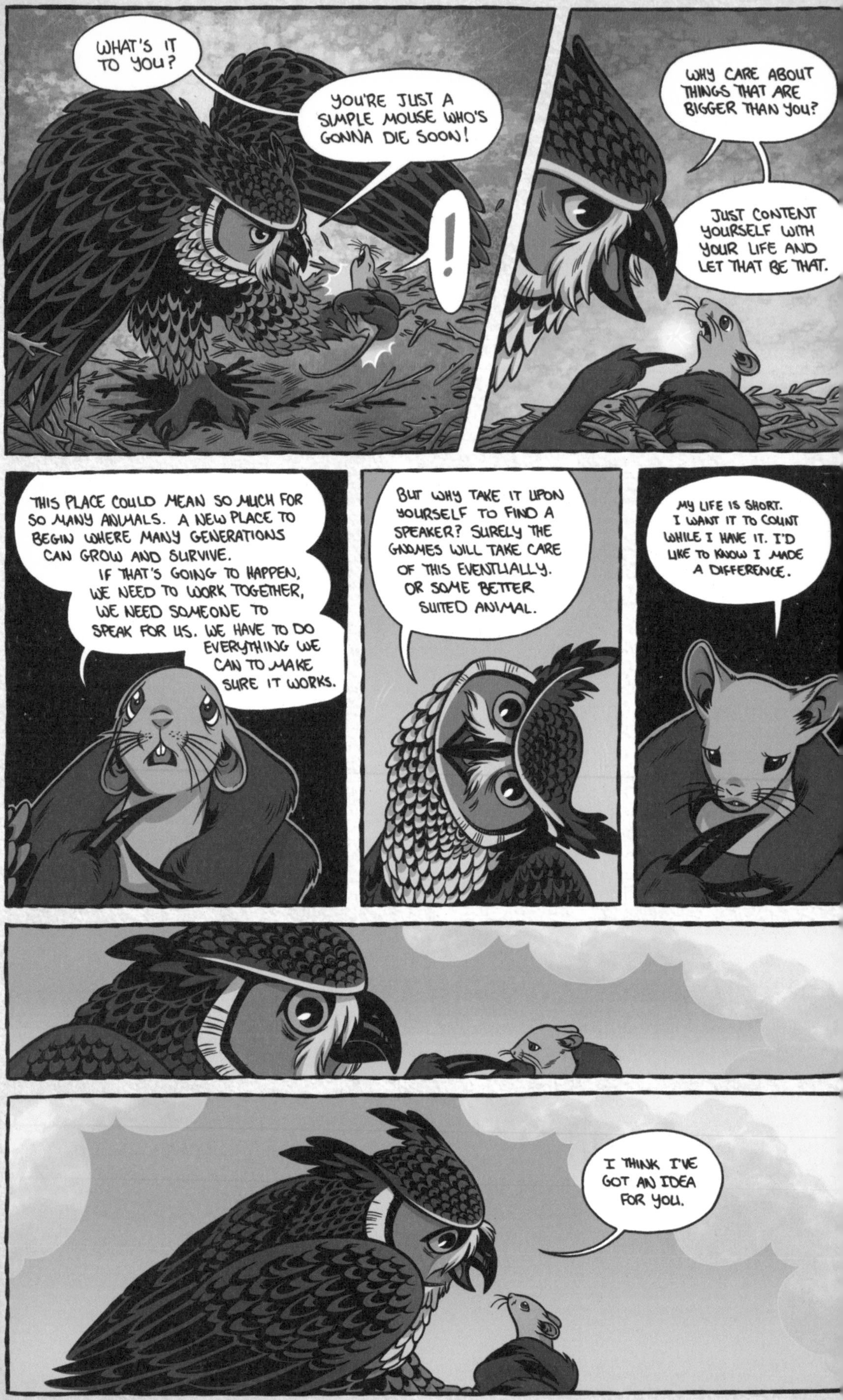
WHAT'S IT TO YOU?
YOU'RE JUST A SIMPLE MOUSE WHO'S GONNA DIE SOON!
!
WHY CARE ABOUT THINGS THAT ARE BIGGER THAN YOU?
JUST CONTENT YOURSELF WITH YOUR LIFE AND LET THAT BE THAT.
THIS PLACE COULD MEAN SO MUCH FOR SO MANY ANIMALS. A NEW PLACE TO BEGIN WHERE MANY GENERATIONS CAN GROW AND SURVIVE.
IF THAT'S GOING TO HAPPEN, WE NEED TO WORK TOGETHER, WE NEED SOMEONE TO SPEAK FOR US. WE HAVE TO DO EVERYTHING WE CAN TO MAKE SURE IT WORKS.
BUT WHY TAKE IT UPON YOURSELF TO FIND A SPEAKER? SURELY THE GNOMES WILL TAKE CARE OF THIS EVENTUALLY. OR SOME BETTER SUITED ANIMAL.
MY LIFE IS SHORT. I WANT IT TO COUNT WHILE I HAVE IT. I'D LIKE TO KNOW I MADE A DIFFERENCE.
I THINK I'VE GOT AN IDEA FOR YOU.

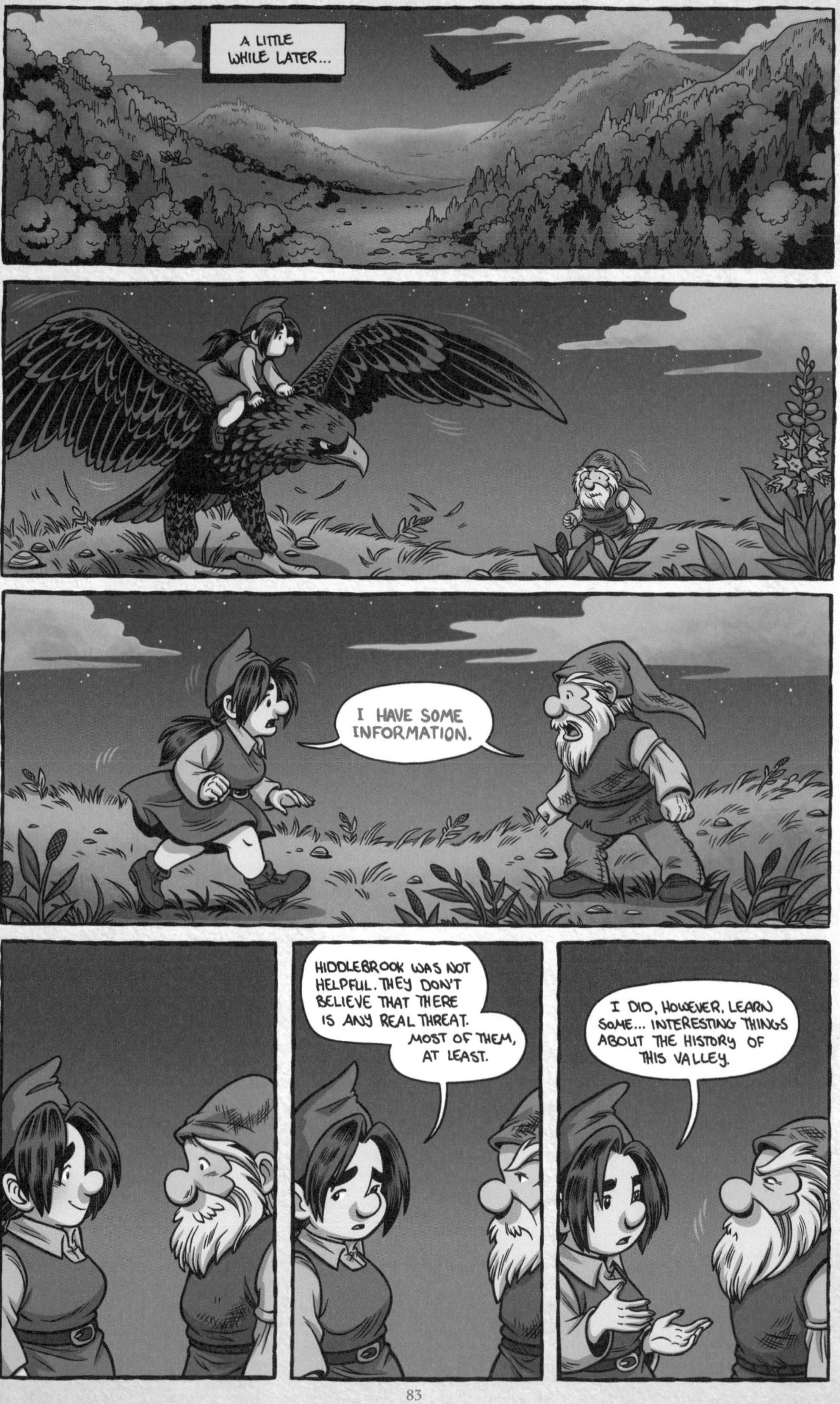
A LITTLE WHILE LATER...
I HAVE SOME INFORMATION.
HIDDLEBROOK WAS NOT HELPFUL. THEY DON'T BELIEVE THAT THERE IS ANY REAL THREAT.
MOST OF THEM, AT LEAST.
I DID, HOWEVER, LEARN SOME... INTERESTING THINGS ABOUT THE HISTORY OF THIS VALLEY.

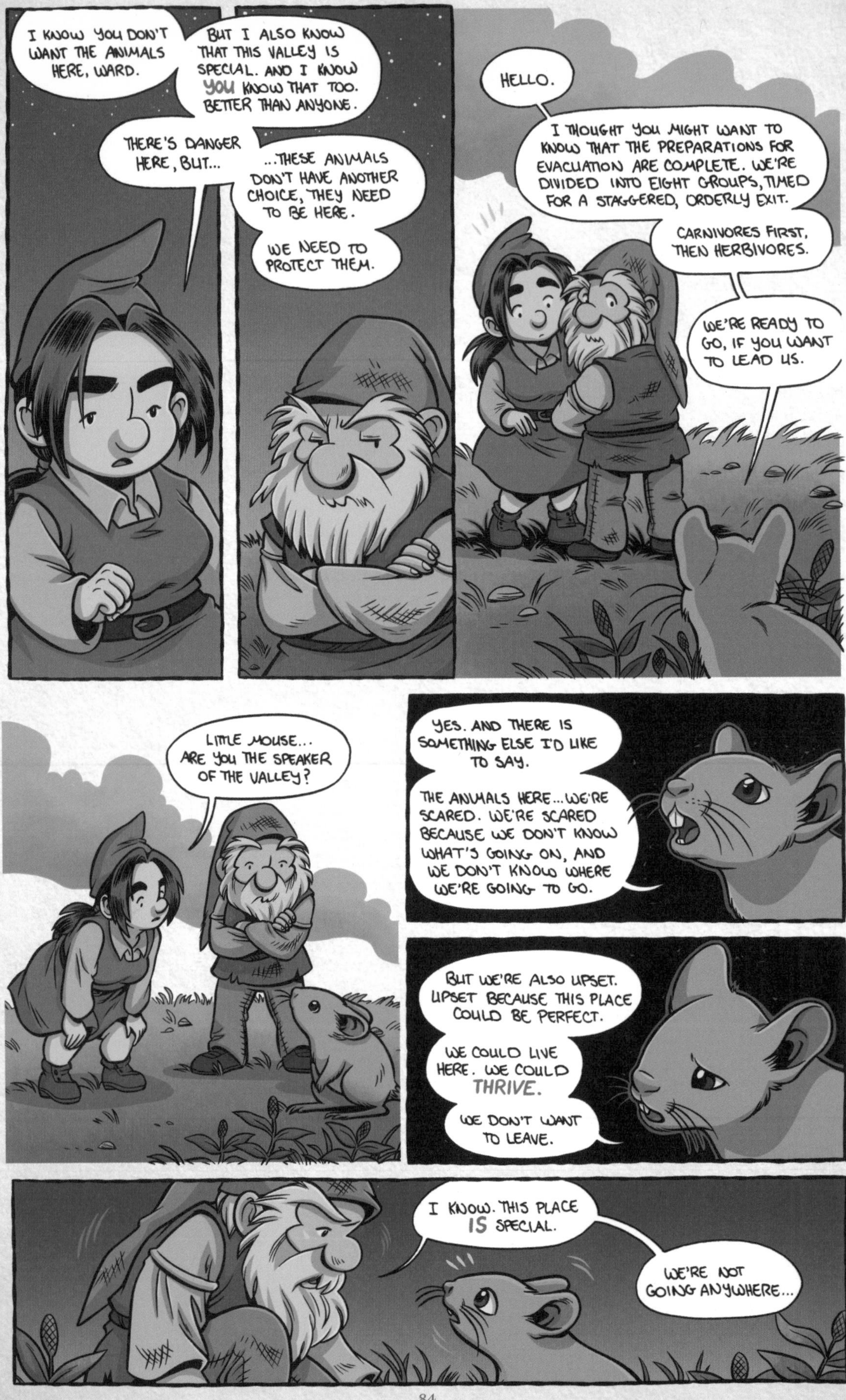
I KNOW YOU DON'T WANT THE ANIMALS HERE, WARD.
BUT I ALSO KNOW THAT THIS VALLEY IS SPECIAL. AND I KNOW YOU KNOW THAT TOO. BETTER THAN ANYONE.
THERE'S DANGER HERE, BUT...
...THESE ANIMALS DON'T HAVE ANOTHER CHOICE, THEY NEED TO BE HERE.
WE NEED TO PROTECT THEM.
HELLO.
I THOUGHT YOU MIGHT WANT TO KNOW THAT THE PREPARATIONS FOR EVACUATION ARE COMPLETE. WE'RE DIVIDED INTO EIGHT GROUPS, TIMED FOR A STAGGERED, ORDERLY EXIT.
CARNIVORES FIRST, THEN HERBIVORES.
WE'RE READY TO GO, IF YOU WANT TO LEAD US.
LITTLE MOUSE... ARE YOU THE SPEAKER OF THE VALLEY?
YES. AND THERE IS SOMETHING ELSE I'D LIKE TO SAY.
THE ANIMALS HERE... WE'RE SCARED. WE'RE SCARED BECAUSE WE DON'T KNOW WHAT'S GOING ON, AND WE DON'T KNOW WHERE WE'RE GOING TO GO.
BUT WE'RE ALSO UPSET. UPSET BECAUSE THIS PLACE COULD BE PERFECT.
WE COULD LIVE HERE. WE COULD THRIVE.
WE DON'T WANT TO LEAVE.
I KNOW. THIS PLACE IS SPECIAL.
WE'RE NOT GOING ANYWHERE...

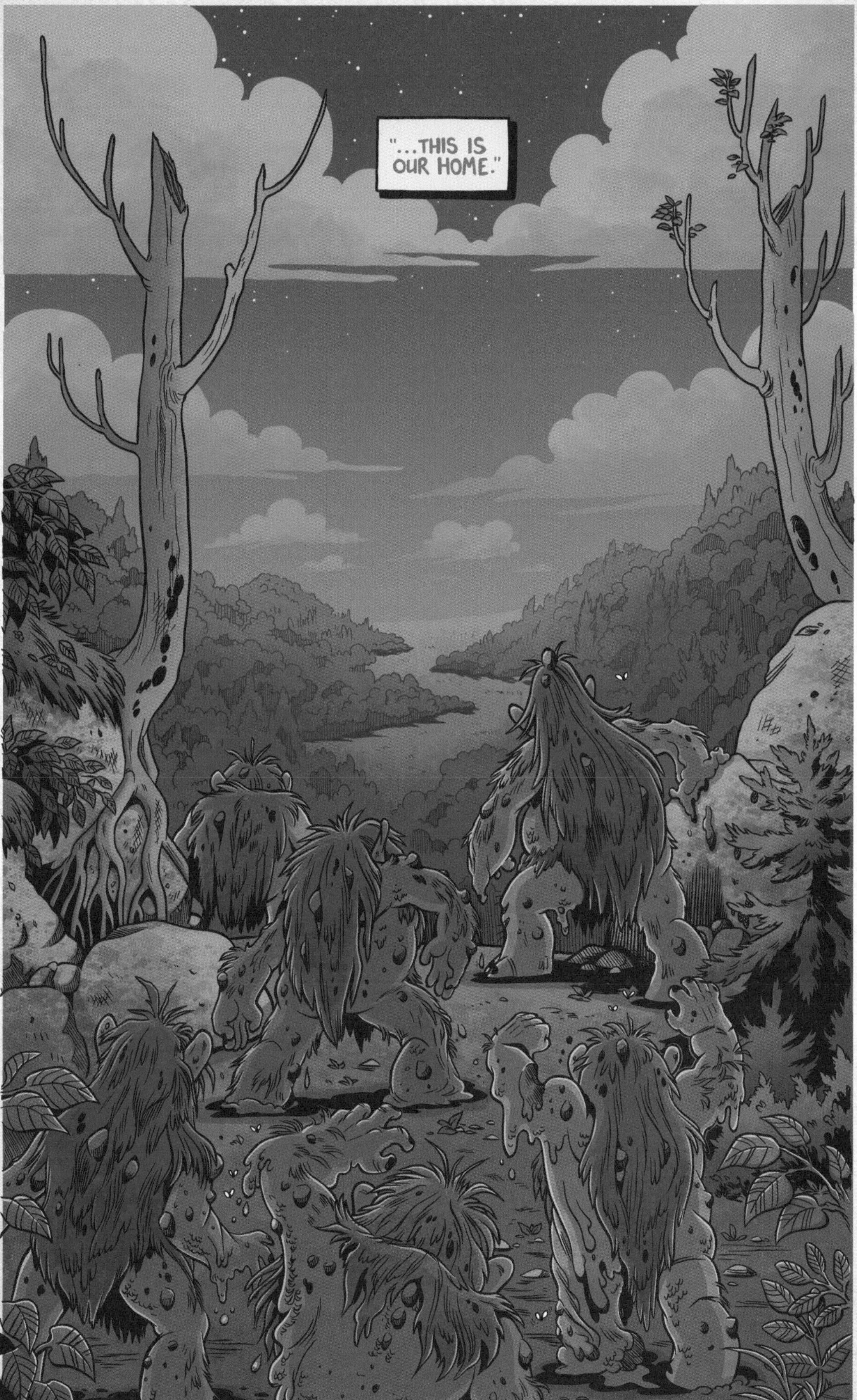
"...THIS IS OUR HOME."

Chapter Four

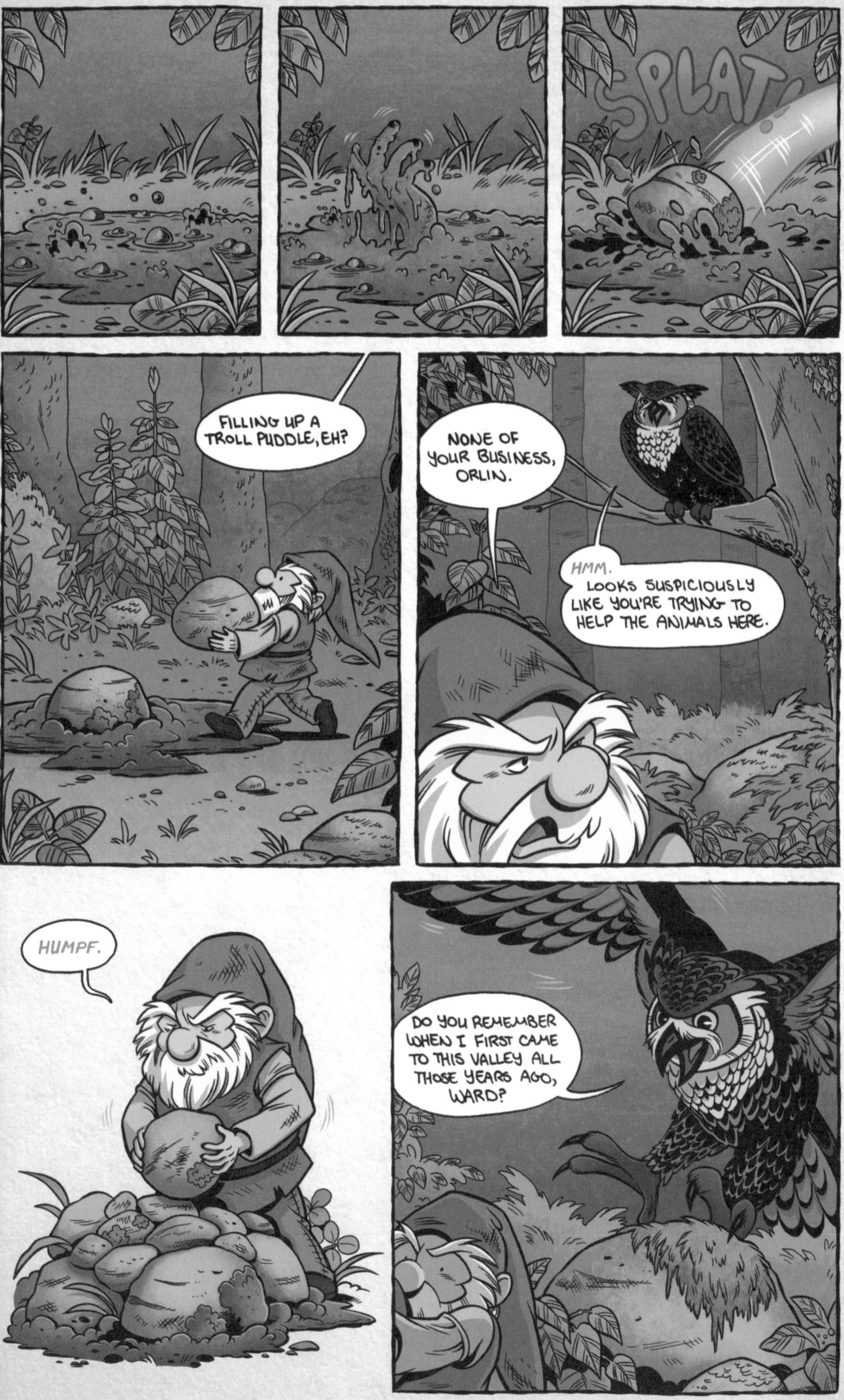
SPLAT!
FILLING UP A TROLL PUDDLE, EH?
NONE OF YOUR BUSINESS, ORLIN.
HMM.
LOOKS SUSPICIOUSLY LIKE YOU'RE TRYING TO HELP THE ANIMALS HERE.
HUMPF.
DO YOU REMEMBER WHEN I FIRST CAME TO THIS VALLEY ALL THOSE YEARS AGO, WARD?

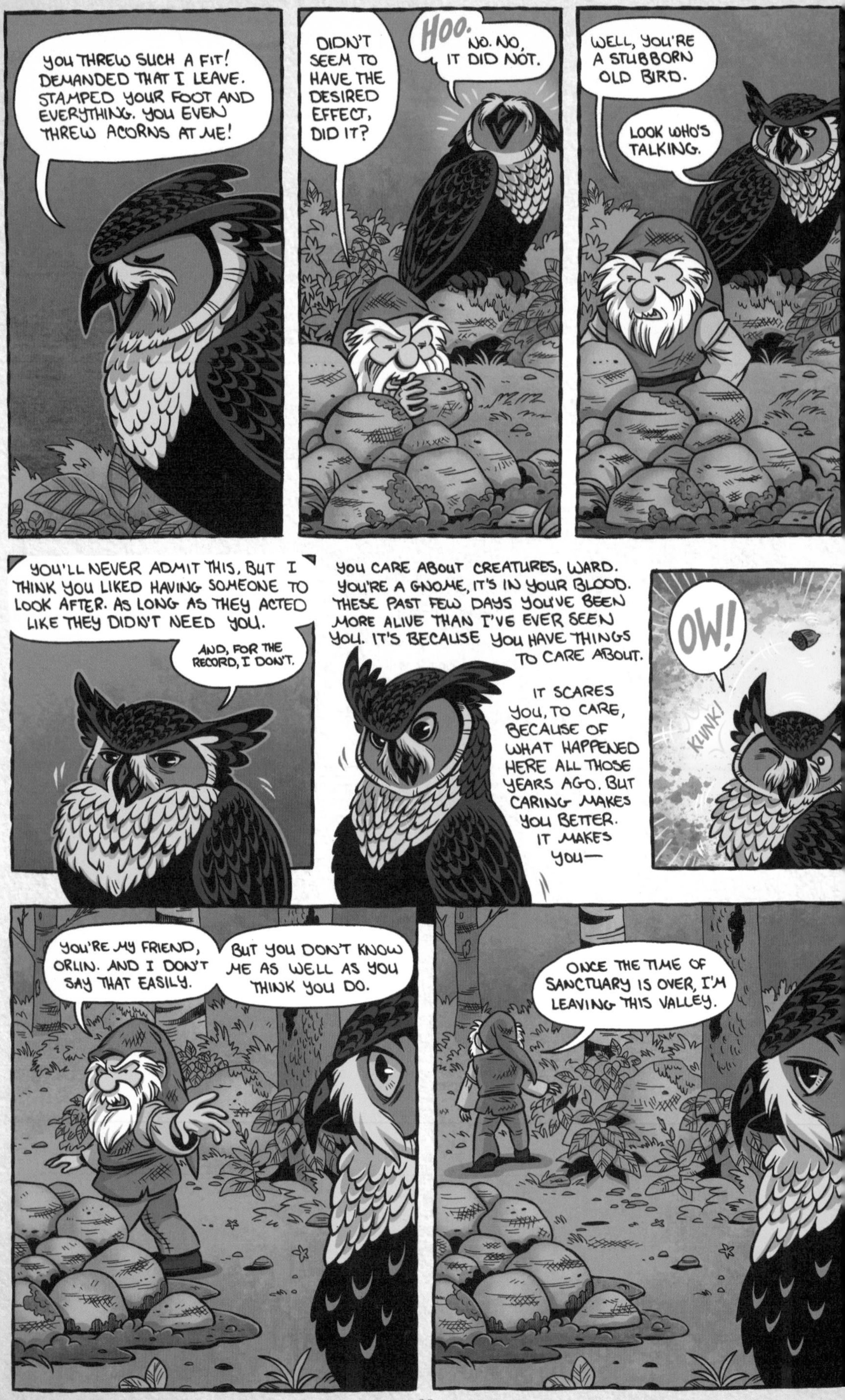
YOU THREW SUCH A FIT! DEMANDED THAT I LEAVE. STAMPED YOUR FOOT AND EVERYTHING. YOU EVEN THREW ACORNS AT ME!
DIDN'T SEEM TO HAVE THE DESIRED EFFECT, DID IT?
HOO.
NO. NO, IT DID NOT.
WELL, YOU'RE A STUBBORN OLD BIRD.
LOOK WHO'S TALKING.
YOU'LL NEVER ADMIT THIS, BUT I THINK YOU LIKED HAVING SOMEONE TO LOOK AFTER. AS LONG AS THEY ACTED LIKE THEY DIDN'T NEED YOU.
AND, FOR THE RECORD, I DON'T.
YOU CARE ABOUT CREATURES, WARD. YOU'RE A GNOME, IT'S IN YOUR BLOOD. THESE PAST FEW DAYS YOU'VE BEEN MORE ALIVE THAN I'VE EVER SEEN YOU. IT'S BECAUSE YOU HAVE THINGS TO CARE ABOUT.
IT SCARES YOU, TO CARE, BECAUSE OF WHAT HAPPENED HERE ALL THOSE YEARS AGO. BUT CARING MAKES YOU BETTER. IT MAKES YOU—
OW!
KLUNK!
YOU'RE MY FRIEND, ORLIN. AND I DON'T SAY THAT EASILY.
BUT YOU DON'T KNOW ME AS WELL AS YOU THINK YOU DO.
ONCE THE TIME OF SANCTUARY IS OVER, I'M LEAVING THIS VALLEY.

YOU'RE OVERREACTING. JUST BECAUSE SOME OF YOUR CHILDREN WILL BE EATEN DOESN'T MEAN ALL OF THEM WILL.

OH, THANK YOU, THAT IS VERY COMFORTING. I'M SURE YOU WILL ALSO BE COMFORTED TO KNOW THAT, IF I BLIND YOU WITH MY ANTLERS, YOU'LL STILL HAVE SOME OTHER VERY FUNCTIONAL SENSES.

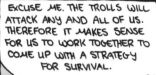

EXCUSE ME. THE TROLLS WILL ATTACK ANY AND ALL OF US. THEREFORE IT MAKES SENSE FOR US TO WORK TOGETHER TO COME UP WITH A STRATEGY FOR SURVIVAL.

WE ARE HERE ONLY TO DISCUSS WHAT TO DO IF WE ARE ATTACKED BY TROLLS.

NOT TO DISCUSS... WHATEVER CONVERSATION WE FIND OURSELVES IN PRESENTLY.

LET US BE CLEAR, MOUSE. WE ARE STARVING. WHILE YOU HERBIVORES CAN NIBBLE AWAY AT YOUR TREE BRANCHES, WE ARE STUCK WAITING FOR THE TIME OF SANCTUARY TO END. WHICH IS TOMORROW.

AND WHILE WE WAIT, YOU EXPECT US TO WORK WITH WHAT WILL SOON BE FILLING OUR STOMACHS?

TO BE AROUND SUCH TENDER PREY IS NOTHING SHORT OF MADDENING.

AWWW, POOR LITTLE WOLVES HAVE TO GO HUNGRY FOR ANOTHER DAY. WHY DON'T WE DEER JUST BAND TOGETHER AND FIGURE OUT A WAY TO GET THE TROLLS TO ATTACK YOU AND NOT US? YOU NEED US.

WE DON'T NEED YOU.

YES, PLEASE ENJOY STARVING TO DEATH WHEN WE'RE GONE BECAUSE OVERPOPULATION HAS STRIPPED THIS VALLEY OF EVERY NUTRIENT YOU NEED!

OH, PLEASE, DON'T ACT LIKE YOU SERVE SOME GREAT PURPOSE.

HEY, WHERE YOU GOIN'? JUST GETTIN' GOOD!

HA! IF THAT'S TRUE, THEN—

WELL, WE DO!

TO GET A GNOME. ANY GNOME. THIS IS NOT GOOD.

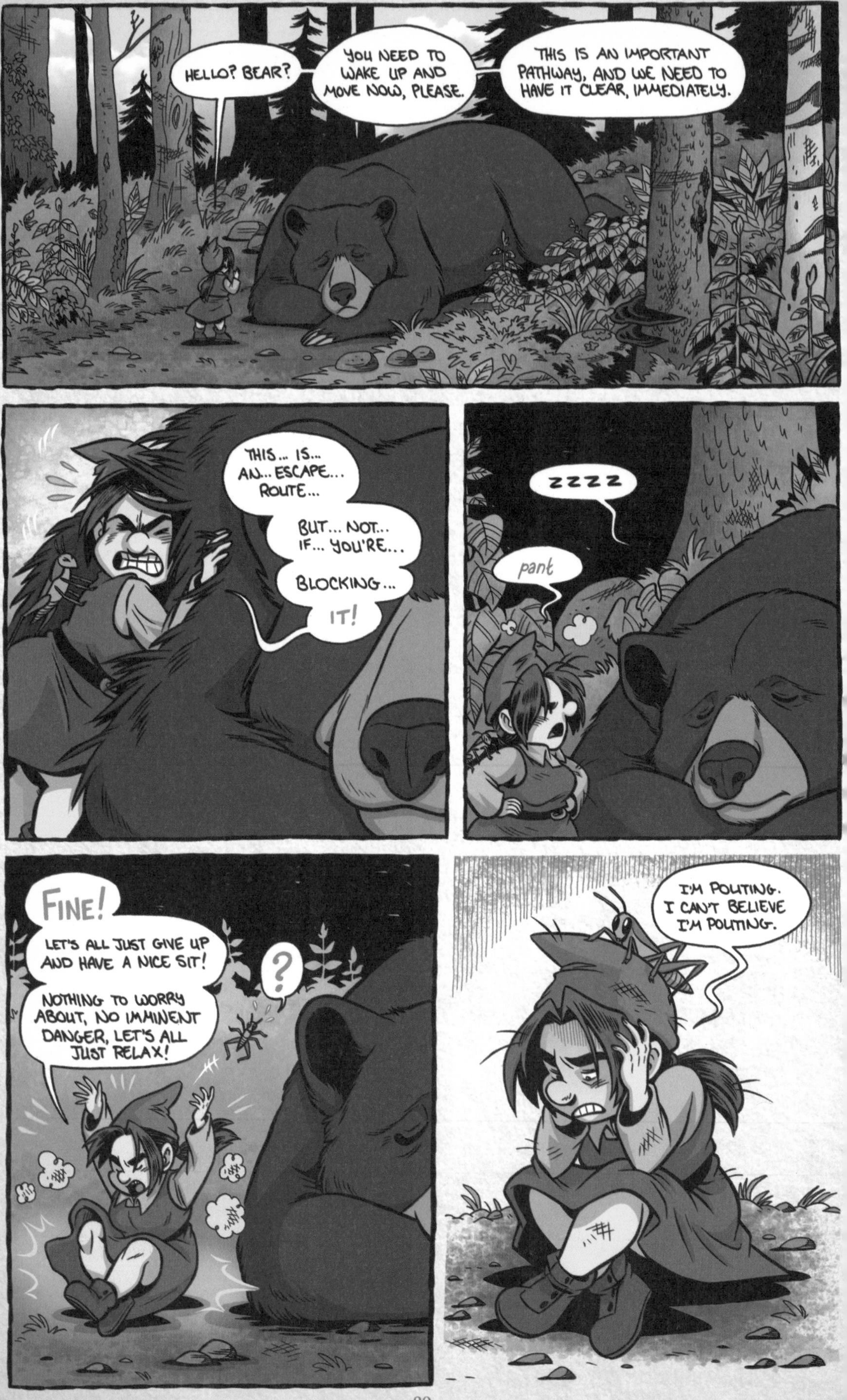
HELLO? BEAR?
YOU NEED TO WAKE UP AND MOVE NOW, PLEASE.
THIS IS AN IMPORTANT PATHWAY, AND WE NEED TO HAVE IT CLEAR, IMMEDIATELY.
THIS... IS... AN... ESCAPE... ROUTE...
BUT... NOT... IF... YOU'RE...
BLOCKING...
IT!
ZZZZ
pant
FINE!
LET'S ALL JUST GIVE UP AND HAVE A NICE SIT!
NOTHING TO WORRY ABOUT, NO IMMINENT DANGER, LET'S ALL JUST RELAX!
?
I'M POUTING. I CAN'T BELIEVE I'M POUTING.

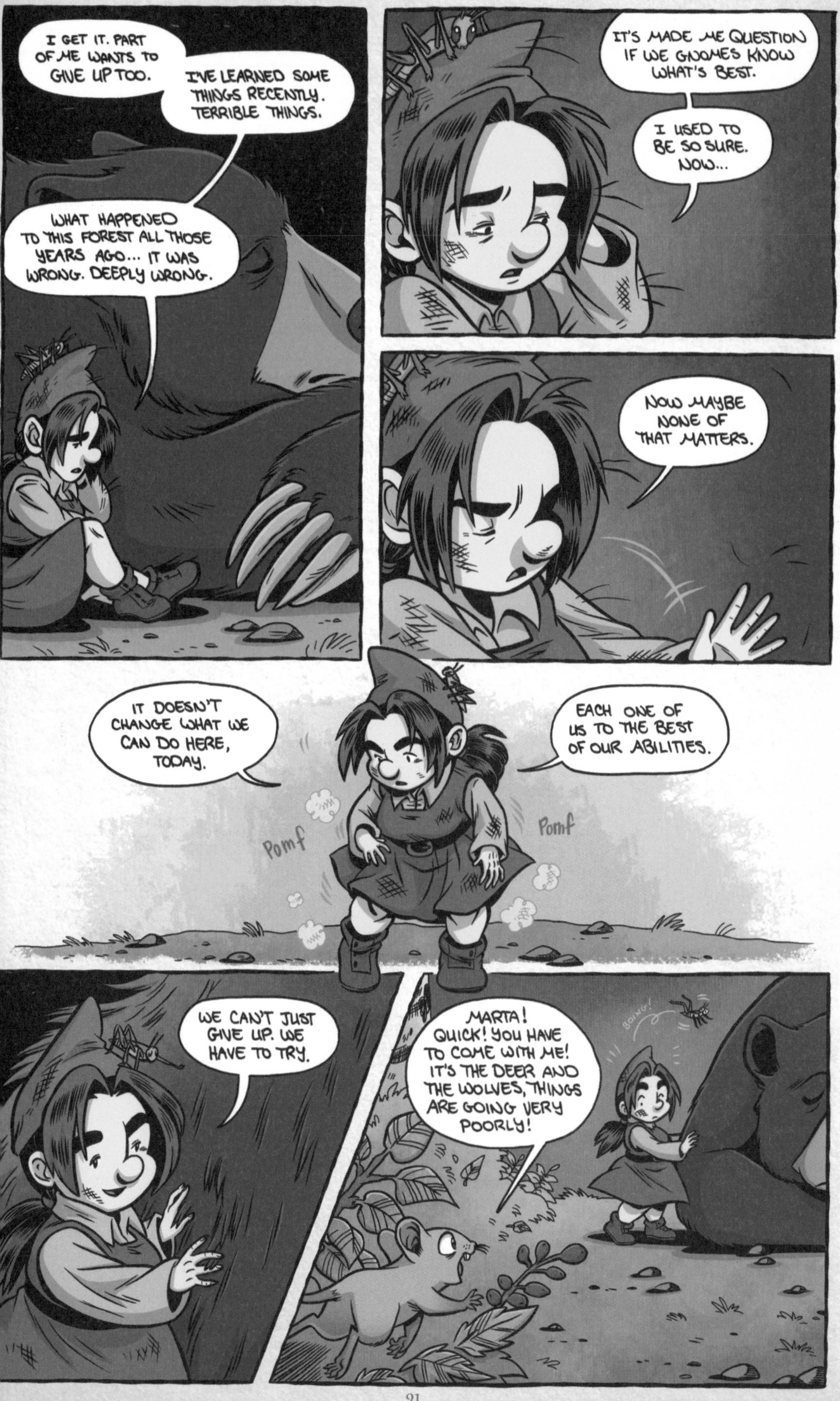
I GET IT. PART OF ME WANTS TO GIVE UP TOO.
I'VE LEARNED SOME THINGS RECENTLY. TERRIBLE THINGS.
WHAT HAPPENED TO THIS FOREST ALL THOSE YEARS AGO... IT WAS WRONG. DEEPLY WRONG.
IT'S MADE ME QUESTION IF WE GNOMES KNOW WHAT'S BEST.
I USED TO BE SO SURE. NOW...
NOW MAYBE NONE OF THAT MATTERS.
IT DOESN'T CHANGE WHAT WE CAN DO HERE, TODAY.
EACH ONE OF US TO THE BEST OF OUR ABILITIES.
Pomf
Pomf
WE CAN'T JUST GIVE UP. WE HAVE TO TRY.
MARTA! QUICK! YOU HAVE TO COME WITH ME! IT'S THE DEER AND THE WOLVES, THINGS ARE GOING VERY POORLY!
BOING!

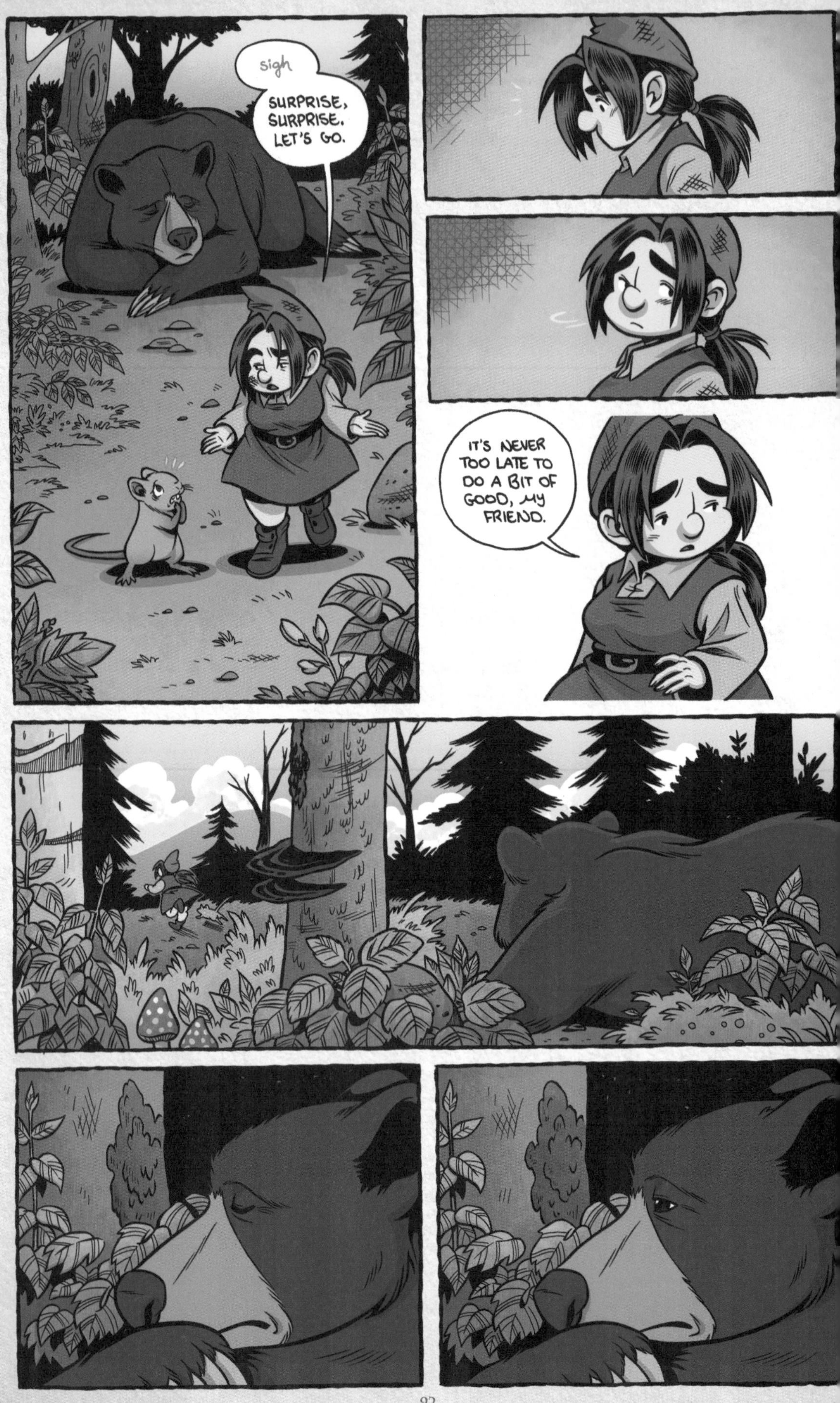
sigh
SURPRISE, SURPRISE. LET'S GO.
IT'S NEVER TOO LATE TO DO A BIT OF GOOD, MY FRIEND.

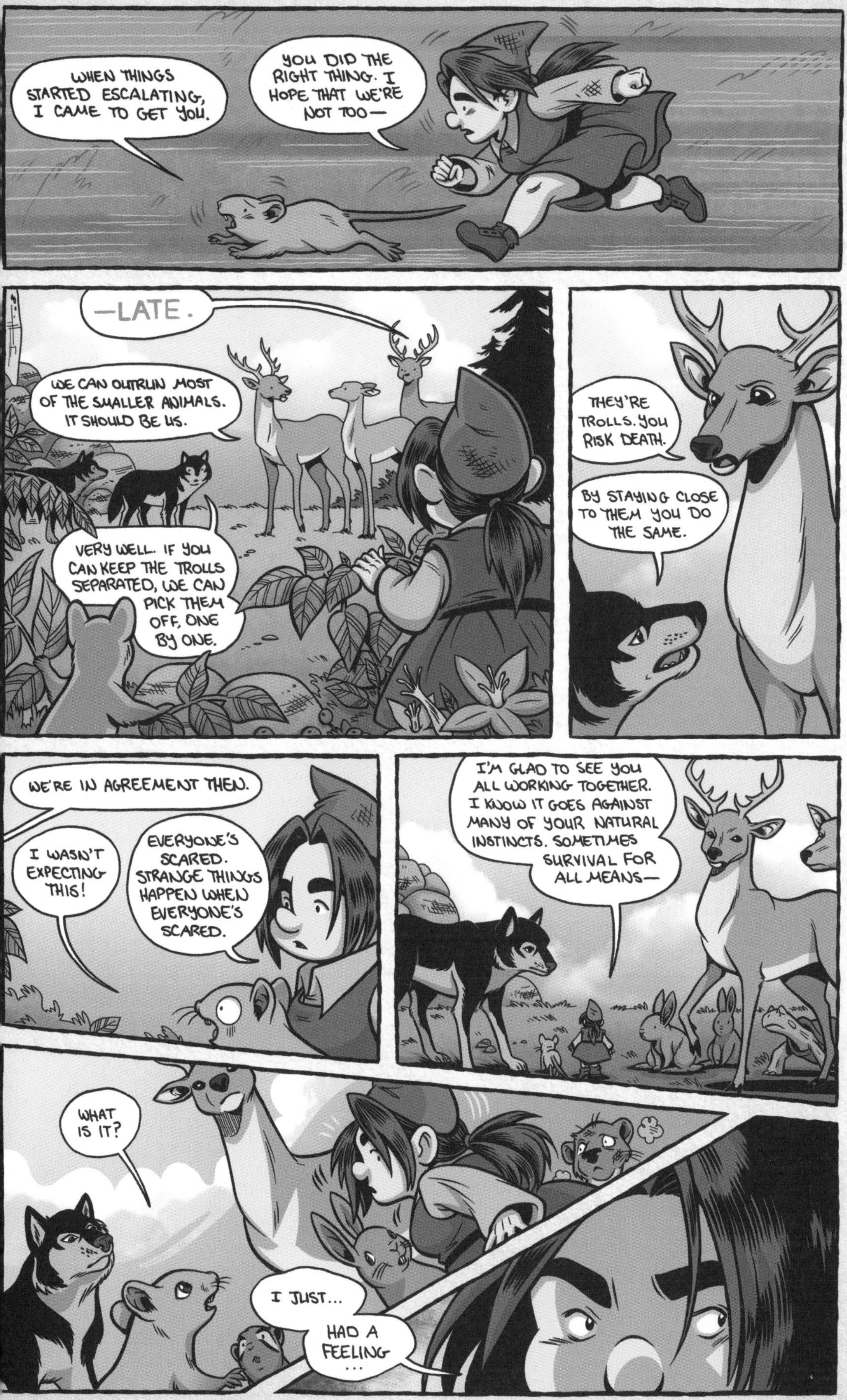

WHEN THINGS STARTED ESCALATING, I CAME TO GET YOU.
YOU DID THE RIGHT THING. I HOPE THAT WE'RE NOT TOO—
—LATE.
WE CAN OUTRUN MOST OF THE SMALLER ANIMALS. IT SHOULD BE US.
VERY WELL. IF YOU CAN KEEP THE TROLLS SEPARATED, WE CAN PICK THEM OFF, ONE BY ONE.
THEY'RE TROLLS. YOU RISK DEATH.
BY STAYING CLOSE TO THEM YOU DO THE SAME.
WE'RE IN AGREEMENT THEN.
I WASN'T EXPECTING THIS!
EVERYONE'S SCARED. STRANGE THINGS HAPPEN WHEN EVERYONE'S SCARED.
I'M GLAD TO SEE YOU ALL WORKING TOGETHER. I KNOW IT GOES AGAINST MANY OF YOUR NATURAL INSTINCTS. SOMETIMES SURVIVAL FOR ALL MEANS—
WHAT IS IT?
I JUST...
HAD A FEELING ...

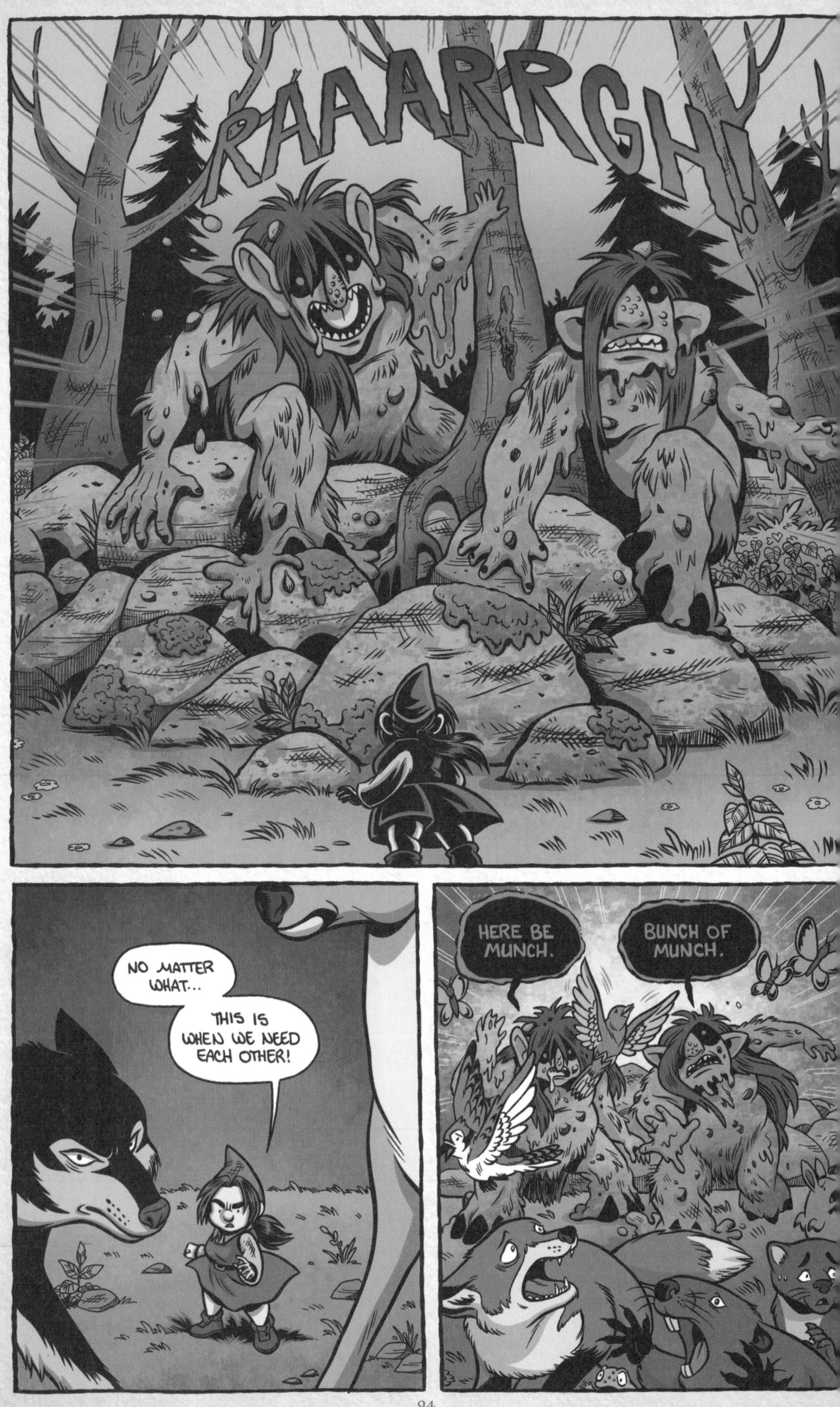
RAAARRGH!
NO MATTER WHAT...
THIS IS WHEN WE NEED EACH OTHER!
HERE BE MUNCH.
BUNCH OF MUNCH.

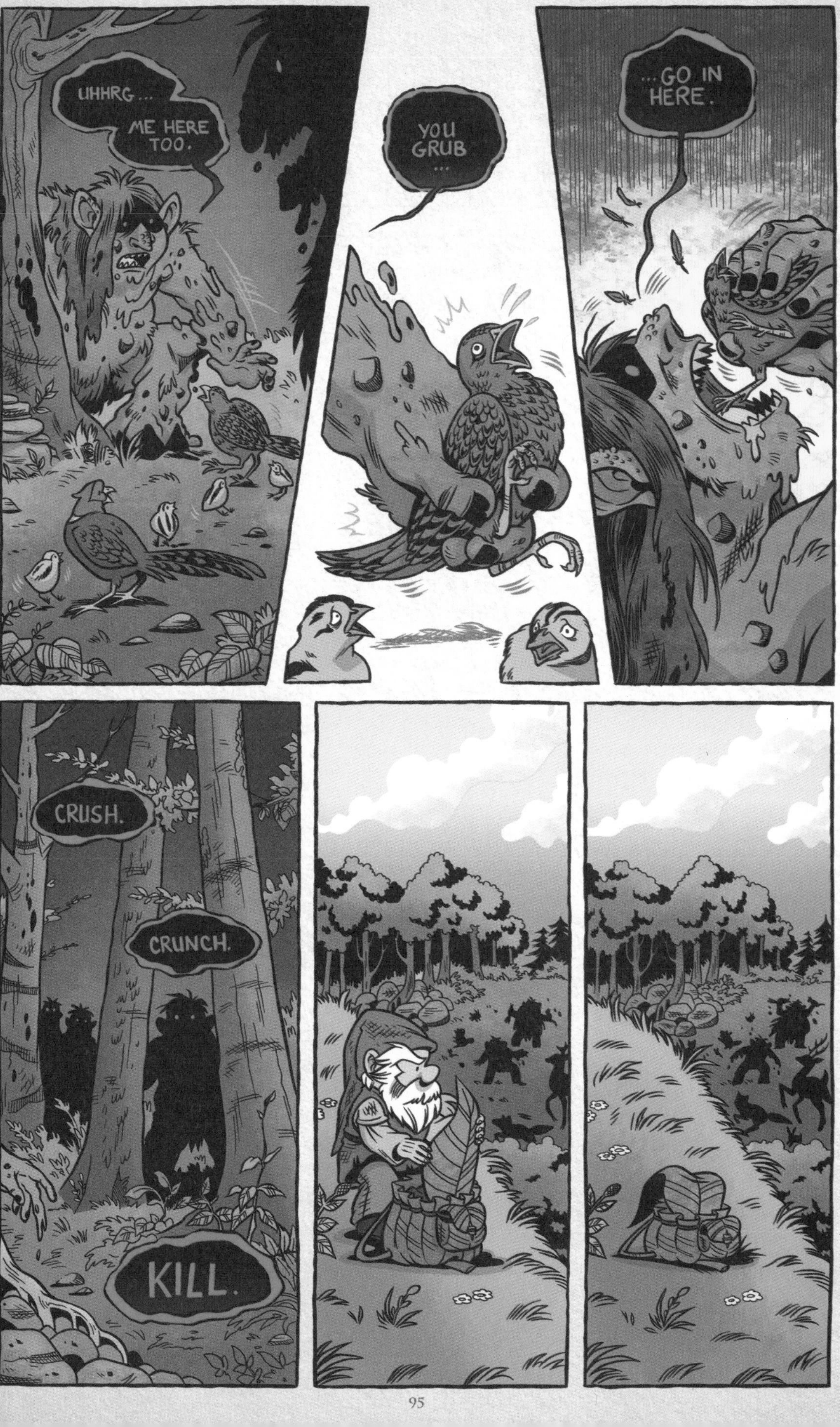
UHHRG...
ME HERE TOO.
YOU GRUB ...
...GO IN HERE.
CRUSH.
CRUNCH.
KILL.

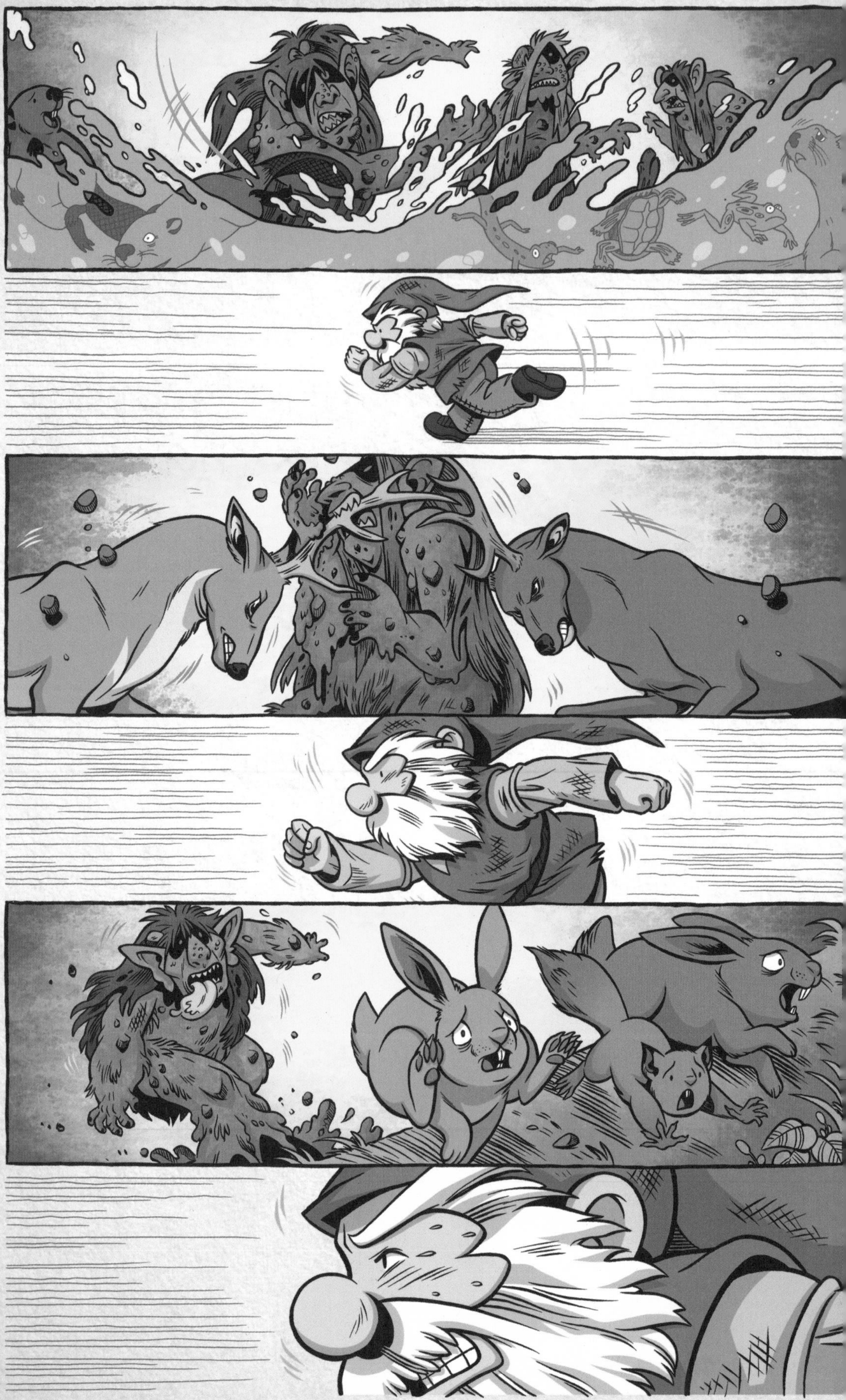

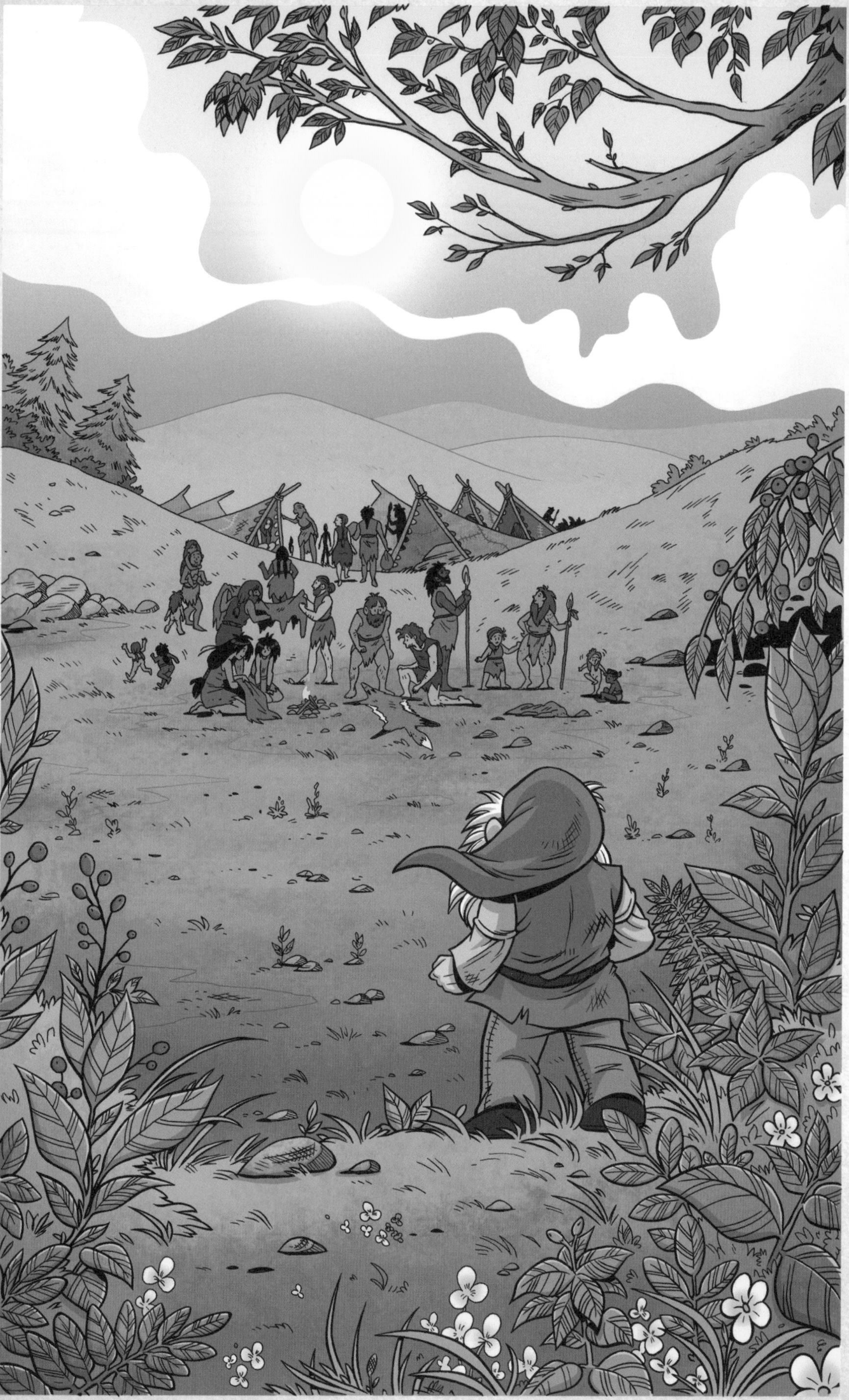

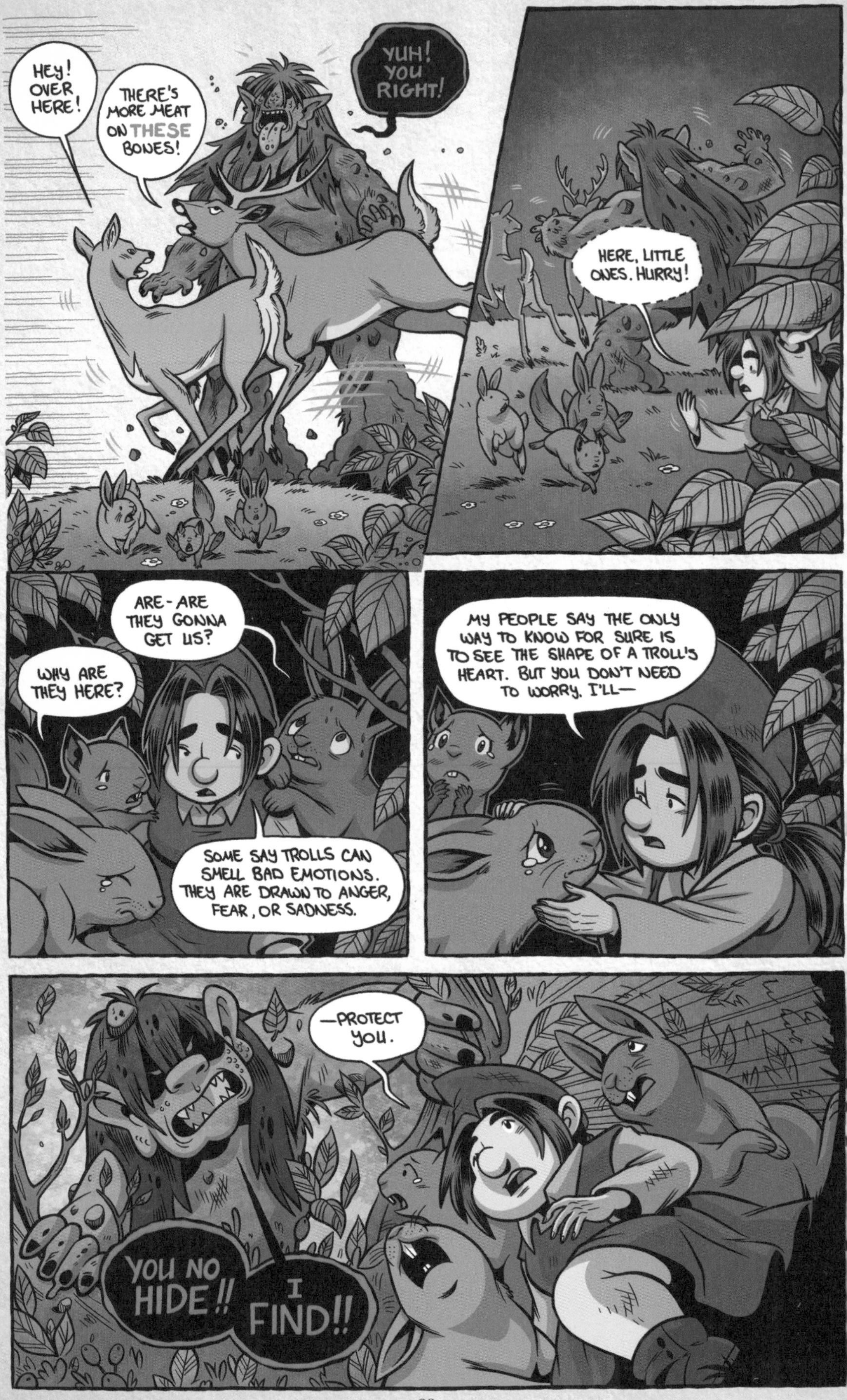
HEY! OVER HERE!
THERE'S MORE MEAT ON THESE BONES!
YUH! YOU RIGHT!
HERE, LITTLE ONES. HURRY!
ARE- ARE THEY GONNA GET US?
WHY ARE THEY HERE?
SOME SAY TROLLS CAN SMELL BAD EMOTIONS. THEY ARE DRAWN TO ANGER, FEAR, OR SADNESS.
MY PEOPLE SAY THE ONLY WAY TO KNOW FOR SURE IS TO SEE THE SHAPE OF A TROLL'S HEART. BUT YOU DON'T NEED TO WORRY. I'LL—
—PROTECT YOU.
YOU NO HIDE!!
I FIND!!

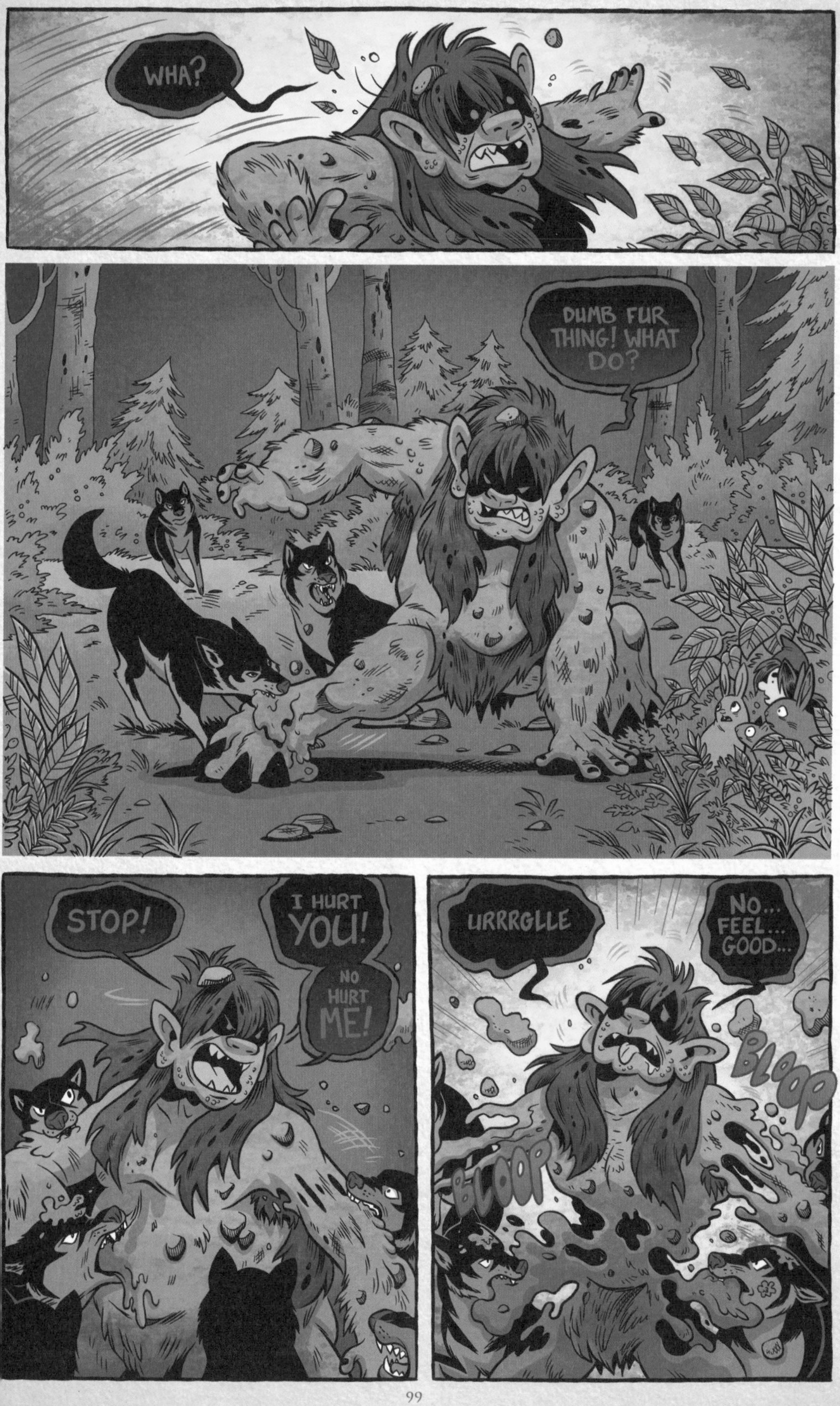
WHA?
DUMB FUR THING! WHAT DO?
STOP!
I HURT YOU!
NO HURT ME!
URRRGLLE
NO... FEEL... GOOD...
BLOOP
BLOOP

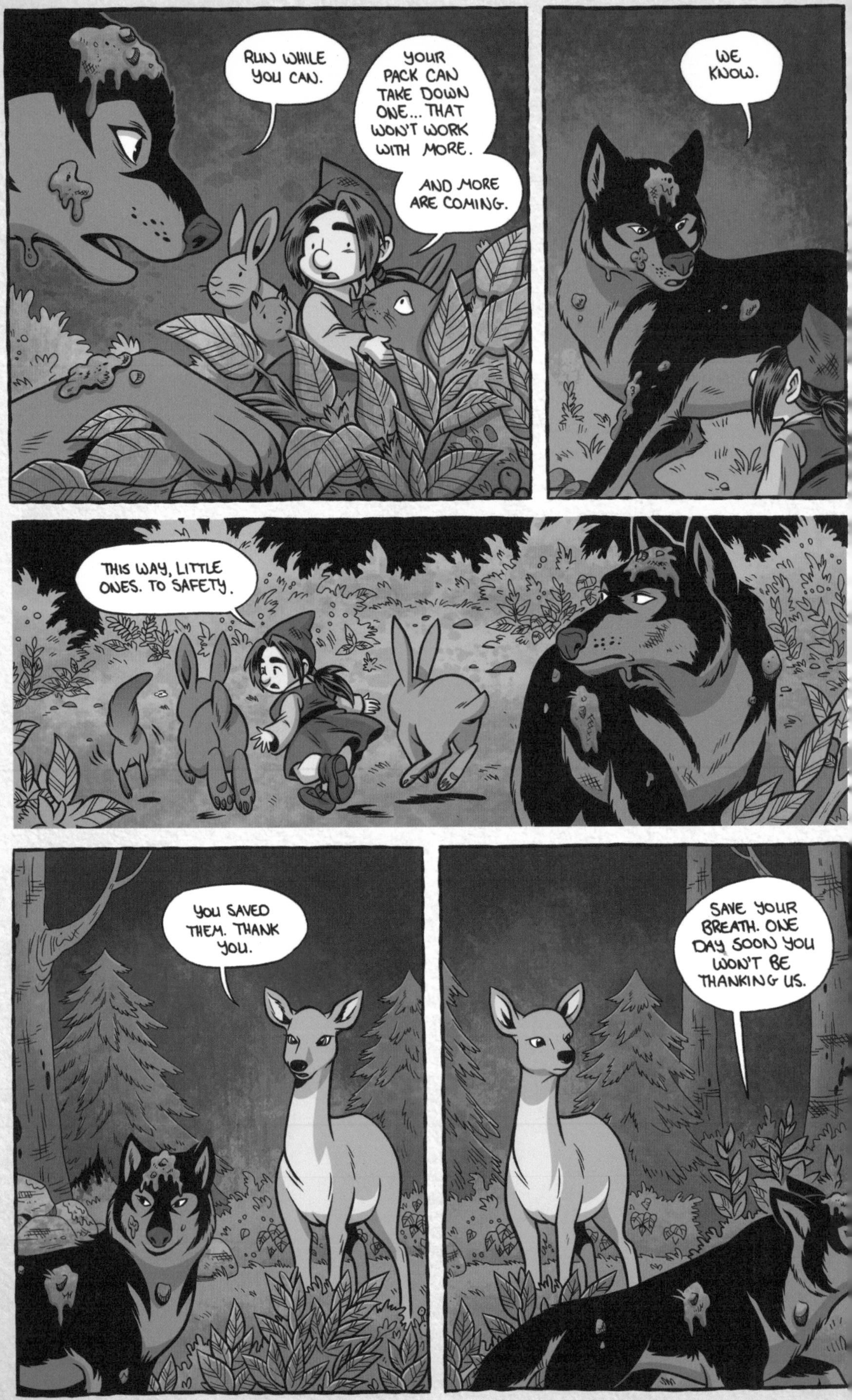
RUN WHILE YOU CAN.
YOUR PACK CAN TAKE DOWN ONE... THAT WON'T WORK WITH MORE.
AND MORE ARE COMING.
WE KNOW.
THIS WAY, LITTLE ONES. TO SAFETY.
YOU SAVED THEM. THANK YOU.
SAVE YOUR BREATH. ONE DAY SOON YOU WON'T BE THANKING US.

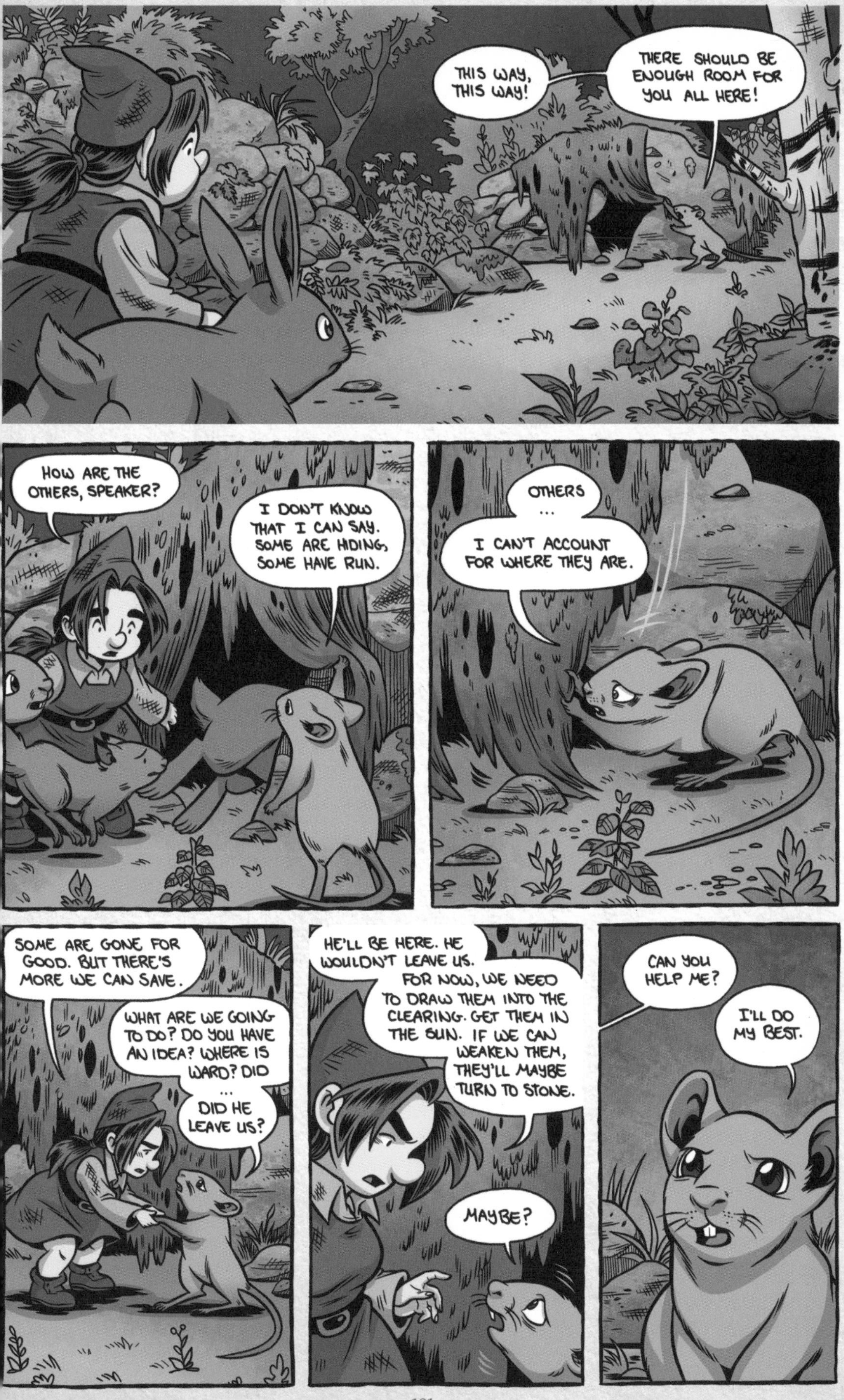
THIS WAY, THIS WAY!
THERE SHOULD BE ENOUGH ROOM FOR YOU ALL HERE!
HOW ARE THE OTHERS, SPEAKER?
I DON'T KNOW THAT I CAN SAY. SOME ARE HIDING, SOME HAVE RUN.
OTHERS ...
I CAN'T ACCOUNT FOR WHERE THEY ARE.
SOME ARE GONE FOR GOOD. BUT THERE'S MORE WE CAN SAVE.
WHAT ARE WE GOING TO DO? DO YOU HAVE AN IDEA? WHERE IS WARD? DID ...
DID HE LEAVE US?
HE'LL BE HERE. HE WOULDN'T LEAVE US.
FOR NOW, WE NEED TO DRAW THEM INTO THE CLEARING. GET THEM IN THE SUN. IF WE CAN WEAKEN THEM, THEY'LL MAYBE TURN TO STONE.
MAYBE?
CAN YOU HELP ME?
I'LL DO MY BEST.

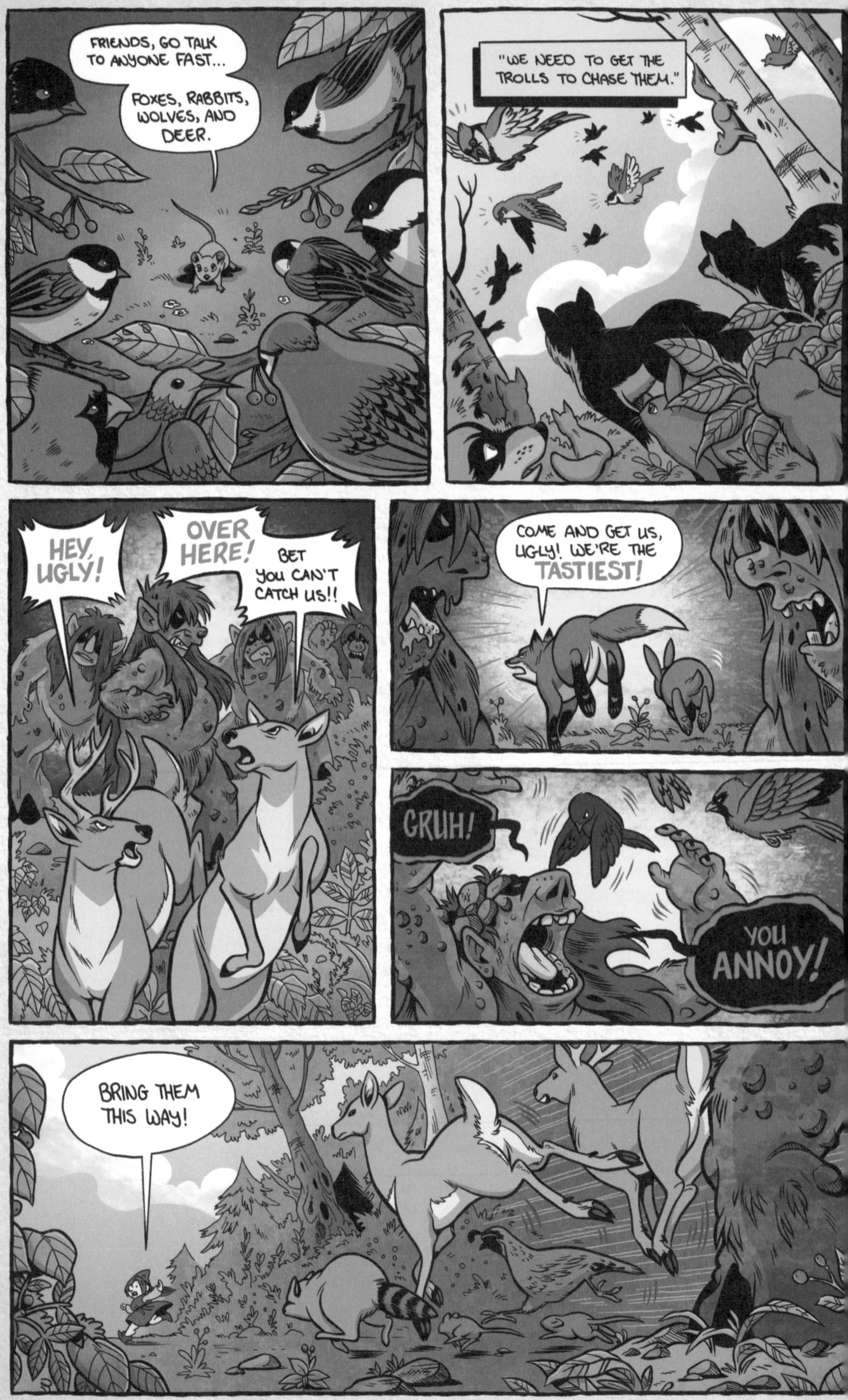
FRIENDS, GO TALK TO ANYONE FAST...
FOXES, RABBITS, WOLVES, AND DEER.
"WE NEED TO GET THE TROLLS TO CHASE THEM."
HEY, UGLY!
OVER HERE!
BET YOU CAN'T CATCH US!!
COME AND GET US, UGLY! WE'RE THE TASTIEST!
GRUH!
YOU ANNOY!
BRING THEM THIS WAY!

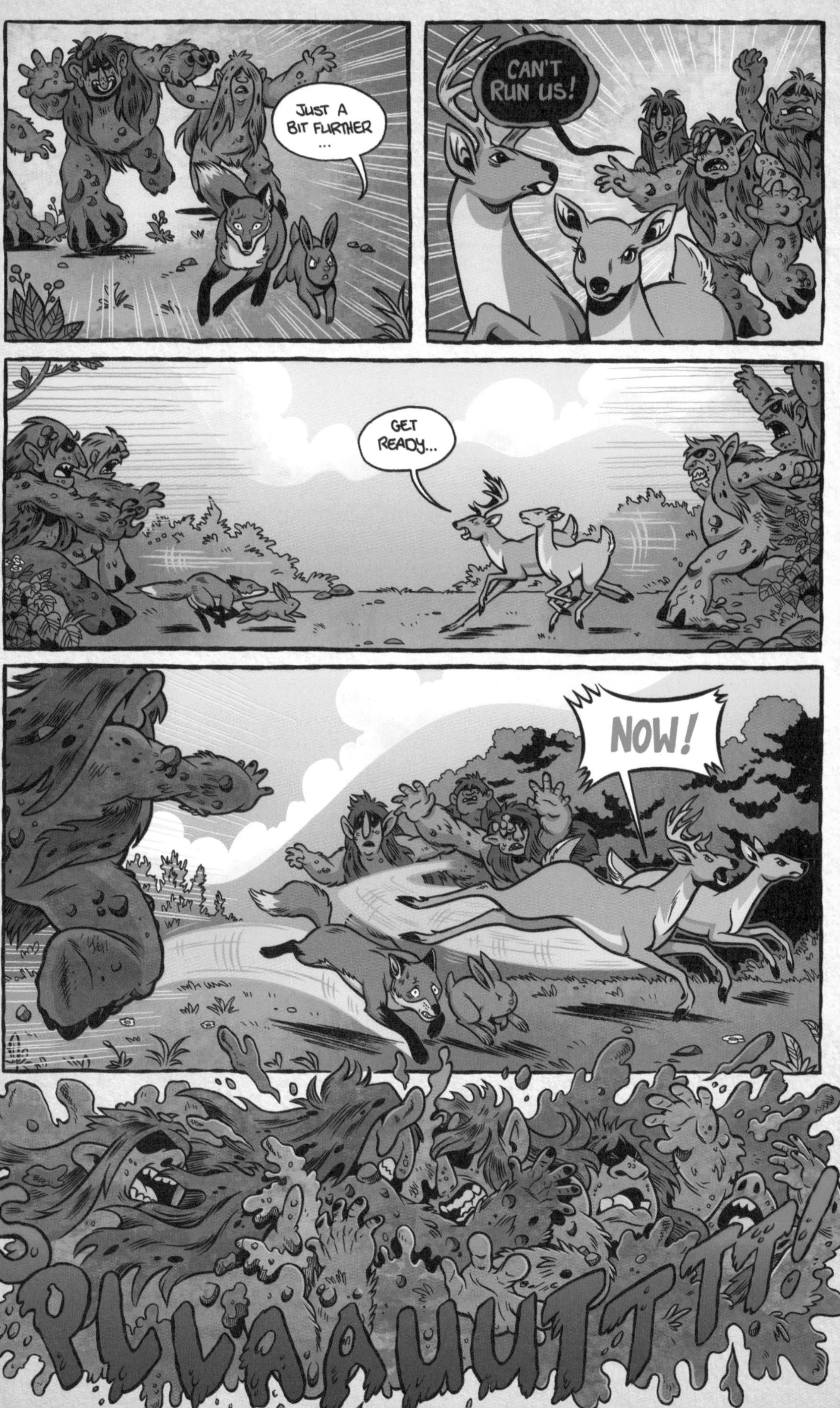

JUST A BIT FURTHER ...
CAN'T RUN US!
GET READY...
NOW!
PLLAAUUTTTT!

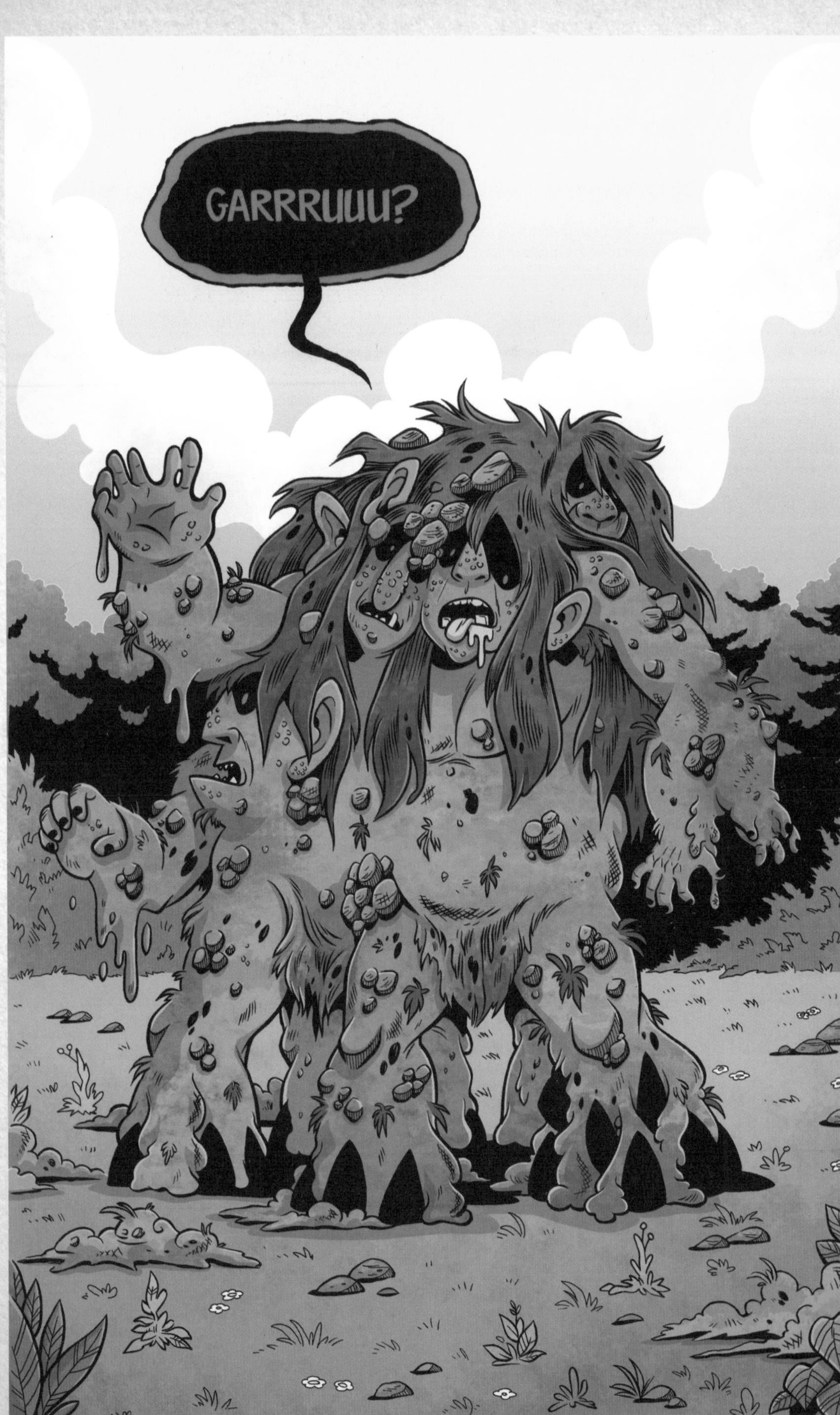
GARRRUUU?

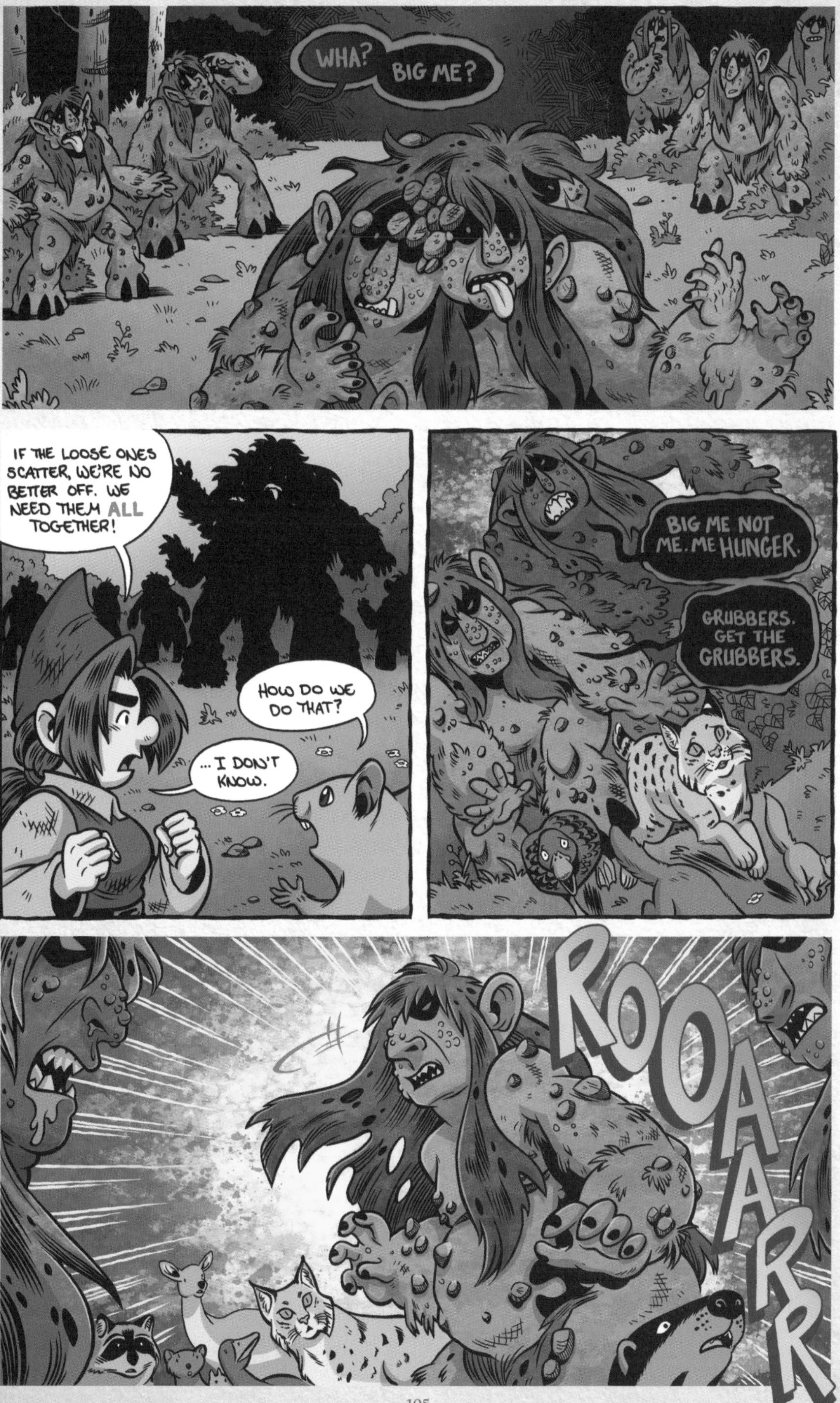
WHA?
BIG ME?
IF THE LOOSE ONES SCATTER, WE'RE NO BETTER OFF. WE NEED THEM ALL TOGETHER!
HOW DO WE DO THAT?
... I DON'T KNOW.
BIG ME NOT ME. ME HUNGER.
GRUBBERS. GET THE GRUBBERS.
ROOAARR

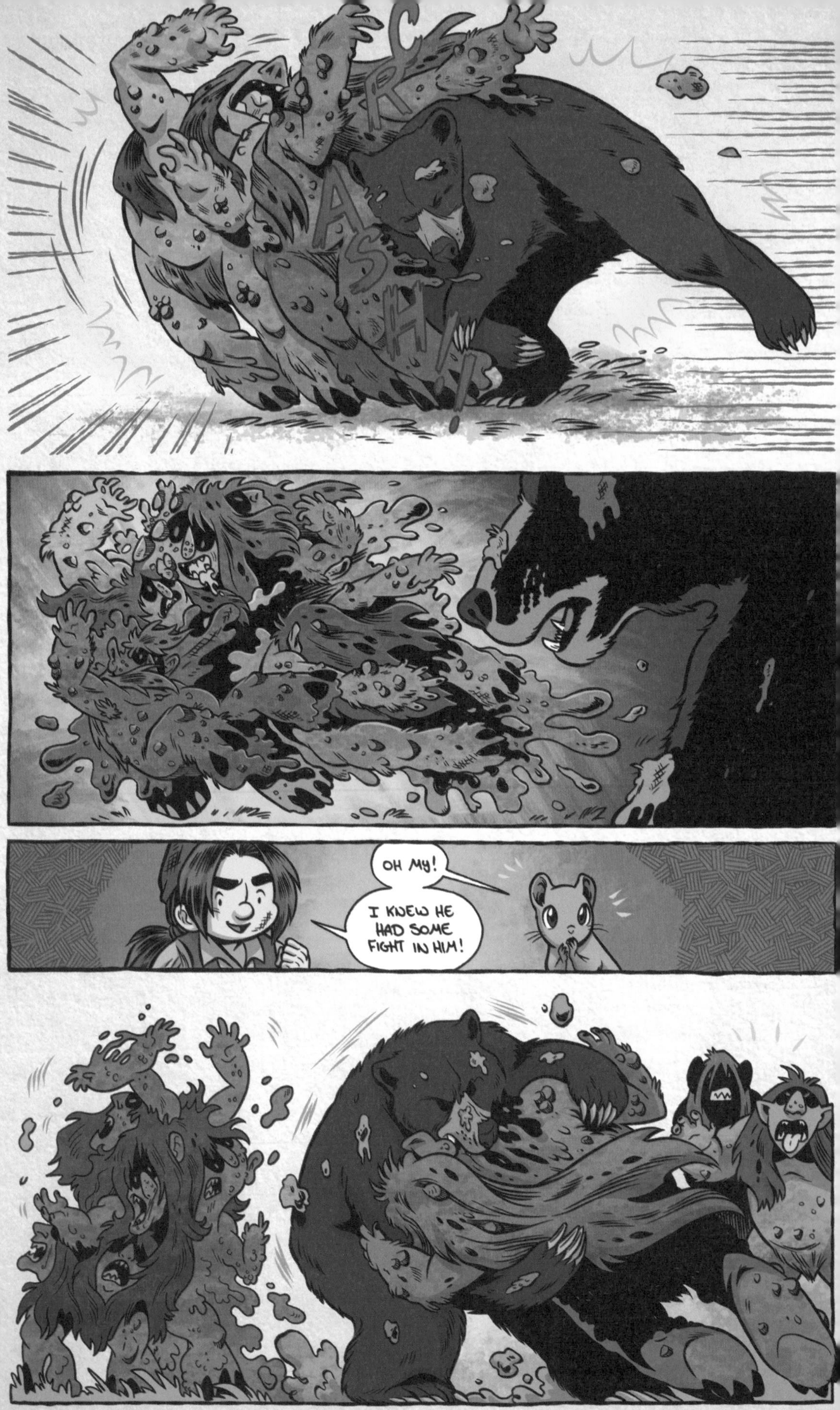
CRASH!
OH MY!
I KNEW HE HAD SOME FIGHT IN HIM!

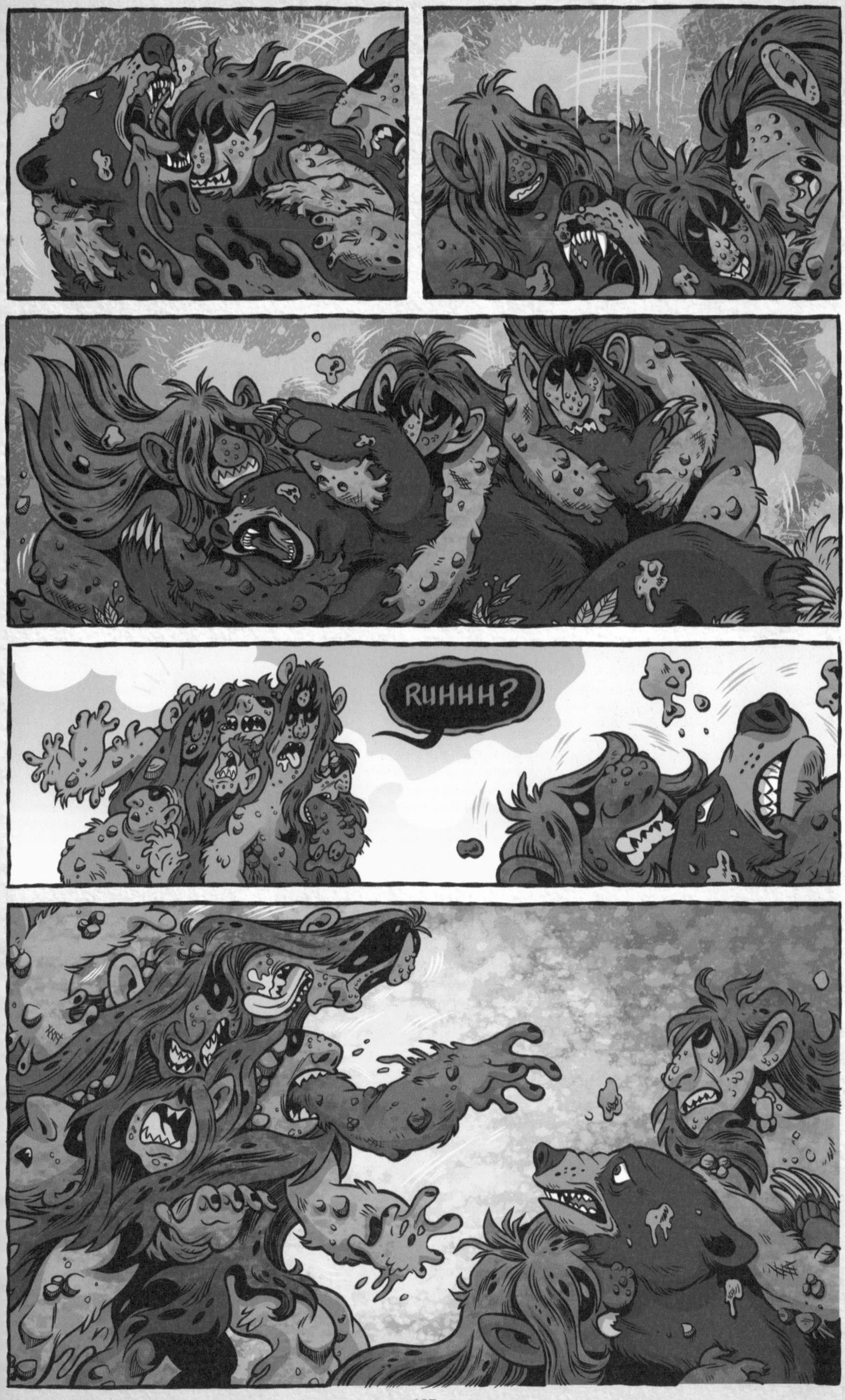
RUHHH?

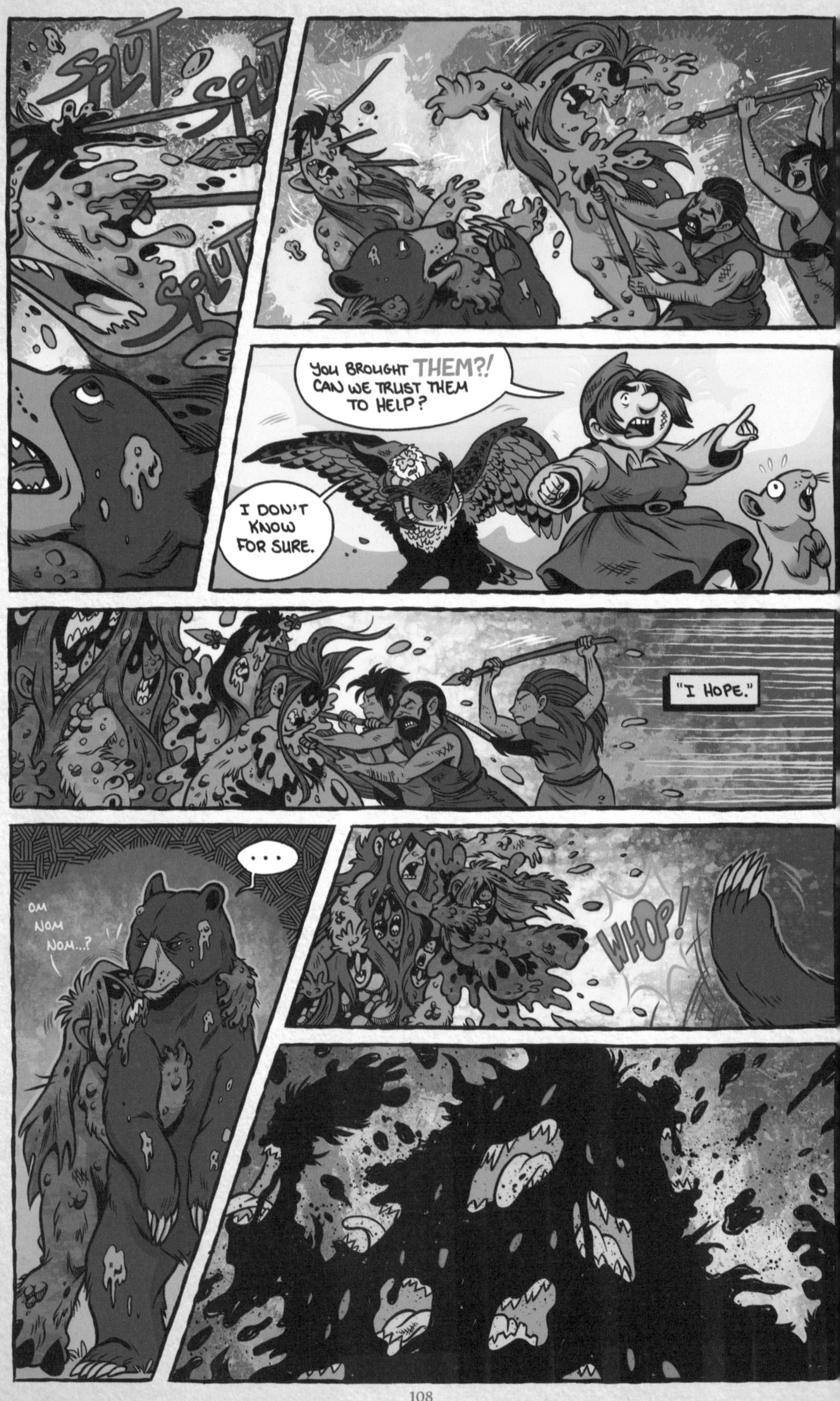

SPLUT SPLUT
SPLUT
SPLUT
YOU BROUGHT THEM?! CAN WE TRUST THEM TO HELP?
I DON'T KNOW FOR SURE.
"I HOPE."
...
OM NOM NOM...?
WHOP!

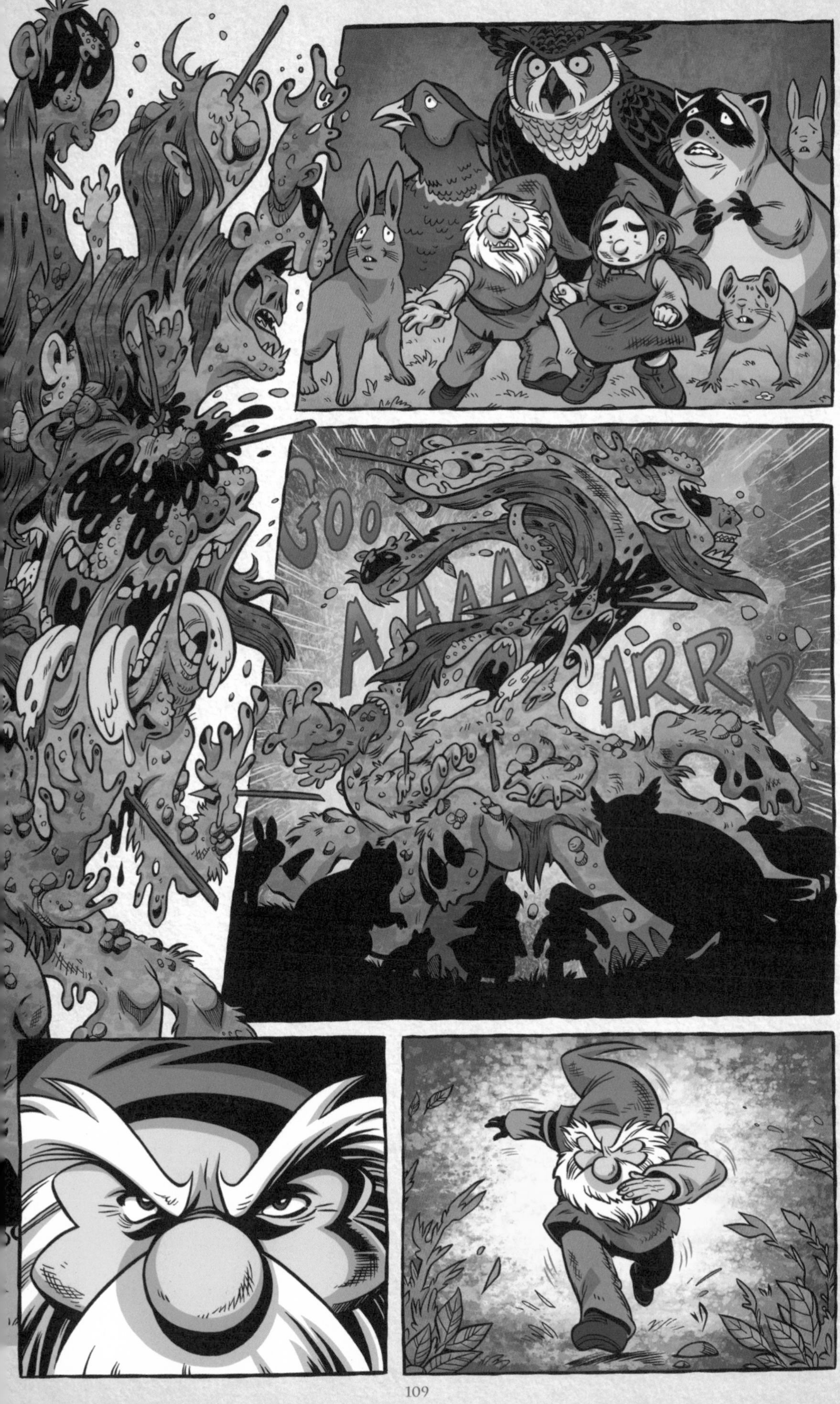
GOOAAAAARRR

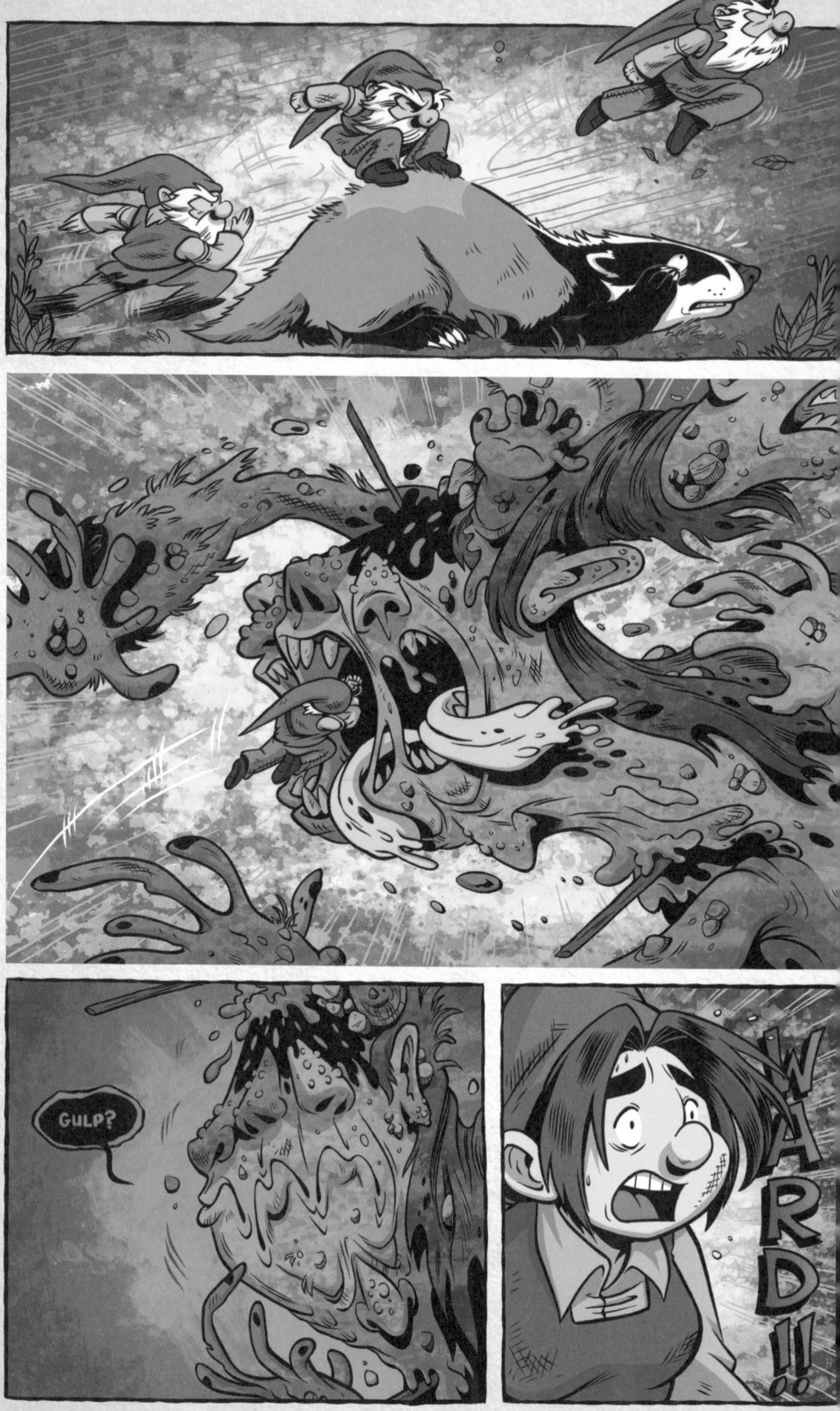
GULP?
WARD!!

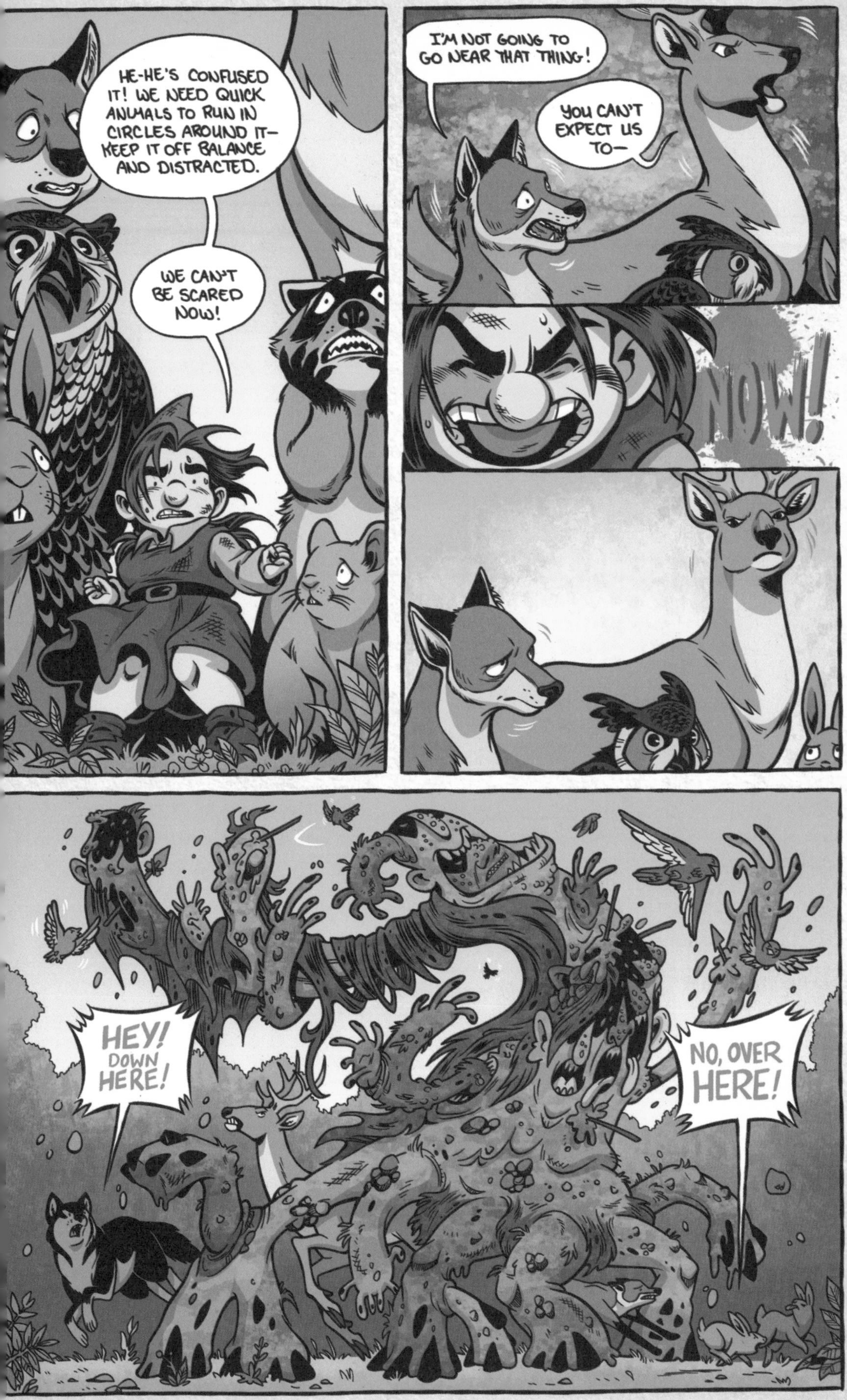
HE-HE'S CONFUSED IT! WE NEED QUICK ANIMALS TO RUN IN CIRCLES AROUND IT-KEEP IT OFF BALANCE AND DISTRACTED.
WE CAN'T BE SCARED NOW!
I'M NOT GOING TO GO NEAR THAT THING!
YOU CAN'T EXPECT US TO—
NOW!
HEY! DOWN HERE!
NO, OVER HERE!

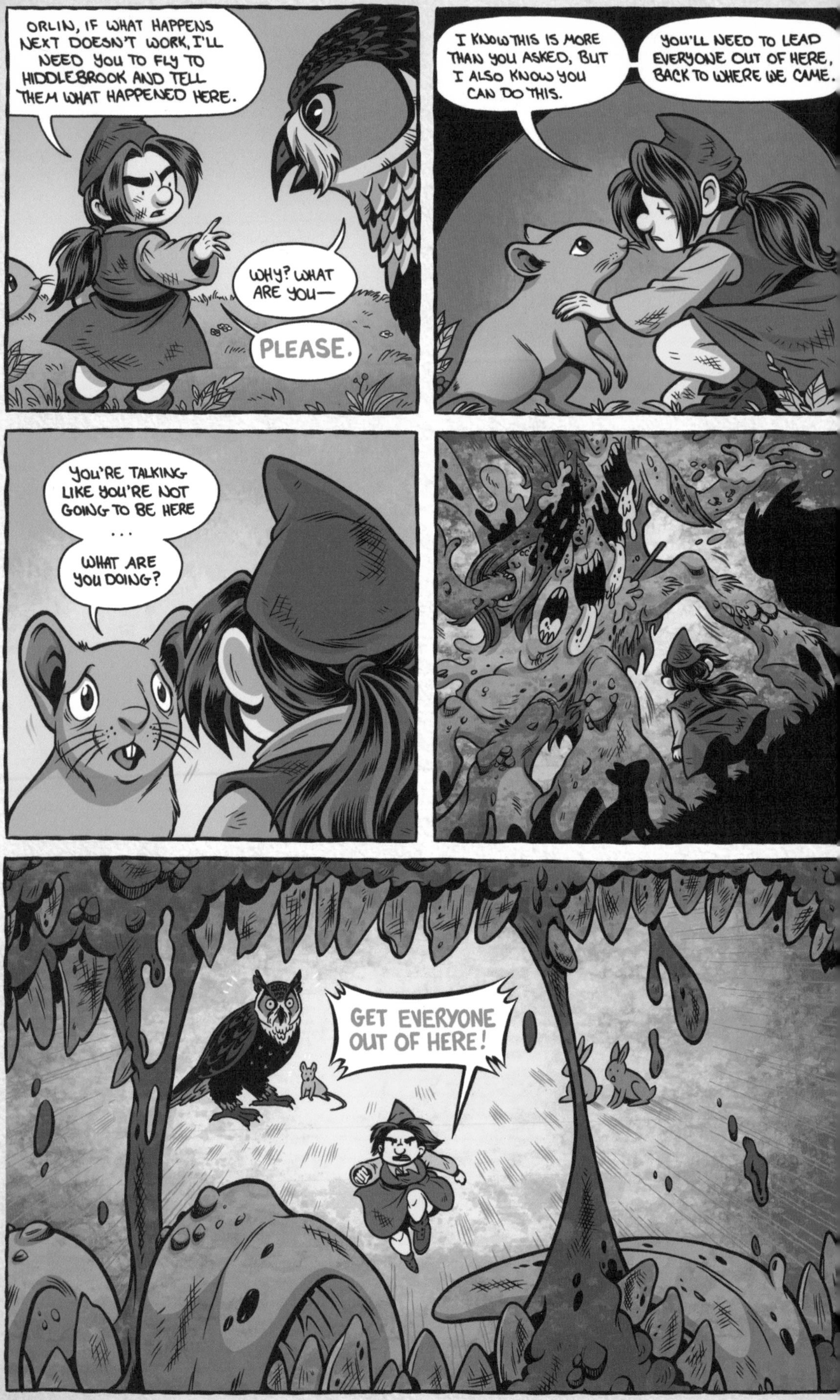
ORLIN, IF WHAT HAPPENS NEXT DOESN'T WORK, I'LL NEED YOU TO FLY TO HIDDLEBROOK AND TELL THEM WHAT HAPPENED HERE.
WHY? WHAT ARE YOU—
PLEASE.
I KNOW THIS IS MORE THAN YOU ASKED, BUT I ALSO KNOW YOU CAN DO THIS.
YOU'LL NEED TO LEAD EVERYONE OUT OF HERE, BACK TO WHERE WE CAME.
YOU'RE TALKING LIKE YOU'RE NOT GOING TO BE HERE
. . .
WHAT ARE YOU DOING?
GET EVERYONE OUT OF HERE!

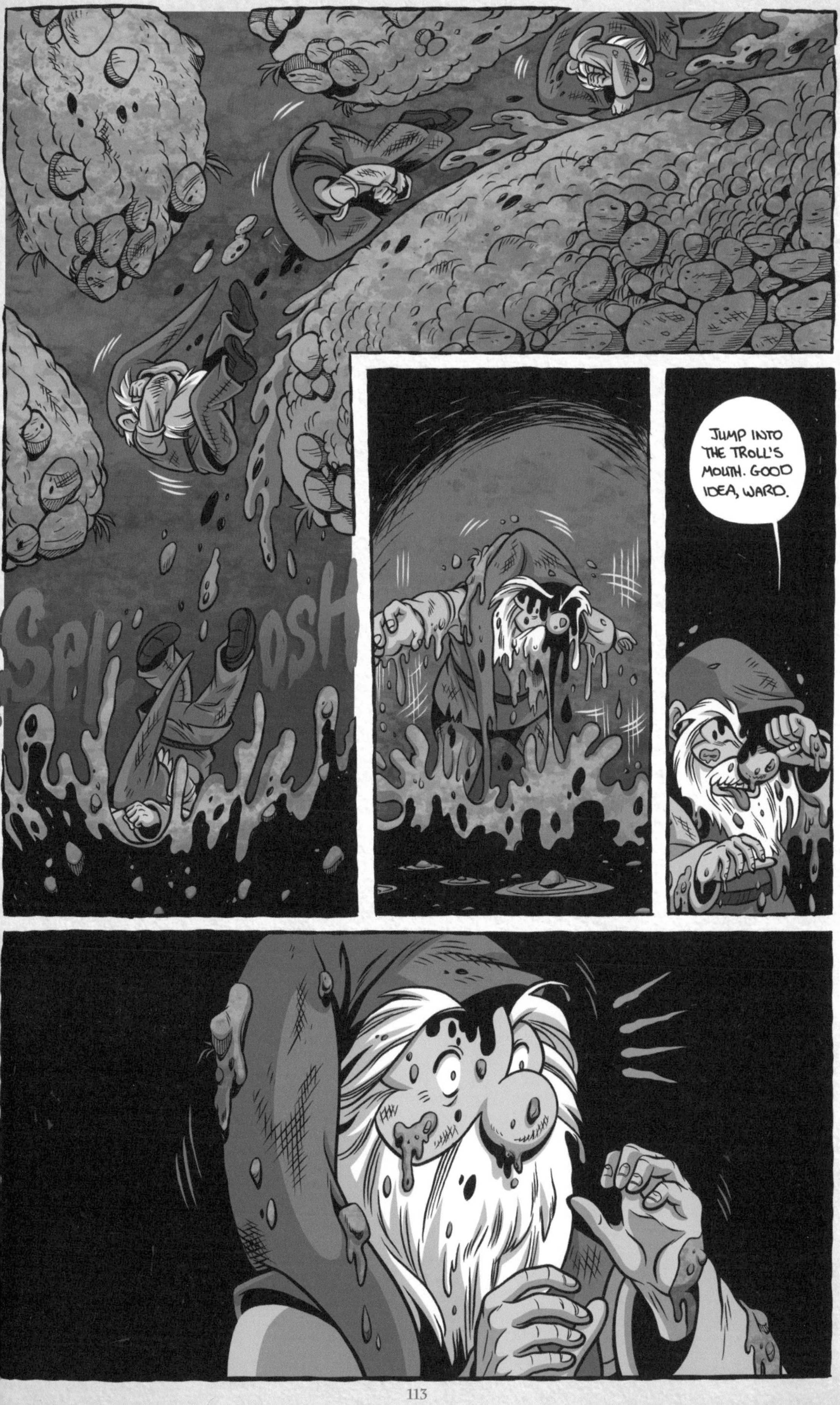
SPLOOSH
JUMP INTO THE TROLL'S MOUTH. GOOD IDEA, WARD.

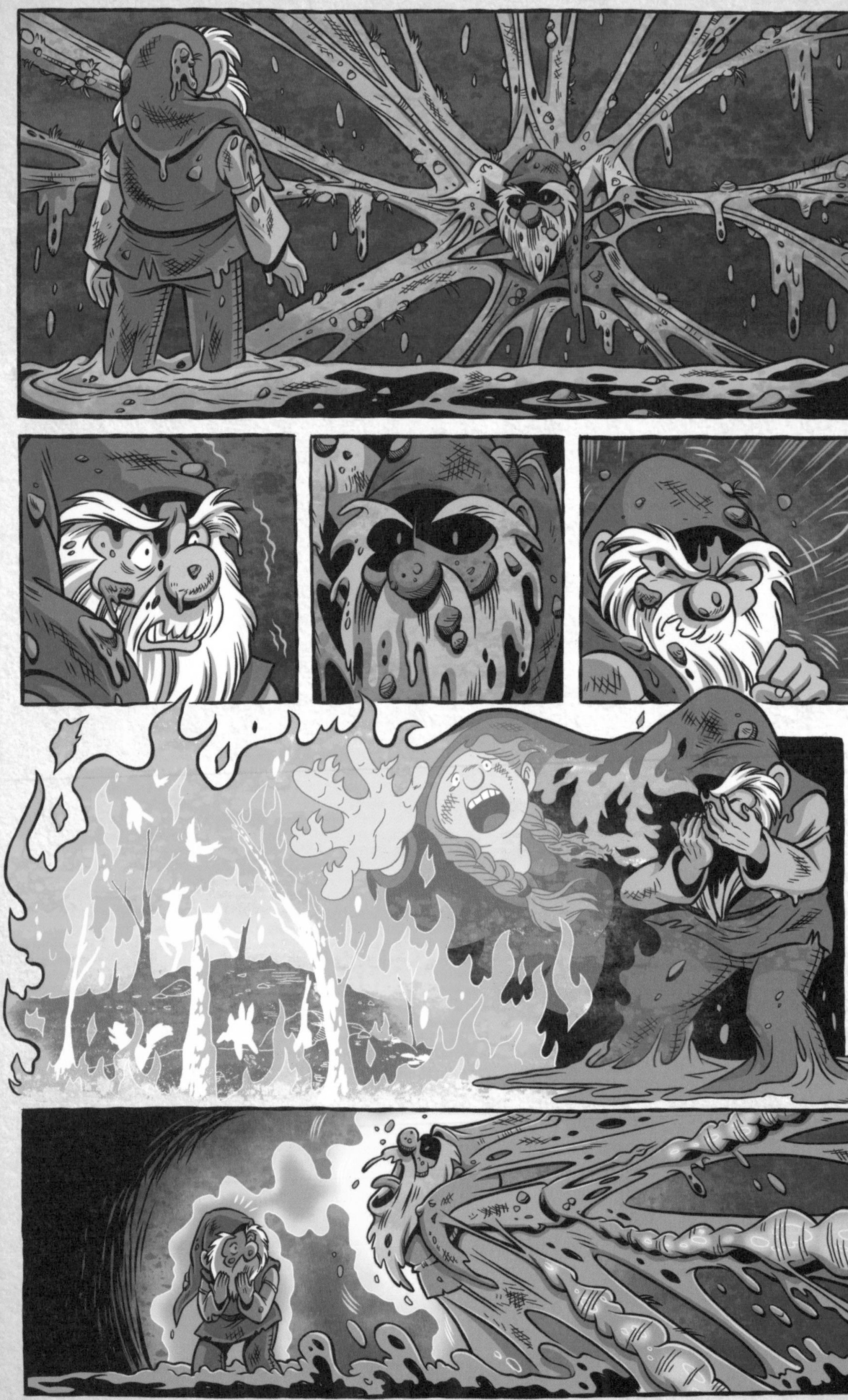

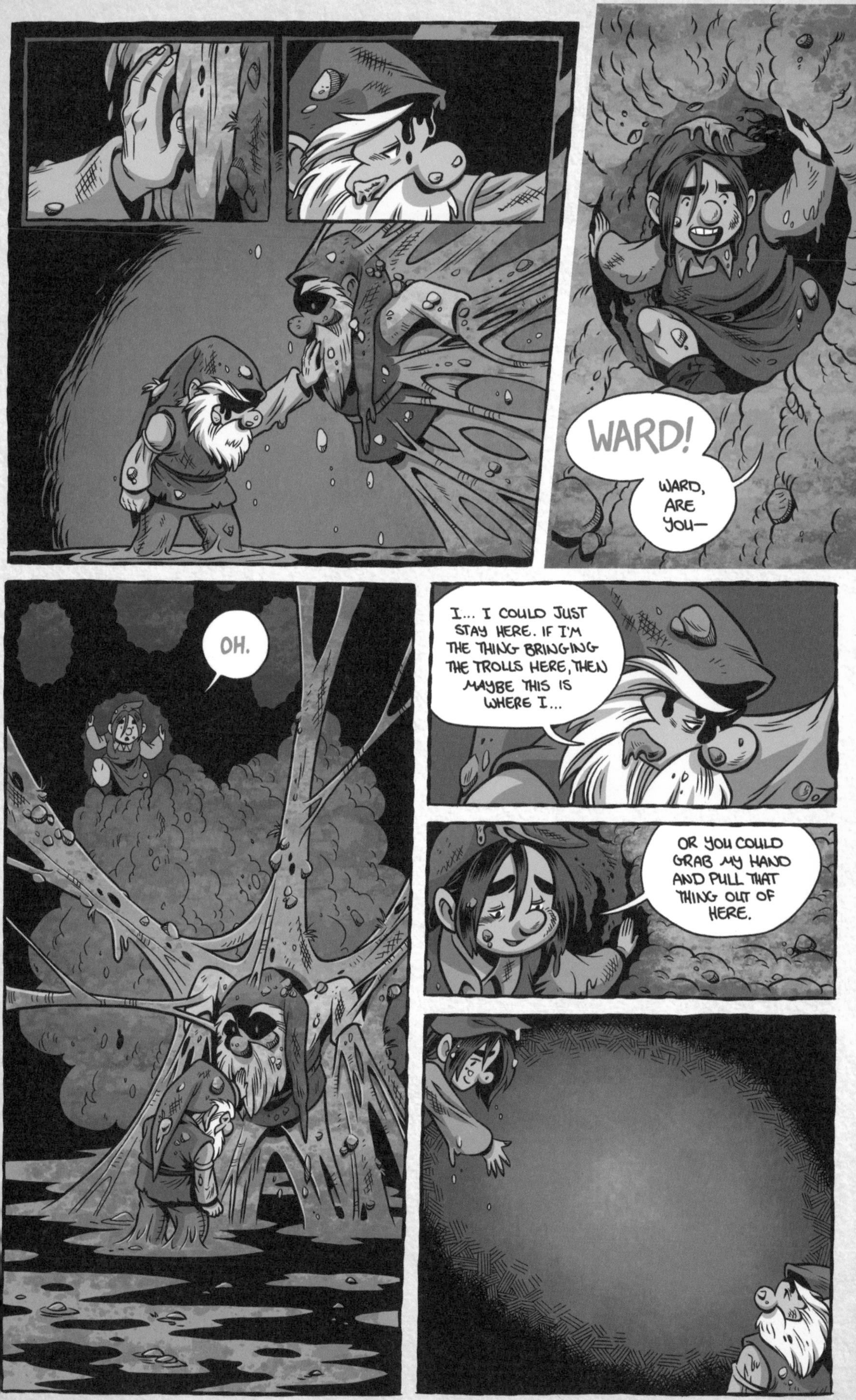

WARD!
WARD, ARE YOU—
OH.
I... I COULD JUST STAY HERE. IF I'M THE THING BRINGING THE TROLLS HERE, THEN MAYBE THIS IS WHERE I...
OR YOU COULD GRAB MY HAND AND PULL THAT THING OUT OF HERE.

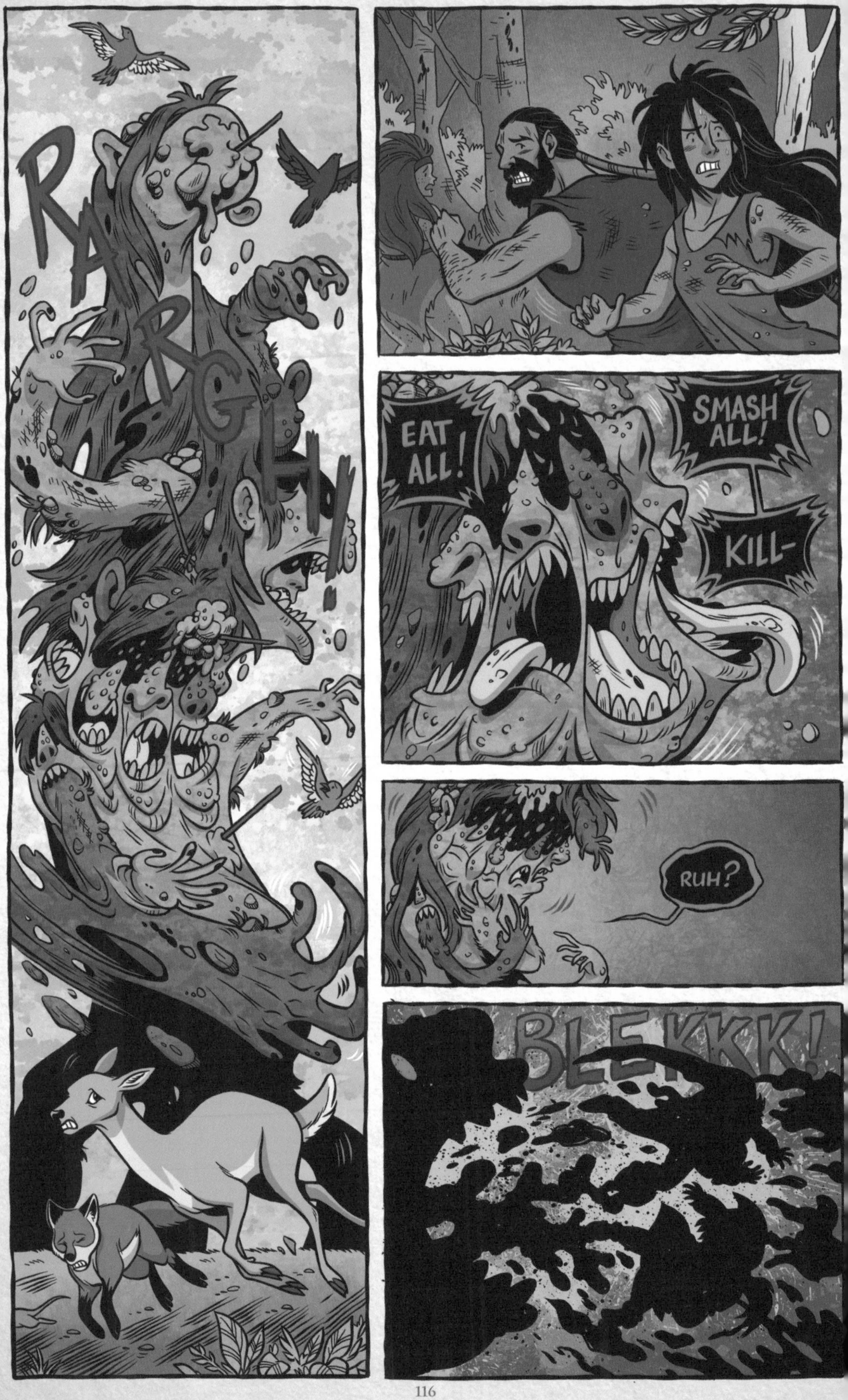
RARRGH!
EAT ALL!
SMASH ALL!
KILL-
RUH?
BLEKKK!

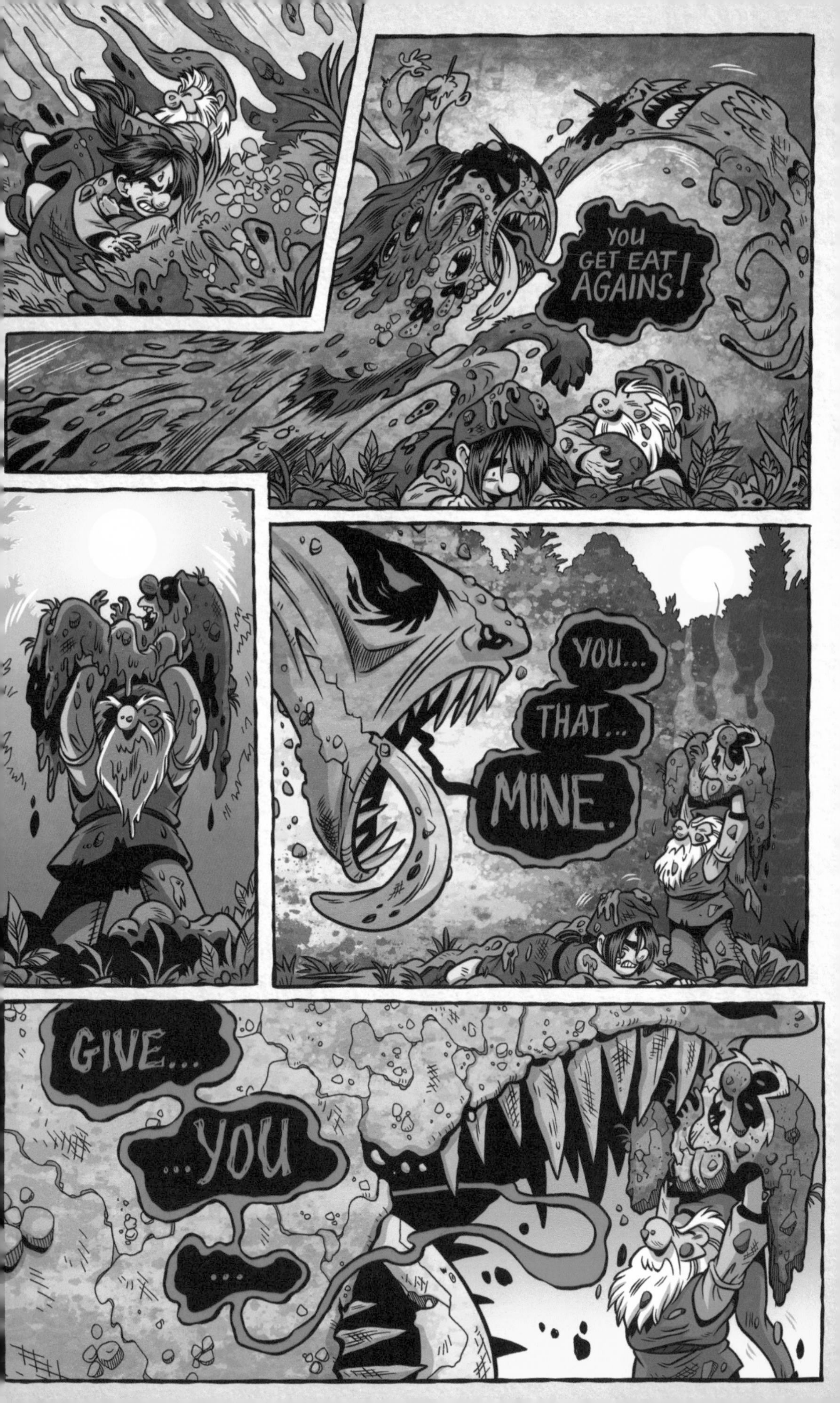
YOU GET EAT AGAINS!
YOU...
THAT...
MINE.
GIVE...
...YOU
...

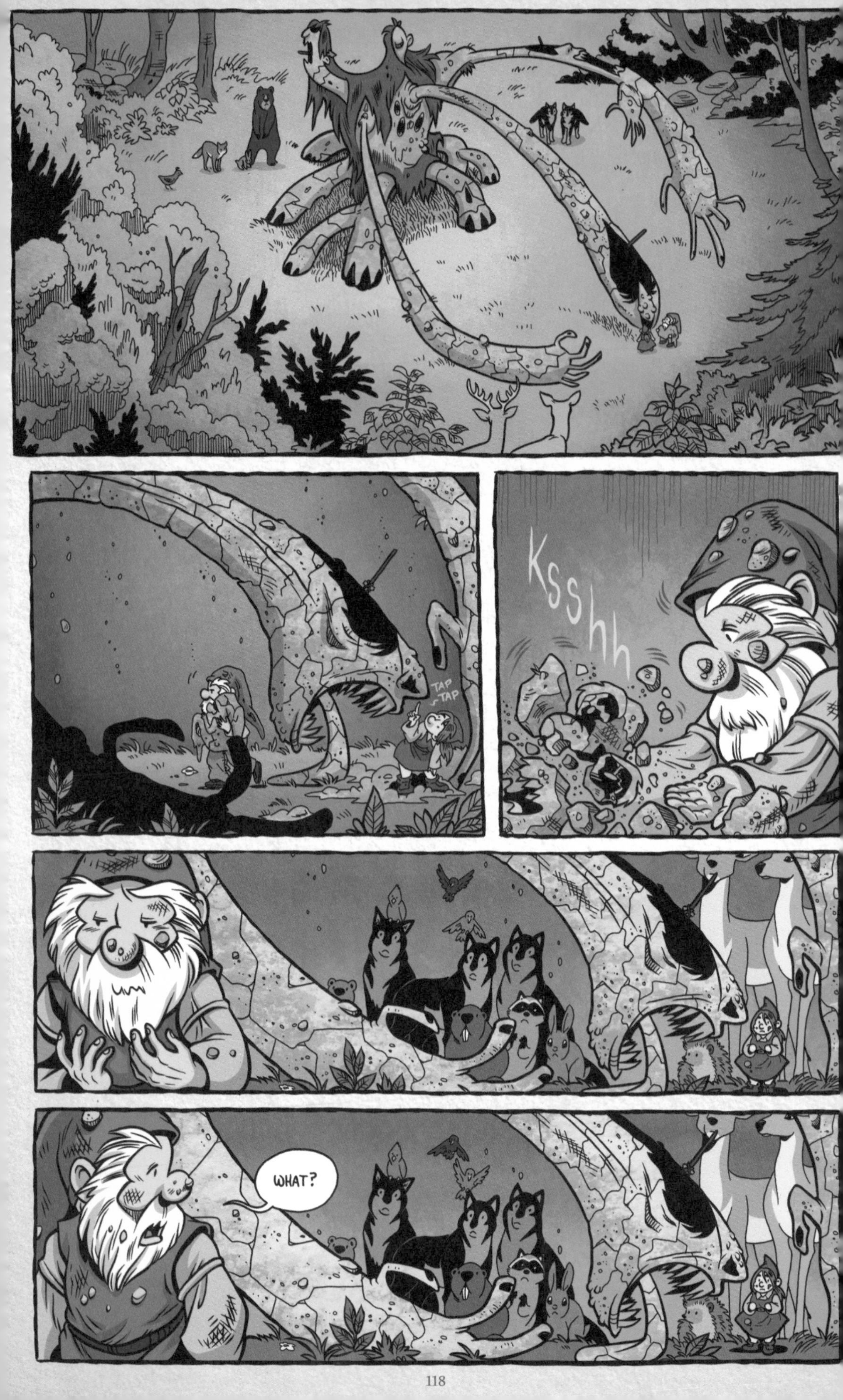
TAP
TAP
KSSHH
WHAT?

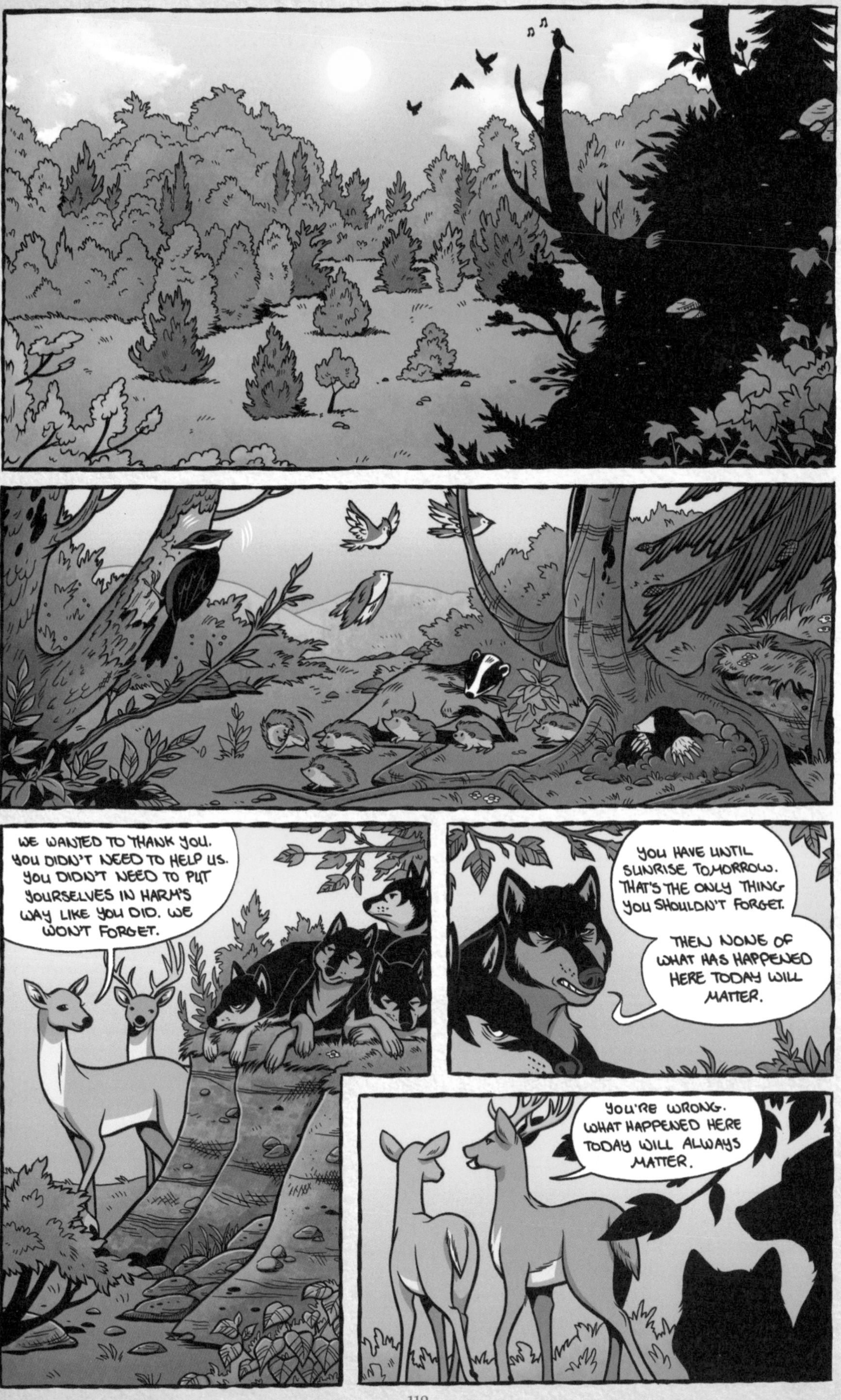
WE WANTED TO THANK YOU. YOU DIDN'T NEED TO HELP US. YOU DIDN'T NEED TO PUT YOURSELVES IN HARM'S WAY LIKE YOU DID. WE WON'T FORGET.
YOU HAVE UNTIL SUNRISE TOMORROW. THAT'S THE ONLY THING YOU SHOULDN'T FORGET.
THEN NONE OF WHAT HAS HAPPENED HERE TODAY WILL MATTER.
YOU'RE WRONG. WHAT HAPPENED HERE TODAY WILL ALWAYS MATTER.

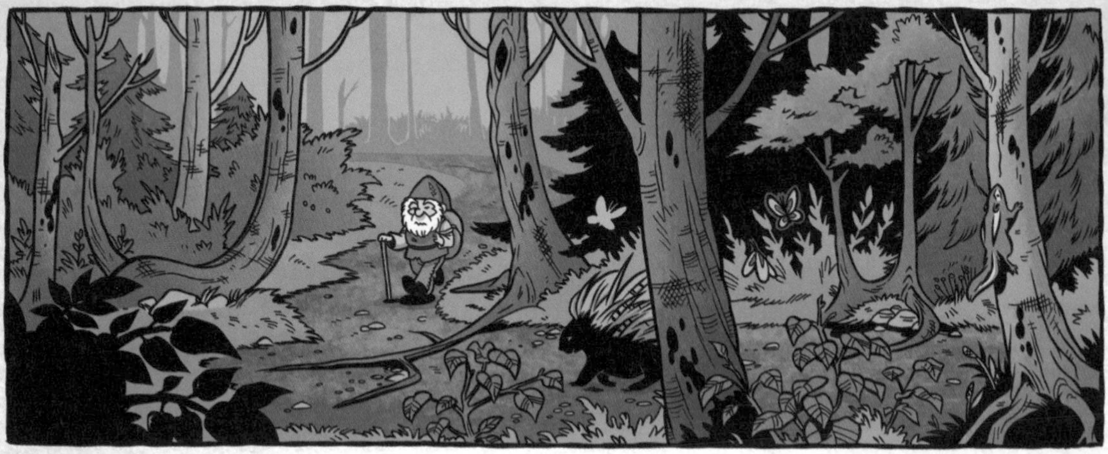

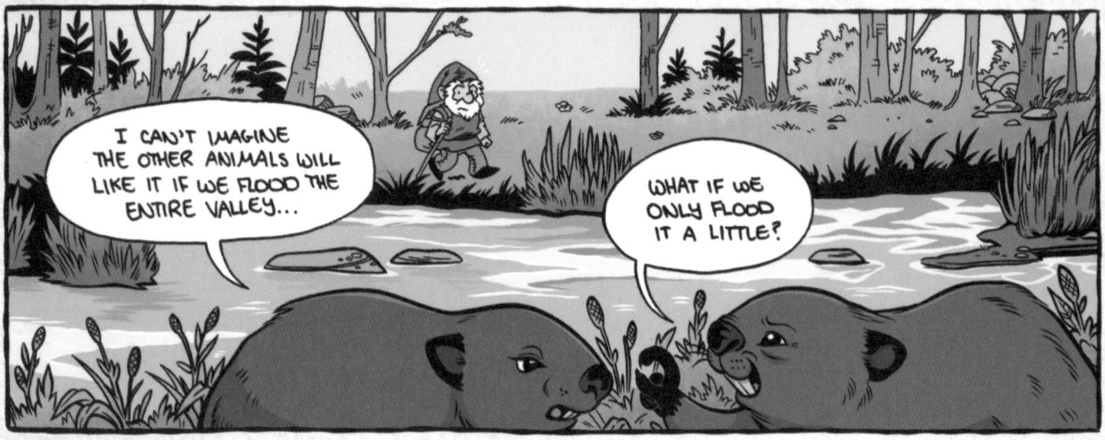
I CAN'T IMAGINE THE OTHER ANIMALS WILL LIKE IT IF WE FLOOD THE ENTIRE VALLEY...
WHAT IF WE ONLY FLOOD IT A LITTLE?

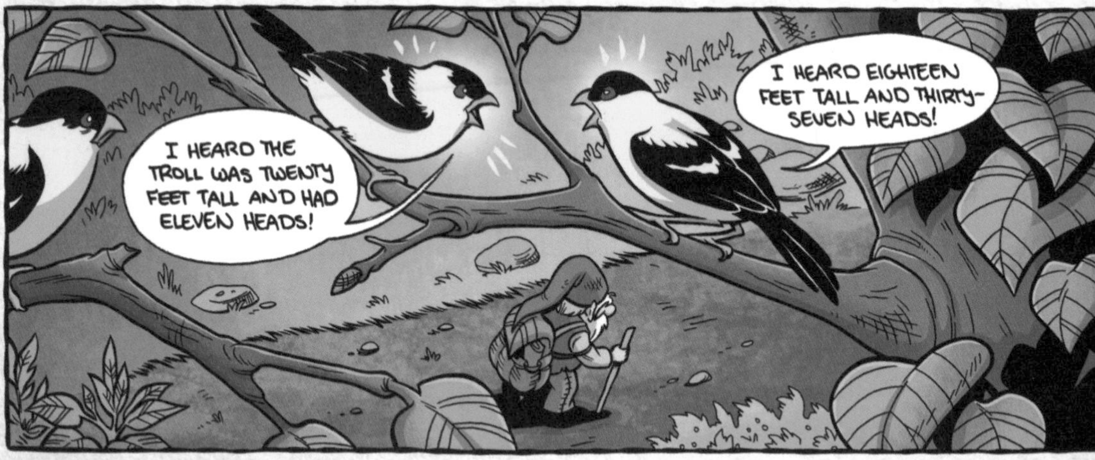
I HEARD THE TROLL WAS TWENTY FEET TALL AND HAD ELEVEN HEADS!
I HEARD EIGHTEEN FEET TALL AND THIRTY-SEVEN HEADS!

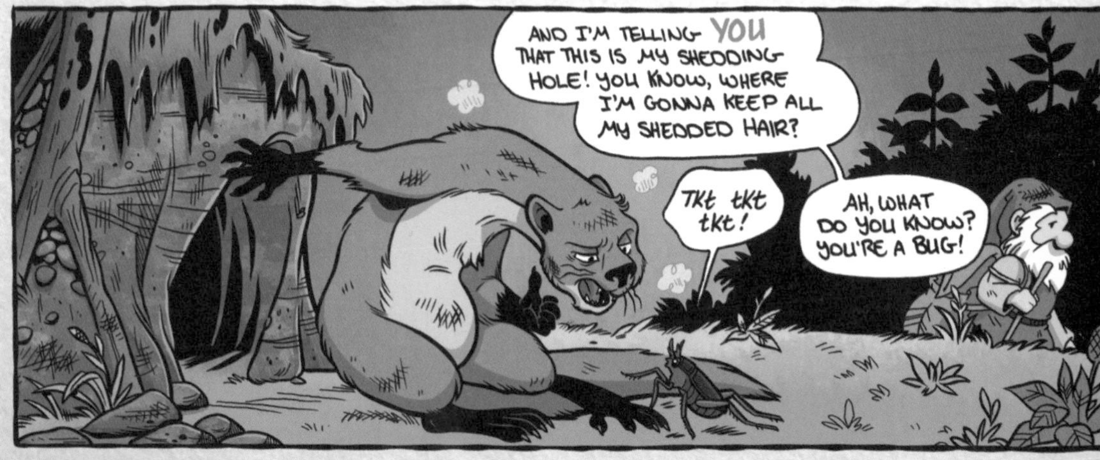
AND I'M TELLING YOU THAT THIS IS MY SHEDDING-HOLE! YOU KNOW, WHERE I'M GONNA KEEP ALL MY SHEDDED HAIR?
TKt tKt tKt!
AH, WHAT DO YOU KNOW? YOU'RE A BUG!

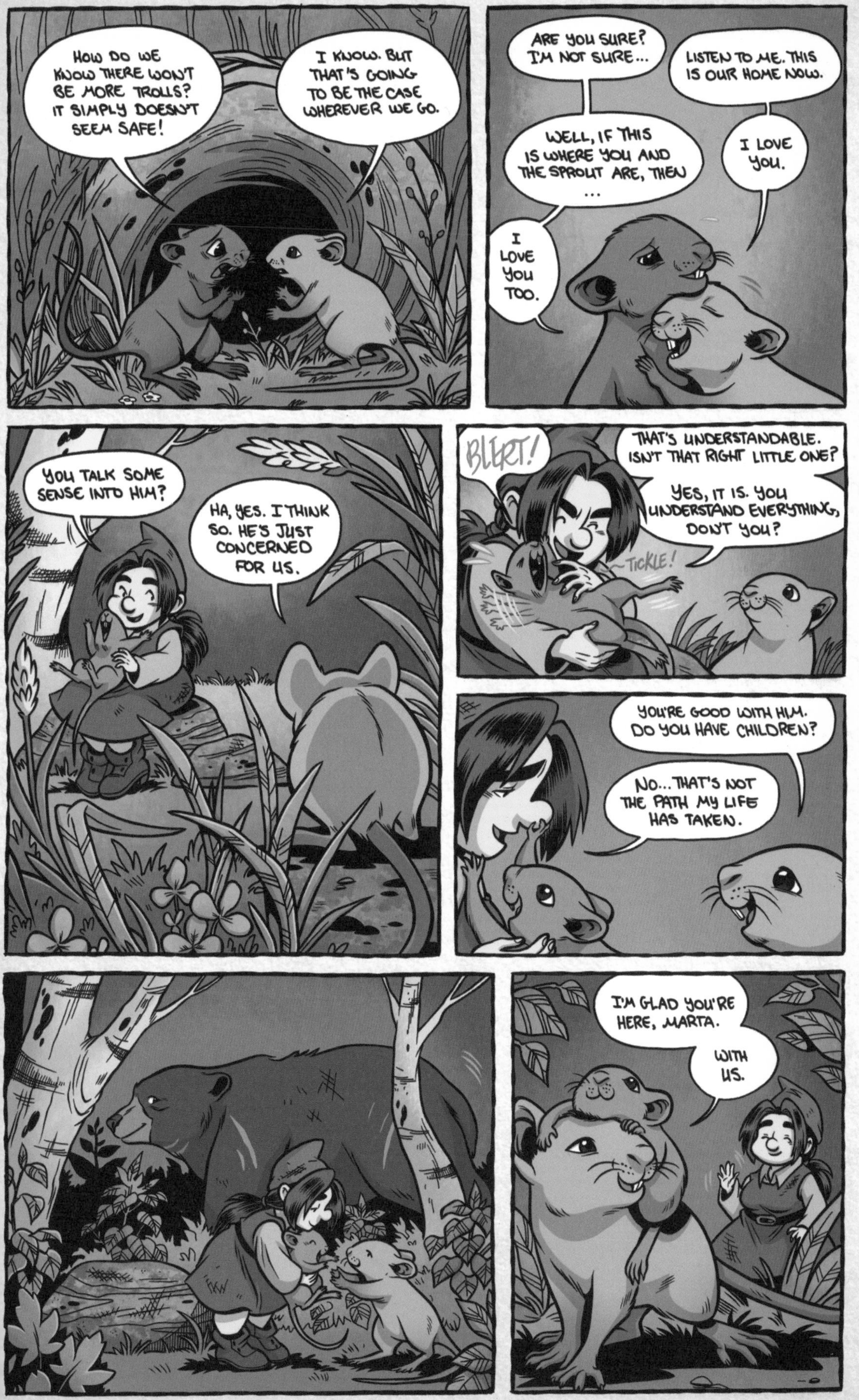
HOW DO WE KNOW THERE WON'T BE MORE TROLLS? IT SIMPLY DOESN'T SEEM SAFE!
I KNOW. BUT THAT'S GOING TO BE THE CASE WHEREVER WE GO.
ARE YOU SURE? I'M NOT SURE...
LISTEN TO ME. THIS IS OUR HOME NOW.
WELL, IF THIS IS WHERE YOU AND THE SPROUT ARE, THEN ...
I LOVE YOU.
I LOVE YOU TOO.
YOU TALK SOME SENSE INTO HIM?
HA, YES. I THINK SO. HE'S JUST CONCERNED FOR US.
BLERT!
THAT'S UNDERSTANDABLE. ISN'T THAT RIGHT LITTLE ONE?
YES, IT IS. YOU UNDERSTAND EVERYTHING, DON'T YOU?
~TICKLE!
YOU'RE GOOD WITH HIM. DO YOU HAVE CHILDREN?
NO... THAT'S NOT THE PATH MY LIFE HAS TAKEN.
I'M GLAD YOU'RE HERE, MARTA.
WITH US.

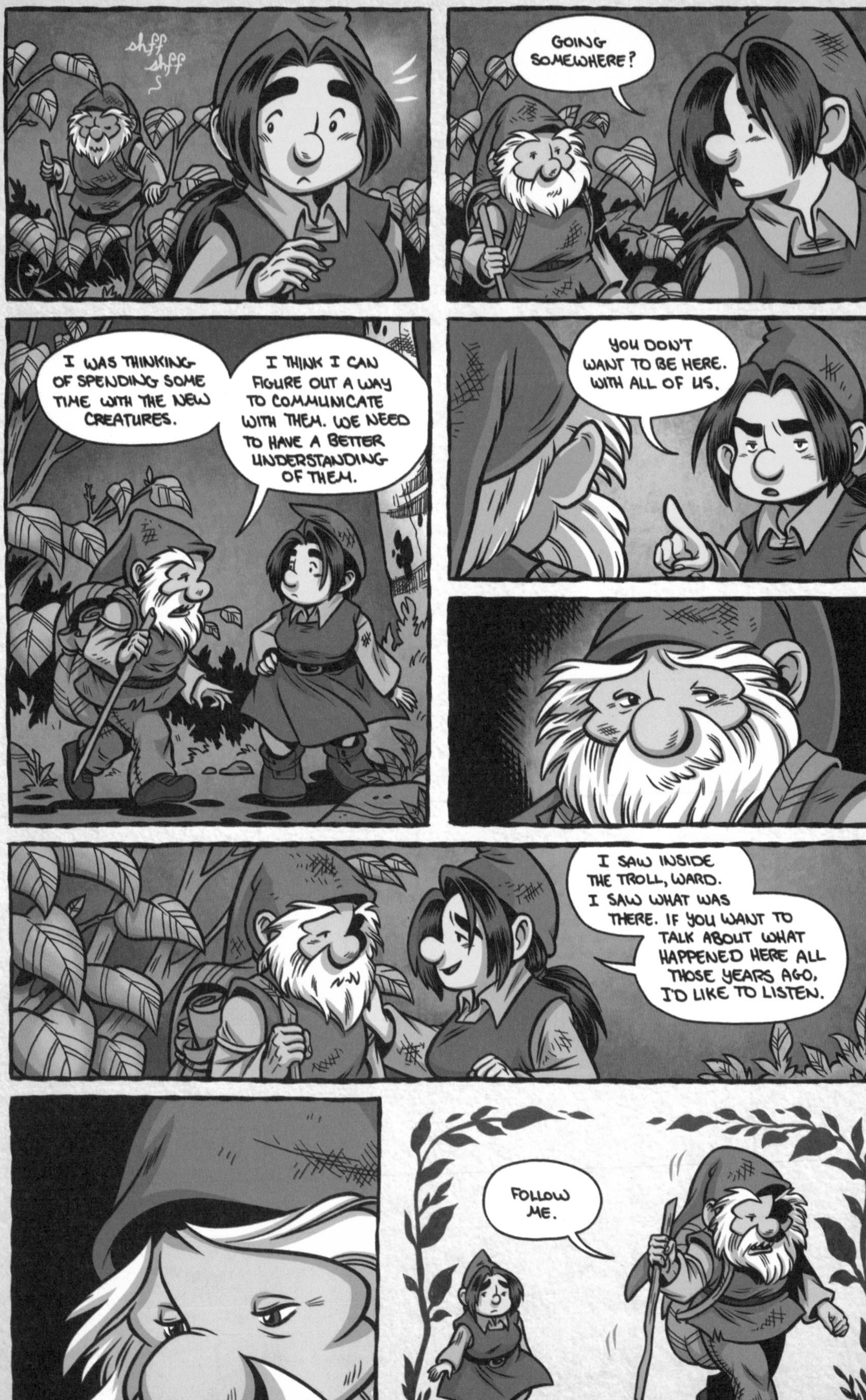
shff
shff
GOING SOMEWHERE?
I WAS THINKING OF SPENDING SOME TIME WITH THE NEW CREATURES.
I THINK I CAN FIGURE OUT A WAY TO COMMUNICATE WITH THEM. WE NEED TO HAVE A BETTER UNDERSTANDING OF THEM.
YOU DON'T WANT TO BE HERE. WITH ALL OF US.
I SAW INSIDE THE TROLL, WARD. I SAW WHAT WAS THERE. IF YOU WANT TO TALK ABOUT WHAT HAPPENED HERE ALL THOSE YEARS AGO, I'D LIKE TO LISTEN.
FOLLOW ME.

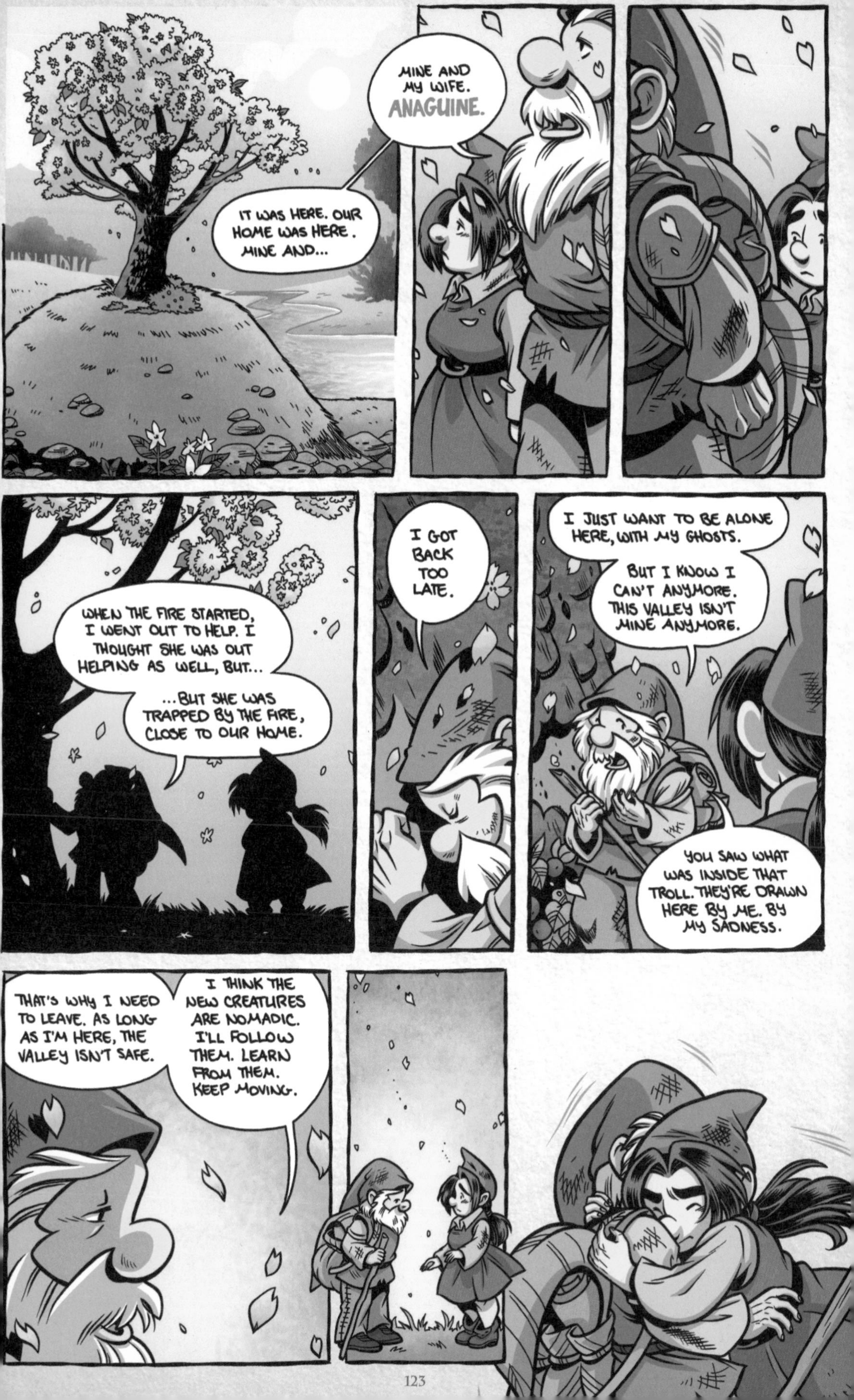
IT WAS HERE. OUR HOME WAS HERE. MINE AND...
MINE AND MY WIFE. ANAGUINE.
WHEN THE FIRE STARTED, I WENT OUT TO HELP. I THOUGHT SHE WAS OUT HELPING AS WELL, BUT...
...BUT SHE WAS TRAPPED BY THE FIRE, CLOSE TO OUR HOME.
I GOT BACK TOO LATE.
I JUST WANT TO BE ALONE HERE, WITH MY GHOSTS.
BUT I KNOW I CAN'T ANYMORE. THIS VALLEY ISN'T MINE ANYMORE.
YOU SAW WHAT WAS INSIDE THAT TROLL. THEY'RE DRAWN HERE BY ME. BY MY SADNESS.
THAT'S WHY I NEED TO LEAVE. AS LONG AS I'M HERE, THE VALLEY ISN'T SAFE.
I THINK THE NEW CREATURES ARE NOMADIC. I'LL FOLLOW THEM. LEARN FROM THEM. KEEP MOVING.

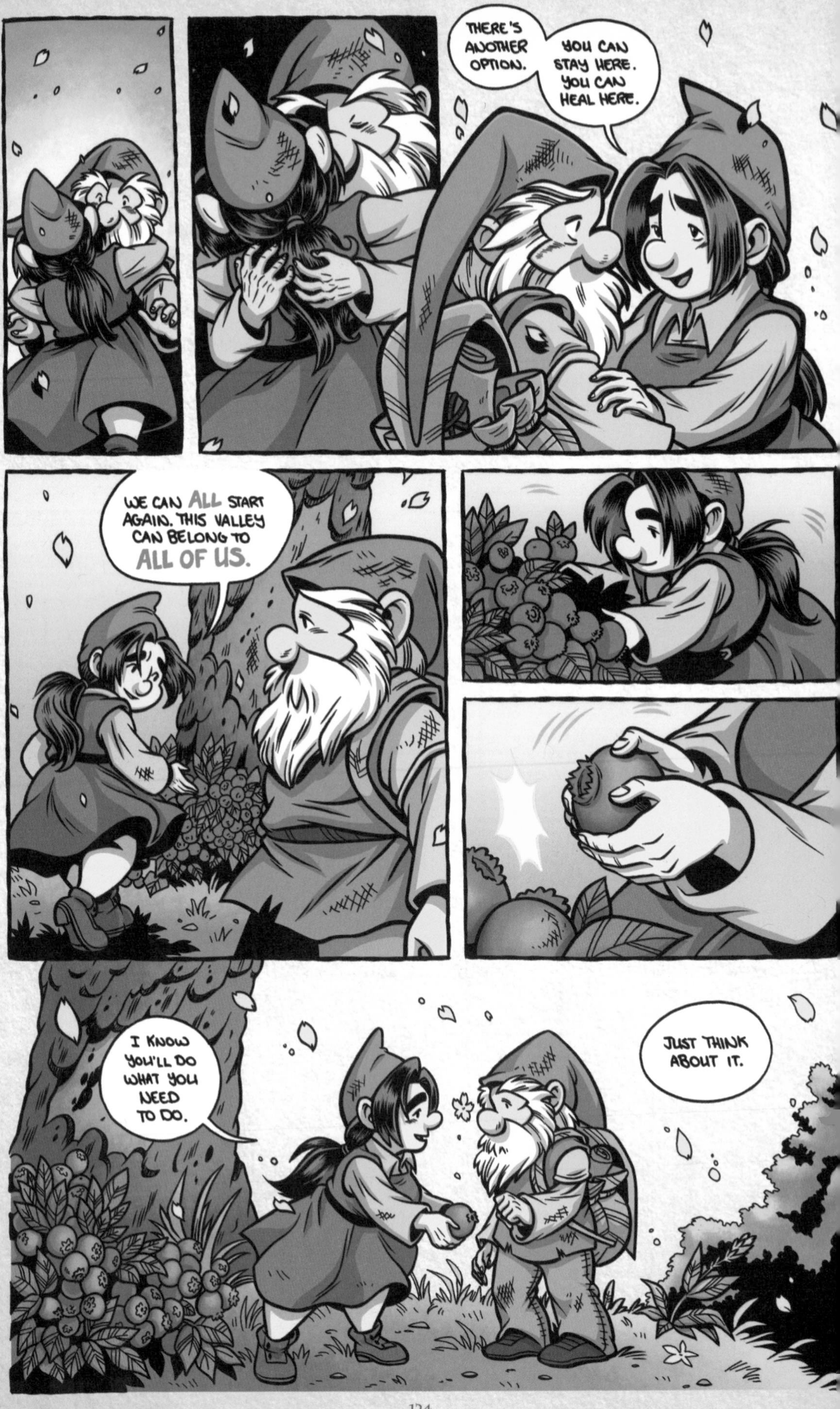
THERE'S ANOTHER OPTION.
YOU CAN STAY HERE. YOU CAN HEAL HERE.
WE CAN ALL START AGAIN. THIS VALLEY CAN BELONG TO ALL OF US.
I KNOW YOU'LL DO WHAT YOU NEED TO DO.
JUST THINK ABOUT IT.

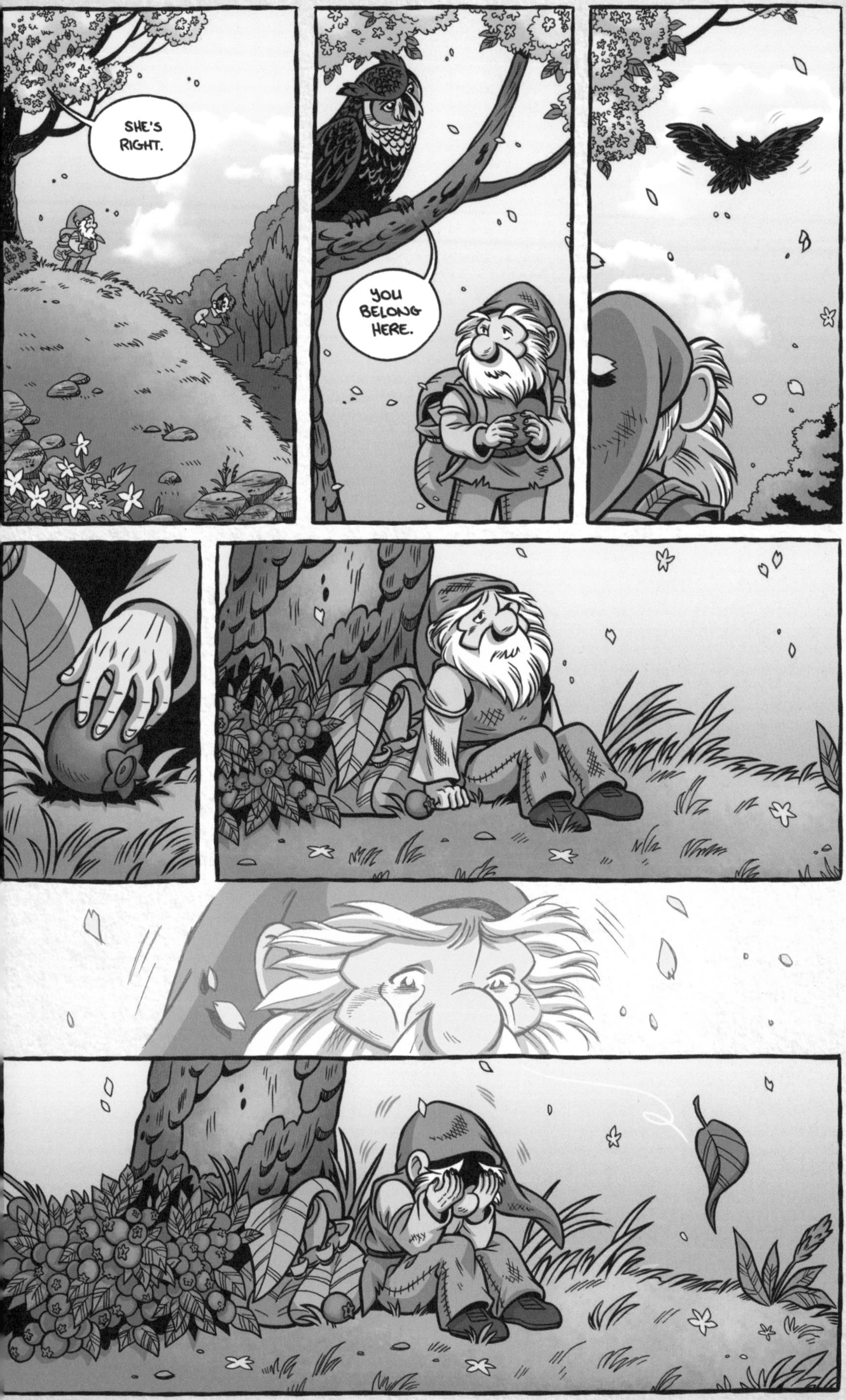
SHE'S RIGHT.
YOU BELONG HERE.

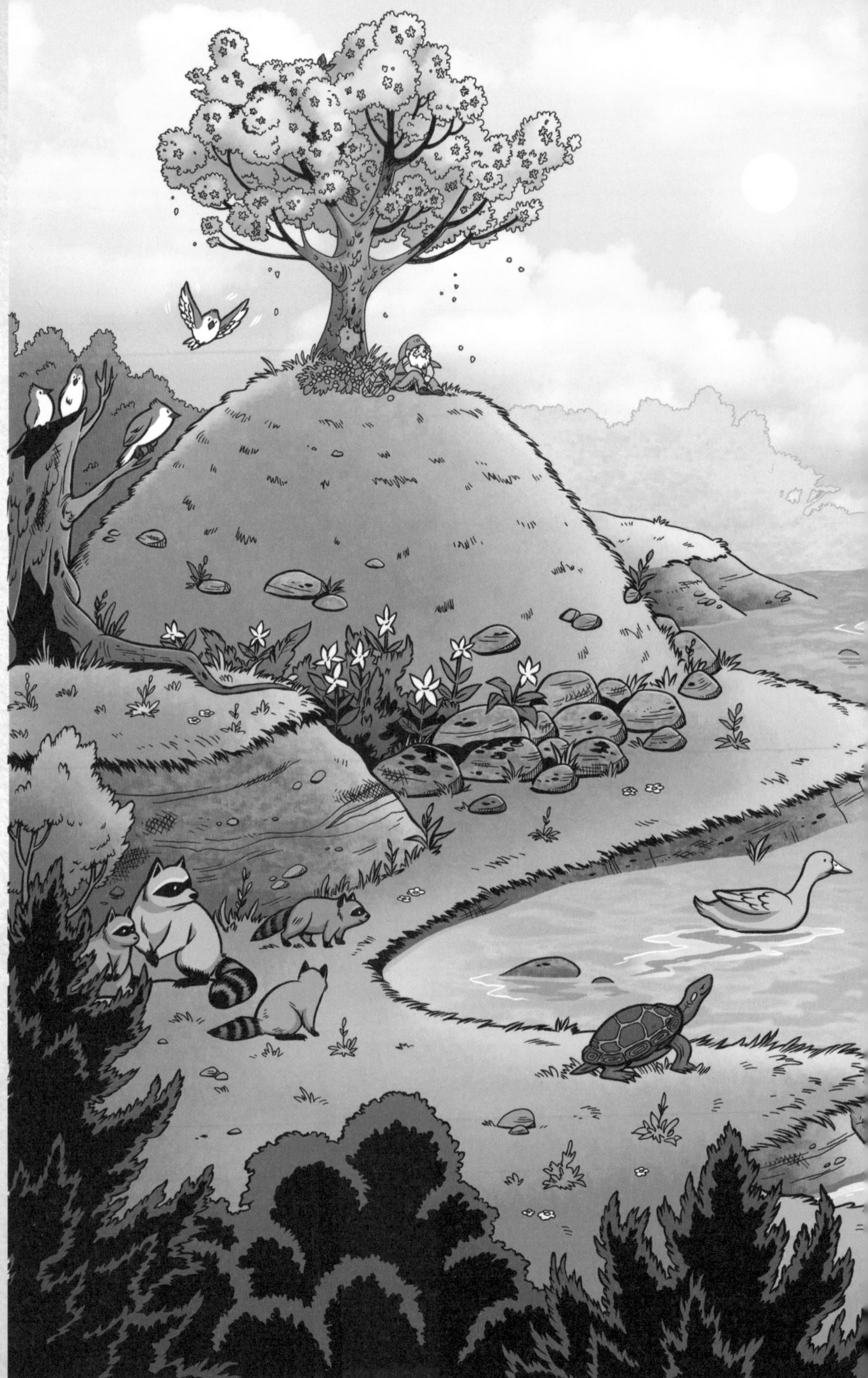

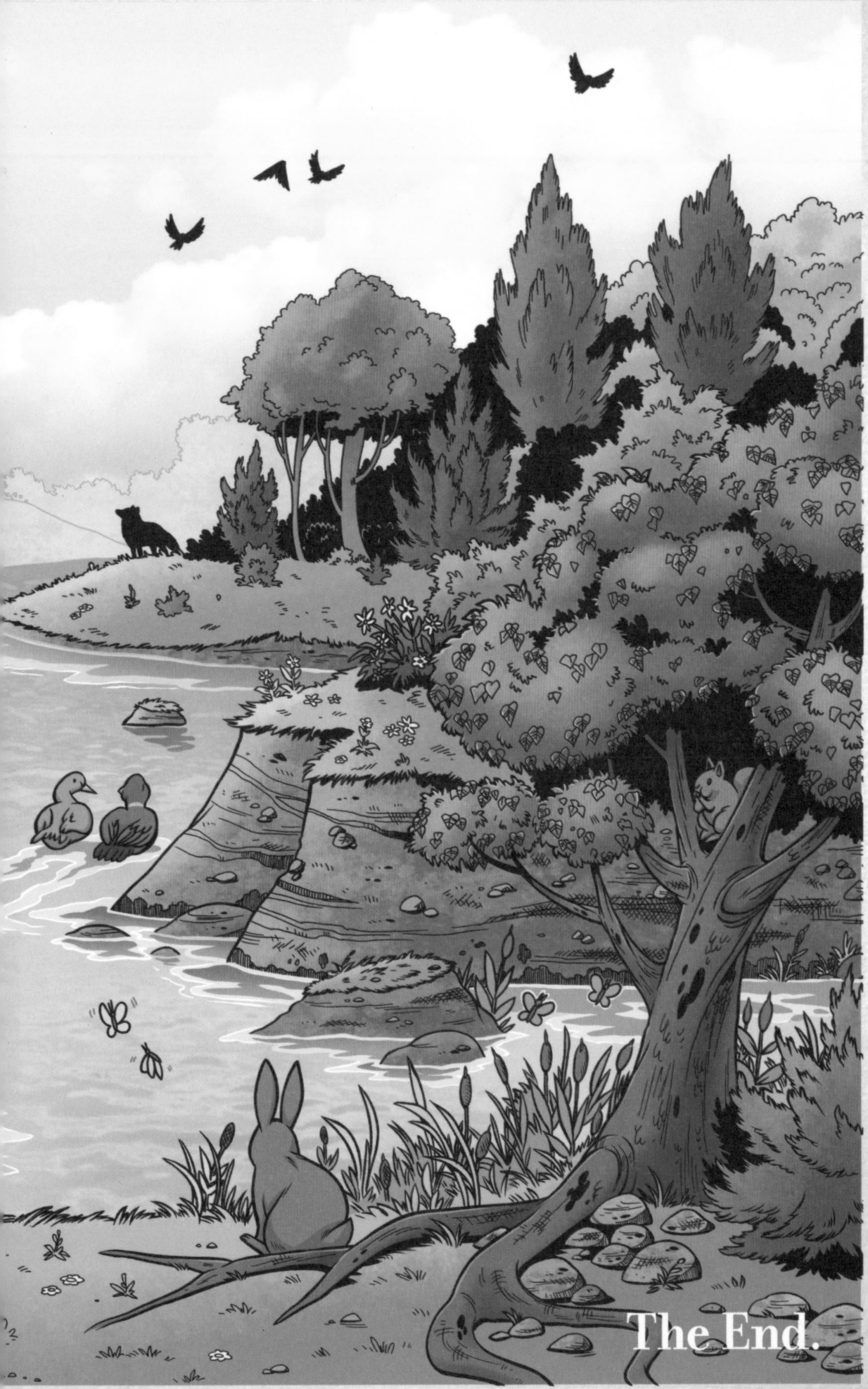
The End.

DEDICATION:

FOR MABEL ROSE
FRIEND AND GUARDIAN OF NATURE

—BOBBY CURNOW

FOR MY SISTERS
LOVERS OF ADVENTURES IN MAGICAL FORESTS

—BRENDA HICKEY

Editor-in-Chief: Chris Staros.
Designed by Gilberto Lazcano.
Edited by Zac Boone.

Visit our online catalog at topshelfcomix.com

ISBN 978-1-60309-424-5   4   3   2   1

Published by Top Shelf Productions, PO Box 1282, Marietta, GA 30061-1282, USA.
Top Shelf Productions is an imprint of IDW Publishing, a division of Idea and
Design Works, LLC. Offices: 2765 Truxtun Road, San Diego, CA 92106. Top Shelf
Productions®, the Top Shelf logo, Idea and Design Works®, and the IDW logo are
registered trademarks of Idea and Design Works, LLC. All Rights Reserved. With the
exception of small excerpts of artwork used for review purposes, none of the contents
of this publication may be reprinted without the permission of IDW Publishing. IDW
Publishing does not read or accept unsolicited submissions of ideas, stories, or artwork.
Printed in Korea.